Thinner Skin

Billie Jean Diersen

Thinner Skin is a work of fiction. Names, characters, places and incidents described herein are either the product of the author's imagination or are used fictitiously. Any resemblance to actual persons, living or dead, events or locales is purely coincidental.

For those who are striving to find themselves. May it comfort you to know that we've all been there.

Prologue

I 'll never forget the night I met the only man I've ever killed. Despite my efforts to erase it from my mind, I remember it as clearly as I do the night my mom died, the day I got married, and the days both of my children were born.

That's not to say I make a habit of committing to memory my every experience—much less the circumstances surrounding each new acquaintance. For example, I have no idea how or when I met my husband. Nor do I recall meeting any of my closest childhood friends. Although I can ballpark the geneses of these relationships, when I try to summon specific dates or memories of the occasions, I draw a total blank.

Maybe that's how it is for anyone who's moved around as much as I have. You come into contact with so many people over the years that you don't stop to document the moment you become aware of their existence. Unless you keep a diary—or have OCD—you don't bother; there just isn't time.

So the kid who sits behind you in fifth grade gradually becomes Tony Zeigler and, later, the first boy you ever kiss, while the girl with the pink-rimmed glasses becomes your science partner and, over time, your best friend, Quinn. You don't remember your initial meeting or when you first spoke. Unless there was something special or significant about the event, you only know that at some point they appeared on your radar and you somehow learned their names. You also learn that relationships are fluid, and you don't expect them to last.

That's how it should have been with Rob Copeland. And yet, although there was nothing at all significant about that Friday, I remember it as if it were yesterday, and in fine detail. I don't recall the date, but I can name the location right down to the zip code. I also remember what he wore, what he was drinking, and nearly every second I spent with him until the moment he was no longer of this earth.

One

I was running late—as usual—that unseasonably sticky October night. Having finally managed to pry myself away from the phone, I burst out the front door with my purse in one hand, shoes and smokes in the other, and raced to the street where the car stood waiting. Breathless, I hopped in, dropped my stuff on the floor, and slammed the door.

"I am *so* sorry," I heaved, fastening my seatbelt as the vehicle crept away from the curb. "I would have never answered the phone if I'd known who was calling. The sitter even offered to get it, but, no—I just *had* to pick it up myself. And what did I get for my trouble? Just the latest chapter in the eternal saga of *Marie's Self-Induced Misery*."

Marie was my cousin, my first best friend, and her own worst enemy.

"So who is it this time?" asked my amazingly patient husband, Kevin, from behind the wheel. "Boss or boyfriend?"

"Neither—although they're now one and the same. And since he's also *married*, we can all about imagine where that's going."

"We sure can."

"I don't even know why I bother," I admitted, waving off the smoke from the cigarette I'd just lit and extinguishing the match. "She never listens to a word I say, and I only hear from her when she's angry or suicidal. Sometimes I'd like to tell her to piss off."

"So why don't you?"

I shrugged. "Probably because she makes me look so stable by comparison."

Kevin laughed.

"So tell me," I continued, lowering my window just a crack, "why are we going to this party again? As I recall, you said Todd's last wasn't worth the tread wear on the tires."

"I guess I'm just a glutton for punishment."

"Speaking of punishment," I said as I tossed the matchbook into the cubby in the dash, "Todd's not going to make us play that stupid Fame Game again, is he?"

"Probably."

Great. "So how about we skip the party and go watch some paint dry? That couldn't possibly be any less fun."

"Sorry. No can do."

"Why not?"

"Because I told Sergeant Copeland we'd be there."

"Sergeant who?"

"Copeland. He's one of the new marines assigned to the NROTC unit this year. I'm sort of helping him get acquainted."

"That's very decent of you. But what does that have to do with me?"

"Well, he's bringing his fiancée."

"Ah. So I'm programming a new Marine Corps Wives Club initiate, eh?" I mused as I kicked through my stuff on the floor, located both black pumps, and slipped a bare foot into each. "Why didn't you say so?"

"That's the spirit, Jackie. I knew you'd find a positive way to look at this. You always come through for me."

"Yeah, well, payback's coming, pal," I promised as I flipped down the visor to access the vanity mirror. Ignoring my hair, which—thanks to the humidity—had taken on a life of its own, I unzipped my makeup kit and returned Kevin's grin in the mirror.

Tall, dark, and handsome really doesn't begin to cover it, I observed privately. With his deep evergreen eyes, rich olive skin, perfect jaw and cheekbones, and tall, athletic build, the man easily could be the next Sexiest Man Alive as a sergeant in the Marine Corps.

And nowhere on earth was there a finer man than this. Smart and drop-dead humorous was how I described him to my friends back in the day, but that told only half of the story. As decent as he was exquisite, Kevin really was more than could be believed, and words could not express how grateful I was for having resisted the urge to write him off as just another pretty face.

"So," I interjected, as I considered said visage, "what can you tell me about this Sergeant Copeland and his intended?"

"He enlisted about five years ago, since which time he graduated third in his class at boot camp; finished both his MOS and NCO schools as company honor man, *and* picked up his last rank meritoriously—all of which undoubtedly explains his selection for MECEP."

MECEP—aka the Marine Enlisted Commissioning Educational Program—was the means by which Kevin was able to trade his job as an avionics technician for a slot at the University of Minnesota Naval ROTC unit two years ago. If everything went according to plan, in two more years it would also earn him a bachelor of science in mechanical engineering and a nice shiny set of lieutenant's bars.

"Damn, Kevin. What did you do? Screen his record book?"

"Of course."

"You're *so* bad," I said approvingly. "So what else did you find?"

"Nothing too juicy. He spent some time with Security Force Company in Naples, where he was until his selection for MECEP in May. Before that he was on embassy duty in Moscow."

"Moscow?"

"Yep—one of the first sent in after that Clayton Lonetree shit hit the fan."

"Wow," I mused, recalling the news reports from 1987 when the disgraced marine and embassy guard was convicted of espionage for providing sensitive documents and information to Soviet intelligence agents. "That's impressive."

"Tell me about it. It's hard enough to get a slot like that under normal circumstances; a guy practically had to walk on water to get one back then."

"Gee, Kevin, it sounds like he's got more officer material than you do."

"I wouldn't go *that* far. But he does seem to have his act together."

"And this fiancée of his?" I asked as I resituated the visor and put my makeup kit back in my purse. "What's she been up to while he was racking up the honors?"

"I have no idea."

"Stop kidding around. If I'm going to do this, you've got to give me something to work with. I can't go in there blind."

"I'm afraid you may have to. I really don't know that much about her."

"That's fine. I just need the basics."

"Like?"

"Like, does she have a name?"

"I assume so."

"You didn't even get her *name*?"

"I didn't think to ask."

"And he didn't mention it?"

"Probably. I just don't remember."

"Fine. Then what *do* you remember?"

"Well, he did mention something about Budapest."

"*Budapest*?" I repeated as if it was a joke. "As in *Hungary*?"

"Yeah. I think he said they met there. Although it may have been Bucharest."

"So what you're saying," I offered by way of clarification, "is that on top of playing Welcome Wagon tonight, I'm working with someone whose knowledge of English may be limited to your five basic obscenities and a handful of phrases culled from pop music lyrics?"

"Unless it was Belfast."

"What?"

"Well, that's a *British* territory, right? So odds are she would speak English."

I shook my head. "This is going to be a disaster. We should just go home."

"Why?"

"*Why*? Kevin, I don't know if you've been counting, but I speak exactly two languages besides English and Pig Latin, neither of which is native to the Eastern Bloc. I'll be of no help here—really."

"I think you're getting just a little ahead of yourself, Jack. I mean, for all we know, she speaks English like a native."

"And if not?"

"Then just do like you would with any other new acquaintance and talk about your period."

"That's quite amusing, Kevin. Truly. But why me?"

"Because you're a welcoming force—when you *want* to be—and you know what it's going to be like for her over the next few years."

"So do either of the other two wives at this command."

"Ah, but they don't have your winning personality."

"You don't actually think I'm going to fall for that, do you?"

"A guy can hope."

"And here's another question for you: what's she doing here in the first place? I mean, honestly, as much as I love it here, why would *anyone* give up Europe for Minneapolis?"

"*Eastern* Europe, Jack—it's practically the third world."

"So now she's a refugee?"

"Probably not. But if she's engaged to a marine, she's definitely not *royalty*."

I conceded the point with a shrug and lit another cigarette.

Kevin sighed as I cracked my window again. "Look, I'm not asking you to make her your best friend. I just want you to hang out and make introductions. If you hit it off—great. If not, no big deal, and I won't ask again."

"Can I get that in writing?"

"You can get it in blood, if that's what it takes."

"That sounds good. Do I get to choose where it comes from?"

Kevin laughed. "Let's see how things go," he suggested, patting my hand. "No point in sweating the fine print just yet."

A few minutes later, he stopped the car in the parking lot of the apartment complex where Todd Van Ault and his roommates lived.

"I just remembered," I announced as he cut the lights and pulled the keys from the ignition. "It's two-for-one night at the gun range tonight. Why don't you teach me to shoot?"

"No, thanks."

"But you've always said you wanted to."

"Maybe. But under the circumstances, that's one skill I think is best left *untapped*."

"Wise man."

Kevin draped his arm over the steering wheel and faced me. "What's going on here?" he asked. "I mean, since when don't *you* like to meet new people?"

"Since you started pimping me out to foreign nationals."

"I am not pimping you out. At most it's a blind date."

"Either way, I'm screwed."

"At least you'll have a fresh audience for your best material," he coaxed like a waiter offering up an enticing dessert. "Isn't that just a little tempting?"

"It would be a lot more tempting if I knew they were *both* going to understand it."

"Come on, Jack. It's only for a couple of hours. And if they're total losers, we can sneak out and make fun of them all the way home."

"Well, *that's* a given."

"So what do you say? Do we have a deal?"

"I guess," I sighed. "But only because of that last part. Not because I expect it to be fun. And in return, you have to promise not to abandon me. No slipping off to talk shop or leaving me with people I'm too polite to ignore or annoy."

"Done. Anything else?"

"Yeah. No Fame Game. I'll play any other game you want, including strip poker, but I do not want to play the Fame Game."

"No Fame Game. No problem."

"And I'm *not* getting dragged into another debate on Iraq," I added as he locked the doors. With Saddam Hussein having invaded Kuwait two months earlier and the United States scrambling to get in position to drive him back out, it seemed all anyone wanted to talk about was Iraq, Iraq, Iraq.

"No Fame Game. No Hussein. Got it."

"I'm serious, Kevin. I'm tired of being called a commie for not agreeing with everything those guys say, and I do not want to get angry."

"But you're at your best when you're angry, Jack. That's what we all love about you."

"Yeah, right. Pull the other one. It has bells on."

Two

A few minutes later, after the buzzer confirmed that our request for admittance had been granted, we walked through the front door, up the stairs, and down the hall to Todd's apartment.

"It's Jackie and Kevin," shouted a voice, apparently in answer to a previous inquiry.

"Finally!" said Connie Opperman, a senior midshipman and one of just five women at the unit this year. "You've got to get in here," she urged in her characteristically hoarse, lower Okie drawl. "Toni, Pam, and I are perilously close to being asphyxiated by the fumes coming off Frazier and Company's white male bullshit."

"And you say the military no longer uses biological weapons," I chided Kevin as we followed the voices to the kitchen, where we joined Connie, fellow seniors Toni Barnes and Pam Alexander, and juniors David Frazier and Brad Burkhart.

"Go ahead," Pam dared Frazier once the greetings had been exchanged. "Ask her."

"Keep your shirt on, Alexander," the latter replied. "Let the woman get a drink first."

"Good idea," I announced, following Kevin to the makeshift bar atop the microwave and examining the selection. "Assuming they're talking about me, that is."

"And even if they're not," he offered.

"Exactly."

"That's about what I figured," Kevin sighed. "Here you go."

"Thanks," I chirped as I accepted the whiskey and cola he'd originally made for himself. "So what are you advocating tonight, Frazier? Tax breaks for people with multiple assault rifles? Gutting public education? Or are you pulling out the big guns and calling for the appointment of a Lactation Czar to stop women from breast-feeding in public?"

"Actually," he said with a grudging smile, "we're discussing the role of female personnel in combat operations in the Persian Gulf. Care to share your two cents?"

"No, thanks. I'm so sick of talking about Kuwait I could scream. In fact, after sitting in class all day listening to a bunch of cake-eaters whine about the devastating blow a draft might deal to their educational goals, and spending nights with this one here," I paused to nudge Kevin's side, "arguing over sovereignty and engagement verses isolationism, what I'd really like is to meet *someone* who thinks Desert Shield is something the Saudis wear under their armpits. I mean, Christ! Doesn't anybody wanna fight about abortion anymore?"

"Jackie's right," Kevin teased as he edged toward the doorway with his own drink in hand. "Never mind the Middle East. Instead of worrying about stability in that or any other part of the world, we should all join hands and start singing songs about rainbows and sunshine."

"Fine by me," I called after him. "I can't remember the last time I attended a sing-along."

Connie laughed. "Count me in," she said. "I won't be doing any singing, but I'd pay a fair sum of money to see Sergeant Thompson play Ring around the Rosie."

"You and me both," I laughed. "And now before I go spreading any more goodwill, I need nicotine. So, should anyone need me—for another opinion perhaps, minor surgery, or to share a charming limerick—I shall be outside reducing my life expectancy with carbon monoxide and a vast array of carcinogens."

As I left the kitchen, I spotted Kevin on the other side of the room talking to Sergeant Copeland—or so I assumed from the fact that I had never seen the dude before and from the half-inch of blondish stubble garnishing the crown of his otherwise bare head—who had apparently just arrived, along with a slender young woman with dark eyes and long brown hair.

"So much for that cigarette," I muttered when they all suddenly faced me as Kevin motioned for me to join them. Weaving my way through the crowd, I approached the trio, who now seemed to be enjoying a good laugh.

"Here she is," Kevin said, slipping an arm around my waist. "Sergeant Copeland, this is my wife, Jackie. Jack, allow me to introduce Sergeant Copeland and his fiancée, Katrine."

The marine nodded. "It's nice to finally meet you, Jackie."

"Same here," I replied, wiping my hand on my pant leg before shaking each of theirs. "Now what's so funny?"

Copeland grinned. "Kevin told us about your conversation in the car earlier this evening and your concern over Katrine's grasp of English."

Oh my God.

"Don't be embarrassed," he added as my cheeks and neck started to burn. "We think it's pretty hilarious."

Clearly. "Care to let me in on the joke?" I inquired. "I mean, it's great that you're all on the verge of wetting your pants, but I'm standing here feeling like an ethnocentric jackass."

Katrine smiled. "Would it help if I told you I'm American?"

"It might." I gulped down half my drink and stared at Kevin.

"I *told* you she probably spoke English," he insisted.

"You also told me she was from Budapest."

"I said I thought they'd *met* there."

"He was close," Katrine offered. "It was Café Budapest—in Paris. But I'm originally from Syracuse."

New York. I shook my head at Kevin. "I sure hope Uncle Sam thinks twice before putting you in counterintelligence."

"Oh, they will," he replied meaningfully. "That kind of thing requires a special security clearance, so that ship sailed when I married you."

"So tell me," I continued, meeting his smirk with my own before facing his companions, "what other embarrassing shit has 007 here revealed to you in my absence?"

Katrine shrugged. "Only that you're bisexual and once had the hots for Justine Bateman."

And with that, they were all laughing again.

With little to do but wait them out, I tossed back the last of my drink and undertook the study of an overtly sexist poster on the wall behind me. Observing my host's right to decorate his home in any offensive manner he chose, I defied the urge to set the paper ablaze and decided instead to solicit another drink from Kevin. Upon turning around, however, I realized that he and Copeland had defected to another group across the room and left me alone with Katrine and an empty glass. Rotating the vessel in my hand, I watched the viscous residue roll slowly around the inside as I cursed his stealth and pondered my options for revenge.

"Looks like you could use a refill," Katrine observed.

"Nah. I'd better wait. I drained that first one kind of fast."

"It's OK, you know. I can manage by myself."

Gnawing on the inside of my cheek, I sized up my companion. She was clearly younger than anyone in the room—definitely not of legal drinking age—and, despite her brave words, totally out of her element.

"Look," I said finally, setting my glass on a nearby shelf, "I'm not about to leave you alone without a court order or a hold-harmless agreement. However, as a nicotine fiend and occasional agoraphobe, I wonder if you'd mind taking our conversation elsewhere—like, say, the garage?"

Katrine shrugged. "OK by me."

"Terrific. Let's go."

Katrine followed me to the opposite wall and watched as I stopped to unlock the sliding glass door to the balcony. "I thought you said we were going to the garage."

"We are—if I can get this damn thing open."

"But we're still on the second floor."

"Yes, we are. And if we were better acquainted, I'd tell you just how sharp you are to have noticed."

"Forgive me, but where I'm from, this would be called a balcony."

"Trust me," I said with two fingers in my mouth, having hurt them trying to pop the lock. "Around here, it's all in how you use it—and with three hundred cubic feet of storage space, this place has everything but the oil stains and remote-controlled opener."

Katrine watched me slide the door aside and then followed me through the densely lined drapes out onto the cluttered cement floor. "So I see."

"Now, since we can't lock this from the outside," I continued as she closed the door, "we're going to need to come up with some other form of defense."

"Against what?"

"Young male warmongers looking to pick a fight with a peace-loving liberal. Now, since ignoring them would be rude and telling them to leave would be mean, our best option is to talk about something that will make them so uncomfortable as to induce or expedite their departure."

"Such as?"

"Bodily functions seem to work best," I offered as I reached into my purse and produced a lighter. "Menstruation, masturbation. Things like that."

"Seriously?"

I nodded. "Believe me. A comment or two along those lines will have an intruder gone so fast he'll disrupt the space-time continuum and be back inside before he ever left."

Laughing, I lit a cigarette and proceeded to choke on my first drag. "Would you like one?" I coughed, offering up the pack. "How rude of me not to offer, since I'm enjoying mine so much."

"Thanks, anyway. Rob doesn't like me to smoke."

"No problem. Of course, having someone tell me not to do something makes me want to do it more often, not less. But suit yourself."

I took another drag as my companion stared covetously at the slim, white cylinder in my hand. "Are you sure you don't want one?" I asked. "I have plenty."

Katrine shook her head and then glanced toward the door. "But I wouldn't mind sharing yours."

"Be my guest."

"Thanks. And thanks for keeping me company tonight."

"No sweat."

"Really—I owe you one."

"Great. I'll remember that next time I can't find a babysitter."

"Babysitter? You guys have kids?"

Nodding, I expertly slipped my wallet from my purse and whipped it open to a set of photographs. "That's Tyler," I said, pointing to a towheaded boy with Kevin's eyes. "He's three. The baby is Lucy. She's three months old there, but she's almost seven months old now."

"Wow. So how old are you, if you don't mind me asking?"

"Twenty-four. You?"

"I'll be nineteen next month."

"No kidding. Well, in case I don't see you, happy birthday."

Katrine regarded me warily. "Is that it?"

"Well, yeah. I mean, I really haven't had time to buy a gift."

"It's not that. I'm just…oh, never mind."

"Never mind what?"

"I'm sorry. It's just that ever since Rob and I got engaged, my age has become this huge issue for everybody. Even my sisters, who once fought their own battles with our parents and should, therefore, be on *my* side, say I'm too young to settle down, that I can't possibly be ready to make that kind of commitment."

"Well, forgive them. It's basically their job to rain on your parade."

"That sounds like the voice of experience. I take it you have older sisters, too?"

I shook my head. "Used to, though—about five in total. All step and, luckily, now all *ex*. So these days it's just my brother and me, although with my dad, that statistic is subject to change."

"So your parents are divorced?"

"Sort of. My dad's divorced from my brother's mom and twice more since. But my mom died before all that, so he's also widowed. In fact, next July, Kevin and I will have been married six years—which is longer than my dad was married to all his wives put together."

"Wow. So you were around my age when you got married."

"Yeah—about."

"And did you guys live together before the wedding?"

I eyed her with mock suspicion. "What magazine did you say you were with?"

"I'm sorry. I didn't mean to pry."

"Don't be silly. I was only teasing."

"Are you sure?"

"Ask anyone in there," I added with a nod toward the apartment. "They'll tell you: the real challenge lies in getting me to shut up."

"I'll keep that in mind."

"As to your question," I continued, "No, we did not live together before we were married. In fact, we didn't live together until a few months *after* our wedding because I decided to stay in Minnesota while Tommy finished his last MOS school."

"Tommy?"

"Sorry. That was Kevin's nickname from high school—short for Thompson. You must've triggered a time warp, because I haven't used it in years."

"At least you can use his real name if you want to. You can't say the same for Rob."

"Why?" I asked, having assumed that by *Rob* she meant her fiancé. "What have you got against *Robert*?"

"Nothing. But then, his name is *Robinson*."

"*Robinson*? As in *Crusoe*?"

"Yep."

"Oh, my. That's unfortunate."

"Yep. Which is why he goes by R. C. Only where I come from, that's a brand of cola, so I call him Rob."

"That's very kind of you. Personally, I would've had a little more fun with it, but to each her own."

Katrine giggled as I crushed out my smoke in a makeshift ashtray.

"So you two met in Paris?" I observed for lack of a better segue. "How did that happen?"

"He and his friends happened to be there on leave the same week my roommate and I were there between terms at the Sorbonne, and somehow we all wound up at the same club."

"You went to school at the *Sorbonne*?" I said, forgetting all about their romance and its origins. "That must've been awesome."

"Everyone says that. But it's no different from any other university, except that everyone there is speaking French."

"I suppose. Still, you got to live in France."

"True. But it's not as if I had a choice. I mean, if I had *asked* to go to France and my parents had let me, it would've been great. But being forced to go somewhere, even if it's France, kind of takes the fun out of it. You know what I mean?"

"I guess. So why didn't you just refuse to go?"

"Because in my family, 'no' is not an option."

"No is *always* an option."

"Maybe for you. But at our house, unless you're willing to endure a steady stream of verbal and psychological harassment, you do exactly what you're told."

"Ah."

"I take it that's not how things worked at your house."

"Actually, that's exactly how it worked at our house—which is partly why I've been on my own since I was seventeen."

"You left home at seventeen?"

"In a manner of speaking. My dad got a new job in the middle of my senior year that required him to relocate. I didn't want to move at the time, so I got a second job and rented the apartment over a neighbor's garage so I could stay behind and finish school where I was."

"That makes sense. I wouldn't want to leave the friends I'd known all my life and start over again just before graduation."

"Don't get too choked up. It was more about having my freedom than being near my friends. Plus, it was smack in the middle of college application season, and I didn't want to have to screw with transcripts and financial aid all over again. Besides, it was only my second year there, which probably set some kind of record since we had moved about twenty times since I started kindergarten."

"What does your dad do that he has to transfer so often?"

"Generally he gets fired, but sometimes he quits."

I nodded as Katrine's mouth formed a silent O. "Yeah. It's a tragic tale with needy women and bad luck playing key roles in the plot," I observed. "Maybe you'll hear it someday. Anyway, a few months later, I graduated— with honors, thank you very much—and, with a scholarship in hand, was set to ignite my career as an investigative journalist. Regrettably, however, at the last minute I decided to chuck that plan and go to a school near my boyfriend's job."

"You obviously don't mean Kevin."

"God, no. Now, he would have been worth giving up a scholarship for."

"So what happened with the other guy?"

"It just wasn't meant to be. He's Catholic; I'm an agnostic. He's a hothead with no sense of humor; I'm a smart-ass with a defective filter. On top of that, he was insanely jealous and had a penchant for booze and access to his father's gun safe—which is a lethal combination by any standard. So, narrowly dodging a future as stable as my past, I dropped out of college after one semester and left him in the dust."

"I see. And when did Kevin enter the picture?"

"I have no idea. It was sometime during high school, but I don't know when or where. All I remember is hanging out and shooting pool with him and thinking he was a great guy. We kept in touch after he enlisted, but since he never hit on me, I assumed I wasn't his type. We lost touch for a while after he joined the marines, but then I ran into him a couple weeks after I had ditched the humorless psychotic. Fearing it was my last chance to get on his radar before he disappeared for good, I invited him over to my apartment and jumped his bones."

"Wow."

"I know. It's not exactly a fairy tale, but there you have it. And of course, that's just my side of the story. You can always go inside and ask Kevin for his version."

"I may just do that."

"Meanwhile," I continued, yanking the brush from my purse and taking aim at the blond mass whose volume had increased exponentially in the night air, "I need a moment to show my hair who's boss."

Katrine laughed. "Here, let me," she instructed as she relieved me of the brush and guided me by the shoulders toward an empty chest cooler.

Unaccustomed to *receiving* instructions from my contemporaries—much less *following* those of strangers—I was inclined to argue but could not find the words to do so. Instead, I lowered myself onto the designated perch and struggled to appear at ease.

"You know," Katrine said as she lifted the hair off my shoulders to smooth the underside, "I've always wondered what it was like to be a blonde."

"Take it from me—it's not all it's cracked up to be. For one thing, I'm supposed to have more fun—which can be pretty tough with a Republican in the White House, believe me—so even when I'm not enjoying myself, I'm obliged to fake it. On top of that, I'm not supposed to have a brain, so people are shocked to discover I'm not only sentient but in fact quite brilliant. I'm telling you, sometimes I'd like to cut it all off and dye it red just to escape the pressure. Still, if you think you can handle the strain, you should give it a try."

"No way."

"Why not? I'm sure it would suit you."

"Maybe—but my mother would have a coronary."

"Not if you don't tell her."

"Believe me, she'd find out. The woman is programmed to detect my every move and boasts a network that spans the globe. I don't know all the parties involved, but if I so much as sneeze, it'll set off a chain reaction, and by sundown there'll be a UPS driver on my porch with a vat of chicken soup; a month's supply of decongestant, cough suppressant, and pain reliever; and a list of instructions from my pediatrician."

"That's hilarious."

Katrine stopped brushing. "You think I'm kidding?"

"No. I just think you're funny."

"You're pretty funny yourself. In fact, you remind me of someone..."

"Oh?" I braced myself as Katrine tried to summon the name of the blonde whose image I called to mind. I say *blonde* because never in my life has anyone said I remind them of a brunette or redhead. In fact, we blondes must all look alike to everyone else because everywhere I go it seems someone mistakes me for some blonde they've seen somewhere, or says I remind them of a blonde from some movie or TV. Sometimes these remarks can be taken as compliments, like the time a woman at the mall mistook me for the gal who played Blair Warner on *The Facts of Life* and asked for my autograph. Others have been less flattering, like when a guy at one of Kevin's unit parties said I looked like Rebecca de Mornay's fatter younger sister.

"Can you give me a hint?" I asked warily. "Or should I just start guessing?"

Katrine laughed. "I'm sorry. I'm trying to think of her name, but all I can come up with is the character she plays on TV."

"Which one?"

"Murphy Brown."

Well, that was a new one. And given all the options, it wasn't too bad. Murphy Brown was sharp, funny, and attractive. I could do worse than remind people of her. Of course, Candice Bergen is twenty years older than I am, has darker hair, and is clearly unfamiliar with the word *frizz*, so the resemblance obviously wasn't physical.

"Candice Bergen," Katrine pronounced as if she'd read my mind. Her thoughts no longer obstructed, she returned her attention to the task at hand. "Jeez," she exclaimed, gathering my unruly locks into one giant handful. "You have a *lot* of hair."

"Tell me about it."

"Can I braid it?"

"Braid it, burn it, whatever—just as long as it's off my face."

"OK, tip your head back."

Not wanting to seem ungrateful, I did as Katrine instructed and pretended I let strangers handle my hair every day. In truth, I do let strangers handle my hair every now and then, but they usually have licenses and don't know the people I gripe about, so it's hardly the same thing.

"So did you ever go back to school?" Katrine asked as she used her nails to part my hair and divided it into four roughly equally bushy sections.

"I took classes here and there until Kevin was selected for MECEP. Once he had settled in, I picked up a scholarship to Hamilton, from which I'm set to graduate this spring."

"And then?"

"And then I'll be an even-more-overqualified housewife."

I grinned toward Katrine in her periphery. "So now, what about you?"

"What *about* me?"

"Anything. So far all I've got is that you quit school and plan to get married."

"Sounds remarkably close to your story, doesn't it? Well, that's where the similarities end. I'm the youngest of three girls who were born two years apart yet who look so much alike that we're constantly mistaken for triplets. Unlike you, I have two parents who've been together since they met, and I lived in the same house all my life until I went to college. I attended the same schools, took the same classes, and joined all the same clubs my sisters did, and I was never allowed out of my parents' sight."

"But they sent you to France."

"Only so I could become the next Marie Curie far from the sin and filth of the American higher education system—and even then I had relatives to keep an eye on me."

"They sent you to France to *avoid* sin? Isn't that just a little backward?"

"Actually, it's a lot backward, but that's my mom. She shipped each of us over the minute we finished high school, expecting us to return educated and employable. Suffice it to say, one of us didn't."

"I take it you didn't like it there?"

"France itself was great—aside from the fact that my mother had chosen everything from the school to my major to my courses without even consulting me. Anyway, I was a good girl and gave it a shot, but my heart just wasn't in it. I was trying to find a way to convey that to my folks when I met Rob, and, well, suddenly France didn't seem so bad anymore."

"That was awfully convenient. Are you sure she didn't engineer it?"

"The thought did cross my mind. Rob was so perfect that I figured there had to be a catch, and paying someone to keep me company would be right up her alley. Of course, when he was selected for MECEP and asked me to move back here with him, my suspicions quickly faded."

"And how did your parents react when you said yes?"

"Horribly. Not only because of my age—which we've already mentioned—or his, which I had somewhat expected, but also, and I quote, 'because your father and I didn't pay for twelve years of private school, six years of English riding lessons, and eight years of classical violin so you could throw your life away for the next Oliver North or Lee Harvey Oswald.'"

"Wow. That's a little unfair."

"Not to mention insulting. But I guess I should have expected that reaction since I was deviating from her master plan. But since that plan was motivated by an interest in my long-term financial security—and since Rob had a good job and I could go to school almost anywhere—I figured it would be no big deal. Obviously, I figured wrong." Katrine patted my shoulders as she finished her summation. "There," she said. "You're done."

I stood to examine my reflection on the patio door. "Looks great," I said stiffly, dropping my brush back in my purse. "Thanks."

"You don't like it."

"No—I do. It's just that I can't remember the last time someone did my hair for me that wasn't getting paid. That's all."

"I'm sorry. I guess I've always taken that kind of thing for granted."

I smiled. "I'd expect nothing less from someone with two older sisters," I reasoned, lighting a pair of cigarettes and handing one to my stylist. "So how do you intend to fill your days in the Land of Ten Thousand Lakes? Do you plan to work, or will you be going back to school?"

"Actually, I started at the U with Rob this fall. I listed international commerce as my major, but I'm not sure what I want to do with it. I basically went back so my mom could stop telling people, 'My older girls are in the sciences, and my youngest is a dropout.'"

"Nice."

"Isn't she though?" Katrine laughed. "So how about you? What are you studying?"

"Communication and poli sci. May as well make the most of that scholarship, you know?"

Katrine nodded. "So are you planning to be a lawyer or just run for office?"

"Neither—although people tell me I'd make a terrific litigator—which I assume is a compliment, but who knows? Truth is I don't know what I'm going to do any more than you do. All I've ever wanted was to write and talk—neither of which pays much unless you're very lucky, already famous, or outrageous, like Howard Stern. Not that money matters all that much to me, but the bills must be paid. So I guess I'll just see what comes along that might involve either or both of those skills and hope for the best."

"Have you considered going into journalism again?"

Before I could answer, the patio door slid open, and Kevin popped his head out through the gap. "Sorry to intrude," he said, "but I figured you'd want to know—the horny have headed for the bar, so the diehards are gonna play Trivial Pursuit."

"Cool," I said, immediately pressing out my cigarette. "The usual partners?"

"Ah, no. In fact, you were invited to play only on the condition that you and Brad are *not* partners."

"But Brad and I are always partners."

"Yep. And you always win, which is why we're separating you. Now, are you in or out?"

I turned to Katrine, who shrugged.

"I guess we're in," I said as we followed Kevin through the door. "So is it the girls against the guys tonight?" I asked hopefully when we reached the coffee table where Connie was setting up the game.

"No," she huffed. "Frazier put the kibosh on that too."

"Even though they outnumber us by two?"

"That's right," Frazier announced. "Two-person teams have been selected at random so that no more obnoxious alliances or battles of the sexes will occur."

I took a moment to roll my eyes behind his back before heading for the kitchen for a diet soda.

"It could be worse," Kevin whispered as he joined me there.

"How so?"

"We could be playing the Fame Game."

"Thank heaven for small favors."

"Actually, you can thank Frazier for that. He hates the Fame Game as much as you do."

"Why did you have to go and tell me that? Now I'm going to feel bad when he loses."

"Don't worry. If he loses, you're going to feel bad anyway."

"And why is that?"

"Because he's your partner."

My partner? "Great. Now if I want to see him crash and burn, I'll have to go down with him." Sighing, I walked back to the living room. "OK, Frazier; where are we sitting?"

"Right there, next to Copeland," he said, nodding to the specified span of floor. "I'll sit on the other side of you. Katrine, I'm afraid you're stuck with Eric. I'll introduce you as soon as he comes out of the head."

Katrine leaned toward Kevin, who had returned from the kitchen. "As soon as he comes out of the *what*?"

"The head," he repeated. "That's Squid for *bathroom*."

"Squid?"

"That's marine for *sailor*."

Katrine nodded. "I have another question," she said uneasily. "Would anyone mind if one of the teams had three players? I'm not very good at trivia, and I don't want anyone to lose because of me, so I'd like to watch for now and maybe join in next time."

"What are you talking about?" Rob demanded. "You can't just watch."

"Why not?"

"Well, you don't want to spoil this for everyone else, do you?"

"Well, no."

"Then you have to play," Rob declared as he assumed his place on the floor. "Right, Jackie?"

I mentally surveyed the crowd, wondering if it would be better or worse for Katrine if I were to back her up. Before I could decide, I felt Rob wrap his arm around my shoulders and give me a squeeze. Stunned by this bold and unwelcome gesture, I sat frozen and awaited release. Watching from the corner of my eye as the offending limb finally retreated and its accompanying palm came to rest atop my knee, I was torn between breaking his wrist and planting my fist in his groin.

"You see," he continued, clearly mistaking silence for consent as he gave my leg a final pat and withdrew his hand to his own lap. "No one cares if you suck. Just play."

Without another word, Katrine slunk to the floor, where she played absently with her shirt cuffs and shoelaces from the start of the game until it was called due to drunkenness, disinterest, and fatigue.

Three

"You're awfully quiet," Kevin observed as we approached the freeway on the way home. "You haven't said a word since we left the party."

"That's because I'm concentrating."

"On what?"

"Willing you not to fall asleep at the wheel."

"Ah. Well, I appreciate your concern, but I can think of better ways to keep me awake than staring silently out the windshield."

"I'll just bet you can. Seriously, though," I added, taking my eyes off the road to face him, "I'd feel better if I was driving. Why don't you pull off and let me take over?"

"No. I'm OK. Besides, I know you don't see too well at night."

"Yeah, but there's no law against driving under the influence of *astigmatism*."

"Well, there *should* be. Oh, lighten up, Jack," he continued with a grin. "I had my last drink hours ago, which means the only influence I'm under at the moment is that of supreme boredom. Now relax and talk to me."

"About what?"

"I don't know. How's school going?"

I narrowed my eyes. "All right, pal—how many fingers?" I demanded as I formed scissors with my hand and snipped the air in front of him.

"Two—why?"

"Because you'd never ask me about school if you were sober."

"Sure I would."

"Kevin, please—whenever I talk about school, your eyes cross and you practically lapse into a coma."

He grimaced guiltily. "OK, so let's talk about the party. Are you glad we went after all?"

"Sure. But then I'm always glad *after*ward."

"I wish you'd remember that—or write it down. Then I wouldn't have to practically put a gun to your head to get you to go every time."

"I can't help it. It's just like I am with needles: the preceding panic is always worse than the actual poke."

"And how about Katrine?" he asked with an air of vindication. "Are you glad you got to meet her?"

"Sure. She's great. Shame I can't say the same of her fiancé."

"I take it you didn't care for Sergeant Copeland."

"That's putting it mildly."

"So what's the problem?"

"Where do I start? I mean, first he bullies Katrine into playing that game and completely humiliates her in front of everyone. Then he continues to embarrass her by insulting and treating her like a child for the rest of the evening."

"Maybe he was just trying too hard to get her to make a good impression. I know I'm not always my sweet, charming self when I'm stressed out."

"Agreed. And I could almost buy that as an explanation if it weren't for everything else. But in addition to treating Katrine like crap, the guy takes himself way too seriously. He can't take a joke, and he can't stand to be challenged or contradicted."

"How do you know that?"

"It was all over his face during the game tonight—like when Pam would talk him out of an answer that turned out to be right, or when Frazier and Burkhart razzed him for knowing the names of all the main characters from *Little Women*. His eyes would go all cold and detached like he was plotting their death and dissection."

"Oh, my," Kevin said with feigned gravity. "Do you think we should warn them?"

"Look, I know it sounds like I've lost the plot, but I'm telling you that man is not right. And I'm not talking about your everyday oddball here. I mean a full-on, poisons-his-ex-girlfriend's-dog, stockpiles-automatic-weapons, and spends-his-free-time-editing-his-manifesto psychotic."

"You got all of that from one night?"

"Yes, I did—and I'm not often wrong in my first impressions."

"Well, I'll give you that. And I'm not going to try to change your mind, since I hardly know the guy, and—more importantly—it could prove hazardous to my health. I just think you should allow for the possibility that you caught him on an off night."

"Oh, I'll allow for that possibility. And because I'm such a good sport, I promise not to gloat even after you're proven wrong."

"Nice to see you're keeping an open mind."

"My mind is no less open than yours. I just happen to have information you don't. But I'm confident that once you get to know him, you'll see past your bias and agree that the man has serious issues."

"*My* bias?"

"Don't take it personally. I'm biased, too. It's just that my bias is well placed, while yours is, well, misplaced."

"I guess I didn't realize there was such a thing as well-placed bias."

"That's because it's so closely associated with racism and, therefore, gets a bad rap. But bias is just one of the mental shortcuts we use to make judgments, predictions, and decisions. Known in communication circles as *heuristics,* these shortcuts evolved over time to hasten the speed at which we assess people and situations, thus increasing our odds of survival. Basically, they help us decide whether someone is friend or foe and whether he or she warrants our time, energy, fear, respect, love, et cetera. Bias can be negative, like when people avoid black men because they think they're all criminals, or it can be positive, like when a guy assumes another guy has a good moral character because he happens to be a marine."

"Is that a fact?"

I nodded. "We all do it. For example, when I was younger, I assumed all Elvis Costello fans were normal people with exceptional taste in music—like me. Then I met this guy at the record store who walked around in horn-rimmed glasses speaking with a phony British accent, and I realized that some of them are freaks.

"My point," I added, because I could see he wanted me to get there, "is that it's reasonable for you to think highly of Sergeant Copeland because he's your brother-in-arms and, as of this moment anyway, you have no reason not to. Right?"

Kevin laughed and shook his head. "If you say so."

"Well, tell me I'm wrong."

"I don't know if you're wrong or not. I'm an IT guy, remember?"

"Then think of this as you do our printer. Since it only acts up when I use it, you always lay the blame on operator error. But when it finally malfunctions when you're using it, you'll realize there's a problem and it needs to be fixed. Likewise, at this moment, you think Copeland is a decent guy with good intentions. But that will change if he says or does something to give you cause to question his character—which, based on what I've seen, he'll manage in short order."

Kevin laughed again. "So now I'm biased in favor of our printer as well?"

"If the shoe fits."

"But it's a Hewlett Packard," he joked.

"Exactly my point. The fact that it's a Hewlett Packard may make it a high-quality product, but that doesn't mean our specific unit won't turn out to be a piece of garbage. Likewise, the fact that Copeland is a marine may increase the likelihood of him having a sound moral character, but that doesn't mean he won't turn out to be a total jerk."

"Fair enough," Kevin admitted as he shifted into park as the car rolled to a halt in front of our duplex. "But I doubt Katrine would be with him if he was a total jerk. I mean, with everything she has going for her, she could toss him back and find someone else."

Interesting. "So you liked her, too?"

"What's not to like? I mean, she's friendly. Pretty. Kind of funny. And she's smart."

"Smart? Are you serious? How would you even know? You spoke to her for all of five minutes before ditching us in the living room and maybe twice after we came in from the patio. Meanwhile, she hardly spoke during the game and didn't answer one question along the way."

"Are you saying she *isn't* smart?"

"Actually, I think she's very smart. But that's not the point. The point is that you ascribed qualities to her without a single shred of evidence. In short, you gave her more credit—because she's attractive—than you would have given a less attractive person who acted the same way."

"And I suppose you didn't notice her looks at all?"

"Of course I did—she's beautiful. But I actually spoke to her and found out she's more than that. She gave no one else Clue One."

"OK. So I tend to judge a book by its cover. What's your point?"

"My point is that, just like you can't assume someone is smart because she's pretty, you can't assume this Copeland is trustworthy because he's a marine. So please keep your eyes open and watch your back. OK?"

"OK."

"Thank you."

"You could have just said that at the beginning, you know," Kevin added with an audible smirk. "You didn't have to draw me a picture."

"True. But I prefer the circuitous route. Besides, you said you wanted conversation."

"I did, didn't I?"

"You did."

Smiling, Kevin took my hand and leaned in for a kiss. "So you think she's beautiful, huh?" he asked with a leer. "Should I be jealous?"

I shook my head. "It means I find her attractive, Kevin—not that I want to sleep with her."

"But would you?"

"Don't be silly. You know you're the only one for me."

"The only *guy*, maybe; you can have as many girls as you like."

"Thanks for clearing that up."

"Then you'll consider it?"

"For God's sake, will you get a grip? You're practically drooling."

"And for good reason."

"Yeah—because you're a deviant letch," I announced, hopping out of the car but stopping short of closing the door. "Which reminds me: would you care to explain that little remark she made about Justine Bateman?"

Kevin stood and grinned across the car roof. "I wish I could. It was damned funny."

"So you don't know where it came from?"

"Not a clue."

"Then you didn't share this little fantasy of yours?"

"Nope."

"Not even with him?"

"That sort of thing usually doesn't come up at work. It tends to have an adverse impact on advancement. But if you want, I'll happily pass it along to Katrine the next time I see her."

"No, thanks."

"Are you sure?"

"I'm positive."

"I wouldn't have to be there, you know. You could just tell me about it afterward."

"Will you stop?"

"Hey, you're the one who said she was gorgeous."

"The word was *beautiful*, Kevin. And it was an *observation*—not a confession. Now will you please be serious?"

"I am being serious."

"By encouraging me to seduce the fiancée of one of your colleagues?"

"I doubt you'd have to seduce her. After all, that joke of hers came from somewhere, right? Maybe she was trying to tell you something."

The man has seen way too much porn.

"I hate to break it to you," I said as I closed the door and joined him on the driver's side, "but in real life, women don't joke about bisexuality in order to convey attraction, just like we don't order pizza in hopes of getting laid."

Kevin shrugged. "More's the pity."

"I know. Life can be cruel. Speaking of which—guess who got roped into helping Katrine find a wedding gown next weekend."

"Frazier?"

"I wish. So now I get to spend next Saturday in a bridal shop. Doesn't that sound like a fun way to spend the day?"

"Depends. Does it mean you'll get to watch her undress?"

I shook my head. "You really are shameless."

"That's true." Smiling, Kevin took me by the hands and pulled me close. "But then, one would think you'd be used to it by now."

"One would."

"So are you going to try to get out of it? The shopping, that is."

"No. I'll probably just grin and bear it. I mean, all I have to do is give my opinion. How hard can that be?"

"For you?"

"Exactly. Now, I'm happy to stand out here and talk all night if you'd like, but one of us needs to take Maggie home. And given your mood tonight, I think it's best if I do the honors."

"You're probably right. I'll head upstairs and start warming up the bed for you."

"Sounds good," I replied as we kissed good-bye, although I doubted he'd be awake enough to close the deal when I returned.

With that in mind, I decided not to go home after taking Maggie home but instead took a detour through the parking lot of the Big Five Motel. Spotting the red Datsun that told me Sera was inside, I parked my own vehicle a few spaces away and made for the lobby.

Sera McKinnon was a friend and classmate I'd known for just over a year. Like me, she was a nontraditional student who grew up on the wrong side of the tracks and thus did not fit in among the well-heeled middle-class ladies and gentlemen at Hamilton University. Unlike me, she was blessed with the silky hair, smooth skin, and Ivy League bone structure that would have allowed her to mix with that crowd were it not for her palpable disdain for "the stupid, the shallow, and the spoiled," as she called them, and her refusal to bow to the rules of convention in nearly every sense of the word.

We met as guests at a luncheon given for Presidential Fellowship candidates the spring before last and again as Presidential Fellows last fall. Given my wholly conventional life as a military spouse and mother, I doubt we could have met under any other circumstances. As it was, however, we had a lot in common when it came to politics and policy, and plenty of time to get to know one another due our similar schedules and the tendency of everyone—including some of our instructors—to pretend we didn't exist.

Prior to transferring to Hamilton, Sera had been an insurance investigator, a telemarketer, and a bartender. At some point she landed at a community college where she developed an interest in law and policy, which prompted her to pursue a bachelor's degree and, later, her juris doctor. Having dropped her other gigs due to a lack of time and interest, she now made ends meet by working nights at the motel, serving champagne and hors d'oeuvres for a catering company on weekends, and—when necessary—selling the odd pint of blood or plasma.

Through the window I could see her at the front desk reading a tattered paperback while absently twirling the coppery locks gracing her left shoulder.

"Oh, concierge," I said as I walked through the door. "Do you rent rooms by the hour?"

"Yep. Condoms, too—although new ones cost extra."

"That's disgusting."

"I know."

We exchanged wicked smiles as I took off my coat and folded it over my arm.

"Historical romance?" I wondered aloud upon spotting the bare, muscled arms and chest that encircled the enraptured woman on the cover of the paperback she had set on the counter. "Are you feeling OK?"

Sera shrugged. "It was in the lost and found, and I was sick of studying."

"I see. So is it doing anything for you?"

"It's not going to make me start dating men, if that's what you mean." Grinning, Sera vacated her perch and signaled for me to join her in the lounge behind me. "So, what brings you here at this ungodly hour?"

"Kevin and I got home from a party a while ago, and since I was out this way to take the sitter home, I came by to shoot the shit with you for a while. Are you busy?"

"Well, as you can see from the sign above the door, all the rooms are full. So unless the cops decide to raid the place or someone sets the place on fire, we can probably talk all night."

"Terrific. Got anything to drink?"

"There may be a soda or two left in the machine."

With a sigh, I approached the front of the dispenser, dropped some coins in the slot, pressed a panel, and watched a root beer tumble out. Sinking into a chair, I popped open the can and took my first desperate sip. "It's warm," I observed with annoyance.

"Yeah. I think the refrigeration component is bad."

"Thanks for the warning."

"No problem." Sera smirked as she plopped down on the sofa. "So whose party was it?"

"Todd Van Ault's."

"That's helpful. So are you gonna tell me who that is, or shall I call the psychic hotline?"

I crossed my eyes and offered a salute.

"Ah…one of Kevin's friends. I thought you swore off those."

"I did. But there's a new guy on board, and Kevin wanted me to meet his fiancée."

"Gotcha. So how'd that go?"

"All things considered, it wasn't too painful. Rob and I didn't exactly hit it off, but his fiancée is pretty cool."

"You sound surprised."

"I am, actually. I mean, after meeting some of the silly things these guys wear on their arms, you learn not to expect too much. But Katrine is great. She's very funny and incredibly bright."

"Pretty?"

"And then some."

"So what does she look like?"

"She's about five-seven, slim; has fair skin, a great smile, and—in the parlance of your recent literary diversion—a cascade of sable tresses that showcase her luminescent, toffee eyes."

"Wow. She sounds like a real hammer."

"A real *what*?"

"Hammer," Sera repeated. "Apparently guys are using that these days instead of *babe*."

"According to whom?"

"My twin brother, Seth."

"Well, I guess that's an improvement. At least it suggests power rather than pedophilia."

"Amen. So do I get to meet her?"

"Meet her?"

"Yeah. You know—as in make her acquaintance."

"I know what the word 'meet' means. I also know you and that you're interested in more than just *making her acquaintance*."

"And do you have a problem with that?"

"Not at all. I just think you'd be wasting your time given that she's already spoken for and, therefore, is probably about as gay as the tile on this floor."

"Well, you know," Sera whispered, cupping her palm around the corner of her mouth, "I have noticed a few of the pink ones sliding back and forth against each other recently."

"That's probably roaches. You might want to call an exterminator."

"Seriously, Jackie. At least think about it."

"Fine. I'll think about it. But you really should get ahold of yourself. I mean, you're about as bad as Kevin."

"Kevin? What does he have to do with this?"

"Katrine made a joke tonight that he has taken totally out of context, and now he's tormenting himself with the prospect of the two of us getting it on."

"The two of you, as in you and Katrine?"

I nodded. "I'd come into the conversation late to find that Kevin had told her and Rob how nervous I'd been about meeting her, since he'd let me believe she was from Eastern Europe and might not speak English. Anyway, with nothing to do but endure my humiliation, I jokingly asked if he had shared any other embarrassing details with them before I arrived, and a dual-directional sexual orientation and a crush on Justine Bateman were what she offered in reply."

I sighed as a smile crept over Sera's face. "Justine Bateman, huh?" she mused. "That's interesting."

"How so?"

"Well, from what you just said, this girl looks a lot like Justine Bateman."

"They have similar features," I allowed after giving it some thought. "But Justine Bateman looks like the pretty girl next door. Katrine looks like that girl's smarter, hotter cousin. Why is that significant?"

"Well, one could argue that she was subconsciously wondering if you found her attractive."

"You sound just like Kevin. But let me assure you, as someone who is frequently compared to celebrities with certain outward features, it's far more likely that when she conceived the joke, she simply said the first name that came to mind, which happened to be one she hears a lot."

"I guess that's equally plausible. Whatever the case, it's a strange thing to joke about with people you've just met—especially military people."

"True. But she's young and probably doesn't know any better."

"You and I would have known better."

"You and I weren't sheltered or smothered by overprotective parents and thus don't have to joke about sex in order to seem smart and sophisticated."

"Touché," Sera said with a laugh. "So I gather from your recap that Kevin's not offended by the idea of girl-on-girl action."

"Are you kidding? You should hear what he'd like to get going between you and me."

"You mean he *knows* about me?"

"Well, sure. I mean, you're out, right? So I didn't think you'd mind."

"Not if he doesn't. So how come he never acts like he knows?"

"What's he supposed to do, Sera? Wear a pin?"

"Point taken."

"I'll tell you what," I added facetiously. "Next time you're at our place, I'll have him ask you about your conquests. Would that make you feel better?"

"Most definitely. Thank you."

Sera and I continued to chat for another hour or so, when a series of progressively stronger yawns told me it was time to mosey.

"Already?" she groaned. "But you just got here."

"I know. But Lucy might wake up and need changing or something."

"But Kevin's home, right? And he's a big boy. Can't he handle it?"

"Of course. If he were awake, that is. But the man sleeps like the dead, which means the poor kid could scream herself hoarse and he wouldn't even stir."

"Fine," Sera sighed. "Leave me alone here with nothing to do but stare at the walls."

"What about your book?"

"Are you kidding? After this conversation, that thing's gonna be a total snooze."

"Romance novels are always a snooze. You should try something a bit more interesting—like the phone book or the ingredient list from a can of ravioli."

Four

*T*he next week was a blur starting with Sunday—when, after a quick
brunch, Kevin headed for the armory, leaving me to cover the laundry
and the kids while mentally plotting out the paper I would be up all night
writing for class on Monday. By Friday, with two midterms, two more
papers, and a presentation under my belt, I was ready to relax. Disgusted,
however, by the condition of the house when I returned to it that afternoon,
I opted instead to spend the two hours sweeping, mopping, and dusting
before picking up the kids from day care at four o'clock.

Kevin walked in at ten after five to find the house clean, dinner in the
oven, the kids playing on a blanket on the floor, and me wiping down the
aquarium stand while Mr. Costello insisted he wasn't angry.

"Hey, babe," he said as I met him at the door and offered him my cheek.
"How was your day?"

"Better now that you're here."

"That's good to know."

"So how was school?" I asked, although I didn't have to. The look of
relief on his face told me he was as glad to be home as I was to have him
there.

"Just peachy," he lied, setting his bag on the floor, plopping down on the
couch, and pulling me onto his lap.

"That good, huh?"

"To be honest, it wasn't that bad. It's just that, with everything going on overseas, it doesn't seem right that so many guys are stuck in Kuwait while my ass sits comfortably on a stool in some science lab."

"*Comfortably*? Kevin, you're busting that ass trying to complete a five-year program in less than four. I'd hardly call that sitting comfortably."

"Fair point. But sometimes I wonder if becoming an officer is really worth it."

"It will all pay off in the end, Kevin. You just have to remember why you wanted this in the first place."

"Why *did* I want it again?"

"Mostly you were motivated by the money," I teased. "But you also liked the idea of retiring in your forties and spending the next half century hunting, fishing, and drinking cheap beer."

"That's right—fishing, guns, and beer. I remember now. What's in it for you again?"

"Silly!" I ran my finger down the center of his face and poked him on the chin. "*I'm* looking forward to hosting wives' coffees and standing beside my marine as he hastens the struggle for capitalism so that people everywhere can enjoy the pollution and rampant consumerism that we've come to take for granted here in America."

"Got it. Thanks for setting me straight."

"You're welcome. Now I need a favor."

"Anything for you, my muse."

"Funny—I didn't know techies *had* muses."

"Well, *someone* inspired the development of shock therapy, and I'm damn sure it wasn't a guy."

Feigning umbrage, I strode to the kitchen and left him laughing on the couch.

"I thought you needed a favor," he teased.

"I've reconsidered."

Kevin stood and hung his head in affected shame. "OK," he sighed. "I guess I'll go upstairs and change."

"You do that," I called back to him as I headed to the kitchen to check on dinner. "Hopefully the kids won't get hold of your bag while you're gone and wreak havoc on your homework."

Pleased with my joke, Kevin's mood, and the fact that the weekend had finally arrived, I giggled all the way to the stove and continued to do so as I opened the oven door to inspect the roast. My mirth came to an abrupt and painful end, however, when the sound of the phone ringing pierced my ears, made me jump, and caused me to smack the back of my hand on the edge of the hot metal rack.

"Hello," I challenged the caller as I picked up the receiver.

"Jackie?"

"Yes?"

"It's R. C."

"I beg your pardon?"

"Sergeant Copeland—from the U?"

"Oh, sure," I sighed. "How are you?"

"Good. And you?"

"I've been better," I admitted, stretching the cord across the room to the sink so I could run water over my burn. "Kevin's busy at the moment. Can I have him call you back in a little bit?"

"No. That's OK. I actually called to talk to you."

"Me?"

"About tomorrow?"

Tomorrow? "Oh, right!" I said, recalling their shopping trip and hoping he had called to cancel. "Wedding gowns—I remember."

"Great. So can we pick you up around ten?"

We? "You mean you're coming along?"

"Of course."

Terrific.

"By the way," he continued as I scrambled to hatch an escape plan. "I want to thank you for doing this. Katrine's kind of out in left field without her mom and sisters around, so we really appreciate your willingness to help."

So much for an exit strategy, I thought in answer to the tug on my heartstrings. *Well, if I can't get out of it, at least I can get* him *out of it.*

"Look, Rob, I know how guys are about shopping. So why don't Katrine and I go shopping by ourselves and save you the time and trouble of dealing with all this girl stuff?"

"I really don't mind," he said to my chagrin. "I don't have anything else to do tomorrow."

What a shame.

"And besides," he added. "I'm paying for everything, so I sort of have to be there."

"I see."

"OK then. Unless something changes, I guess we'll see you at ten."

Lucky me.

"Who was that?" Kevin asked as he stepped into the kitchen, having swapped his uniform for a pair of jeans and a yellow sweatshirt with "USMC" printed in red.

"Sergeant Copeland. He was calling to firm up our plans for tomorrow and let me know they would be by to pick me up at ten tomorrow morning."

"They?" he repeated. "You mean he's going with you?"

"Evidently. I tried to talk him out of it, but he said he has to come because he's paying for everything."

"I see."

"So do you still think he's perfectly normal?"

"Why wouldn't I?"

"I don't know. Maybe because he's going shopping with two women when he could be doing just about anything else."

Kevin shrugged. "Maybe that was Katrine's idea. Maybe she wants his input."

"OK. Then *maybe* because he and Katrine have been shacked up and engaged for months, and she still can't write a check or use a credit card."

"Maybe they're waiting until the wedding to get joint accounts. Military banking institutions usually won't let you add someone to your account who isn't a spouse or a relative."

Damn. I hadn't thought of that.

Assuming from my silence that he'd won the volley, Kevin winked at me and then went to collect the kids and get them ready for dinner. "So did you tell him you couldn't make it?" he asked when he returned. "Or have you finally managed to psyche yourself up for the occasion?"

"If by psyching myself up you mean accepting my fate, then yes. Much as I'd love to get out of it, the fact is, I have to go."

"I still don't understand why you don't *want* to go. You never seem to mind shopping with Lynette."

That wasn't strictly true. A marine wife and former college classmate, Lynette was the person I most recently had called my best friend. And while we used to spend a lot of time together—much of it at garage sales and thrift stores, which I suppose qualifies as shopping—over the last year that had begun to change. When we did manage to get together, our conversations felt strained and forced, and although I continued to make myself available in the hope that things would turn around, I looked forward to our meetings less and less every time.

But I wasn't going to go into all of that now.

"This is different," I said instead. "For one thing, Lynette has never asked me to go shopping for wedding dresses."

"That's only because you were both already married when you met."

"That's true. But if she had, I would've refused because—and you know this, so I shouldn't have to explain it—I think it's crazy to spend thousands of dollars on a single event when you can use it for something useful, like a car or an education. Plus, it's hard for me to be excited about helping Katrine shop for a gown so she can marry a man who is loathsome and revolting."

"So, call her up and tell her that."

"Yeah, right. Why don't I just ring up the neighbor's kid and tell him he's adopted?"

"No—let me."

"Seriously," I said, crossing my arms, "there's a fine line between honesty and cruelty, and I'd rather put up with a little personal inconvenience than shatter her illusions."

That settled, we turned our attention to dinner and made the usual inquiries of Tyler as to his and Lucy's adventures at day care. After eating his food and sharing the news about Miss Betty's new couch and the tree they'd seen cut down at the park, the preschooler asked to be excused.

Smiling, Kevin watched him climb down from his seat, wipe his hands and face, and head for his room. "So what would you like to do after the kids go to bed?"

"I'm not sure," I said hopefully. It seemed like ages since we'd gone to bed early enough to make the earth move, as it were, and Kevin's lack of interest in using the bed for anything other than sleeping was starting to rattle my confidence. "What do you have in mind?"

"Nothing," he replied as he lifted his backpack off the floor and set it on the table. "I was just wondering if there was anything you wanted me to do before I hit the books."

So much for subtlety, I thought as I squeezed his hand and headed to my office upstairs.

Five

*H*aving spent the first half of the next morning oversleeping and the second half racing around getting ready, I failed to notice that the faded pewter Nova had not arrived on time until I was climbing into the backseat.

"Sorry we're late," Rob said as he held the driver's seat forward for me. "We stopped off to clean out the car."

"That's sweet," I said with a nod to Katrine, "but you shouldn't have bothered. It just reminds me that my own vehicle is a fire hazard."

After we'd buckled in, Rob put the car in gear and took off down the street. He drove with a hand on the gear shift, tapping it in time with the unidentifiable noise coming from the tape deck.

I remember thinking at the time that it was strange for him to be driving a beat-up Chevy with a cassette player. Given all other indications, I had expected him to show up in a BMW or Mercedes convertible with a state-of-the-art sound system and a five-disc CD changer. Although the CD was not yet commonplace—this was only 1990, after all, and the MP3 format was still but a collective twinkle in some engineers' eyes—his clothing, shoes, and outerwear gave the impression that Rob was accustomed to nice things, while his affinity for words like *audiophile* suggested he was what marketing folks would call an "early adapter" when it came to entertainment and technology.

"So how's the music back there?" he asked after a while.

Loud was the first word to come to mind, although I kept it to myself.

"It's OK," I said instead, both despite and because I could tell he wanted me to approve.

I can be that way sometimes.

"So you don't like it?"

"Not really. But listen to whatever you want. It's your car."

"Don't be ridiculous. We're not going to subject you to something you don't like."

And yet, you're still here.

"Put that in its case," Rob directed Katrine, having ejected the tape and set it onto the bridal magazines on her lap. "Then give Jackie the box so she can find something more to her liking."

"I don't believe you," she complained. "You never let *me* pick the music."

"That's because *you* can listen to the stuff you like any time you want on the radio at home. The only way I can hear what I like is when we're in the car."

"Well, maybe if you had bought a new stereo instead of that TV, you wouldn't have that problem. We don't even have cable."

"Don't mind Katrine," Rob said via the rearview mirror. "She hasn't quite woken up yet."

"It's OK," I replied, more to her than him, as I retrieved Squeeze's *Singles—45s and Under* from the bin and handed it over. "Kevin and I have the same problem when we ride together. The minute he gets behind the wheel, he pops out whatever I had in the tape deck and tunes in to the local classic rock station."

Rob smiled at me in the rearview mirror. "So what do you normally listen to?"

"It varies," I replied, training my gaze out the window to avoid his. Even though I'm prone to car sickness, it beat looking at his arrogant mug. "I like Squeeze, the Replacements, the Talking Heads. I also like the Smiths and U2; but mostly I listen to Elvis Costello."

"Who's that?" Katrine asked as Rob rolled his eyes in the mirror.

"Just another Brit with a guitar," I replied before he could insult her taste or intelligence. "He doesn't get much airtime here, and he's currently boycotting the media, so I'm not surprised you haven't heard of him. But he's got a great way with words and a real gift for arrangements."

"He is quite a talent," Rob agreed. "Ever seen him in concert?"

"I was hoping to see him while he's on tour this spring, but his nearest venue is Madison, Wisconsin, and Kevin would sooner die than drive five hours for that."

"I'll go with you. When will he be there?"

"I'm not sure of the exact date," I lied. As much as I would have hated to miss the concert, I knew *I'd* rather die than spend even one hour alone in the car with Rob.

"Well, you let me know when you find out, and we'll see what we can do. Meanwhile, we should check out the local club scene. I understand a lot of area bands like to cover him."

"Thanks anyway, Rob. Kevin's not much into crowds, and he's even less into dancing."

"So let's you and me go."

I could tell from the set of her jaw that this appealed to Katrine about as much as it did to me, but she clearly wasn't going to tell him that. "I don't think so," I said. "But thanks anyway."

"Why not? Kevin doesn't seem like the kind who'd mind, and Katrine is too young to get in anyway, so she won't care."

"I appreciate the offer," I demurred, watching her flip through a magazine as if she weren't listening. "I have neither the body nor the wardrobe for that anymore, and I can't stand to be any place where everyone is cooler than me."

"Are you serious?"

"As a heart attack."

"OK. But let me know if you change your mind."

"Will do. Just don't hold your breath."

On second thought…

Five or six songs later, we arrived at the bridal shop, which occupied an old Victorian on St. Paul's Grand Avenue. Like many others in the area, it recently had been restored to look like it would have in its prime, including high ceilings, tall windows, and an impressive set of hand-carved double doors with original brass hardware.

Jogging up the front steps to the wraparound porch, having left Rob and Katrine to canoodle at the curb, I opened one of the doors and froze.

"What's wrong?" Katrine asked as she caught up with me a few moments later.

"I need to leave."

"What? Why?"

"I don't belong here."

"You're not making any sense," she observed, waving a hand in front of my eyes. "And what are you looking at?"

A blinding white nightmare was the only way to describe it. There was tulle, silk, and satin as far as the eye could see, reflecting light from ceiling lamps like sunshine off of snow.

In retrospect, I should not have been so surprised. This wasn't a trip to the lumberyard, after all. I guess I'd just never thought it could be so much worse than I had imagined.

"I'm sorry," I said sincerely. "I can't go in there."

"Why not?"

"Would you believe I'm allergic to taffeta?"

"No."

"What about organza?"

Katrine crossed her arms. "Jackie, what's going on?"

"I told you: I can't go in there."

"Why not?"

"Because I'll just wind up breaking something."

"No, you won't. Now come on. I'm getting cold."

"You're making a big mistake," I warned as she grabbed my hand and dragged me through the door. "They're just going to kick us out."

"No, they won't."

"She's right," Rob offered, having returned from parking the car. "In fact, they'll barely know we're here."

"Look, I wasn't kidding," I told him as Katrine walked away to find a clerk. "I honestly don't belong here. And if you don't let me out, eventually someone is going to *put* me out, which—take my word for it—ranks right up there with going to the grocery checkout with a cartload of food and realizing you don't have enough cash to cover the bill."

"I'm really not worried."

Realizing I wasn't going to get anywhere with Rob, I looked around and took stock of the contents of the store. Although I fully understand the desire to make a wedding memorable and special, to this day I can't comprehend how "special and memorable" for some equates to ostentatious and obscene.

I had vowed long before Kevin and I decided to tie the knot that my wedding would bear no resemblance to the traditional monstrosities that every other girl I knew wanted. It wasn't just the cost; although I could hardly see the point of spending as much on one day as some people made in a year, my objection was to the waste. Even if you happened to have thousands of dollars lying around, why would you spend it on a party that might last a few hours when you could buy a car that would likely run for years? Or put it toward an education, which would last you a lifetime?

Fortunately, Kevin agreed. Thus, we were married by a justice of the peace in a park near the river with only our two best friends and immediate family in attendance. Even with the reception and the dance that followed, the whole thing had cost barely a grand.

Glancing toward the gift registry, I saw Katrine waving from the first of three sets of stairs. "Come on," she stage whispered as if conveying a state secret. "The fitting rooms are up here."

Seeing the excitement on her face, I decided to be a good sport and headed toward the stairs behind Rob. I followed him until we got to the first landing, where he planted himself on a royal blue, crushed velvet divan.

"What are you doing?" I asked as he pulled a handheld video game from his pocket.

"Killing time."

"Can't you do that upstairs?" Not that I wanted him along, but if there was a loophole that would get *me* out of going up there, I wanted in on it.

"He's not allowed," Katrine announced from two flights up. "See?"

I followed her point to a sign that urged grooms and fathers to remain on the lower floor.

"That way, men can still come to the store," she explained, "without breaking the rule against seeing the bride in her gown before the wedding."

So much for getting in on that loophole, I groused as I tromped up the stairs, regretting—for the one and only time in my life—the fact that I didn't have a penis.

On the second floor, Katrine and I were approached by a woman in a periwinkle suit and matching pumps. I figured her to be about forty-five and ruled her medium-blond bob a dye job, but I decided not to hold it against her. *If the rest of me looks that good at her age,* I concluded as she greeted Katrine, *I'll probably be on the bottle myself.*

"Hello," she murmured in a voice that screamed good breeding. "My name is Sandra. Are you the bride-to-be?"

"Yes." Katrine beamed, clasping her magazines to her chest. "How could you tell?"

Well, it sure as hell didn't require a crystal ball, I thought. *If that grin on your face didn't give it away, that rock on your hand certainly would have been a clue.*

I imagined the clerk was thinking roughly the same thing but was trained not to show it.

"In this business, you learn to recognize the signs," she said, tilting her head indulgently and lacing her fingertips in front of her waist. "Now, how can I help you ladies today?"

Katrine opened a magazine to a marked page. "I'd like to see this dress," she announced. "I called last week and was told you carried this line."

"I'm sorry," the clerk replied with genuine regret as she recognized the item in question. "We do carry that line, but we haven't any samples of that particular item in stock at the moment. Can I show you something similar, perhaps, or is there another dress that you liked as much?"

A diamond tennis bracelet dangled from the woman's wrist as she indicated with a sweep of her arm the array of gowns positioned along the other three sides of the room. Realizing that I'd been staring at it, I blinked and turned to Katrine, who now appeared to be sulking.

"I don't understand," she was saying. "They *told* me you had this dress."

"Well, I don't know to whom you spoke, but perhaps they had the wrong item number."

"That can't be. I had them repeat it back to me."

"I'm truly sorry. There has obviously been some kind of misunderstanding, because I sold the last sample of this dress myself two weeks ago."

"You *sold* the sample?"

"I'm afraid so. You see, like you, many of our clients are rather anxious to have exactly what they want for their special day. So occasionally, we'll sell them a sample since it saves them time and we can always order another one."

"What about all your *other* clients?"

"It's rarely a problem. Since we have so many other beautiful gowns, our ladies generally find something that makes them happy, even if it's not the item they originally had in mind."

I observed this exchange uncomfortably and then watched another clerk approach and speak quietly to the first.

"Would you excuse me for a moment, please?" she asked when her associate had gone. "Evidently I'm needed below."

"Well, how do you like that?" Katrine asked as we watched the women glide down the stairs and out of view. "What am I supposed to do now?"

Her attitude only increased my discomfort, but knowing I was trapped until she found a dress, I thought it prudent to approach things in a way that would lead to that end.

"Excuse me, ma'am," I began when the clerk reappeared.

"Please—call me Sandra," she said, relieved to be dealing with someone less emotional.

"Thank you, Sandra. Now, did I hear correctly that another sample of this dress could be ordered?"

"Yes. In fact, we generally order a new sample at the same time we sell the last one. Unfortunately, that did not happen with this item since it was part of our summer stock, and we don't replace our summer samples once the winter line comes out. The dress itself can still be ordered, but only as a purchase—which requires a fifty percent deposit."

"And once it's ordered, how soon can the item be ready?"

"Well, it generally takes about four to six weeks for the item to arrive, and from there it really just depends on how many alterations are required."

"We don't have that much time," Katrine interjected. "My wedding is in December."

"That's no problem. We'll just arrange for priority handling. It will involve an additional fee, but it would save a week or two."

"That won't help! The wedding is in New York, and I'm leaving on the fifteenth."

"I see. Well, in that case, you're right. An express order won't do us much good."

I watched Katrine bite her lip, hoping it wasn't a harbinger of a looming tantrum.

"Look," I said carefully. "It seems we got into this game a little late. I mean, even if you could try this dress on tonight, you would have had to buy the sample in order to have it fitted by the fifteenth. Right? So why don't we look around and see what they have in stock? I'm sure there's something here that you'll like. If so, you can buy it today and not only save yourself time but get a discount as well."

Katrine sighed and considered my suggestion. "All right," she said finally, closing her magazine and setting the stack on the counter. "I guess it can't hurt to look at some other things as long as I'm here anyway."

"Wonderful," Sandra said with a grateful smile. "I'll assemble some samples with designs similar to this one and a few others I think might suit you. I'm sure we can find something you will like. You look to be about a size eight. Is that right?"

"Usually. Although sometimes I have to go to a ten."

"That should be no problem. We have plenty of samples in both sizes, and your figure is very well proportioned. There won't be much to do in terms of alterations."

That was as much of the conversation I heard for a while as Sandra and Katrine drifted down toward the rows of samples at the other end of the room.

After they had gone, I strolled around in search of something to help me pass the time. My options were great if I was planning a reception or romantic getaway, since there were racks of brochures and other materials positioned about the place. Having neither the interest nor the inclination to even mock them, I resisted their myriad charms and decided instead to investigate the magazines I'd spotted on the coffee table, in the dim hope of finding one concerned with something other than honeymoon retreats, cake designs, and floral arrangements.

Several minutes later, Katrine reappeared carrying an armload of dresses.

"What are you doing?" she asked as I was settling into one of the chairs with a recent copy of *Wine Enthusiast.* It was either that or *Modern Game Breeder*—which had to be someone's idea of a joke, surely. In any case, my gut told me I'd sooner take up wine drinking than bestiality, so I went with that.

"Just relaxing," I replied. "Why?"

Before Katrine could respond, Sandra arrived with a second bundle of gowns.

"Here you are," she announced, drawing back the curtain on the nearest open fitting room and depositing them inside. "You ladies just let me know if you need anything else."

When Sandra had gone, Katrine hung her own load of dresses on the fitting room rack, and then returned to the doorway and faced me.

"What?" I wondered aloud.

"I'm ready."

"For what?"

"I thought you were going to help me."

"Help you what?"

"Change."

Change? I cast my glance from Katrine to the fitting room and back. "Look, I came along today to provide advice and moral support. You didn't say anything about manual labor."

Katrine eyed me sympathetically. "You don't often shop with other women, do you?"

"Now and then. But since I'm perfectly capable of dressing myself— as are most of my friends—I've never had to enter a fitting room with anyone, much less help them change."

"OK. Well, I don't know how many of those excursions involved copious amounts of satin and lace, but I can assure you that it's at least a two-man operation."

"That will be tricky," I mused, "since men aren't allowed on this floor."

Katrine could not suppress a smile. "You *know* what I meant."

"Perhaps. But in the interest of clarity and inclusivity, I suggest that in the future you use the word 'person' instead of 'man' except when referring to a specific adult male."

"It'll be my pleasure. And now that we've cleared that up, let's get this show on the road."

"I'm serious," I announced as she continued to watch me. "I have no intention of going inside that fitting room."

"Why not?"

"Because we barely know each other, that's why. And I don't know about you, but I don't make a habit of taking off my clothes in front of people I don't know; nor do I make a habit of watching them undress."

"Fine. So keep your eyes closed."

"And how am I supposed to help you with the dresses if I can't see anything?"

"Beats me. I guess you'll have to use the Force."

"Now you're just being silly."

"*I'm* being silly?" Katrine repeated. "Look, I'm sorry this is weird for you. But I've been looking forward to this all week, and I do not want to have waited so long and come so far just to go home empty-handed. So whatever your problem is, do me a favor and get over it *tout suite*."

Get over it? I repeated privately. *What the hell was there to get over?* This wasn't a cold, the flu, an ear infection, or an irrational fear of heights. This was a matter of modesty, which, last I checked, was a virtue to be prized, not a disorder to be defeated.

I was about to say as much when I noticed a hint of fear in Katrine's eyes, as if she half expected me to tell her off and walk away. It occurred to me then that it had taken all the nerve she had to assert herself and that it wasn't something she did often. It occurred to me as well that, in fact, I was being silly and, perhaps, a bit selfish. Here was this sheltered kid trying to plan a wedding without her mom, her sisters, or even a best friend to help her. I was the only person she knew for miles, and instead of making things easier, I was raining on her parade.

At that point I decided to dispense with the drama and get on board with whatever Katrine had in mind. To that end, I surrendered my magazine, retrieved my purse from the floor, and nodded for her to lead the way.

Once inside the fitting room, Katrine yanked off her shoes and coat and tossed them onto the settee in the corner. A sweater and jeans soon followed. Although she obviously wasn't worried about what I could or could not see, I kept my eyes on the pile as it grew, and then jumped as a white blouse landed on top like a dollop of whipped cream.

"Are you all right?" Katrine asked. "You look warm."

"Yeah. I guess they keep the heat on pretty high—since people are changing, I mean."

"Should I ask them to open a window or something?"

"And have you freeze to death between dresses? Certainly not."

"Really, Jackie. You look like you're burning up."

I turned and faced the mirror. My chest and neck were awash in red blotches. "See?" I said with a shrug. "I *told* you I'm allergic to taffeta."

"I doubt that. But you should probably have something to drink. Shall I ask Sandra for some water?"

"No, thanks. I'll be fine."

"Are you sure?"

"I'm positive."

"OK," Katrine said, turning and reaching for the ceiling. "Then let's get to it."

Assuming from her position that these things went on from the top, I slipped a gown from its hanger, lifted it over Katrine's head, and tugged it into place. Naturally, the first one I chose *had* to have a choker neck and a closure consisting of a line of tiny faux pearls running from the nape to the hip that had to be pulled through even tinier elastic loops. To facilitate this, Katrine drew her almost waist-length hair to the side and over her shoulder, but while that gesture made it easier to *see* the pearls, it did nothing to improve the skill or the speed at which I handled them.

What kind of psycho designs a dress you can't get in and out of on your own? I griped to myself. *And, more importantly, what kind of idiot would buy it? I mean, what if the thing caught fire and you had to get out of it quickly? And haven't these people ever heard of zippers?*

"How are things going back there?" Katrine asked hopefully.

"Fine," I lied as I continued battling the beads. "Although if I ever come to you for career advice, be sure to steer me away from surgery. I'm a walking malpractice claim."

After what seemed like an eternity, I finally finished fastening the buttons. "There," I said, letting my aching hands fall to my sides. "You're done."

"Great!" Whirling around, Katrine shook out the folds of the skirt and faced the mirror behind me. "So what do you think?"

"I'm not sure. I mean, the sleeves are a little, uh, puffy for my taste, but otherwise, it seems OK. What do you think?"

"I think I look like I've been taking steroids."

"Oh, it's not *that* bad."

"Yes, it is," Katrine argued as she posed and pretended to flex her satin muscles. "These sleeves make me look like a linebacker."

"So you don't like it?"

"Are you kidding? It's heinous."

"It's a good thing you didn't order the other dress, then. Those sleeves were even bigger."

"True." Giggling, Katrine dropped to one knee and crouched over an imaginary line of scrimmage. "So shall we punt, or try for that first down?"

"How 'bout you just get your ass off the floor and into another dress?"

"OK. OK." Still giggling, Katrine stood and turned around. "Say," she said as I started to unbutton her, "when we're done looking at these, we should find something for you to try on."

"I don't think so."

"Come on, Jackie. It could be fun."

"Sorry, Katrine, but trying on clothes that rarely fit is not my idea of fun—especially since big fluffy dresses make me look like a guy in drag. Now turn around and let's get on with it."

The buttons were more easily unhooked than fastened, and before I knew it, Katrine had leaned forward, shaken the dress off her arms, and stepped out of it through the back.

"Now hang on just a minute," I ordered, fixing my eyes on the wall to her left to avoid seeing her exposed flesh in the periphery. "If you can step out of it, why couldn't you step *into* it?"

"Because that way I also run the risk of stepping *onto* it," she explained, "and then I couldn't have pulled it *up*."

Shaking my head, I returned the gown to its quilted hanger and pulled another from the rack. This one opened on the side and, although it involved a zipper and a clasp instead of ridiculously tiny buttons and elastic loops, having to work under Katrine's left arm made it almost as much of a challenge as the first.

And so it went for the next hour and a half. Having become intimately acquainted with nearly every form of bridal hardware known to mankind, I was rewarded with a break as Katrine considered her options with a view of narrowing the field from eleven to three. Finally, after she had tried on the remaining contenders each twice more, my torment was over.

As Katrine changed into her own clothes, I took her selection to the anteroom to check out the headwear. In no time I had found the perfect item—a simple tiara encrusted with rhinestones and crystal beads from which flowed a single-layer veil made of sheer tulle and embellished with tiny embroidered leaves. This I presented to Katrine without mentioning that it was on clearance, since, as I confided to Sandra, not everyone appreciates a bargain the way I do.

As we drove back to South Minneapolis—more than three hours after we'd started out—Rob listened with pride and uncharacteristic patience to Katrine's version of our adventure on the second floor.

I, meanwhile, was near shock over the cost of the day's purchases. Even with the discount on the sample and the clearance price of the veil, Rob had spent over twelve hundred bucks on them and a host of accessories that Katrine insisted she would need for what I figured would amount to five hours in December.

My calculations were interrupted by the sound of the car being shifted into neutral and coming to a halt.

"Here we are," Rob announced as he parked in front of our house. "Safe and sound."

"Wonderful," I replied, although I had really expected nothing less. "You're a gem."

"Don't mention it."

OK. Next time I won't.

"So, what are you and Kevin up to tonight?" Rob continued as he and Katrine faced me after a whispered exchange. "Do you have any plans?"

"I'm not sure," I stalled. "Why?"

"We thought you might like to get together—for drinks and maybe dinner. It would be our treat—as a way of saying thanks for your help today."

"That's not necessary, guys. Really."

"Yes, it is. You've been very generous with your time. Let us do something for you in return."

"OK. But I should check with Kevin before we go any further. I mean, we didn't have any plans as of this morning, but something may have come up while I was out."

"No problem." Turning off the engine, Rob leapt from the car and pulled the seat forward to release me. "We should plan to do it at your house," he said as if it were a done deal, "since our place is kind of small and you guys have the kids. We'll take care of the booze, of course, and whatever else you want as if you were our guests, so it won't be as much of an imposition."

I considered Rob and Katrine's invitation as they followed me up the walk. Despite a nagging sense that I would one day bludgeon the man for his grating self-importance, I was inclined to accept. With Lynette—and, by association, her husband Josh—largely out of the picture, we didn't have much of a social life anymore, and hanging out with and eventually murdering a condescending ass sounded vastly more entertaining than cleaning house or watching television.

"I doubt anything has changed since this morning," I admitted as we reached the door. "Our friends Josh and Lynette are the only people we see outside of unit functions, and since she and I already have plans to meet for brunch tomorrow, I doubt she would've called except to cancel."

As I was voicing this prediction, the door opened to reveal Kevin standing in the living room holding Lucy to his chest. "Hey, babe," he said, kissing my cheek before thrusting the child into my arms. "Hi, Rob. Katrine. How was shopping?"

"Highly successful," Rob replied, as he handed his coat to Katrine, even though he was standing closer to the closet, "thanks to Jackie, who saved the day in more ways than one. And with that in mind, we'd like to show our appreciation by treating you to dinner. It doesn't have to be tonight, but since Katrine and I have nothing going on, and Jackie said you were free as of this morning, we thought we'd run the idea by you and see what you think. So what do you say?"

Kevin looked at me as if looking for a clue.

He had reason to be confused. On the one hand, he knew I didn't care for Rob. On the other hand, if I wasn't interested in having dinner with him and Katrine, I could have put the kibosh on the idea outside instead of leaving it for him to decide.

"I know we sprung this on you kind of late," Katrine said, having sensed his hesitation, "so if you want to skip it and make plans to do it another time, we're totally cool with that. Or if you want some time to talk about it, we'll go home, and you can call us when you decide."

"Actually, tonight's fine," Kevin said suddenly. "In fact, I could use a drink and some adult contact. I'm losing the ability to form complete sentences."

"Christ, Kevin. It's only been three hours."

Kevin pointed to his watch. "Almost four."

I shook my head. "Isn't Daddy funny?" I asked Lucy as I lifted her into the air. "He's trained to lead men into battle, but he can't handle full-contact child care."

Rob laughed and slapped his hands together. "OK," he said as if we were football players in a huddle. "It sounds like we're a go. Now, what would you like to drink? We've got a fully stocked bar over at our place, so you can pretty much name your poison. Never mind," he added before anyone could answer. "We'll just bring everything. If we don't use it tonight, we'll just leave it here for next time."

"OK by me." Kevin shrugged. "I've never been one to turn down free booze."

"Great! Now what about dinner?"

I turned to Kevin. "Did you take anything out of the freezer?"

"Did you tell me to?"

"That's what I thought," I mused. "Well, I'd offer to cook something, but it seems that would require me to wiggle my nose, and Darrin here doesn't like it when I use witchcraft."

"No problem," Rob said, having pulled their coats from the closet and tossed Katrine's in her direction. "We can grab burgers, Mexican, Chinese—whatever you want. You decide."

Kevin nodded. "Chinese sounds good."

"Chinese it is!" With a flourish, Rob opened the front door and waved Katrine toward him. "I know a great Chinese place just down the street from our place. We can run home and give them a call, and then grab the liquor and pick up the food on our way back. How does that sound?"

Kevin shrugged. "OK by me."

"Great. Back in a bit."

Kevin closed the door and stared at me after Rob and Katrine had gone. "What the hell was *that* all about?" he asked. "I mean, a few hours ago, you wanted to pulverize the man, and now you're agreeing to have dinner with him? What gives?"

"I tried to put them off in the car, but Rob wouldn't hear of it. So I told them I needed to talk to you, assuming they'd wait outside or go home and wait for a call. But instead they followed me, and, well, you know the rest."

"Ah. Undone by your own good manners again, I see."

"It's the story of my life. Then again, it's only fair I let them compensate me for spending all day in that damn bridal shop. Plus, as you recall, I did promise to give the guy another chance."

Kevin eyed me with suspicion. "In other words," he said with a grin, "you're going to give me the opportunity to see the side of Rob I missed at the party last weekend."

"One could look at it that way, too, I suppose. Do you object?"

"Not at all, provided it's a clean match. In other words, no baiting the bear and no poking the snake with a stick."

"Kevin, I'm offended. When have you known me to be unkind to animals?"

"Never. But there's a first time for everything."

Six

"My God, you look awful," announced Lynette as I dropped into the seat across from her at brunch the next day.

"Shhhhh. Not so loud," I begged, leaning forward and resting my head on the table. "My brain left a wake-up call for tomorrow morning."

"Sorry. So…where were we last night?"

"At home."

"With who? Jack Daniels?"

"Him, Jose Cuervo, and Rob and Katrine."

"Rob and Katrine?"

"Rob's one of the new marines at the unit this year," I offered as I used my nose to write an obscenity in the steam my breath had left on the table. "Katrine is his fiancée."

"So did they wear out their welcome or what? You look like you were up all night."

"Thanks," I said as the server deposited two glasses of water on the table and promised to return in a few minutes. "What you don't know is that they got there at six—which, if you've done the math, gave me seven hours over which to acquire and sustain a blood alcohol level just this side of a coma. Plus, this is only the second time I've had anything alcoholic to drink since Lucy was conceived. So, to be clear, this fabulous look isn't achieved through sleep deprivation so much as by rapid fluid depletion."

"Well, then I guess you don't look as bad as you should."

"Is that your professional opinion as a registered nurse? Or just a friendly observation?"

"Both."

"Great. And, again, thanks."

"Don't mention it. So what did you and your new friends do last night, anyway? Besides drink, that is."

"I was hoping you wouldn't ask me that," I said with affected remorse. "But since you did, I'm just going to put it out there: we played spades."

Lynette gasped and put her hand to her heart. "You got drunk *and* played spades?"

"Yes."

"With someone else?"

"I'm afraid so."

"How could you do that?"

"I don't know. I mean, we didn't plan it. It just sort of *happened*."

"How does something like that just *happen*?"

"Again, I don't know. But it meant nothing—I swear. You and Josh are still our best friends, and we can still get together and drink and play spades just like we used to."

"As long as by 'drink,' you mean milk or juice," Lyn advised, breaking character to pat her abdomen affectionately. "I'm off the hard stuff for a while, remember?"

"Sorry. I forgot."

"Again?"

"It's only my second offense since you told me—and this time I'm hung over."

Lynette shrugged as the server returned to take our orders. "I'll have the eggs Benedict over medium," she announced, "and a large OJ."

"I'll have the same—except instead of OJ I'll have coffee and a vat of water with lime."

"So, are they any good?" Lynette asked when the server had gone. "At cards, I mean?"

"Uh, no. Katrine has never so much as played *Uno* before, and although Rob claims to have played for years, he has yet to master the art of bidding one's hand. I can only hope they get better with practice."

"Are you saying this wasn't a one-time thing?" Lynette asked with feigned anguish. "That you're going to see them again?"

"What choice do we have? I mean, you and Josh are always busy working or something."

"We're not that busy."

"Yes, you are. In fact, you're so busy that Kevin and I are starting to think you're the same person. I was just saying to him last week, 'Have you ever noticed how you never see Lynette and Josh in the same place at the same time?'"

Lynette laughed but did not contradict me.

"Anyway," I continued between gulps of water, "we'll still play with you and Josh when you have the time. We just figured, with your schedules, it would be wise to train a second string."

"Well, good luck with that."

"Thanks. From what I've seen so far, we're going to need it."

"So what do you think the problem is?"

"I have no idea. He's in some engineering program at the U, and she studied biochemistry in Paris before they moved here."

"So they're obviously not stupid."

"No. In fact, Katrine is hands down one of the brightest people I've ever met. In addition to having been a science major, she has a huge vocabulary, knows all there is to know about poetry, and is fluent in French and Spanish."

"Wow."

"I know," I enthused, although I could tell from her expression that Lyn wasn't as impressed as her remark implied. "So we entertained ourselves by talking about random things in different languages until we had the guys convinced we were cheating or talking about them. They didn't find that as amusing as we did, of course—even though they were winning—so they banned us from speaking anything but English. So then we switched gears and decided to make them crazy by conversing in haiku and alliteration. It was so much fun."

Lynette forced a smile. "Sounds like it."

If it had been anyone but Lynette, I would have sworn she was being sarcastic. But Lyn doesn't have a bitchy bone in her body, so although she couldn't see foreign language, poetry, or literary devices as anything but components of a high school curriculum, neither would she have mocked me for thinking otherwise.

"It sounds silly to me now, too," I allowed, "but at the time it was hilarious."

Lynette nodded. "And her fiancé? What's he like?"

"Annoying. Irksome. Frustrating."

"I take it you don't like the guy."

"No. And for the record, I have tried. He's clearly bright, which is normally a plus, but he's the type who needs you to notice, which just gets on my nerves. On top of that, he's constantly asking my opinion and kissing my ass, which tells me I can't trust him. Plus, he's kind of rough on Katrine, which will earn him no points with me. For example, we were talking about the last election when she made a remark echoing one I'd made about President Bush. Well, apparently Rob thinks the man hung the moon; but instead of simply voicing his dissent, he lights into her right in front of us and, after bringing her to the brink of tears, snipes, 'Of course, you couldn't have known that since you were still in high school,' which was a pretty low blow. She's super conscious of her age and lack of sophistication, and Rob reinforces that at every opportunity."

"What a jerk."

"I know. And I would have told you that when you first asked about him, but I didn't think you'd believe me."

"That's only because you think all men are jerks—except, of course, for Prince Kevin."

"Not true. I think Alan Alda and Richard Gere are wonderful men—as were Mohandas Gandhi, and Charles Ingalls."

"That's great, but you've never met any of those men. So they don't count."

"Well, I have met my new mailman, and I like him so far. And the guy who runs the new convenience store down the street seems pretty nice."

I had no choice but to treat the topic as a joke. If I had named even one of the men I knew and liked, Lyn would have wondered why I hadn't included Josh, which would have opened up a whole new can of worms. For although I'd never said as much to her, I liked Josh even less than I did Rob and tolerated him only slightly better. Another engineering major, Josh was tactless and condescending to everyone except the women he worshipped—which, sadly, included Pam Anderson and Farrah Fawcett but not Lynette—and the men he felt were smarter than he was and those he knew could kick his ass. In fact, the only thing that set Josh Latimer apart from Rob Copeland was that, whereas Rob was a narcissist with a pathological need for attention and approval that rendered him at times obnoxious and overbearing, Josh was so convinced of the superiority of his actions, abilities, and opinions that he wouldn't deign to engage or argue with anyone and, therefore, left me alone.

"Anyway," I continued with a view to getting the dialogue back on solid ground, "this one really is an ass. In fact, on a scale of one to ten, Rob ranks right up there at eleven with that Steff guy from *Pretty in Pink*— although I'm sure he doesn't look nearly as good with his shirt off as James Spader did in 1986."

"Does Katrine know you don't like him?"

"I don't think so. And I see no reason to tell her."

"I thought you said she was clever."

"She is."

"So how long do you think it will take her to figure out you can't stand the man she loves?"

Well, it's been more than four years since I met Josh and you still haven't caught on.

Clearly that was not the way to prove my case. Even if the statement was both completely true and my strongest evidence for how skilled I am at hiding my feelings, I wasn't about to hurt Lynette by speaking it aloud. Things between us were tense enough as it was.

"I'll just have to be very careful," I said instead, hoping she wouldn't think too hard on it and realize she had been similarly deceived. "Meanwhile," I added, hoping to steer things in a completely different direction, "how are preparations for the baby coming along?"

"Pretty well," Lynette replied excitedly, before embarking on a detailed account of all the deals and steals she'd found thus far en route to outfitting her nursery.

I found it hard to share in her thrill of the hunt. I attributed this, in part, to the fact that I'd been down that road a few years ago myself and was way over it, and to the fact that no matter how frugal she was trying to be while putting together her child's layette, I knew her and Josh's families were going to spend a fortune and then some on the new little one, who would be the first grandchild on both sides of the family. Still, it was her first baby, and she deserved to be excited, so I made all the right inquiries and all the right comments in all the right places along the way.

"Well, I suppose we should wrap this up," Lynette said upon glancing at her watch twenty minutes later. "I start a double shift in a few hours, and I want to get a nap in before I leave for the hospital."

"No problem. I've got the check if you can get the tip."

"It's a deal."

"What are you guys up to this Friday?" I asked warily as we headed for the lobby. Although I had a feeling my goodwill would come to nothing in the end, I figured it couldn't hurt to ask.

"I don't know yet. Why?"

"Kevin and I are going to a Halloween party at the armory. If you'd like, you and Josh can join us."

"Is it a *costume* party?"

"Yep."

"And *Kevin* wants to go?"

It was a fair question. As great a guy as he is, there are three things that irk me about Kevin: He doesn't dance. He won't sing. And he doesn't do costumes or Halloween. Usually.

So I nodded. "Can you believe it?"

"No."

"Me either," I admitted as I accepted my credit card and receipt from the guy at the till. "But since he's willing, I plan to go all out. So, are you in?"

"That depends. What do you mean by *all out*?"

"I'm not sure yet. I'm waiting for inspiration to hit me. Meanwhile, Kevin was hoping to borrow the Minnie Mouse costume you made for your party last year."

Lyn stopped in her tracks. "Are you telling me that Kevin—as in Kevin Thompson, and not Kevin Bacon, Kevin Costner, or Kevin Kline—intends to wear a blue polka dot dress with tights and a tutu?"

"Yep."

"In public?"

"Yep."

"Is there money on it or something?"

"Sort of. Grand prize is a portable CD player."

"Is that all?" Lynette marveled. Although at the time a portable CD player was quite a hot commodity, it still seemed grossly insufficient as an incentive to get Kevin to abandon his military bearing. "For him to wear tights, I would have expected it to be an AK-47."

"Holy God. You can't even imagine what he'd do for *that*."

"And I don't want to, thank you very much."

"Me either," I laughed, as much because of the fun we were having as because of Lyn's joke. At that moment it felt almost like the old days—

when the four of us were still just a bunch of teenagers and everything seemed open and real. "So do you think you can make it?"

"I don't know. I'll talk to Josh and get back to you."

"Sounds good. Just let me know by Thursday so we can sort out the transportation."

Seven

On the day of the dance, to which Lyn and Josh—surprisingly—had agreed to accompany us, I was a basket case. I had come up with what I believed to be an ingenious costume, and I was worried I might not pull it off.

The outfit itself wasn't the problem; it was the hair. Not since I had to sit for two and a half hours while Michelle Benson's mom transformed my preternaturally coarse tresses into a ten-inch beehive befitting Pauline Morris Anderson Strubel Cain—whom I was playing in my high school drama competition—had I worn anything so complicated or so completely out of character. And, in truth, I was far more nervous about this dance than I had been about the play.

It bears mentioning here that I didn't expect to win any prizes for my effort. I was perfectly happy to let Kevin take home the CD player and whatever other items were up for grabs that evening. Although I would have been tickled to place in the top five, all I really wanted was props for creativity and to maybe get a laugh or two.

Fortunately, I had had the presence of mind to take steps to increase my chances of success in this department. For example, the night before the dance, I had called Maggie and arranged for her to come over a few hours earlier than originally planned so I wouldn't have to divide myself between the kids and doing my hair. I also arranged for her to take them to the park after their naps so I could put myself in the right frame of mind—

that is, play the stereo loud enough to hear Mr. Costello's latest release over the bathroom fan.

I was just patting myself metaphorically on the back for all this forethought when, during a pause between songs, I heard the sound of someone pounding on the front door.

"Hang on!" I bellowed as I dashed, half-dressed, down the hall and through the kitchen to the living room. "I'll be right there!"

I had locked the front door behind Maggie and the kids—more due to force of habit than any concern for my safety—but they weren't due back yet. I couldn't imagine who else it could be, but whoever it was seemed determined to gain entrance.

"Oh, just keep your shirt on!" I ordered the unknown party, pausing quickly to punch the stop button on the tape deck on my way to the door.

"What if I'm not wearing a shirt?" Katrine asked as she walked through the door wearing a black and orange fur leotard with a five-foot tail, two ears, black whiskers, and a smile.

I crossed my arms and considered my visitor. "Tigger, I presume?"

"Yeah. How'd you know?"

"Well, you're too thin to be Garfield, and Heathcliff was a little before your time."

Katrine shrugged. "So what took you so long to answer?" she continued as I shut the door. "Judging by your attire, you didn't stop to throw something on."

I yanked the bottom edge of my swim robe to cover my underwear. "I was in the bathroom, if you must know."

"For that long? You poor thing. Have you tried bran?"

"I was *doing* my hair."

"And you couldn't stop to get the door? What if this had been an emergency?"

"Then I guess you would have died out there, because I couldn't hear you. The fan runs when the light is on, and I can't work in the dark—or without music."

"Well, we all have our priorities. So who are you supposed to be?"

Quickly, I withdrew from the closet the shiny brass curtain rod and green fabric that I'd scored at the Goodwill after brunch with Lynette on Sunday, and arranged them strategically across and over my shoulders. To this I added a gaudy gold rope, which, tied at my waist, completed the ensemble.

"*Starlet* O'Hara," I announced as I modeled my creation.

"Well, that explains the 'do,'" Katrine observed as she tugged one of the ringlets hanging from the crown of my head. "What's with the curtain rod?"

Suppressing a sigh, I looked out the window and tried to hide my dismay. I had hoped her remark about my hairstyle meant that she got the joke. Even if she hadn't heard of Carol Burnett and had mistaken my parody of the "dress made of curtains" scene from *Gone with the Wind* as original comedy, I would have been thrilled. Her question about the rod, however, confirmed she was a fan of neither Ms. Burnett nor Margaret Mitchell and left me somewhat sad for both of us.

"Let me summarize," I said, choosing to view the situation as an opportunity rather than a challenge. "*Scar*lett O'Hara is the daughter of a plantation owner in antebellum Georgia."

"That much I know."

Thank God.

"So, left devastated and destitute following the Civil War, Scarlett decides to ask Rhett Butler—whom she despises—for a loan to save her home, on which she now owes back taxes. Needing the money but not wanting Rhett to know she's desperate, Scarlett feels she must wear something other than rags to go meet him. Unable to afford a new outfit, she decides to make one out of the velvet draperies that hung in the parlor."

"And this is your version of her outfit?"

"Not exactly. You see, Carol Burnett parodied that scene on her variety show back in the seventies, renaming the main character *Star*let and hilariously incorporating the curtain rod into the outfit."

I paused to allow Katrine to appreciate the humor, but she seemed unimpressed. With a sigh, I removed the rod from the slot over my shoulders and started toward the stairs. "I have to run up to my room for a bit," I said. "Make yourself comfortable."

Moments later, I met Kevin outside our room in full Minnie regalia.

"Hey, Jack," he said, adjusting the band that held on his ears. "Who was at the door?"

"You know, you wouldn't have to ask that question if you had bothered to answer it."

"I assumed *you* would get it."

"Well, I did."

"Whaddaya know? I'm a goddamn prophet."

"Then you should have no trouble divining who it was," I said, tossing the curtain and rod onto our bed and throwing open the closet doors. "Better yet, divine me something to wear."

"What do you mean? I thought you were almost ready."

"Me too," I moaned, admiring my makeup and period hairstyle in the mirror. "Unfortunately, I have to find a new costume."

"Why? I thought that one was great."

"Me too. But apparently no one but you and I will get the joke."

"What makes you say that?"

"Katrine."

"So that's who it was," Kevin mused, checking his watch as I considered the items before me. "Well, not to rush you or anything, but we need to be at Josh and Lyn's in under an hour."

"I know. I'll be ready as soon as I can. In the meantime," I added, sensing the time Nazi hovering behind me, "why don't you go down and chat with Katrine? I'm sure she'd appreciate the company."

"She's still here?"

I nodded. "And she looks terrific."

"Oh? Is she in costume?"

"Oh, yeah."

"What kind of costume?"

"A very nice costume that was apparently inspired by a well-known publication. It includes soft, furry ears and an unmistakable tail, and suits her figure right down to the ground."

"Oh my God," Kevin gasped, having clearly developed the image of the infamous bunny suit I was aiming to conjure. "This I've got to see."

"Hey, Katrine!" I shouted as he launched himself down the hall. "Come over to the stairs. Kevin wants to see your costume."

Stifling my laughter with my hands, I watched him stop in his tracks as Katrine appeared at the foot of the stairs.

"What do you think?" she asked, twirling to allow him a view of all sides.

"It's very nice," he said politely as he paused and then resumed his descent at a much more casual pace, "and very funny, Jackie!"

Leaving the two of them to chat, I returned to the bedroom in search of alternative attire. It would have been simple if I could have just fallen back on one of my previously discounted ideas. Unfortunately, they were all in the same vein as Starlet O'Hara—an aging, jilted Miss Havisham from

Great Expectations; the soot-smudged, crazed arsonist Mrs. Rochester from *Jane Eyre*—and thus would have been equally unsuited to the impending event. Nonetheless, I was determined to find something out of the ordinary to wear, and eventually came up with a concept I hoped would not require a degree in literature to comprehend.

"So what's R. C. up to?" I heard Kevin ask as I started down the stairs several minutes later.

"He's at home getting ready. He's going as a member of the Foot Clan—you know, from the Ninja Turtles movie? I was too jazzed to sit around waiting for him, so I decided to come here and visit for a while before we head for the armory."

"I see."

"So what happened to Jackie?" Katrine asked carefully. "She's been gone quite a while."

"She's getting a new costume together. She should be down shortly—I hope."

"Who's Jackie?" I asked from behind them.

I had been standing there waiting for them to notice me and had begun to fear they never would. Especially with Katrine in her striped bodysuit, I figured interrupting was the only way I was going to get Kevin's attention.

They turned around to find me at the foot of the stairs dressed all in black save the two strands of leis hanging around my neck and the blank "HI. MY NAME IS" sticker I had pasted diagonally above my left breast. My hair was still in curls, but the clip was off-kilter, giving me the appearance of an escapee from a beauty salon for the criminally insane.

Katrine approached me slowly. "What's that on your forehead?" she asked, reaching up to touch the red blotch above my eyebrow.

"Lipstick."

"I think you missed."

"It's *supposed* to look like I took a brick to the face."

"A brick?" Kevin repeated. "So who are you? The big bad wolf post–house blowing in?"

Katrine shook her head. "He couldn't blow that one in," she stage whispered. "Remember?"

"OK, smarty pants. Then who do *you* think she is?"

"I have no idea."

"Come on, you guys," I groaned. "Think about it! I've been hit on the head and have no memory. What do you suppose that means?"

Kevin shrugged. "That whoever attacked you will probably get away with it?"

Sighing as he and Katrine exchanged a high five, I slipped past them and into the kitchen.

"OK, we've established that you have amnesia," he said as they followed me. "But what I'm asking is whether you're supposed to be any one amnesiac in particular."

"I don't know."

"Then what should we call you?"

"That's a good question," I observed, taking my cigarettes from my purse and tapping one from the pack. "For now I guess Ms. Doe will have to suffice."

"Ms. Doe it is. And now that we're acquainted, let me inform you that you don't smoke."

"Really?" I marveled. "Then why on earth would I have all these cigarettes?"

"Because you're donating them to science."

"Are you sure you're not just some antismoking crusader bent on ruining my day?"

"Negative."

"That's funny," I said as he snatched my Bic before I could flick it. "Because you sound like one to me."

"Ah, but you're delusional."

"That's fair," I laughed. "So you're not going to give it back?"

"I will if you go outside."

"Can you believe this guy?" I asked Katrine. "You may be interested to know that we never had to smoke outside before he quit."

"That's true," Kevin interjected. "But that was also before we had kids."

He was telling the truth, of course. I had talked him into quitting when I found out I was pregnant with Tyler because I hoped that would make it easier for me. Not that either of us had a hard time of it, since we were never what you'd call heavy smokers. We generally only smoked when we were drinking or playing cards, and rarely did we light up before dinner. I tended also to smoke in response to anxiety, such as before a party or a visit with my father. In fact, I bought my first pack in almost four years on the way to visit my dad a few weeks after Lucy was born. At the time I had assumed Kevin would join me; to my surprise, he never did.

"Speaking of the kids," he added now, "when are they and Maggie due back?"

"In about five minutes."

"Perfect. Did you remember to ask her about New Year's Eve?"

I nodded. "Unfortunately, she's already booked, so I guess we'll just have to tend to the kids ourselves this year."

"I don't mean to intrude," Katrine interjected, "but what's happening New Year's Eve?"

"We're having a party."

"We have one every year," Kevin explained, "and we generally hire a sitter to come watch the kids so we can attend to our guests, but apparently that's not in the cards this year."

"I see. Well, I won't be much help when it comes to the kids, but I'm happy to assist elsewhere if you let us come."

"That would be nice," I said. "But won't you still be in New York on the thirty-first?"

"We will. But our flight leaves late that afternoon, so—barring any weather issues or traffic problems—we should be able to make it here by nine or ten. Which reminds me," Katrine added after glancing at her watch. "Rob's probably ready by now, so I'm going to take off and let you finish getting ready. See you at the armory."

Twenty minutes later, Kevin and I were pulling up to the curb in front of Josh and Lynette's place—an eight-unit apartment building just south of Powderhorn Park.

The neighborhood had seen better days. In fact, as we arrived we noted that another home had been boarded up on Josh and Lynette's block since we'd moved out of the building next door late last year. I would have happily stayed in our old place—despite the growing blight—and continued to enjoy the park and all the unique features of our quarter of the ancient brownstone, which boasted original oak woodwork, hardwood floors, a built-in buffet, a claw-foot tub, antique cast-iron sinks, and ultrahigh ceilings. News of Lucy's impending arrival, however, made it necessary for us to find a bigger place, so we opted for the duplex a couple miles south, which offered a garage, a more modern floor plan, and a yard for us to enjoy whenever we wanted.

We wondered to ourselves how long Josh and Lyn would stick it out in their building. There had been two robberies there the previous summer—both in broad daylight—and Josh was constantly reminding Lyn not to leave the doors unlocked or her car running, so Kevin figured it was just a matter of time before they retreated to the suburbs. I reminded him, however, that they were managing the building for Lyn's great-aunt and uncle in lieu of paying rent and that Josh's financial OCD made it unlikely they would move until the place was falling in around them.

"I sure as hell wouldn't wait that long," Kevin replied. "Some things are more important than money. Like safety and personal security."

"Please, Kevin. We're talking about property crimes. It's not like anyone's been murdered."

"Yet."

Laughing, I unhooked my seatbelt and pushed open my car door. "You stay here and keep watch," I directed facetiously before beginning my journey to the entrance of Lynette's building. "If I'm not back in five minutes, call the police."

"Yes?" inquired Josh's voice over the intercom after I'd pressed the button to alert him and Lynette to my presence a minute or two later.

"Yes?" I repeated.

"Jackie?"

"Jackie?"

"I don't know," I heard him say—presumably to Lynette—in the background. "I mean, it sounds like Jackie; but she also sounds a little strange."

"That's nothing unusual," she replied. "Tell her we'll be right out."

As I waited for them in the lobby, I examined the fraying tassels on the ancient cranberry velvet draperies and considered resurrecting Starlet O'Hara.

"You're not in costume," I observed when Lyn and Josh appeared a few minutes later.

"Sorry. We didn't really have time to put anything together."

"That's OK."

"What about Kevin? Is he really wearing it?"

"Tights and all."

"Wow. We were sure he'd chicken out."

"Me, too."

"Speaking of costumes," Lynette added, having stopped to scan my outfit as Josh shut and locked the front door. "Is this yours, or are we crashing a funeral on our way to the party?"

"What party?" I said with a smile as I drew my hair back behind my ear.

"Oh my God!" Lynette exclaimed upon seeing my counterfeit wound. "What happened to your head?"

"I have no idea."

Lynette faced Kevin as we approached the car. "What the hell is going on?"

"Don't ask. You'll only be more convinced she's crazy, and if word gets out and she's committed, I'll be stuck with her forever since the law prohibits you from divorcing someone while they're institutionalized."

"I'm not sure you have room to talk," Josh said as he held the rear door for Lynette to climb in. "You're wearing a dress."

"*I* have an excuse, my friend: material gain. She, on the other hand, is certifiable—which, incidentally, is my second excuse: I've been living with her."

Josh laughed. "Speaking of living with her—I bet it's been pretty interesting at your place these days, what with Desert Shield and everything."

"Why would you say that?" I asked. "Just because I happen to prefer peace and love to death and destruction doesn't mean I'd waste my breath talking to Kevin about it."

Josh looked doubtfully at Kevin's smirk in the rearview mirror. "Is she for real?"

"Which part? That she believes it, or that she doesn't waste her breath on me?"

"Either."

"Well, I wish I could tell you it was part of the costume, but unfortunately, if she was in character, she would have forgotten both Kuwait *and* her treasonous leanings."

"Well, there's your answer," Josh observed. "Have her arrested as an enemy of the state. I'm pretty sure you're allowed to divorce a convicted felon."

"Very funny, you two," I huffed. "Believe it or not, you can love your country and still disagree with your government. And I happen to think Bush and Company should spend a little more time on domestic issues and less time meddling in the affairs of oil-producing nations."

Josh nodded derisively. "And exactly which domestic issue would you say is more pressing than the world's energy supply?"

"The economy, for one."

"And you don't think the economy will be influenced somewhat if Saddam Hussein takes control over the entire Persian Gulf?"

"Speaking of golf," Kevin interjected as we pulled into the armory parking lot. "That Wayne Levi has had quite a year."

Who?

"Sorry," he said with a chuckle to as Josh and I looked at each other. "I just don't think this is a conversation we want to have now. So how about we drop it and try to have some fun?"

"What a great idea," I said. "In fact, let see what the guys in Iraq think of that one. Hey, guys!" I added, jumping out of the car and facing east. "We're sorry you're stuck in the middle of the fucking desert and could get your ass shot off at any moment, but we're all getting kind of sick of hearing about it. So we're just gonna forget about you for a while and try to have some fun. Thank you for serving the interests of big oil, and enjoy your heat-resistant chocolate bars!"

Kevin smiled at Josh across the hood as he locked the car doors. "See how rarely she shares her opinions with me?"

The gym was nearly full when we arrived, but the DJ—dressed as a vampire—seemed to be having trouble getting people on the dance floor.

"Why is it so dead in there?" Lynette asked as we peered through the doorway.

"Don't ask me. The music's great from out here."

Lyn shrugged. "Well, it's still pretty early, I guess."

"Yeah, they probably just need to get a few beers in them."

"That'll be a neat trick," remarked the tuxedoed monster that was stamping hands at the entrance to the gym, "since it's a nonalcoholic function."

I looked at Kevin. "He's kidding, right?"

"'Fraid not," he replied. "Colonel Keane's rules. No more alcohol at unit events."

"Since when?"

"Since his son went into recovery. I'm sure I told you."

I shook my head. "Must've been during one of my blackouts."

"So are we still going in?"

"Why not?" I asked. "It's not like you or Lyn were going to be drinking anyway."

That decided, Kevin handed over our admission fees, and we all walked through the door.

"Looks like they have a pretty good stock of soda and juice," he observed, pointing to the concessions table. "Would anyone care for something to drink?"

"Nothing for me, thanks," Lynette replied. "I'll grab something later if I change my mind."

"Me too," I said. "But you two go ahead. Lyn and I will go find a place to sit."

As the guys drifted off, I spied Katrine waving at me from the other side of the gym where she stood with Rob—or so I assumed, since all I could see, thanks to the breath muffle and other accoutrements, were his eyes.

"There's Katrine," I said, gesturing toward the girl who was now indicating, à la Vanna White, toward the array of folding chairs she'd assembled to accommodate our group. "Looks like they're expecting us to join them."

"You didn't tell me she was so pretty," Lyn said as we got closer. "From here she could be Brooke Shields."

Or Justine Bateman, I mused as we approached Katrine and Rob. "Hey, guys. How's it going?"

"Better now that you're here," the girl replied. "Besides you, Kevin, and Rob, I don't know another soul in the place."

"Then allow me. Lynette, this is my friend Katrine and her fiancé Rob. Rob and Katrine, allow me to present Lynette Latimer."

"In case you're wondering about *l'ensemble maternité*," I added facetiously as they exchanged nods, "that is *not* a costume; this woman is actually *with* child."

"That's funny," Katrine observed with feigned confusion. "I don't *see* a child."

Rob rolled his eyes as he pulled the bottom of his mask up over his forehead. "It's nice to meet you, Lynette," he said, bowing slightly. "Now, forgive me, but since I don't recognize you from the armory or any of the unit functions I've attended so far, I must ask: how is it that you and Jackie are acquainted?"

"We were classmates in South Carolina when my husband, Josh, and Kevin were stationed there. In fact, we didn't know it at the time, but they worked in the same shop on different shifts. Anyway, Jackie and I got to talking before class one day and realized not only that we were from the same home state but also that the guys worked together."

"What a coincidence," he observed. "And where are you stationed now?"

"Nowhere. Josh got out after he did his four, and we moved back home to go to school."

"I see. And are you still in school? Or have you taken a sabbatical in light of your condition?"

"No. In fact, that was one of the conditions *of* my condition," Lynette laughed. "Josh said I had to have a degree and a job before I could have a baby, so I did everything in my power to make them both happen."

I feigned distraction as Lynette shared the details of their procreative arrangements. I was personally and thoroughly disgusted by the whole thing and not the least bit interested in hearing about it for the tenth time. It took a certain kind of nerve for a guy—much less one as odious as Josh Latimer—to dictate the career and reproductive choices of his wife, and it disturbed me to see her letting him get away with it—not to mention admitting it so eagerly to others.

"I know how it sounds," she had argued upon seeing the dismay on my face when we first discussed it a few years ago, "but he just wants me to be successful, and he knows how to keep me motivated."

"Hey, that's between you and Josh," I had replied. "If you're happy with the plan, you needn't explain anything to me."

No such exchange occurred this time, of course, since I had learned to better control my facial expressions in recent years. Although I rarely held back when it came to sharing my thoughts and opinions with my friends, I made a point to do so with Lynette. I knew that she was far too enamored with playing the role of wife and mother to concern herself with such silliness as equity and that my words would only amount to so much wasted breath. And while I also knew she would come to regret having surrendered so much power to her spouse, I had vowed in the meantime to grit my teeth, bite my tongue, and perform whatever other oral and verbal gymnastics were necessary to avoid hurting Lyn's feelings and keep the peace.

"At any rate," I said to that end after an appropriate pause, "Lyn is now gainfully employed as a pediatric nurse—which means, in addition to being able to hold all the babies she wants while she waits for her own to arrive, she can be counted on to deliver an impromptu forum on the dangers of cigarette smoking should this party get to be a drag."

"I don't think so," Lynette sighed. "It's my day off. Besides," she added, dropping into a folding chair, "this isn't really that bad."

I nodded. "At least the music is decent."

"I was just thinking the same thing," Rob interjected. "Care to see what else he's got?"

"Who?" I wondered aloud.

"The DJ."

Smirking, I took the seat next to Lynette. "What's a DJ?"

Katrine laughed. "See what I mean? She was supposed to come as Scarlett O'Hara, but now she has amnesia."

"Actually, it was *Star*let O'Hara," I objected in a haughty southern drawl. "With a *T*."

Rob nodded. "Well, Miz *Star*let," he said, mimicking Harvey Korman's Ratt Butler. "Would you care to dance?"

"No, thank you."

"Why not?"

"Because I don't feel like it."

"Oh, go on and dance with the man," Lyn urged. "It won't kill you."

"You never know. I could drop dead of a heart attack right there on the floor."

"Well, rest assured—if that happens, I'll be ready and willing to perform CPR."

"I'm not falling for that. You already told us it was your day off."

"It is, but in truth I'm bound by law to intervene. So get your butt out there and dance with him. You know as well as I do that Kevin won't ask you."

Rob nodded. "You heard the lady," he ordered. "Let's cut a rug."

"I don't think so."

"Why not?"

"I repeat: because I don't feel like it."

"Well, I do," he insisted, hooking his arm under mine, "and I'm not taking no for an answer."

"I'm afraid you are," I replied, gripping the seat of my chair with both hands and wrapping my feet around the bar that connected its legs, "because I'm staying right here."

"We'll just see about that."

I laughed triumphantly as Rob tried to pull me to my feet and succeeded only in moving my chair. "I told you I'm staying."

"Not for long," he replied, continuing to tow me sideways across the ancient gym floor. "Once people start to notice you sitting out in the middle of the room with me dancing around you like a lunatic, you'll be off that chair and on your feet in no time."

"To avoid embarrassment, you mean?"

"Exactly."

"That shows how much you know," I scoffed as he released my arm and began to twist and twitch freakishly. "I'm far too accustomed to making an ass of myself for *that* to bother me."

"I see yet another fool has made the mistake of underestimating just how stubborn my wife can be," Kevin observed as he and Josh joined our party in time to catch Rob storming off the dance floor with me limping a few steps behind calling "math-ter, math-ter" while clutching my chair to my bottom. "Someone should have warned him."

"I tried to," I said with as I returned the chair to its original position. "He wouldn't listen."

Katrine nodded. "It's true—he wouldn't. Meanwhile," she continued, thrusting a hand toward Josh, "since Kevin's being rude and won't introduce us, I'm Katrine."

"Josh Latimer," he replied uncertainly. "It's, ah, nice to meet you."

"Same here. So would you like to dance? I'd ask Kevin, but from what I've gathered, I'd be wasting my breath, and Rob's probably tired from his recent attempt at tripping the light fan-spastic."

Josh shrugged at Lynette, who waved them off.

"I need to use the restroom," Rob informed Kevin when they had gone. "If I'm not back before Katrine is, let her know, will you?"

Kevin nodded.

"So?" I asked Lynette as soon as he was out of earshot. "What do you think?"

"I think you're mean," she chided. "Letting the poor guy embarrass himself like that, when he was nice enough to ask you to dance."

I crossed my arms. "Not about *me*," I huffed. "About *them*."

"Ah. Well, he's a little pushy, but otherwise they seem OK to me."

"A *little* pushy? The man dragged me thirty feet and tried to humiliate me into dancing with him. I'd say that makes him more than a *little* pushy."

"He doesn't mean to be pushy," Kevin interjected. "He's just trying to have a good time."

"So he's not quite the jerk Jackie described to me last weekend?"

"He can be. It's just that the jerky things he does happen to bother her more than they do the rest of us. Isn't that right, my sweet?"

I nodded. "But oddly not as much as you're bugging me now, my darling."

"You're terrible," Lynette laughed as I ducked to avoid the kiss Kevin had blown my way. "Why can't you just be nice for once?"

"I'd love to," I replied, pointing to the sticker on my chest. "But I don't remember how."

Rob returned from the restroom as the opening bars of "Unchained Melody" were filling the gym. Bypassing Jackie, Lyn, and Kevin, he approached Katrine, who, along with Josh, had rejoined the group, and escorted her back to the center of the gym.

"Come on," Lynette called to Kevin as she and Josh—and seemingly hundreds of other couples—almost reflexively migrated to the dance floor. "Grab Jackie and join us."

"No, thanks."

"But this one only requires you to turn in small circles," Josh added, demonstrating with Lynette. "You don't even have to move your arms."

Kevin laughed and faced me as the others were absorbed into the crowd. "So...are you having a good time?"

"So far. You?"

"Yep."

"That's good."

Kevin sighed. "Well, can I get you something to drink?"

"No, thanks," I replied, following his gaze toward the cluster of active duty staff standing near the refreshment table. "But you go ahead."

In truth, I had more than martyrdom in mind when I sent him away. I had never told Kevin, but it embarrassed me to no end that he would never dance with me, and I didn't want to subject him to the anger that always welled up inside me in response to my abject humiliation.

I stayed in my chair for few minutes after he had gone, and then slipped away to snoop around the armory. Although I had felt a genuine, if mild, curiosity about the historic facility for quite some time, my primary motivation was self-preservation. I needed to disappear before some well-intentioned person compounded my embarrassment by trying to make me feel better.

My tour was fairly short since every door in the place was locked and the hallways were fairly empty. My curiosity unsatisfied, I nevertheless headed back to the gym and arrived in time to find Josh and Lyn standing with Kevin just outside the door.

"The wife is craving sugar," the former announced, "so we're going to duck out for a while and get some ice cream. You guys want to come along?"

Kevin looked down at his legs. "Like this?"

"Why not?" I asked. "It's Halloween. Lots of people are out in costume."

"Well, I don't intend to be one of them. Besides," he added, fluffing the tulle supporting his skirt, "I don't want to miss the contest."

I shrugged. "Looks like it's just going to be us," I said. "Lead the way."

I soon realized it had been a mistake to go with Lyn and Josh. The man watches everything she eats, and he's so tight when it comes to money that his ass squeaks when he walks, so I had to bite my tongue as he harangued her about the caloric and monetary extravagance of a second scoop—even after she acquiesced and ordered only one. Needless to say, I was glad that the trip lasted but forty minutes.

"We're gonna head home," Josh told Kevin when we returned to gym only moments after he'd won first prize in the costume contest. "Lynette's pretty wiped out from our trip to Dinky Town, so we called my friend Jeff from the pay phone downstairs, and he's coming to pick us up so we can get home and go to bed."

"No problem," Kevin said. "You guys have a safe trip."

"Will do. Congratulations on the CD player, by the way. We'll see you around."

As we watched them leave, I noticed Connie waving and walking our way.

"Oh my God!" she cried as she approached. "You should have seen it, Jackie. Kevin was such a scream! He actually lifted his skirt and shook his booty for the judges."

"Well, it helped that the lightbulb's battery died," Kevin demurred, referring to a finalist who'd shown up with a clear plastic dome attached to the top of his head that lit up with a switch he held in his hand. "He might've had a shot if he'd been able to keep it from shorting out."

"No way!" Connie argued. "It may have been a dead heat up until the point at which you showed some leg. But after that, the lightbulb didn't have a prayer—with or without juice."

I patted Kevin on the back. "So what's it like to have traded your body for material gain?"

"I feel so cheap," he lamented, covering his face with his hands. "So used."

"Well, you'd better get used to it, since the only way we'll be able to afford CDs on our budget is for you to sell your body."

Kevin shrugged. "Whatever. Just as long as I don't have to cut back on porno rentals."

"I did not need to hear that!" Connie cried, cupping her hands over her ears and doing an about-face. "I will talk to you guys later."

"I can't believe you!" I said, poking him in the chest as we watched Connie join her roommates. "I hope she knows you were kidding."

"Was I?"

"Anyway," I added, having privately observed the increase in the number of people on the dance floor since my departure. "I'll see you around."

"What do you mean? Where are you going?"

"I haven't decided yet."

"Jackie," he said with a degree of concern.

"I'm not planning to steal any state secrets, if that's what you're worried about," I assured him. "I'm just going to find a place to relax."

"And you can't do that in the gym?"

"I suppose, but I don't see the point. In a few minutes, you'll be off talking to someone else and I'll be stuck sitting by myself anyway."

"What are you getting at?"

"It's no big deal," I continued with as much dignity as I could muster. "I have no problem with you hanging out with the guys. I just prefer to cut to the chase and find something to do instead of sitting by myself making everyone wonder what's wrong with me. It's embarrassing."

"Embarrassing?"

"Yes. And it's ten times worse during slow songs, when *everyone* hits the dance floor and I'm stuck sitting here like a wallflower at the prom."

"I'm sorry, Jack. My intent has never been to embarrass you. I just do *not* like to dance."

"I know that, and you know that, but none of these people know that. And although they'd never say so, they have to be wondering what kind of loser I am if my own husband won't dance with me."

"And how do you know that's what they're thinking? For all you know, they're wondering what kind of a jerk won't dance with that gorgeous blonde."

"It doesn't work that way, Kevin. In this demographic, it's never about the man."

"I don't know what else to say, Jack. Other than I'm sorry."

"Don't sweat it," I said, rolling onto my tiptoes to give him a kiss. "I just need to accept things the way they are and stop setting myself up for disappointment."

That shouldn't be hard, I added as I set off in search of distraction. *I did it all the time before you came along. I can do it again.*

Eight

"Knock-knock!" called Lynette as she let herself in the front door two days later. "Anybody home?"

It had been ages since she had dropped by unannounced and almost as long since I'd seen her three times in one week. Still, I didn't want to make her feel unwelcome or make things between us any more awkward by highlighting that fact, so I decided to go with the flow and see if she offered anything of her own accord to account for the unexpected visit or the recent uptick in her interest in seeing me.

With that in mind, I met her in the living room with the batch of laundry I'd just taken out of the dryer. "Hey, Lyn. I figured you'd be working today."

"I am. But Josh is off helping my dad cut firewood today, so I thought I'd kill an hour or so with you before I have to leave for the hospital. Do you mind?"

"Not if *you* don't mind watching me fold."

"Not at all." Lynette shook off her coat and followed me to the kitchen. "So did anything exciting happen after we left the dance last Friday?"

"Sadly, no. But if it's any consolation, Rob and I almost got arrested afterward."

"Oh, no. What did you do this time?"

"Nothing. It was just a minor misunderstanding that sort of snowballed out of control."

Lynette looked at her watch. "You're going to have to give me the condensed version," she said after a moment. "I only have an hour."

"OK. Well, we took both cars to the restaurant to avoid a trip back by the armory on the way home. Then Rob and I dropped Katrine and Kevin at the door so they could pop into the restrooms to change since they had the foresight to bring another set of clothes.

"So Rob and I are standing in the lobby for a while when I realize that no one has come out to greet us. This doesn't concern me all that much because we're not ready to sit down anyway, but—and purely for the sake of conversation—I remark to Rob about how odd it is that no one is running the counter. He agrees, adding that someone might try to leave without paying or walk off with the till or the ATM. Now, I'm no expert, but I'm pretty sure these things are bolted down or at least weighted to prevent them from being stolen—not to mention impossible to crack even if you could get them off the premises. Still, my point was that it's bad business to make people wait as long as we had been there—either to pay or to be seated. So I present these arguments to Ninja Boy, who agrees that it's bad business to make people wait but disagrees with me on the security features of an automated teller machine and proceeds to argue that two people could make off with the machine in the amount of time the lobby has been unattended. I tell him he's crazy, and then—as if to prove it—he walks over to the ATM and starts looking for something to grab on to so he can pick it up.

"So now I'm shaking my head because, one, I think he's an idiot, and, two, he's obviously showing off. I try to talk him out of it, but he won't listen, and I'm convinced that any minute someone is going to walk into the lobby and get the wrong idea. About this time, the manager appears at the counter. Now, I've been to this place a few times, but I've never met this guy before, so I don't know if he's someone with vigilante tendencies or not. What I do know is how this looks, and as much as I can't stand Rob, I did not want to get tied up with the cops all night when I had kids at home with a sitter whom I'm paying by the hour. So, hoping to avert a major crisis, I say, 'Hello. Are you the manager?' Only Rob thinks I'm joking, so he doesn't even look up. He just says, 'Very funny, Jackie,' and, having finally found a grip, starts trying to lift the machine off the floor. So I smile at the manager and say, 'I don't know who he's talking to. My name is Cynthia.'"

Lynette gasped. "Oh my God."

"Well, what was I supposed to say? I didn't want the guy to think I was in on whatever shit he thought Rob was pulling. I mean, I told him not to do it and then tried to get him to stop. It's not my fault he wouldn't listen. And it doesn't matter anyway," I added, raising my voice so Lyn could hear me as I carried the freshly folded towels to the linen closet in the hall, "because just then he finally looks up, sees the manager, turns white as a sheet, and lets go of the ATM. 'It's not what you think,' he says, approaching the counter. 'Yeah,' I laughed. 'It really just looks like a ninja is trying to steal your ATM.'"

Lynette put her face in her hands. "What were you thinking?"

"I have no idea. I guess I just couldn't help myself. I mean, the situation was that ridiculous. Anyway, so Rob cuffs me on the arm for being a smart-ass, which forces me to retaliate. This leads to a brief game of tag, during which he trips over my purse, loses his balance, and falls on his face in front of the counter."

"Oh my God," Lyn repeated.

"I know. But it was hilarious. So now this manager, whose name—I discover from the tag above the pocket of his shirt—is Skip, gets his knickers in a twist and orders us to leave. Well, I'm laughing too hard to say anything in my own defense, but Rob, who's still on the floor, decides to get up and explain. That's when Skip grabs the phone and starts brandishing it like a weapon."

"You're kidding."

"No. And what's even better—Rob actually *backs away from him*!"

"Get out."

"Seriously. I honestly have never laughed so hard in my life. I mean, here is this marine—who is trained to kill with his bare hands—held at bay by some dweeb holding a phone. It was just too much. So I asked him, 'What do you think he's he going to do, Rob? Dial you to death?'

"Now, by this point even the two dudes who had come in from the kitchen were smiling, but there stood Skip holding that phone, invoking his right to refuse us service and threatening to call the cops. Meanwhile, Rob is still trying to explain that we haven't been drinking; that we had a bet on whether the ATM was too heavy to lift, et cetera, and promising we'll behave if he'll let us stay. Well, you can see Skip's not buying it, and just when I'm convinced we're going to have to hit the street or stand trial for disorderly conduct, Kevin walks out of the bathroom looking like Mr. Clean Marine himself and clears everything right up."

"Just like that?"

I nodded. "All he had to do was flash that all-American smile alongside his military ID. That got Skip all warm, fuzzy, and patriotic. Suddenly he starts laughing like he was in on the joke all along. Next he's telling Kevin how proud he would be to serve him and his friends and how he had planned to enlist himself but couldn't pass the physical because of his vision."

"As if you care."

"Oh, believe me—we did at the time."

Lynette laughed. "So can I assume you finished eating without incident?"

"Basically. Although since Katrine had missed all the fun—having been forced to futz with her hair because the headband to which her ears were attached had given her a hat head, so to speak—I naturally had to fill her in. Needless to say, Kevin was not amused."

"Can you blame him? You nearly cost him breakfast."

"I know. The poor bastard. I still think things got blown way out of proportion. I mean, it was almost midnight, for God's sake, and I sincerely doubt we were the strangest people they've seen at that hour on any other Friday night. Besides, I think anyone who's required to work with the public on the night shift should be required by law to have a sense of humor and nerves of steel."

"I agree. With all the craziness I see at the hospital, I couldn't survive without either one."

"I'll bet."

"So what's on the agenda for tonight?"

"French cuisine, apparently. Rob and Katrine are cooking for us."

"They are?" Kevin asked as he came around the corner with Lucy in his arms and Tyler in his wake. "Oh, hey, Lynette," he said, tipping an invisible Stetson with his free hand.

"Hi, Kevin."

"Hey, babe," I said, glancing at the clock over his head. "Have you guys finished cleaning out the garage already?"

"Not quite. But we'll finish up after we've had something to drink," he added as he held the refrigerator door and waited for Tyler to pull their juice boxes from the shelf. "When did you talk to Katrine?"

"I didn't. Rob called after you went outside. I knew we didn't have plans, so when he offered to cook dinner, I said yes. But since we did just see them Friday night, I can call him back and cancel if you like."

"No, that's OK. But if I'm going to have time to clean up before they arrive, I'd better get my tail back outside. Good to see you, Lyn."

"You too, Kevin." Lyn rose as the door shut behind them. "I'm gonna take off, too," she said with what sounded like regret. "I just realized I left my lunch at home, so I'll need to stop by the apartment and pick it up before I hit the freeway."

"OK," I said, although I doubted her lunch was the sole cause of her distress. Still, she was a grown woman, and if there was something she wanted to talk about, it was up to her to tell me. "Well, thanks for stopping by. It was good seeing you."

"You, too. Have fun tonight."

"Thanks."

I watched Lyn settle into the front seat of her little white Lumina, waited for the trademark half-wave that always accompanied her departure, and then turned and crossed the lawn to the garage where Kevin greeted me with a kiss.

"So you're finally warming up to Rob, huh?"

"Where on earth did you get that idea?"

"Maybe from the fact that you keep making plans to get together with him and Katrine."

"Don't let that fool you. I only keep making plans with them because you two work together and I like Katrine. I find him just as irritating as ever—and I still don't trust him."

"Why not?"

"Think about it, Kevin: I met him a month ago. Within a week he'd invited me to go clubbing, bought us dinner, and stocked our bar. Since then, he's bought us breakfast; offered to proofread all my papers, and brought me a stack of his favorite novels—which I have neither the time nor the inclination to read. Last week he lent me his copy of the Cure's new CD and his collection of *Peanuts* paperbacks because I happened to mention how much I'd enjoyed them as a kid, and tonight they're cooking for us and bringing wine. Now add all that up, and what do you get?"

"Lots of free stuff?"

"Will you please be serious?"

"I'm trying, Jackie; but I honestly don't see a problem with any of that."

"Would you see a problem with it if the roles were reversed and I was doing all those things for him?"

"Yes. But that's only because I'm a cheap bastard who wouldn't want you spending money and lending our things to someone we barely know."

"Exactly. But set aside the cheap bit for a moment, and ask yourself: why on earth would I be doing favors and giving my things to people I barely know?"

"Because you're a kind and generous person."

"True. But Rob's actions go beyond simple kindness and generosity. Kindness is doing someone a favor, like changing a tire or picking up a carton of milk if you're going to the store anyway. This guy is rotating my tires every eight thousand miles and going to the store just so he *can* buy me milk. It's hardly the same thing."

"But if he wants to do it, what's wrong with that?"

"Nothing—except that it's weird. There are things you do for people at various levels of familiarity and according to the degree of urgency. People generally don't want others doing things for them that they wouldn't be comfortable doing for them in return. And when someone breaks that unspoken contract, it makes people uncomfortable and suspicious."

"Understood. But that aside, isn't it possible Rob is a genuinely nice guy?"

"Sure. But based on my experiences, it is far more likely that he's a creep with an agenda."

"Despite the fact that you've never seen a shred of evidence to that effect?"

"There may not be any evidence of an agenda, but there is ample evidence of his status as a creep. Like the dressing down he gave Katrine the first time we played cards with them and the way he dismisses almost everything she says as stupid or unnecessary."

"OK. Let's say he does have an agenda. Have you assembled any theories about his intentions, or haven't your paranoid fantasies progressed that far yet?"

"No," I admitted, crossing my arms. "But my homicidal tendencies seem to be thriving."

"Well, we can deal with those next if you like," Kevin laughed. "For now let's focus on this agenda issue. And since you claim to have no theories of your own to put forth, I'd like to suggest, somewhat foolishly perhaps, that you consider the very legitimate possibility that he likes you and wants us all to be friends."

"Why in the hell would he want to be *my* friend? We have absolutely nothing upon which to build a friendship."

"Maybe he doesn't see it that way."

"Then he needs glasses."

"Fine. Maybe that's not it. Maybe he's not the least bit interested in you as a person, and he's only being nice to you because of Katrine. That would explain why he seems so phony to you and, thus, why he gets your hackles up."

I considered the thought as a satisfied smile crept over Kevin's face. "I could buy that theory if we weren't talking about the man who's constantly insulting her and embarrassing her in front of people."

Kevin shrugged. "Even jerks have their redeeming qualities. I mean, he may not realize how he comes across toward her. Or maybe he knows exactly what an ass he can be, and cultivating a friendship with you is his way of making that up to her."

"No way," I scoffed. "There has to be more in it for Rob. He's not the altruistic type."

"Well, if it's easier for you to believe the guy's out to get you than to think he'd try to please the woman he loves, that's your prerogative. It just seems a tad paranoid to me."

"*Paranoid?*"

"Oh, don't be cross," he chided as I folded my arms. "At least you won the 'agenda' point. That's more ground than I planned to give at the outset."

"*Give?*"

"Give. Grant. Whatever. Meanwhile, if you're so annoyed by his behavior, why not just tell him? He'll be here tonight, right? So you'll have ample opportunity to explain how much his favors and compliments irritate you, and that you'd feel more comfortable if he would ignore and criticize you instead."

With a ripple of self-amusement, Kevin opened the car door and reached into the glove compartment. I watched him until suddenly the mail truck rolled up to the end of our driveway. Happy for the distraction, I walked out to retrieve whatever treasure our mail carrier would have left for us by the time I got there.

"What's this?" I asked, accepting a brochure from Kevin in exchange for a handful of junk mail when I returned to the garage.

"It's from the Marriott downtown."

"I can see that. Why do we have it?"

"That's where they're holding the ball this year."

"*The Marine Corps Birthday Ball?*" I asked, though I didn't have to. I'd been expecting the subject to arise since before Halloween and hoping against hope that the fates would intervene and we wouldn't have to go this year.

My aversion wasn't to the event itself. In fact, I applaud the fact that every November, marines around the globe get together and celebrate the birth of their corps, and that, where possible, they do so by way of a fancy dress affair. The problem was that fancy dress affairs usually feature dancing, which Kevin wants no part of, and they always require fancy dresses, which are hard to find when you have big boobs, a short waist, and almost no hips.

So I had been looking forward to November with the zeal of a convict awaiting sentencing. Which is why, when Halloween came and went without a word about it, I managed—somewhat foolishly, perhaps—to convince myself that this year I would be spared the twin agonies of trying to find a gown and spending an entire evening watching other people cut the proverbial rug, and that Kevin would finally be spared the drama that arose from my efforts to avoid it.

"In the top-floor ballroom," he was saying now, having set a stack of junk mail on the trunk and opened up a glossy new catalog advertising hunting equipment and supplies. "Two weeks from, well, yesterday."

"Wow. That's soon. How do they expect people to make plans on such short notice?"

"They don't," he countered as he flipped the catalog to a clearance sale on riflescopes. "The invitations came out two weeks ago. I just forgot to bring mine home."

"Gee. That's too bad. I'm not sure I can find a gown on such short notice."

"Don't give me that. I've already bought our tickets, and there is still plenty of time for you to get a dress."

"And he thinks *I'm* paranoid." I told Lucy as I handed her the brochure, which she eyed intently for the twenty or so seconds that elapsed before Kevin noticed.

"I'm serious," he said, dashing toward the playpen and gently rescuing the paper from her drool-moistened hands. "I've even booked our room."

"A room? I don't know, Kevin. I don't know if we can afford that."

"You say that every year."

"Well, it's true every year. And staying over means hiring a babysitter for the whole night, which will be even more spendy."

"Already taken care of. My sister said she'd stay with the kids. We just have to cover her gas."

"So we're paying for Laurie's gas instead of paying for a babysitter?" I asked as he picked up the broom to resume sweeping. "How does that equate to savings?"

"It doesn't. But at least the details are covered, so all you have to do is find something to wear."

I sighed. "You really want to do this, huh?"

"Unless you prefer I go alone."

"Are you crazy? You know I couldn't stand to stay home and hear about it later."

"Then you'd better plan to come along, because I'm going—with or without you."

"Fine," I said, recognizing the familiar sensation of a barrel pressed against my head. "I'll check my closet tomorrow, and if I can't make something work, I'll go to the mall next week."

"Jeez, Jack. Don't get too excited—I wouldn't want you to have a stroke."

"Only because you'd be stuck schlepping me around in a wheelchair."

"Don't be silly. I'd hire someone else for that. But I would be stuck paying the bills." Kevin paused as we exchanged wicked smiles. "Come on," he said. "It'll be fun."

"It would be even more fun if I could get you to dance."

"No, it wouldn't."

"Why not?"

"Because it would mean I'd lost my mind."

"Seriously. What would I have to do to get you to loosen up and dance?"

"Attach marionette strings to my limbs and have someone maneuver me from the rafters."

"That could be arranged, you know. In fact, I know a few people at the unit who would enjoy making that happen—and several more who would pay to see it."

"No doubt."

Laughing, Kevin set the broom against the wall. "So, what's left to do before Rob and Katrine show up?"

"Not much. I finished folding the laundry while Lynette was here, so all I need to do is straighten up the living room, take a shower, put on a face and some clothes, and dry my hair."

"OK. Well, Tyler and I still need to run those movies back to the video store. Should I take Lucy along so you can shower?"

I shook my head. "It's time for her nap anyway. I'll change her and put her down."

"OK, then. We'll see you when we get back."

Having seen Kevin and Tyler off, I lifted Lucy from the playpen and carried them both into the house. After removing her coat, hat, and shoes, I took her down the hall to her and Tyler's room, and then changed her diaper and sat down to rock her for a while. Once she was asleep, I put her in the crib and went to shower, leaving the door ajar so I could hear her if she started to fuss.

I had just turned on the water when the phone rang. Afraid the sound would disturb her, I shut off the faucet, grabbed a towel, and raced to the kitchen to answer it, only to find it was a wrong number. "Figures," I sighed as I headed back down the hall.

Bypassing the bathroom, I stopped outside the playroom and listened. Satisfied Lucy had not been disturbed, I returned to the bathroom and turned on the shower.

I was halfway in the stall when the phone rang again. With my right side dripping, I grabbed the towel again, sped to the phone, and dislodged the receiver.

After verifying for a second time that although ours was the number the party intended to dial, it would *not* put him in touch with anyone named Barry, I hung up the phone once more. Rather than chancing another aborted trip to the shower, however, I lingered in the kitchen for a moment, with a view to launching a verbal attack on the caller's cerebral function.

"Look, you idiot," I hissed when it rang again, "your friend doesn't live here. I don't know who he is, and, frankly, I don't care. So would you please do us both a favor by calling Directory Assistance, or kindly fuck off."

"Janet?"

Oh, for Christ's sake.

The receiver was almost to the cradle when I recognized the voice of the only person who still called me by my given name. "Dad?"

"I can't believe you answered the phone that way. What if I'd been Kevin's commanding officer?"

"I don't know. I'd probably ask him how to handle an imbecile who calls the same wrong number three times in a row."

"Well, you might try asking the party to check the number he was dialing."

"He *or* she," I corrected him. "And thank you for the advice, but I already did."

"Well, then I guess all you can do is shout at him—or her—until he—or she—realizes that he—or she—doesn't want to talk to you anymore."

"Does that mean you want me to let you go? If so, I have plenty of other things to do."

"Oh, my industrious daughter."

"That's me," I sighed. "Care to make any additional character assessments?"

"No. That one will suffice."

"Great. So to what do I owe the honor of your harassment?"

"Well, I hadn't heard from you in a while, so I thought I'd call and see how you're doing."

"OK. Well, we're here and we're alive. And you?"

"Oh, I'm fine. Just fine."

"That's great. Is there anything else?"

"Ahh…Janet Kathleen. As prickly as ever, I see."

"I thought you said you were done making character assessments."

"So I did. Please accept my apologies."

"Done. Now, what do you need?"

"It sounds like you're in a hurry. Have I caught you at a bad time?"

"As a matter of fact, you have. The baby is napping, and I'm trying to catch a shower before she wakes up."

"Then, again, I apologize."

"Not necessary. You couldn't have known. Now, what can I do for you?"

"Well, I was wondering if you and Kevin have plans for the evening of the tenth."

"The tenth of November?" I offered hopefully. I didn't know where he was going with this, but it wasn't like him to inquire as to our plans unless he had something in mind.

"Yes."

"I'm afraid we do," I said with feigned regret. "We're scheduled to attend the Marine Corps Birthday Ball that night."

Although I couldn't show it then, I was filled with relief and bursting with gratitude. Never before had I been so happy to have that commitment on my calendar, and never again would I try to get out of it. Of course, like my father's sudden interest in my social calendar, I knew my gratitude would fade over time, and by next year I'd be singing a different tune.

"I guess I hadn't realized it was that time of year," he was saying now.

"Yeah. Sorry."

"Don't be. It can't be helped. And, in truth, that will probably work out better anyway."

"Better how?"

"I had planned to invite you and Kevin to join me for dinner that night, but the Marine Corps Ball might be an even better place for what I had in mind."

"What exactly did you have in mind?" I asked. Having assumed previously that he'd called to ask for our help with a project or to borrow something—like cash, our car, or a kidney—I was thrown by the idea that the Marine Corps Ball would somehow facilitate his goals, and suddenly as intrigued as I had been apprehensive.

"I was hoping to introduce you to Eleanor."

Eleanor? Last I knew, my dad was dating someone named Linda who, incidentally, looked about ten years older than me but dressed about five years younger. Although I hadn't expected their romance to last long owing to the fact that Linda had an estranged husband in the picture, I had expected to hear about it—if only from my brother, Ricky—if they'd broken up.

Given his history, Eleanor was no more likely to resemble her predecessor than she was to look completely different. Although my dad didn't have a type when it came to hair color, eye color, age, style, or occupation, his tastes ran fairly consistent when it came to one thing: the more broken the better. How else could you explain why so many of the women he got involved with were on the brink of divorce, experiencing legal or financial problems, battling addiction or mental illness, running from an abusive spouse, or embroiled in some other drama of the sort you can find portrayed on any given day on either Lifetime or the Oxygen network?

I don't know if my dad prefers that kind of woman because he finds them easier to please, or if he's just trying to avoid those who remind him of my mom. Although I was too young when she died to have known much about her personality, I remember her being funny and funky, and people who knew her back in the day say she was goofy and full of piss and vinegar. Of course, while in my opinion these are qualities to be embraced, for a widower trying to forget the apple of his eye, they are to be avoided at all costs, which, sadly, doesn't leave much other than damaged, deranged, or dimwitted to choose from.

"Yes, that would definitely work out better," the widower was saying now. "We could go to the ball with you and Kevin and make a real evening of it. Do you think Kevin would mind picking up two extra tickets? I would reimburse you, of course."

"I'm sure he wouldn't mind buying the tickets—assuming there are any still available. But with less than two weeks until the event, they may be sold out. And even if there are tickets available, there's not guarantee we'll be seated together."

"Understood. But if Kevin would pick them up, I would appreciate it. And if we wind up at different tables, I'm sure we can manage to spend a fair portion of the night at the same table."

"OK. I'll talk to Kevin and let you know what happens."

"I would be much obliged."

"No problem. Now, much as I hate to," I added upon hearing Lucy starting to cry, "I have to go. Lucy's awake, and she's bawling her head off."

"Oh, leave her be. It won't hurt her to cry for a while. In fact, I've heard it's good for her lungs. Besides, you can't let her grow up thinking she's the center of the universe. I made a point not to let that happen to you and Ricky…"

You sure did, I thought as he rambled atop his soapbox. *We were just insignificant little satellites—especially whenever you were looking to make another conquest.*

To his credit, our dad did see adequately to our basic needs. Although we ate poorly due to his ignorance of nutrition and lack of time and cooking skills, we never went hungry. And while we spent time in government housing and trailer parks and occasionally had to live with friends or relatives, we always had a roof over our heads and clean clothes to wear.

Where he was less successful was in tending to our emotional well-being. A man who neither reads nor believes in psychology and for whom everything is either black or white, my dad had no patience for tears or fears, whatever their source, and since I was prone to both, he often ridiculed and chastised me and Ricky instead of reassuring or comforting us. Moreover, he was so focused on pleasing the women in his life that he would change everything about the way we lived—from what we ate and wore to how we celebrated holidays—to suit them, and, if they had children, take their side against us whenever there was a dispute. So while he never put us in danger or failed to meet our basic needs, it would not be unfair to say our interests and comfort were often subordinate to the desires and preferences of his latest squeeze or her offspring.

"It's a policy more people should adopt," he was saying as I tuned back in to the Richard Jackson show. "Far too many people are focused on immediate gratification, which is getting us nowhere, and that's a damn shame."

"I'm sure it is. Listen, Dad, I don't mean to be abrupt, but I really have to run. I promise I'll ask Kevin about the tickets and get back to you next week. I'll talk to you later."

Before he could reply, I hung up, ran down the hall, and lifted Lucy from the crib.

As I settled into the rocker near the window, I marveled again at how different Lucy was from her brother. Aside from a brief colicky phase, Tyler's first year had been a breeze. He slept hard, rarely cried, and was alarmingly comfortable with strangers. It was sometimes hard to get him to go to bed, but once he was down, he would sleep through the night and coo in his crib until I came to greet him in the morning. Lucy, however, could best be described as intense. She would smile for me, Kevin, and Tyler, but stared warily at virtually everyone else she encountered and would scream bloody murder if they looked her in the eye. She fell asleep easily as long as Kevin or I were near but would kick up a fit if we left before she nodded off or if she woke up alone. Things hadn't changed much since she started going to day care, and—unlike Tyler—it had taken her weeks to warm up to Miss Betty and the other kids. To this day she could still produce the most heartrending, earsplitting wail known to mankind.

Not that anyone would believe that if they could see her now. For instead of screaming at the top of her lungs, the child was laying in my arms, contentedly sucking the thumb of one hand and covering her nose with the other such that the sound of her breathing approximated that of an asthmatic Pekingese.

I hoped I had done the right thing by picking her up. I didn't want to spoil the kid, but neither did I want her to feel unwanted, unimportant, or unloved. Such concerns were probably common to all thoughtful parents, but they were especially challenging for me since, having grown up without a mother, I felt completely unqualified to be one. I had a solid grasp on the basics—like health, safety, and nutrition—but when it came to everything else, I had only my instincts to go on, and I was terrified that wouldn't be enough.

At the heart of my anxiety was the knowledge that at any moment, I could be wiped off the planet, and my babies would have to go it alone. Although Kevin loves them and would do right by them if I dropped dead, deep down I viewed them as my responsibility, and for my own peace of mind I needed to know they could survive without me.

I had few worries about Tyler. He was born confident, articulate, and resourceful and displayed a great balance of pensiveness, assertiveness, and resilience. I had no doubt that, while he would miss me if I were to vanish, he would still thrive in my absence.

His sister, however, was a different matter. It was clear she would struggle to adapt to the world—with or without me in it. She had no interest in connecting with anyone else besides her immediate family, and unfamiliar situations put her on edge. She had definite preferences in what she allowed on, in, or near her body, and anything she didn't like the look, smell, taste, touch, or sound of was immediately and unceremoniously dispatched to the floor or across the room. She was even sensitive to clothing and would pull at offending articles and cry if she couldn't get them off.

I tried to view these tendencies as strengths she had working in her favor rather than as deficiencies that would hold her back. I hoped that intolerance for discomfort and refusal to accept the unacceptable would prevent her from settling when it came to her education and career and help her avoid unhealthy relationships.

Still, I had my doubts. Because it's one thing to thing to know how to stand up and assert yourself when something is wrong; it's another to balk at every little thing that doesn't go your way. If this kid was going to have a shot at a happy, satisfying life, she would have to learn to recognize when it's time to go to battle and when it's time to negotiate, and while it's OK to get riled up about some things, others you have to let roll off your back.

"You're just perfect as far as I'm concerned," I told her as I rose to join Kevin and Tyler in the kitchen, "but if you're going to make it in this world, we need to get you some thicker skin."

Nine

"Sorry we're late," said Rob as he stepped into the kitchen through the back door. "It was a bit of a challenge finding all the ingredients for tonight. We had to stop at three different places before we found everything Katrine needed."

"No problem," Kevin replied, relieving him of an armload of bags after nodding at Katrine, who waved back.

"Hope you don't mind us coming in the back," she said as she closed the door. "Rob parked in the driveway so we wouldn't have to carry stuff so far."

"No problem," Kevin repeated into the bags, which he'd arranged on the counter and was surreptitiously inspecting like a kid out to spoil a surprise.

"Don't worry about unpacking that stuff," Katrine advised, shaking off her coat. "I'll do that as I'm using it."

"You give him *way* too much credit," I said over the running water as I rinsed out a dishrag. "He's only trying to figure out if there's something he can steal now or if there will be something for him to sample later."

Kevin shrugged unrepentantly and popped open the beer he'd just taken from Rob.

"See?" I mimed from behind Lucy's highchair as I reached around to wipe her face.

"Don't tell me you gave up on us already," Katrine exclaimed, having spotted the dirty dishes on the table as I moved on to Lucy's hands.

Kevin shook his head. "We just fed the kids. That way I can bathe them while you're cooking and put them to bed just before we eat."

"Is that a good plan or what?" I asked of no one in particular. "I especially like the part where I don't have to get wet or clean up the flood afterward."

Kevin shot me a parting smirk before disappearing around the fridge accompanied by the kids and the toys Tyler had gathered and staged just before Rob and Katrine arrived.

When he returned an hour later, the kitchen was in total disarray. Pans of varying shapes and sizes covered the entire stove except for the burner at the rear left, which, from the smoke still rising from it, was the source of the odor he would have noticed upon entering the room a few seconds ago. I followed his eyes to the counter next to the burner where lay a wad of wet dishtowels, a partially melted plastic bowl, and two charred oven mitts, and then to Katrine, who stood sweating by the sink holding an index card. Like her baby blue shirt, the card had entered the house unblemished but would leave it bearing a smattering of tiny spots that matched the color of the puddle Rob was now wiping from the floor in front of her.

I knew Kevin would have questions, so I continued to work on the salad I was making as I waited for him to decide where to start.

"What the hell happened in here?" he asked finally.

I grabbed a celery stalk and stepped back to survey the scene behind me. "Well, first she turned on the wrong burner, which led to the initial casualty—the plastic bowl. Then she turned on the right one but unfortunately had set the flame too high. That led to the second and third casualties—the mitt and her shirt—as well as the collateral damage to the floor, the stove, and the counter.

"I'm not one to jump to conclusions," I added quietly, "but I'm starting to question her skill with twentieth-century appliances."

"I heard that."

"Anyway," I continued as Katrine continued to contemplate the index card. "So now she's trying to read the rest of her mom's recipe, which—incidentally—is not only written in French but also illegible. Apart from that minor challenge," I said, biting off the end of a chunk of celery and popping the remains into Kevin's open mouth, "we seem to have everything under control."

"If you say so," he replied as I resumed chopping. "Anything I can do to help? Say, locate the fire extinguisher or put nine-one-one on speed dial?"

"I wouldn't go there if I were you," I advised. "But if you're really looking to help, I could use a drink."

"Coming right up. I'll keep it on the weak side," Kevin added before shooting a wink at Katrine. "In case that's all you're able to get into your stomach for a while."

"I would be careful if I were you," Katrine warned, grabbing her wooden spoon and wielding it menacingly. "Your food is in my hands, and therefore so may be your life."

Rob stepped back from the stove after wiping the floor for about the fifth time. "All jokes aside, Katrine. It is getting late. Is this almost finished?"

"I think so. I know I put in all the ingredients; I just can't figure out what to do next."

Kevin laughed. "How about serve?"

Katrine stuck her tongue out at him as she wiped her hands with a swatch of paper towel.

"Do you think your mom would remember what it says?" I asked.

"Maybe," Katrine replied, glancing at the clock. "What time is it in New York?"

"Who cares?" Kevin asked as he handed her the phone. "If she complains, tell her it serves her right for having such lousy penmanship."

Rob pulled out a chair and sat down to my left. "Shouldn't have done that," he sighed. "Now we may *never* eat."

Kevin watched Katrine stretch the cord around to the living room. "What do you mean?"

"Well, either her mom will seize the opportunity to have a good long bitch, or she'll get mad and hang up. Either way, we'll all starve to death because Katrine will be too upset to finish cooking."

"Sorry, man. I had no idea."

"It's OK. You couldn't have known."

Taking Rob's words with several grains of salt, I tried to follow Katrine's conversation as I worked on my dinner assignments. It was soon clear that the person on the other end was indeed the infamous mother, who was, as Rob had predicted, giving her an earful.

"Why don't you guys go downstairs and watch some TV while Katrine sorts this out?" I suggested. "I promise I'll call when we've made progress on the meal."

I watched as both men got to their feet without argument. Turning my attention back to the conversation in the other room, I found that my effort to follow it would be in vain, as it was being conducted in French. Despite my best efforts, my comprehension was poor due to having only Katrine's side of the conversation to work with and the speed at which she was speaking. Unable to make sense of the exchange, I accepted defeat and decided to await the summary.

Several minutes later, I had finished the salad, the garlic bread, and my cocktail. I was just about to pour myself another when Katrine suddenly slammed the phone down and strode back to the stove.

"Can you tell me how this works?" she asked, indicating to the microwave. "I need to reheat the chicken and the pasta since the sauce is apparently done."

I wiped my hands on the dishtowel that lay over my shoulder. "But you haven't done anything to it?"

When Katrine did not respond, I stood up, pressed a few buttons on the microwave, and started to set the table. "So what did your mom say?"

Katrine sighed and grabbed the spoon in the sauce. "Well, after complaining about the timing of my call and taking a full account of my myriad faults, sins, errors, and omissions—among them the all-too-familiar charge that I don't call often enough—she went on to tell me about my sister Nicole's latest professional accomplishments and Yvette's new boyfriend, the physician. When I finally got a chance to speak, she insisted that I do so in French because I no longer use it on a daily basis and probably need the practice. Once I'd run the grammar gauntlet, she said that she couldn't recall what was written on the card but that whatever it was, it *certainement* wasn't *important* enough to call her so late or delay the meal. In addition, she said I should know better than to serve something to others that I've never made before; that she could have stopped me from embarrassing myself like this if I'd only keep her apprised of my activities like my sisters do; and that even if she could remember what was on the card, she wouldn't have told me what it said because I don't show her the proper respect and therefore don't deserve her help."

Holy family dysfunction, Batman, I said to myself. *And I thought I had it bad.*

"I'm sorry," Katrine added between sobs as I joined her at the stove. "It's just that I really wanted things to work out tonight, and instead I've made a complete mess of everything."

"No, you haven't."

"Yes, I have," she snapped, smacking the spoon handle with the back of her hand. "And this will probably be crap anyway."

"Well, now you have," I laughed as I watched the sauce splash up and over side of the pot and onto the burner. "I'm only teasing," I added, turning off the flame under the pan as Katrine put her face in her hands and started to sob again. "I'm sure it will be fine."

"I'm sorry," she repeated, wiping her eyes with the hem of her shirt until I offered her a paper towel. "You must think I'm an absolute child."

"The thought never crossed my mind. Now let's get this stuff to the table."

Within a few minutes, dinner was served and Kevin was eagerly stuffing his face with *Paillards de Poulet avec Purée de Poivrons Rouges*—also known as Chicken Breasts with Red Pepper Puree—which Katrine had tried in vain to teach him to say phonetically but which he insisted on calling "pie art doo poo poo avec doo doo" instead.

Although I knew he'd been brought to the brink of starvation waiting for dinner and was now too busy eating to think about much else, I nevertheless looked repeatedly at him and Rob—as Katrine stared at her own plate—trying to induce one of them to say something complimentary that wouldn't sound forced or insincere.

The screech of chair legs sliding over the floor cut through the silence as Kevin stood to get a second helping. "Anybody need anything while I'm up?"

I raised my hand. "I'll have some more bread."

Rob seconded that request with a nod.

"I can't believe no one wants more of this chicken," Kevin enthused as he heaped his plate again. "It's delicious."

"It's OK, Kevin," Katrine replied. "You don't have to stuff yourself just to make me feel better."

"Don't worry. I wouldn't."

"Let me assure you," I added when Katrine appeared unconvinced, "Kevin wouldn't do *anything* for the sake of sparing *anyone's* feelings. In fact—and this is not a comment on the meal you have so graciously prepared for us—Kevin defines the term 'edible' rather loosely and will eat just about anything that isn't burned to a crisp or frozen solid."

A piece of garlic bread hit Rob on the side of the head as I finished my statement.

"What was that for?" he inquired.

"Sorry, man," Kevin laughed, pulling another chunk from the basket. "I was aiming for Jackie. Now this time—duck!"

"Well done," I declared as the bread landed flat on my plate and splattered my shirt with red sauce. "I was thinking as I was getting dressed this afternoon that this blouse needed a splash of color. Thanks for helping me out with that."

"My pleasure."

"So Jackie," Rob interjected as Kevin returned to the table, "Katrine tells me that you're on scholarship at Hamilton."

"That's right," I said, after taking a moment to privately grumble about the abrupt change in subject. "I have a two-year fellowship for transfer students with associate degrees."

"How did you come by that?"

"The usual way. You know, an application here, a transcript there. Same as any other."

"I figured that. I'm wondering about qualifications, to be more specific, and eligibility."

"OK. Well, the scholarship is available to all community college students with two years of undergraduate study and a decent grade point average. To apply, all I had to do—apart from submitting an application and official copies of my transcripts—was provide two letters of recommendation and submit a three-to-five-page essay on a topic of my choosing."

"Sounds like a sweet deal. What did you write about?"

"Women in combat."

"No kidding." Rob wiped his mouth and set his napkin on his plate. "I'd like to read that."

"Well, it's on file in the archive room at Hamilton, so feel free."

"You don't have your own copy?"

"Nope."

"Not even on computer?"

"Sorry. We didn't get a computer until *after* I got my scholarship. In fact, it's because of my scholarship that we even have a computer."

"Well, in that case, why don't you just tell me about it?"

"I don't think so. It's a contentious issue, Rob, and I'm really not in the mood for a fight."

"Why on earth would there be a fight?"

"Because you're a marine, and I know where most marines stand on this issue."

"Well, maybe I'm an exception."

"I doubt it."

The participation by women in combat activities is now a nonissue thanks to legislation enacted by Congress and the removal of restrictions by Defense Secretary Leon Panetta in 2013. But in 1990, the idea of allowing women to openly serve in combat roles generated as much controversy as does the matter of gay marriage today. And despite the fact that women had been taking part in combat—honorably and competently—on an ad hoc basis for decades before Saddam Hussein tried to reclaim Kuwait as part of Iraq, the thought of allowing them to do so in an official capacity in Iraq led to much handwringing by aging politicians, religious leaders, and conservative commentators and was the subject of a multitude of independent policy papers, impassioned newspaper editorials, and unemotional but wholly unobjective military journal articles. It was also a topic of much heated debate among male military personnel and those of us who knew and loved them but thought their views on women needed serious updating.

"No offense," I added as I took my dishes to the sink. "It's just that whenever I try to discuss this with a military man, all I get is a bunch of BS about morale and discipline."

"Are you suggesting that morale and discipline are *bullshit*?"

"No—I'm saying the *argument* is bullshit. Don't get me wrong. I understand the importance of morale and discipline to military effectiveness. I just don't think gender poses as big a threat as some say it does. It's the same argument that was used to justify keeping black people out of the service, and it's no more valid now than it was then. It's just a big smoke screen for prejudice and fear, only this time we're dealing with sexism instead of racism."

"So you don't think morale suffers when men are forced to work beside those they deem inferior? Or that discipline fails when men are expected to take orders from those whom they feel are unqualified to lead them?"

"Absolutely. But blaming women for that kind of crap makes about as much sense as blaming teeth for tooth decay. Because problems with morale and discipline aren't born of the mere presence of women—or gays or minorities, for that matter—in the military; they stem from the pathetic need some men have to feel superior to others and the insidious sexism, homophobia, and racism that still pervade our culture and say it's OK for men to dominate and disrespect them."

Rob looked toward Kevin for evidence of agreement but got a look of amusement instead. "Jackie," he nevertheless persisted. "We're talking about a situation in which people must function at their optimum level or someone's going to die."

"Exactly. Which is why they should focus on the mission and not give a thought to whether or not their comrade has a vagina."

"Combat is stressful enough, don't you think? Why would you want to do anything that has the potential to cause more trouble or increase the tension?"

"These are grown men, Rob—men who've supposedly been trained to follow orders and live by a code of honor. If they can't put that training and that code above their own prejudice and insecurity, they don't belong in the military in the first place. Meanwhile, if women are qualified to serve, we should let them."

"Well, if enough of them could make the grade without the services having to lower their skill, speed, and strength requirements, I'd say fine. But given the risk it would pose to others, we cannot abandon our standards to please a bunch of women with something to prove."

"And naturally that's the only reason women want to be in the military."

"Why else would they bother?"

"How about to serve their country?"

"They can serve their country without going into combat."

"So could you. The difference is that when a man sets out to do something great or important, you assume it's because he's strong and noble. When a woman does the same thing, you label her a ballbuster with an axe to grind."

"You have to admit, there are women who want to fight just to prove they can."

"Is that a crime? Was it a crime when Kennedy wanted to put a man on the moon? No—we called him a hero. Was it a crime when a beekeeper from New Zealand wanted to climb Mount Everest? No—it earned him a place in the history books. In fact, whenever a man sets out to do something unusual or risky, we call him brave and daring; but if a woman undertakes something unusual or risky, she's called an idiot or a troublemaker—which is both sexist and unfair."

"OK, say we allow women on the battlefield," Rob allowed "How do we protect them?"

"They'll have *guns*, Rob. They can protect themselves."

"Jackie, if a grenade lands nearby, what kind of a man wouldn't throw himself over a woman to keep her from harm?"

"I think the question is, what kind of a *person* wouldn't do everything *he or she* could to save *any* member of his or her unit? After all, guys were saving other guys' asses left and right in Vietnam. Did we pull the men who needed saving from combat? No. We gave everyone a medal and sent them back to work. Maybe if you guys would stop thinking about our breasts long enough to listen, you'd realize we expect help only to the extent you'd provide it to another man."

"Well, call it sexist," Rob replied, taking his own plate to the sink, "but most of us still see women as mothers, wives, sisters, and daughters. And regardless of your utopian gender politics, most guys cannot treat women like they treat men, because they know they're not."

"Are you one of them?"

"Honestly? Yes. Knowing that most women are weaker than me, I would feel inclined to protect them and would have a hard time trusting them to have my six when things got hairy."

"Let me ask you another question. When you were with MP Company in Naples, did you notice any differences in the skill levels of your unit members?"

"Of course."

"So, you had assessed the members of your unit individually? And you knew on whom you could count and one whom you couldn't?"

"Sure."

"So why the hell can't you do that with women?"

"Because, like it or not, men and women are different. My body is built for strength, and yours is designed to…well…have babies."

"Never mind that some of us can't, right? Or don't want to? But we'll come back to that. Meanwhile, let me remind you that physical differences exist among members of the same sex as well. That's why there are minimum standards for each job category. For example, Kevin will never be a Navy SEAL because he floats like a rock, and my brother will never pilot a jet because he pukes if he walks too fast. Yet, because of that precious Y chromosome, they're allowed to try—and recycled, reassigned, or discharged if they fail. Women, on the other hand, are rejected without regard to their skills or abilities."

"That's because most of them wouldn't pass. It doesn't make sense to let them in if they're just going to wash out anyway."

"What a load of crap. Men wash out all the time, too. The bottom line is that men like you want to keep women out of certain fields because you don't want to believe they're as strong or as capable as you. Of course, what you *should* be afraid of is what will happen to your *cajones* if too many women gain access to assault rifles, grenades, and rocket launchers after centuries of sexist subjugation."

Rob shook his head. "So you'd be OK with sending women to the Persian Gulf right along with the men? Where they would face the potential of not only being shot and killed, but also rape, torture, and mutilation by Muslim extremists?"

"Personally, I don't think anyone should go to the gulf. But yes, if women are willing to fight, men should applaud their commitment or get out of their way. And for the record, women don't have to go to war to be killed or raped—we're at greater risk of that in our own homes than we are sitting in the middle of the desert with M-16s in our arms and knives on our belts."

"Are you serious?"

"Of course I'm serious—just look at the statistics."

"Not about that. I mean about the gulf."

"Yes," I said, recalling his original question. "But that's not the issue. You asked if women should go alongside the men. I said yes."

Rob looked at Kevin, who shrugged. "But the UN has the authority," he insisted, "and NATO an obligation, to step in on behalf of sovereign member nations. As members of both bodies, we are obliged to defend our allies—regardless of the policies by which those nations function internally."

"I understand that. And I happen to find the whole thing pretty damned convenient."

"Convenient or not, we cannot allow Hussein to get control over Kuwait's oil reserves."

"Give me a break. Hussein isn't after oil. What he wants is a port on the gulf so Iraq can become a player in the world economy. That's not to say I condone what he's doing, but neither do I buy the need to keep Kuwaiti oil out of his hands as a motive for US intervention."

"Fine. Then what about the Kuwaitis and the Kurds? Don't they deserve our support?"

"The Bush administration doesn't give a damn about the Kuwaitis or the Kurds, and neither do you. That's just the kind of stuff conservatives like to throw around to shame liberals into supporting their wars. And, for the record, it would be a lot easier to buy their concern for the poor and oppressed if they didn't only feel it for people in the countries they want to invade. Meanwhile, if the US *is* going to justify invasion on the pretense of concern for the Kuwaitis and the Kurds, we should at least make an effort to appear consistent and show as much support for the Bosnians. Of course, there's no interest in the former Yugoslavia because corporate class hasn't found a way to exploit their resources yet."

"That's also a civil war, Jackie."

"And what do you call what's happening in El Salvador, Nicaragua, and Guatemala?"

"I suppose you don't think we belong there either?"

"Do you?"

"Of course."

"But you said we're not supposed to get involved in other nations' internal politics."

"We're not."

"You can't have it both ways, Rob."

"They're entirely different issues."

"Not to me. And I think it stinks that conservatives will use any rationale they can come up with to justify taking action overseas, but they can't be bothered to address the problems we have right here at home."

"I'm sorry to interrupt," Katrine said before Rob could respond, "but are you guys going to fight all night?"

Until she spoke up, I was unaware of how long Rob and I had been at it or of the impact it was having on her. Although Kevin was, as per usual, having fun watching me spar with someone other than himself, Katrine was visibly frustrated and bored with the whole thing.

"We're not fighting," her fiancé replied. "We're just having a friendly discussion."

"Well, it sounds like a fight to me."

"Whatever." Rob rolled his eyes and then faced me again. "Let me get this straight: are you suggesting we abandon our allies until we solve all our domestic problems?"

"No," I said in spite of my guilt over having ignored Katrine since dinner, and vowing to end our discussion as quickly as possible. "I just have this strange aversion to wasting American lives so the president's pals in defense and big oil can make money."

"Lives lost in battle are not wasted when the fight is for freedom."

"Nice sound bite, Rob. But what good is freedom to someone without opportunity? Or to the woman who can't afford to feed her children? Or to the kid whose neighborhood is so dangerous that she can't even play outside?"

"So you'd say screw the Middle East," Rob accused, facing me again, "and let Hussein annex all the land he wants? Because that's what will happen if we aren't involved. Countries like Kuwait haven't the personnel, supplies, or the training to defend themselves against a military force with the manpower and weaponry that Iraq has."

"That's not our problem. Maybe instead of padding their pockets with oil profits, they should throw some of them in that direction. Meanwhile, what this country needs is to put more of its resources toward curing our own social and economic ills. I know it's nowhere near as sexy as, say, blowing Iraq to smithereens, but, to many people, it's more important."

"So you think our Americans are more important than say, the Contras or the Kurds?"

"As far as our government is concerned, yes."

"What a hypocrite."

"Excuse me?"

"I said you're a hypocrite. You rail against racism but value Americans over people from other countries. That makes you a racist and, therefore, a hypocrite."

"Actually, that makes me an ethnocentrist, if anything," I clarified. "And call me names if it makes you feel better, but that will do nothing to improve the strength of your argument."

Katrine turned to Kevin. "Do you think this means the fight's over?"

"I told you we're not fighting!" Rob barked.

"Fine," Katrine replied. "But while you two were *not* fighting, Kevin and I managed to clear the table, wash the dishes and the stove, *and* put away the leftovers. Now can we please do or talk about something else before Kevin and I die of boredom?"

"Well, if you're that bored by this conversation," Rob growled, "you should probably rethink that career path of yours, since you won't get very far in international relations without some semblance of an interest in foreign policy."

"Katrine's right," Kevin interjected upon seeing her redden and turn away. "This is getting old. Why don't we drop the politics and play some cards?"

"Good idea," I agreed, grabbing a deck from the drawer and tossing them to him. "Then we can argue over something really important—like whether you cheat or not."

Grinning, Kevin shuffled the deck, offered up the cut, and dealt out the first hand of spades.

"I guess I'll bid four," I announced after assembling my cards according to suit. "Five if my partner's on the fence."

Rob sighed. "I'll go three."

"Well, that's seven out of thirteen tricks claimed," I announced, picking up a pen to record the bids. "Katrine?"

"One second—I'm still sorting."

Rob sighed again. "And we're still waiting."

Ignoring him, Katrine continued to arrange her cards. "We should do this every weekend," she said instead. "Only maybe from now on, we should order pizza."

Kevin shrugged. "OK by me—although we'll have to find a new pizzeria. Jackie's boycotting Gianni's."

Rob folded his cards into a stack and smiled. "You boycott pizza parlors?"

"When they deserve it. Why?"

"I just think it's funny. I mean, really—a one-person boycott?"

He was clearly taking the idea more seriously than I ever had, which I found amusing. If he had known me better, he also would have known that I'm typically boycotting five or six people, places, or products at any given moment. Still, he was having such a good time imagining what a fool I was that I decided to leave him to it. He wasn't hurting my feelings, after all, and watching him wrestle his desire to discuss my folly definitely beat arguing about military policy.

"Actually, this is the first pizza place she's declared off-limits," Kevin informed him. "She normally sticks to televangelists, dolphin-killing tuna packers, movies, and celebrities."

"I hate to interrupt your mockery, darling," I said sweetly, "but we're waiting for *your* bid."

"Yes, my love," he gushed back. "I'll go three, too."

Rob watched me record the bids. "You boycott movies?"

"Sometimes. It's your go, by the way. I led diamonds."

"Why?"

"Well, primarily because it's my strong suit, but also because they're just so darned pretty."

"No. I mean why do you boycott movies?"

"Why not? And why do you care, anyway?"

"I don't. I'm just curious to know why you'd boycott something as meaningless as a movie."

"It may be meaningless to you, Rob, but I'd rather not throw my money at creeps who produce things that offend me."

"How can you be offended by a movie you haven't even seen yet?"

"Just lucky, I guess. Now will you leave me alone and play? It's your turn."

As I waited to play my next card, I picked up my cigarette lighter and used it to light a candle on the shelf behind me.

"How do you live with yourself," Rob asked as I put the lighter down and returned the votive to its perch, "knowing you're promoting the conservative agenda by giving money to the tobacco companies, who in turn give it to people like Jesse Helms and Trent Lott?"

"It's hard," I admitted, "but then I just have a cigarette and a couple of drinks and forget about it."

Scowling, Rob studied his hand. "Oh, I can't stand this!" he cried finally, slapping the cards on the table in front of him two silent rounds later.

"Me either," I replied. "I move for a misdeal."

"Not that! This crap about the movies."

"Christ, Rob, will you let it go? And if it makes you feel better, just pretend I'm boycotting cornflakes instead." The hand complete, I grabbed the cards and began to shuffle. "Why the hell does this matter so much to you, anyway?"

"Because it's not like you to be so evasive. There's obviously a reason you won't tell me."

"Yeah—because it's none of *your* fucking business. Now can we please drop it?"

Rob crossed his arms and watched me set the deck down in front of Kevin for the cut. "You know, it's too bad you weren't born a century earlier," he said as I started to deal. "It must kill you to have missed the Red Scare, the Nazi book burnings, and the Hollywood blacklist. About all you can do now is join Tipper Gore in her fight against the record industry, or start your own country and model your government on the theories and policies of Enver Hoxha."

I looked at him from behind my cards. "I haven't said a word tonight in support of censorship or socialism, and I've never told anyone else where they can eat or what they can read, watch, or listen to. I just happen to be very selective about where I spend my money. The way I see it, if the movie industry wants to make a buck off of me, all they have to do is offer a product or service that I need or want."

"They're offering you entertainment!"

"And I have to accept it? I don't get to choose? Who's the censor now?"

Rob glared at me. "I don't get it," he said. "You're reputed to be such an intelligent person, yet there you sit with your ridiculous little boycotts and your goofy little causes trying to make the world run according to your stupid utopian ideals."

"That's it." I folded my hand and tossed the cards to the center of the table. "I've tried to be a gracious host," I said as I tried to control my volume. "I've allowed you to goad me into not one, but two conversations that I didn't want to have, because I ran out of polite ways to resist. I've tried to remain genial, despite the fact that I find your politics and your demeanor offensive, and I've done all I could to make you feel welcome and to make this a pleasant evening. In return, you've called me a racist and a hypocrite and compared me to Tipper Gore and one misguided despot—though I'm unsure as to which is the greater affront. In addition, you've mocked my values, questioned my ethics, assailed my principles, and attacked my integrity. And now, after all that, you have the nerve to sit here and insult my intelligence?"

Before Rob could answer, I turned to Kevin, who tossed his cards on top of mine in the center of the table. "Have I left anything out?" I asked him.

"I don't think so."

Rob rubbed the back of his neck. "Look, Jackie, I didn't—"

"No, Rob. Please," I said, standing. "You've said more than enough."

Katrine looked terrified. "Tell her you didn't mean it," she whispered.

"I didn't. Honestly. I guess I just got carried away."

"Carried away?" I raised my brows and smiled. "Is that what happened? You know, it seems to me that's just what they said about the people who shot Anwar Sadat. Of course, this here is just character assassination. How manifestly fortunate I am to know I'll recover."

"OK, so now chew my ass and get it over with," I said to Kevin as we climbed into bed thirty minutes later. "Tell me how I overreacted and ruined what's left of our social life."

He kissed my forehead. "That's your nightmare, babe. Not mine."

"So you wouldn't have been upset with me if I'd put a dent in his head and thrown him out on his ass?"

"No. But I'm glad you saved me the weekly drive up to the state prison by letting him excuse himself in one piece."

"Me, too. I'd look awful in prison orange. Still, the man is going to have to pay."

"What are you going to do, Jackie? Hire someone to break his kneecaps?"

"I won't have to do a thing because it will happen all by itself. Fate will see that he gets what he deserves. I might try to stop it if I thought I could, but it's out of my hands."

"Oh, the suspense is killing me." Kevin laughed as he set the alarm and switched off the light.

"Will you stop laughing?"

"Will you stop with the melodrama? It was an argument, Jack, not the sinking of the Pacific Fleet. He'll get over it, and so will you—eventually."

"I wouldn't bet on that."

"Still," he added, placing a peck on my cheek, "I think I'll call him tomorrow morning and warn him to check his brakes on the Nova before he or Katrine tries to drive it again.

Ten

"I suppose you're not real happy with me," Rob offered—as per Kevin's account of their conversation at the armory the following Monday.

"What makes you say that?" Kevin had replied without looking at him.

"Well, I *know* Jackie isn't."

"That's true. I haven't seen her *that* pissed off since the doctor tried to circumcise Tyler."

"I'm sorry, man. I didn't mean to upset her. I'm not even really sure how it happened."

"Well, it didn't help that you used the word *stupid*."

"That's what Katrine said."

"You should listen to her once in a while," Kevin advised as he stopped to scan the bulletin board outside the lounge. "It might keep you out of trouble."

"You in the doghouse with your fiancée, Sergeant Copeland?" asked Joel Dixon, a third-class midshipman who had joined them at the board.

"No, with Thompson's wife," Rob replied grimly. "We had an argument."

"You had a fight with Jackie? Man, are you insane?"

Dixon and Kevin traded jovial nods behind Rob's shoulders, and the former strode away.

"I couldn't have phrased it any better than that." Kevin shrugged as he stepped into the lounge to collect his belongings from the table.

"Meanwhile," he said to Rob, who now occupied the doorway, "if you *are* going to argue with her, at least try not to *insult* her."

"I didn't *mean* to insult her *this* time."

"Understood. But that doesn't undo the deed."

"I suppose not," Rob said gravely. "So what happens now?"

"Well, I'll survive and—provided none of *her* vengeful fantasies become *your* painful reality—so should you."

"You're joking."

"Am I?"

Rob studied Kevin's face. "OK," he said finally. "So what can I do in the meantime?"

"Well, you *could* try throwing yourself at her feet and begging for forgiveness. Or you could just steer clear of her for a while and let this all blow over."

"And what would you do if you were in my shoes?"

"Never put them on," Kevin laughed. "Seriously," he added sagely. "Jackie may look like a cuddly blonde, but she holds the equivalent of a third-degree black belt in verbal warfare."

"So I've seen."

"Actually, you've only seen the tip of the iceberg. She cut you some serious slack."

"Why would she do that?"

"Probably because she knew you didn't know any better and she felt sorry for you. Or maybe it's because we have to work together. Either way, you got lucky."

"So, again, I ask—what would you do in my shoes?"

"I don't think you understand. As her husband, I have options at my disposal that you don't. It would be ungentlemanly of me to elaborate, so let's just say that if you tried any of the tactics I use when I'm in trouble with Jackie, it would make matters way worse. So, as I said: the best way to get out of trouble with Jackie is to never get *in* trouble with Jackie."

"You can say that again," called Dixon as he passed by the lounge door again on his way back down the hall. "When it comes to her shit list, an ounce of prevention is worth untold volumes of cure. Aye, Sergeant Thompson?"

"Aye."

"Unfortunately," Kevin continued, stepping past Rob and into the hall, "having already risen meteorically to the top of said list, about all you can do is learn from this experience, and take comfort in the fact that she's afraid of guns and has no connections to the Mafia."

"Oh, great!" I exclaimed after Kevin merrily reported this exchange to me as we washed dishes that evening. "So they're all *afraid* of me over there? I don't know whether to be flattered or offended."

"Come on, Jack. Dixon wasn't serious. He was just helping me rattle Rob's cage."

"Yeah? Well, you know as well as I do that there's a grain of truth in every joke."

"OK," Kevin admitted as I rinsed a plate and offered it to him. "But before you go rushing off in search of an image consultant, consider how you'd feel if they all worshipped you the way Rob does."

I cringed as I handed him another plate, and then stopped to stare in disbelief upon catching sight of him wiping it on his shirttail. "What are you doing?"

"Helping?"

"OK. But would you mind using a towel please? I mean, call me crazy, but I thought the point of washing the damn things was to have them *clean* for the next meal."

Feigning shame, Kevin yanked a dishtowel from the drawer. "My shirt is clean. Besides, you didn't say anything the first time."

"I didn't *see* it the first time."

"Well, maybe someone should pay more attention."

"And maybe *someone* wants to do dishes by *himself*."

Kevin threw the towel around his neck like an aviator scarf and wrapped his arms around me. "You know, you're awfully cute when you're all wound up."

"Well, that explains why Rob finds me so irresistible. Between the two of you, I'm cute nearly twenty-four hours a day."

Two nights later, I was startled by the sight of Katrine standing at the sink when I returned to the kitchen after a visit to the bathroom.

"Holy crap!" I breathed as I caught my breath. "You scared me half to death."

"I'm sorry. Guess I should have let you know I was here."

"That might have helped," I admitted, retrieving the cookbook I'd dropped, narrowly missing my foot. "How long have you been standing there?"

"Just a minute or two. I saw Kevin outside, and he told me to go on in. What's he doing out there anyway?"

"Trying to find the fuel pump on the Ford."

"In the trunk?"

"What?" Approaching the window, I saw Kevin with his hands on his hips staring into the open rear end of the LTD. "Oh, my. That's not good."

"What's not good?" Katrine asked, following me back to the counter.

"I'm not sure," I admitted as I grabbed the knife and set a freshly peeled onion on the cutting board. "But whenever he gazes wistfully at the trunk like that, it usually means he's debating whether to fix the damned thing or drive it into a lake."

"I see."

"So, to what do I owe the pleasure?" I asked before laying the now halved onion on the flat edge and slicing it into curved slivers.

"Nothing really. Rob had an errand to run, so I thought I'd come here and visit with you. Do you mind?"

"Not at all. Have you eaten dinner yet?"

"No, but carry on. I'll be out of your hair shortly, I'm sure. Rob said he'd be back for me within the hour."

"OK. Well, it's just a stir-fry, so we could always wait."

"That would be great, Jackie. Thanks." Katrine beamed as she unzipped her coat. "You know, after last weekend, I was afraid you'd never invite us back again."

I stared at the vegetables in front of me. I never imagined she'd interpret my words that way. With her having declined my invitation to dinner, I'd abandoned all thoughts of including her and had offered to delay the meal only to avoid eating in front of her. Still, as disquieting as the prospect of dining with Rob was, to withdraw the perceived invitation would have been impolite.

"That *is* what you meant?" she clarified.

"Of course," I lied, ruing my obnoxious social graces. "I mean, we're in no hurry, and it'll give me a chance to test this great new arsenic recipe I've been working on."

Katrine laughed warily as she arranged her coat over a chair. "You are kidding—right?"

"Of course, silly. Arsenic is expensive—and, more importantly, traceable."

Katrine studied me now—as if giving serious consideration to the possibility that behind my unexpected hospitality might lurk such a plan or similarly sinister intention.

It occurred to me that inviting them both to dinner might inspire the same thought in Rob as well. Given a choice, of course, I preferred not to dine with him at all, but using the occasion to make him squirm would be a close second among the options and a potentially more gratifying way to repay him than avoidance, so it would be a shame to let the opportunity go unexploited.

"Trust me, Katrine," I said upon concluding my wicked reverie, "if I wanted to harm Rob, I wouldn't do it quickly or quietly. I'd make it painful, slow, and obvious, and worth every last minute of my prison sentence."

Katrine seemed to accept this as both logical and believable, and she laughed despite the regret in her eyes. "You know," she said, leaning her back against the fridge to watch me work, "he feels pretty lousy about what happened last weekend."

"Does he?"

"He really didn't mean to insult you."

"You mean by calling me a stupid, racist, fascist hypocrite, he was intending to pay me a *compliment*?"

Katrine sighed. "No. I'm saying he was frustrated and spoke without thinking."

"It's OK, Katrine. I honestly don't care what he thinks of me."

"Maybe not. But he *does* care what you think of *him*."

"Well, I'd be happy to tell him, but I'm afraid we're not speaking at the moment."

"Not speaking? Then why did you invite us to dinner?"

"Because I'm cursed with good manners."

"So you really *don't* want us here?"

"Actually, I rather like having *you* here."

"And Rob?"

"Well, I haven't taken out a restraining order, if that's what you're worried about."

"But you don't want to see him."

"Not actively, no."

Katrine stared at the floor. "So where does that leave us?"

"Same as before, as far as I'm concerned."

"How can you say that?"

"Let me put this in perspective for you," I said, grabbing a bell pepper from the counter and positioning it for decapitation. "I have many friends. Some Kevin likes; others he does not. Some of them, in return, would like nothing more than to have his baby; while a few would jump at the opportunity to personally ensure that he never reproduces again. Occupying the middle ground are those whose feelings range from loving to loathing, via tolerance and indifference. Naturally, I'd prefer them all to adore him as much as I do, but that's the way it goes sometimes. The fact that some of them don't—and vice versa—doesn't prevent us from being friends; and this thing with Rob and me doesn't change things for you and me—that is, unless *you* feel differently."

"No. Of course not."

"Great. Then there's nothing to worry about."

"I'm not so sure about that."

"What do you mean?"

"It's just that, under the circumstances, I'm not sure Rob will feel comfortable here."

"I'm sorry, Katrine, but I'd say that's his problem. Wouldn't you?"

"I suppose. But if you two don't find some way to coexist, it will likely be mine as well. I mean, if he doesn't feel welcome here, he'll start hanging out with his friends from high school like he did when we first moved here, and I'll be stuck watching them play Dungeons & Dragons every weekend, just like I did until we met you and Kevin."

"Not necessarily," I sighed as I set aside the chopped pepper and placed the knife in the sink. "It's not as if you're joined at the hip, after all. So, the next time they get together, tell Rob to have a good time, and then go do something you enjoy—like see a movie or come over here."

"Alone?"

"Well, unless you'd prefer to bring a date."

"I'm being serious, Jackie."

"So am I."

"But what about Kevin?"

"Kevin's a big boy, so he'll either sit back and bask in the company of two lovely women, or find something else to do, just like he does when I'm with my other friends."

"Won't that be weird for you, though? I mean, what would we do?"

"Same thing we do with the guys around I suppose—eat, talk, play games."

"But I suck at games. And I don't know anything about politics or music, or any of the stuff you and Rob talk about."

"Perfect. Then we don't have to worry about fighting over it."

"But then what *will* we talk about?"

"I don't know. What would you like to talk about?"

Katrine sighed. "To be honest," she said, blushing, "it would be nice if I *could* talk about the kind of things you and Rob talk about."

"So what's stopping you?"

"Fear of looking like a moron."

"Katrine, you're intelligent, rational, and uncommonly articulate. You'd have to work pretty hard to look like a moron."

"Not according to Rob. He says I have no business talking about policy or politics because I don't have the knowledge or experience to form an opinion or to make a reasoned argument."

I gritted my teeth as the words came out of her mouth.

Maybe he wasn't trying to insult her, I allowed as I snatched a fresh knife from the block and attacked the mushrooms as if they were Rob's flesh. *Maybe he was genuinely trying to help her avoid looking naïve or uninformed. Or maybe he's saying something entirely different, and this is just her interpretation of his words.*

But try as I did to give Rob the benefit of the doubt, I couldn't shake the feeling that Katrine had heard and interpreted his words exactly as he'd intended them. Thinking back to how he'd spoken to her the night we first met them, I had no trouble picturing him talking to her like that or imagining her standing there as if he had every right to do so. In fact, the only thing I could *not* fathom about the situation was why. *Why wasn't she outraged? Why wasn't she hurt? Why wasn't she threatening to cut off his balls—or at least call off the wedding? Why? Why? Why?*

In truth, I could think of at least two explanations for Katrine's casual acceptance of Rob's rudeness and insensitivity. First, she loved the man—for reasons beyond my comprehension—and trusted him to act in her best interests. Thus, she let him criticize, chastise, and correct her, believing that he did so for her own benefit rather than because he was an insufferable ass. Second, and probably more important, she'd been raised by a mother who subjected her to unbridled censure, emotional blackmail, and abject shame. Thus, she'd come to the relationship with Rob skilled in the art of absorbing an insult and trained in the science of bending to others' will.

As scary as it was to imagine Katrine going into a relationship with someone who treated her so poorly, it was scarier still to watch her repeating Rob's words as blithely as one would remark on the weather. Even more alarming was the fact that it clearly had never occurred to her that she didn't have to take it.

Under different circumstances, I would have been more than happy to educate her on that front. Having escaped a similar situation myself, I had little difficulty identifying unhealthy and potentially abusive relationships and no qualms about advising people to end them.

Unfortunately, Katrine technically hadn't complained to me about her relationship with Rob, nor had she shared with me any doubts she had about marrying him or sought my advice on how to change things. Even if she had opened the door to a discussion about the way Rob treated her, anything I might have said on the subject would not have been taken seriously. Instead, it would have been seen as retaliation for his behavior last weekend and summarily dismissed.

Even without that potential complication, I would have hesitated to speak my mind. Having been down this road with other friends in the past, I was well acquainted with the scenery and none too eager to court the resentment that inevitably results when you speak the truth to those who aren't really ready to hear it. I may as well save my breath.

What a shame, I thought as I pushed another load of mushrooms into the pile. I wished Katrine knew how much better off she'd be without Rob. If she only knew how much happier and more confident she seemed when he wasn't around. Although shifty and restrained in his presence, she was a different person on her own—the irksome fidgeting disappeared, and her movements became more natural and relaxed. Like at the bridal shop a few weeks ago when, despite having met me only once before, and over my strenuous objections, she made me help her try on gowns. And like now, as she stood playing with a few stray chunks of pepper that had bounced onto the counter and rambled on in a voice like coffee-colored suede about some new recipe she'd found. Having been reminded of it by some force known only to her, she was suddenly and so wonderfully unaware of herself.

"For the record," she said somberly, having finished describing the recipe, "I'm pretty upset with Rob over this myself."

I suppressed a frown as the question transported me back to our original conversation. "I would think so. I'd kill Kevin if he behaved that way toward one of my friends."

"Would it help if he apologized again? One-on-one, I mean. Not with me or Kevin there."

"I don't know, Katrine. To be honest, I don't care enough to want an apology, and I can't imagine anything he could say or do that would change that."

"But it's worth a shot, though. Right? I mean, you can't stay mad at him forever."

"Actually, I can."

"Come on, Jackie. Wouldn't you want him to cut you some slack if the shoe were on the other foot?"

"Probably, although I generally don't go around picking fights and calling people names."

"Maybe not, but I'm sure you've pissed off your share of people in your time. I mean, no offense, but I can't believe someone as outspoken as you are hasn't found herself in hot water now and then."

"That's true—but Rob didn't just run off at the mouth. He acted with deliberate malice."

"I'm asking, Jackie. Please."

"That's just it, Katrine. You shouldn't have to make this appeal for him."

"I'm not doing this for him. I mean, it's not as if he asked me to talk to you."

"But he did drop you off."

I nodded as Katrine shrugged in surrender. *Poor kid*, I thought. She desperately wanted this problem to go away—even if that meant simply sweeping it under the proverbial rug. In truth, I wanted the problem to go away as much as she did, but my version of the fantasy involved duct tape, a shallow grave, and a plastic tarp—or at least a much, much bigger rug.

"So are you staying for dinner or what?" I asked before rapping a row of garlic cloves with my knife handle to facilitate their unsheathing.

"That depends. Are you just changing the subject, or is that you way of saying we can work things out?"

"Neither and both."

"What does that mean?"

"It means," I said, setting down the knife and wiping my hands on a towel, "there's an invitation on the table and I'm not rude enough to take it back, but that's as far as I'm willing to go right now. In the meantime there are some conditions that must be met if Rob and I are going to occupy the same room in the future. For example, from this point on, I expect him to treat me with the same courtesy I do him. That means minding his manners and thinking before he opens his mouth. It also means keeping his lips zipped when I say I don't want to discuss something."

"I understand—and after last weekend, I'm sure Rob does, too. I think he just wanted to impress you so badly that he lost his head."

"Impress me? By pissing me off?"

"Of course not. I don't even think it occurred to him that he was pissing you off. In fact, I myself didn't realize you were that upset until the moment you put your cards down."

"That's because I was trying to control my temper and keep the peace—which is what civilized people do in social settings."

"Be that as it may, Rob knows he screwed up, and he's eager to straighten things out."

"I get that, Katrine. I really do. What I don't get is why. I mean, Rob and I may not have argued before, but we aren't exactly pals."

"Because he considers you a friend, I suppose. At least that's how it seems to me given how he raves about you whenever your name comes up. You have no idea how much he admires and respects you."

This sounded like a snow job to me. No one had complimented me like that since I quit the bar scene, and it seemed as much like a load of crap now as it had back in 1983. What wasn't clear, however, was who had manufactured the flakes.

"Has he actually said that?" I asked.

"Several times."

"To whom?"

"People from the unit, mostly. But also to his friends."

"Why would he do that?"

Katrine shrugged. "He says it's refreshing to meet a woman who can converse on his level."

Why that fucking sexist son of a—I thought, literally gritting my teeth to stop myself from speaking the words.

"What's the matter now?" she asked, having sensed—correctly—that I wasn't happy.

"Nothing. Never mind."

"No. Tell me."

"Katrine, if you're not offended by Rob's remarks, you probably won't understand why I am, so there's little point in my explaining."

"Offended?" she sniffed, facing me again "I just told you Rob thinks you're smart. How on earth can you be offended?"

"Because he makes me sound like a novelty, Katrine, and that is simply not the case. There are plenty of intelligent women in the world, and to suggest that I'm unique among my gender is an insult to all women everywhere—including you."

"I see. Well, for the record, I never would have repeated it if I'd thought Rob meant it as an insult."

"I know that."

"I hope so."

"Now, I'm afraid we'll have to go over the rest of my terms later," I advised, having heard voices and snow crunching on the back porch and nodding at the door. "We have company."

"Hey, girls," Kevin interjected a moment later as he held the door for Rob, who nodded as he set a box on the table. "Guess who I just found outside."

"Hi, Jackie," the newcomer said cautiously as he offered his hand. "How are you doing?"

"Fine, thanks."

"That's good."

Curious, I nodded toward the box. "What's this?"

"My CD collection. As you know, I still haven't replaced my stereo, so I thought you and Kevin may as well enjoy these for a while."

Really? I mouthed to Kevin over Rob's shoulder.

"Now, this wasn't an entirely selfless act," Rob admitted. "I was also hoping at some point you might let me come over sometime and record them onto cassettes. That way I can listen to them in my car until I have my own CD player."

"I see."

It was clear that everyone was waiting for me to say something else, but I didn't dare utter another word. I will still too angry about what Katrine had said to be nice to Rob, and he was being too genial for me to say what I was really thinking. Only Katrine had the information to explain the fix I was in, but I doubted she fully understood my dilemma.

"Well," he said finally, "we should get going, Katrine. Are you ready?"

"I'm not sure," she replied delicately as I pushed up my sleeves and pulled my apron over my head to protect my blouse. "Jackie was just whipping up a stir-fry, and she's invited us to stay."

Rob looked at me. "Thanks for the offer, but we should hit the road."

"Are you sure?" Kevin asked. "After all, Jack knows her way around a wok, and there's always enough to go around."

"Sounds great, but I promised to take Katrine out for her birthday, and I'm late by over a week. Maybe some other time."

"Well, that was weird," I said as Kevin closed the door behind them. "Katrine didn't mention anything it being her birthday either last week or today."

"Maybe she thought you knew."

"Then how come it didn't look like *she* knew?"

Kevin yanked my ponytail playfully. "Oh, give the old noggin a rest, Jackie. You're thinking way too hard."

Although I had hoped that would be the end of Rob's campaign to curry my favor, I was soon disappointed, as the following Sunday brought yet another bizarre twist to this already screwy tale.

Kevin and I were sitting on the couch reading when we heard a car briefly pull up out front, followed by a knock at the door.

"Hi, guys," Katrine said excitedly after we'd waved her in. "Hope you don't mind me barging in on you again."

"We're getting used to it," Kevin teased. "So where's Rob off to tonight?"

"Oh, he'll be right back. He just went to pick up Scott."

"Scott?"

"One of Rob's old friends from high school," she explained as she sat noncommittally on the edge of the recliner. "They want to play Risk, but I have homework to do, and since it's no fun with only two players, Rob asked me to pop in to see if you guys are up for a game."

"Sounds great," Kevin exclaimed. "We haven't played Risk in ages."

"Then you're in?"

"Sure."

"Hang on a minute," I interjected, sensing a plot. "Nobody starts a game of Risk at eight p.m. on a Sunday night—at least no one who goes to school or works for a living. What's really going on here?"

Katrine shrugged. "I don't know what you mean."

I scanned her up and down and decided she was telling the truth. Perhaps she didn't know what Rob was up to, or she just didn't know she knew. Still, I knew there was a conspiracy afoot, and I was determined to find out what it was.

"This Scott," I said to kick off my interrogation, "what's he like?"

"It's hard for me to say since I don't know him very well. From an appearance standpoint, he seems like sort of a cross between a stoner and an audio-visual geek, because he wears Hawaiian shirts and cheap sneakers with dark glasses and a leather jacket, and drives an El Camino. Of all of Rob's old school friends, he's not the most offensive. At least he has a steady job and his own wheels."

"Sounds like a real winner," Kevin laughed. "He and Jack should really hit it off."

"Rob thinks so."

There it was. I knew she was too guileless to lie to me. She just didn't know she had the information I wanted.

"So in other words," I said, crossing my arms, "he's bringing some poor schmuck over here hoping I'll like him so much that I'll forget the past and declare Rob awesome by association."

"Say what?" Kevin asked.

Spoken aloud, the charge did sound a little preposterous—even to me. Still, I had grounds to have my guard up. *As they say, just because you're paranoid doesn't mean nobody's out to get you,* I reminded myself. *And don't these people know how to use the phone?*

The sound of the Nova pulling up outside saved me from having to explain.

"They're back," Katrine announced unnecessarily. "What should I tell them?"

I looked at Kevin, whose expression suddenly resembled that of a chocolate lab puppy.

"Fine," I sighed, like the sucker I am. "Tell them to come on in."

Katrine beamed. "OK. I'll be right back."

Kevin regarded me with mild consternation as she stepped out to hail the new arrivals. "Do you really mind?"

"I guess not."

"Then stop looking like you do."

"I can't help it, Kevin. It's just so pathetic!"

"Maybe—but if you're going to let them in, you're obliged to make them feel welcome."

"I know." *Dammit.*

"And don't write this guy off just because he's Rob's friend," Kevin admonished further. "You might actually like him."

Oh, I was going to like him all right. I had already made up my mind about that. The man could have been an underachieving, overbearing, pro-life, anti-Semite, and I was determined to adore him. For at that moment, I could see no better way to get on Rob's nerves than to shower his friend with attention and admiration.

"I have no intention of writing him off," I promised with a big, juicy grin. "Now let's go to the door and meet our new friend."

Fortunately, Scott wasn't hard to love. He was a writer and a fan of all my favorite musicians, including two old-school country artists I'd never even mentioned to Rob. He was also funny in a charming, Bob Newhart kind of way, and he loved Monty Python. He may have been Rob's friend since middle school, but they were as different as night and day. In fact, Scott wasn't the least bit arrogant or pushy. And best of all, he did not suck up to me at all.

About the only thing not to love about Scott—aside from his association with Rob—was his personal hygiene. The guy clearly needed to brush his teeth and to become intimately acquainted with, soap, shampoo, and deodorant. I was willing to overlook this, however, since it was only obvious if you sat right next to the guy, and I wasn't planning to sleep with him.

We had a pretty good time chatting when neither of us was shaking dice. Conversationally, he was more awkward than I'd expected, but he was closer to becoming a professional writer than anyone I knew. He had two science fiction manuscripts completed, plus one in progress, and several short stories that he was shopping to various magazines. Having never read his work, I can't speak to its quality, but given that his sole purpose in life was to become a published author, it was easy to see why he had trouble committing to a day job.

I was also having a pretty good time watching Rob, who appeared to be having second thoughts about introducing me to his friend. He became especially edgy when the topic turned to John Cleese, and Scott and I started talking about our favorite episodes of *Fawlty Towers* and the best scenes from *The Life of Brian*. I couldn't tell if this was because *Fawlty Towers* and the *Monte Python* movies were two of their "things" and he didn't appreciate me horning in on his territory, or if he simply hadn't expected me to be a fan and was now kicking himself for not discovering and exploiting that fact before bringing Scott in to play Cyrano de Bergerac to his Christian de Neuvillette.

As much fun as it was to annoy Rob, I eventually grew tired of both games and, thus, was uncharacteristically blasé when Kevin wiped out the last of my armies in the eighth round and knocked me out of the game.

"Uh-oh," he said, shaking the crumbs at the bottom of the chip bowl as I handed him my victory cards. "We're out of chips."

"So?" I replied. "You just took what little power I had left in South America—use some of your clout to extort some tortilla strips."

Laughing, Katrine sat upright in her chair on the other side of the room where she was trying—or, more accurately, pretending—to read. "I'll get them for you," she offered. "Since we never have you guys over to our place, I can at least play hostess here once in a while."

"That's OK," I said, taking the bowl from Kevin's hand. "I should check on the kids anyway."

After looking in on Tyler and Lucy, I took a detour via the bathroom, where I spent some time reviewing my notes for a quiz I had in the morning, and came out to find Rob standing in front of the fridge reading the collection of comic strips, articles, and editorials I had clipped from recent papers and magazines.

"Interesting display," he observed as I approached. "I noticed it the first time we came over and have been watching it ever since."

Perceiving no question and, thus, no duty to respond, I walked past him to the cupboard, grabbed a bag of cheese curls, and dumped them into the bowl I'd set on the counter.

"So how do you decide what goes up?"

"Depends. I put some things up because I find them funny, others because they are timely or well written, or because they piss me off."

"I see. So why did this one go up?"

I didn't even bother to look where he was pointing. "I don't remember."

"Sure you do."

"No, I really don't."

"You're still mad at me, aren't you?" he asked sincerely. "About last weekend, I mean."

I considered making a full disclosure as I crumpled up the empty cheese curl bag and tossed it in the trash. He had opened the door, after all, so it seemed rude for me not to walk through it. Besides, it might do him good to know I despised him—and had since the day we met.

Then again—it probably wouldn't. People like Rob never see themselves as the problem. He might feel bad about what he'd said and honestly want to make up, but I knew he would always be a rude, condescending ass, and nothing I could say would ever change that.

"No, Rob, I'm not mad at you," I said, truthfully. "I just don't want to talk about it."

"That was very restrained of you," Kevin said after I recounted the conversation to him as we straightened up the kitchen before heading up to bed.

"Tell me about it," I griped. "I haven't wanted to tell someone off so bad in my life."

"I find that hard to believe, but thanks for resisting the temptation."

"Yeah, well, don't get too used to it," I warned as I edged toward the bathroom. "Because one of these days I'm going to forget I'm a lady and really let him have it."

Once in the bathroom, I raced through my evening toilette, hoping to make it upstairs before Kevin fell asleep. We hadn't been intimate in several days, and the impromptu Risk game had blown my plan to make a play in the living room. Still, as late as it had gotten, I stood a fair chance of persuading Kevin to stay up, provided I put the right ideas in his head before he got too comfortable.

It was, therefore, both a surprise and a disappointment to find him and Lucy in the kitchen as I passed by there on my way to our room.

"She started crying as I was halfway up the stairs," he explained as he grabbed a bottle from the fridge. "Guess we were wrong about her sleeping through the night."

As he tried to settle the baby, I sat down on the floor to rummage through the box of CDs Rob had brought over earlier in the week.

"Anything good in there?" Kevin wondered aloud.

"Nothing you would like, but a few things look interesting me."

"That's what I meant. After all, it's not as if I ever get to use the stereo."

"Don't give me that. You're welcome to change the station or the CD anytime you like. All you have to do is get off your butt."

"I know—but I'd rather harass you about it."

"Obviously."

Kevin grinned. "So does that mean you'll be contacting fate to call off the hit?"

"Don't be silly."

"But he just lent you his CD collection."

I nodded. "And his friend. Next time it'll probably be his TV."

"That would be sweet," Kevin mused covetously. "Maybe we should invite them over and talk about the war again. We might wind up with a new car."

"So you find this whole thing funny, do you?"

"That he keeps trying to win you over? Yes. That he insulted you in the first place? No."

"You could have fooled me."

"What does that mean?"

"Just that you seem to enjoy stirring things up between me and Rob."

"Are you saying your fight was my fault?"

"No. But if you hadn't egged him on, things may not have gotten so ugly last weekend."

"What are you talking about?"

"I'm talking about my boycotts. If you hadn't mentioned them, he might have left me alone."

"Hey—I was only playing around. How was I to know he'd take me so seriously—or that you would choose that night to be coy about your causes?"

I shook my head. "Why do you that?" I asked, taking care not to raise my voice.

"Do what?"

"Ridicule me."

"Ridicule you? When have I ever ridiculed you?"

"Just now. You sound like you respect me about as much as Rob does."

"Well, I don't."

"*What?*"

"You know what I mean. And I wasn't ridiculing you by mentioning your causes just now. I was merely remarking on your reluctance to talk, which—you must admit—is pretty unusual."

"I guess. But I can't help it, Kevin. I just don't trust him enough to let him know me that well, and I didn't want to give him more grist for the mill."

"I understand—although given all the people you've trusted already, he could probably find all the grist he wants without ever talking to you." Kevin laughed as I silently conveyed a threat to his existence. "You know, woman. Sometimes you take me way too seriously."

"That's because I want you to take *me* seriously."

"All the time? Even when you're joking?"

"Well…no."

"Right—neither do I. In fact, I wish you'd just blow me off a little more often."

I raised my brows. "I'll just bet you do."

"See?" Kevin laughed again. "Now that's more like it."

"All right, fine. I get your message. I'll try not to take your remarks so personally."

"Great—and I'll try to make my jokes a little easier for you to understand."

"I beg your pardon?"

"And," he continued as I stared at him with crossed arms, "to demonstrate how quickly I can reform, I promise to behave at the ball next weekend."

"Yeah, right. I'll believe that when I see it."

Eleven

According to my father and several other reliable sources, the United States Marine Corps was born at Tun Tavern in Philadelphia on the tenth of November in 1775, when the proprietor—and newly appointed commandant—Nicholas Mullan began recruiting his young male patrons to fill two companies of marines as authorized by the Second Continental Congress five days earlier.

These and countless other militarily significant facts were drilled into my head long before I met and married Kevin, thanks to my father's having served in the Corps and to the numerous lectures and oral quizzes he administered to me and my brother during long car rides through central Minnesota.

Although the Marine Corps was disbanded after the Revolutionary War and not reestablished until July of 1798, since 1921, jarheads around the globe have officially recognized the tenth of November as the birth of their beloved Corps. This they have done in a variety of ways involving food, drink, and general merrymaking.

These days, with the entirely reasonable exception of those in combat zones, marines—aka jarheads, devil dogs, and leathernecks—celebrate their founding by way of the Marine Corps Birthday Ball. This is a formal affair that typically features a social hour, dinner, and dance, plus a structured program of events incorporating traditions that have evolved over time since the first one was held back in 1925. The program generally includes the presentation of the colors, an invocation, a speech by the guest of honor, a video message from the commandant, and the retiring of the colors. It will also include a performance of the national anthem and the Marine Corps hymn, often by a band of bagpipers; a cake-cutting ceremony recognizing the oldest and youngest marines in attendance; and an empty place set in honor of those who are gone but not forgotten. The whole thing is enough to induce a pacifist to pick up a flag and make even the thick of skin and hard of heart reach for a box of tissues.

As if all that wasn't enough to put me in the fetal position with an Evening Primrose drip, this year's program also included a video entitled *Uncommon Valor Was a Common Virtue*, a production featuring scenes from Marine Corps life with Bette Midler's version of "Wind Beneath My Wings" playing in the background. As Mike Myers's alter ego Linda Richman later would have put it, I was a little *verklempt*.

By the time the program was over and the smoking light went on, I decided I needed something stronger to drink than the chardonnay I'd had with dinner, so I excused myself from the table and walked over to the bar near the main doors from where I happened to see Connie near the table that held what was left of the hors d'oeuvre buffet.

"We sure could've used you at the Dining Out last night," she said as I joined her there after picking up the extra dry double vodka martini that the Howie Mandel look-alike behind the bar had made.

I nodded as I smoothed the waist of my tea-length gown with my free hand. It was the second time I'd worn the royal blue number to a ball in Minneapolis, but I doubted anyone would have paid enough attention to notice. Besides, I figured, if the men could wear the same uniforms and tuxes year after year, certainly I could wear the same gown twice in three.

"Yeah, Kevin said it was kind of a snooze," I replied, referring to the annual all-hands dinner the unit held, to which—as per tradition—spouses and significant others were not invited.

"A snooze would be putting it too kindly. It was really much more like a coma."

"That bad, huh?" I cringed. "Well, at least you had Zane there to help you through it."

Zane was Connie's boyfriend and not a bad guy for a bodybuilder cum sports physiology major. Although his status as Connie's significant other wouldn't have gotten him into the Dining Out, his status as a fourth-year navy midshipman would have made it mandatory for him to attend.

"Speaking of Zane," she said, holding out her left hand, "look what he gave me before we came over here tonight."

Without a thought as to why, I did as I was told and found myself nearly blinded by the gleam of the giant diamond solitaire occupying her third finger.

"Oh my God, Connie," I gasped. "Congratulations."

"Thanks. You're the first person besides our parents and my roommates we've told. Not that we're trying to keep it a secret—since anyone who looks at my hand is going to notice—we just didn't want to make a big deal of it tonight."

"Well, I'm sure everyone will be thrilled for you when you tell them—as am I. So when is the wedding?"

"Next August. Zane wanted to do it at the end of next month as part of a New Year's celebration, but there is no way I can pull off even a simple wedding on such short notice. Plus, this way we can both stay focused on completing our last year of school and not steal any of Sergeant Copeland's thunder by getting married so close to his and Katrine's big day."

I bristled at the mention of Rob's name but forced myself to continue smiling. Although I would have loved to ruffle her feminist feathers by telling her what I thought of the man and why, I knew it would be somewhat self-serving and more than a little underhanded to talk about him when he wasn't around to defend himself.

"How is she feeling, by the way?" Connie inquired—referring, I assumed, to Katrine, who had come down with some kind of bug, prompting Rob to leave the Dining Out early the night before and to cancel their plans to attend the ball this evening.

"I have no idea. Rob called Kevin just after three today to ask if we knew anyone who might want to use their tickets, but he didn't offer any information as to what was wrong."

"Did someone say my name?" Kevin asked as he stepped between us from behind.

"Oh, hello," we replied in unison.

"And how are you ladies this evening?"

"Fine, thank you," Connie replied. "And yourself?"

"I'm great—now that I have a real drink."

"Speaking of—" Kevin said, addressing me specifically. "When you said you were going to get one, I assumed you were coming right back."

"I was going to," I lied obviously, "but then I ran into Connie, and we started talking…" With a smile, I picked up a toasted round. "Cracker?"

"No, thanks."

"Suit yourself." With a shrug, I stuck the item in my mouth and dusted off my hands. "Now, much as I hate to break this up," I said when I could speak without blowing crumbs all over the place, "I need to use the ladies' room."

"Oh, no, you don't," Kevin warned. "I know that look."

"What look?"

"The one that says you're going to sneak off and disappear again."

"I don't know what you're talking about."

"Fine. Then allow me to accompany you."

"Never mind. I can hold it."

"I know that look too," Kevin warned as I scowled at him for derailing my plan. "It's the one that says you're considering shortening my life by several years."

"Wow." Connie laughed. "Is it just you," she asked me, "or can he do that with everyone?"

"I have no idea—but sometimes I wish he'd take his act on the road."

Connie laughed again. "So, who's the gentleman you were talking with at your table just before you came over, Kevin?"

"Jackie's dad."

"No kidding."

I wasn't surprised by her reaction. No one ever thought he looked old enough to be my dad. Some said it outright; others just stared. Connie appeared to be taking the second option.

"Is he a marine," she finally asked, "or is he just here as your guest?"

"Both," Kevin replied. "He was a maintenance clerk back in the sixties."

"Well, he looks great. Hardly seems old enough to be Tyler and Lucy's grandpa."

"I know," I sighed. "I'd like to say it was due to his youthful outlook and natural vitality, but in truth it's down to an unchecked libido and all the sprinting he has to do whenever someone's husband or father discovers what's really keeping him looking so hale."

Kevin shook his head. "He's dated a few that were close to her age," he said, "and liberated a few from bad marriages, but he's not quite the letch or the Lothario she makes him out to be."

"I see," Connie said with a grimace that said she wished she hadn't asked. "Well, I should probably see what Zane is up to. Nice talking to you guys."

"Same here."

"And congratulations," Kevin added with a nod toward her hand. "Zane's a lucky man."

"Thanks," Connie replied. "So are you."

"So you heard about the engagement?" I asked when Connie had gone.

Kevin nodded. "Word gets around—especially when people are drinking."

"And have you heard any *word* about Katrine?" I asked.

"Not one."

"Don't you think it's strange that she's suddenly so ill?"

"No. But I take it you do."

"Of course I do. I mean, she was fine on Sunday."

"Jackie, that was six days ago. People can catch and die from pneumonia in half that time."

"Well, aren't you just the bluebird of happiness."

"I don't mean to be morbid. I'm just saying that it's not unusual for someone to be fine one day and then be too sick to leave the house six days later. Then again, we don't know for sure that she's caught something. For all we know, something else is going on."

"Like what?"

"Maybe she's pregnant."

"Bite your tongue!"

Kevin smiled and leaned forward to kiss me. "I'd rather bite yours."

"I'm serious," I said before our lips connected. "It would be the end of her life."

"Why?"

"Because having his kid would bind her to him permanently."

"Funny. I always thought that's what marriage vows were for."

"It is, but having a kid will seal it. I mean, it's hard enough to escape a lousy marriage when it's just you to worry about. It's even more difficult when you have children to support."

Kevin stepped back but held on to my hands. "If you think having kids is such a risk, why did you want so badly to have them with me?"

I smiled and brushed a few loose fibers from the shoulder of his uniform. "Because you, my darling, are what they call a keeper."

"Why, thank you. You're not so bad yourself."

Kevin pulled me closer, and I held him tight. Behind him I could see my dad and his date heading back to the table after having danced to a set of classic country-western tunes.

She wasn't nearly as bad as I feared she'd be. At least she dressed her age, which I could confidently state was closer to my father's age than mine. Her hairstyle was a little outdated, but it worked for her—which is likely why she continued to wear it—and her dress fit well and covered everything it should.

That was all I had gleaned about Eleanor since arriving at the ball tonight, and it was about all I wanted to know at this stage of the game. If the two of them stayed together long enough for me to see her again, I might be able to muster a bit more interest in her, but for now I was going to keep my distance.

Women came and went from my dad's life too often for me to bother getting to know them, and those who stuck around almost always wound up hating or disappointing me. When I was younger, I used to wonder how my dad managed to attract so many dysfunctional women. It wasn't until after I married Kevin that I realized that the problem wasn't a tendency to attract crazy women but a gift for driving all the normal ones away.

"So how about another drink?" I asked in an effort to delay our return to the table.

Kevin raised my hand along with his own to check his watch. "I guess it won't hurt, since it's only ten thirty and we're not driving."

"Excellent."

"You may think I'm working off a double standard when it comes to Katrine," I continued as we walked to the bar. "But you can't compare our situations at all. For one thing, she's marrying an arrogant bastard who seems bent on destroying her confidence. And second, even if I had as much going for me as she does, you would never try to hold me back."

"What are you talking about? You have far more going for you than Katrine does."

"That's not true," I said, trading nods with Howie as Kevin pulled out his wallet and placed our order. "She's beautiful. She's brilliant. And she has two educated parents who want the best for her and who are willing to sacrifice anything to see that she gets it."

"Sure, but on their terms."

"At least they're interested," I argued as I accepted the martini that Howie had presciently made for me in place of the Cape Cod that Kevin had ordered. "Unlike my dad—who had neither the will nor the means to help me with homework, much less become an accomplished anything; whose employment history and nomadic lifestyle afforded me a fractured education with little chance of getting into any college without the word 'community' in its title; and whose own lack of interest in anything other than women, fishing, and football left both me and Ricky culturally and socially illiterate."

"Now hold on a minute," Kevin all but ordered. "You may have had to work for it, but you have an excellent education and have more than overcome the limitations of your upbringing. And rather than focusing on where you started, I think you should focus on how far you've come and who gets the credit for it. After all, Katrine doesn't have a thing on you that her parents' money didn't buy, and, frankly, if she's willing to give that up to be with an arrogant bastard, it either means she knows something about them that you don't, or she's just not as smart as you think she is."

"Kevin, the girl speaks multiple languages and understands mathematic and scientific terms I can't even *say* without risking a cerebral hemorrhage. You don't get a brain like that from rich parents."

"No—but it helps."

"OK, so maybe she was exposed to things she otherwise would not have been without their resources," I allowed. "But rejecting them isn't what will ruin her life. It's Rob. And if it weren't for him—with or without her parents' money—Katrine could do and have anything she wants."

"Maybe she's like me and only wants love."

I eyed him doubtfully. "Is that really all you want?"

Kevin smiled and kissed my forehead. "Well, that and to take a leak," he said with a laugh. "Meet you back at the table?"

Without waiting for an answer, he turned and headed for the men's room. Since I hadn't agreed to meet him anywhere, I stayed right where I was. Dad and Eleanor were out dancing again, but I wasn't about to go back to the table and risk them joining me there before Kevin did.

Dinner, like Eleanor, hadn't been as bad as I had feared. Dad had been too wrapped up in seeing to her comfort to pick me apart, and I'd been too busy drinking wine to say anything that would draw fire.

It was only after dinner—while Kevin was off enjoying his Macanudo and Eleanor was off powdering her nose—that things had gone sour. The problem boiled down to my refusal of his invitation to attend Thanksgiving dinner with him and Eleanor at her daughter's home in New Brighton.

Having already committed to spending the holiday with Kevin's family, I politely declined and offered him and Eleanor dibs on next year's celebration—despite my unspoken doubts that she would be in the picture twelve months from now—at which point I was subjected to a diatribe that included no profanity but did feature accusations of selfishness and disrespect and other unflattering and wholly undeserved evaluations of my behavior. Unwilling to meet insult with insult, I sat there and let him have his say. I knew the things he said to me in anger would bother him more when he replayed them in his head tomorrow than they bothered me. Moreover, I knew those words—combined with my indifference—would bother him far more than anything I could have said in reply.

And so, after he'd run out of steam—which, conveniently, was about two seconds before Eleanor reappeared—and the two of them had moved to the dance floor, I had poured myself the remains of both the red and white wines at our table. When I finished them, I did the same with the bottles of the tables in my vicinity that had been abandoned for the night. Kevin returned to the table about twenty minutes later but, sadly, not far enough ahead of my dad and Eleanor for me to tell him what had happened. And so, rather than watching my dad attempt to maneuver Kevin into changing our plans—and knowing Kevin would never agree to altering our plans without consulting me—I excused myself to the bar and let Howie talk me into my first martini.

Having since finished my second, I decided to head back to the bar for a third, keeping an eye out for Kevin in case he returned from the men's room before I could get back. I was so focused on the main doors that nearly I walked right into him.

"Hi, there," I said, making a point to appear as if I was on my way specifically to join him. "Everything come out OK?"

"Just fine."

"Great. So whaddaya say we *blow* this pop stand and *head* to our room?"

Kevin raised his brows. "Sounds good to me."

"I hoped it would."

Nodding, he took my hand, pocketed a few plastic coasters embossed with the eagle, globe, and anchor, grabbed the commemorative glass steins we'd received as mementos of the event, and started walking toward the dance floor. Realizing we were headed straight for my dad and Eleanor, I stopped short.

"I thought we were leaving," I said, releasing his hand.

"We are. I just thought we'd say good night to your dad first."

"OK, well, I'll see you back at the room."

"Jackie, wait."

I didn't give him a chance to argue but continued walking briskly in the opposite direction.

"What's going on?" he asked when he'd caught up to me in the hall a few minutes later.

"Nothing. I'm just ready to go to bed."

"Then why wouldn't you come with me to say good night?"

"What difference does it make now?" I asked as the elevator stopped and disgorged a boot private and, presumably, his high school sweetheart. "You said good-bye for both of us, right?"

"Of course."

"Perfect," I said as he followed me into the empty car. "Now I have a question for *you*."

"What's that?"

Grinning, I hit the stop button behind him and put my arms around his neck. "Ever wanted to do it in an elevator?"

Twelve

"*Y*ou didn't!" declared Lynette as we chatted about the ball by phone two Sundays later.

"You're right. We didn't." I sighed. "But had there been a condom dispenser in that elevator, things would have gotten pretty interesting—let me tell ya."

I decided to leave her with the impression that a lack of contraceptives was the only barrier to what I had in mind and that the fun continued once we got to our room. I couldn't bring myself to admit out loud that Kevin had fallen asleep while I was getting out of my dress and brushing my teeth, or that I had lain awake for hours after he passed out wondering why we'd bothered to get a room if we weren't going to make the most of it.

"Maybe you should drop a note about that in their suggestion box sometime."

"Good idea. I may have to do that."

"So you had a good time, huh?"

"It wasn't bad," I said, leaving out the part about my dad, "unless you count the next morning when I got stuck cleaning the entire house again because Kevin's sister did little more than keep the kids alive while we were gone. I would have made Kevin do it, since it was his idea to let her babysit, but he was stuck at the armory again all day."

"On a Sunday?"

"Yeah. He had a lot of homework to do so he drove over there after Laurie left so he could work in peace and quiet. Anyway, I had just finished cleaning when I realized we were out of milk. So I had to run to the store, and, well, let's just say this is the last time I let him talk me into staying overnight. I can't believe I paid over a hundred bucks for the privilege of sleeping in a strange bed and cleaning my house twice in thirty-six hours."

"I don't blame you. So did Rob and Katrine stay over too?"

"No. In fact, they never even made it to the ball. Katrine was sick, so they skipped the whole thing."

"What's wrong with her?"

"No clue. It looks a lot like the flu, but if that's what she had, you'd think we all would have caught it since she was here both before and after she was symptomatic."

"Maybe it's a strain you've all had before. If she just moved here this summer, she wouldn't have the antibodies."

"I guess. All I know is that it hit her hard. I stopped by their place on my way to the store Sunday morning to see how she was doing, and she was soaked in sweat and so weak she could barely hold her head up. I was so worried I wound up bringing her home with me."

"Weren't you afraid of exposing the kids?"

"Sure, but what choice did I have? I couldn't leave her there by herself."

"Where was Rob?"

"I have no idea—nor do I know how he could have left her alone like that—but I wasn't about to wait around for him to ask. Instead, I found her a clean shirt and some dry sweats, made her drink about a gallon of water, left Rob a note, and practically dragged her out to the car, where she slept while I ran into the store with the kids."

"What did he have to say when he called you back?"

"That's just it. He never called. In fact, when I hadn't heard from him by the time Kevin got home, I called their house to make sure he'd found the note."

"And?"

"He said yes, and thanks."

"That's it?"

"Yep."

"Well, is she OK now?"

"I assume so. I mean, she was still pretty pale when she left Monday evening, but she was doing much better than when I found her."

"So Rob did eventually come for her."

"No."

"Then how did she get home?"

"She walked."

"You let her *walk*?"

"What was I supposed to do, Lyn? Put her in restraints and post a notice of quarantine? She was well enough to kick my ass at Scrabble by Sunday night and to stay at our house alone all day on Monday. So when she said she needed to get home to cook dinner for the creep she calls a fiancé and that I didn't need to pack the kids and drive her, I wasn't going to argue."

"Dinner!" Lyn gasped. "Crap, I almost forgot. We'll have to finish catching up later. Josh will be home any minute, and we're going to my folks' for an early Thanksgiving since I have to work on Thursday. But call me later in the week—maybe we can get together."

"OK. See ya."

I replaced the receiver and stepped back to the counter to heat three bowls of leftover ravioli, one by one, in the microwave.

A few minutes later, Kevin entered the kitchen with Lucy in his arms and Tyler by the hand. "Here we go," he said. "Two hungry babies—all washed up in time to smear tomato sauce from toe to chin."

Tyler crossed his arms. "I'm not a baby."

"A thousand pardons, sir. Make that one baby and one big guy."

Kevin set Lucy in her carrier and buckled her in. "So who was on the phone?"

"Lynette. She called to find out how the ball went."

"Did you tell her about Katrine?"

"Yeah. She said she'd be sick too if she were weeks away from marrying Rob."

Kevin laughed. "No, she didn't."

"Oh, right. That was me."

Kevin shook his head. "You know," he said as I pulled the last bowl from the microwave. "As I recall, some people didn't give our marriage more than a snowball's chance in hell either."

"True—but then Katrine isn't marrying the most patient, charming, supportive, handsome, and understanding man on the planet."

"OK. What do you want?"

"I was hoping to get a jump on my homework," I admitted. "Would you mind holding the fort for a while?"

"I guess not."

"Thanks," I said, bending down to plant a kiss on his sculpted cheek. "By the way, I'm turning off the ringer on the phone up there because I have an exam in the morning, and I don't have time to talk to anyone. So unless Pat Schroeder calls with visions of job offers dancing in her head, I am indisposed."

"Got it. Does this mean you're planning to pull an all-nighter?"

"No. In fact, I should finish in time to put the kids to bed at eight. What about you?"

"For a change, I managed to finish everything I need for tomorrow apart from printing. If I do that while you put the kids down, I should finish in time for us to get some snuggling in."

"Works for me," I practically rejoiced. "See ya in a bit."

Upstairs, I raced through my speech outline, scanned a few notes for a political science quiz, and stapled together a paper I'd run through the printer. When I finally tossed it all in my backpack, the clock showed 7:47 p.m. Four minutes later, after brushing my hair and changing into a flirty nightshirt, I skipped down the stairs to find the house quiet and Kevin, Tyler, and Lucy sprawled on the floor beside the playpen in the spare room. All three were fast asleep.

I stood in the doorway waiting for Kevin to stir. "Pssst," I whispered, but succeeded only in rousing the boy, who then rolled over and burrowed his face into Kevin's side.

With a frustrated sigh, I pulled the door almost closed and switched off the light.

"So much for that," I murmured, wondering how I would kill the next couple hours until fatigue took over as my prevailing mood and drove me to bed.

I padded down the hall and picked up the phone in the kitchen. Stretching the cord across the room to the counter, I pressed a few buttons and listened for the ring on the other end as I poured myself a glass of Tyler's sugar-free fruit punch.

"Thank you for calling Big Five. Can you hold, please?"

"I don't think so," I teased. "I know this trick."

"Jackie?"

"Yeah, it's me. And I will hold, but not for very long."

"Never mind. Whoever was on his way up the walk must've needed to use the phone, because he turned around the minute I picked it up."

"Maybe he's wanted and thought you recognized him."

"Good thing you called, then," Sera laughed. "So what have you been up to tonight?"

"These days, just homework. Did you finish your paper, by the way?"

"Almost. I still have to print it in the computer lab tomorrow morning. What about you?"

"Signed, sealed, and almost delivered—for all the good it did me to rush."

"What do you mean?"

"Oh, I whipped through the paper and all my other work tonight thinking Kevin was waiting to spend time with me after the kids went to sleep, and instead I found all three of them asleep on the floor in the playroom."

"How sweet."

"Excuse me?"

"Well, it is."

"Sera, you're starting to worry me. First I find you reading romance novels, and now you're saying things like 'How sweet?' What's that about?"

"I don't know. All I can say is that you really got lucky with Kevin."
I wish.

"Women of earlier generations got no help from their husbands," she continued, "and yours does laundry, washes dishes, and helps take care of the kids."

"As he should, since they're his kids, too."

"True."

"What gets me is that you'll never find my ass sprawled on the floor sleeping at eight o'clock at night, or slumped in a chair in the middle of the afternoon when I'm supposed to be studying. In fact, I've been known to stay up all night—sometimes two or three nights in a row—to keep all my shit in one sock, and yet he can't stay awake the one night we planned to go to bed early and—well, you know."

"Ah. So that's what has you so riled up."

"Yes. But, Sera, I swear one of these days I'm going to fix that narcoleptic's wagon. One of these days instead of dragging his ass upstairs or moving his alarm down for him, I'll go to bed and let *him* worry about how he's going to finish his homework and get to work in time for morning muster."

"Seems fair."

"I know. Unfortunately, the plan has a fairly significant flaw."

"What's that?"

"Me and my lack of willpower."

"That's actually two flaws."

"Thank you."

"Welcome."

"Anyway," I continued, "the point is that I've tried this before—twice, in fact. Both times I wound up lying awake for hours—caught between my concern for him and my need to make a point—before giving up and hauling our alarm clocks and an armload of blankets downstairs to join him."

"Christ, Jackie. Why don't you just take his first morning piss for him, too?"

"Tell me about it! But I'm so afraid he's going to sleep through a test or miss an important meeting that I can't rest until I've done everything in my power to prevent that from happening. And of course, the man doesn't come to full consciousness until he's had his shower, so he never remembers where he wakes up, much less how he got there. But once he's showered and dressed, it's 'Gee, I'd like to stay and visit, but as you can see by this exquisitely pressed uniform, I'm an extremely busy person on my way to some exceptionally important place. I love you, and have a nice day!' leaving me wanting to set his clock to a different time zone and make him late three days in a row."

"Have you talked to him about this?"

"No."

"Why not?"

"Because it only started when he got his new billet assignments this fall, and I'd hoped it would go away as he got used to a new routine."

"Well, that's very reasonable of you, but I think it's time you tell him he's pissing you off."

"I know. But it seems so stupid and petty. I mean, he wouldn't fall asleep if he weren't tired, right? And I'm not high-maintenance enough to expect him to stay awake for the sheer pleasure of basking in my presence. My only gripe is that I work my ass off and sometimes forego sleep altogether just to stay ahead of the game, while he can crash when and wherever he likes without worrying that he's gonna sleep in or not be where it is he is supposed to be the next day. I guess I'm really more envious than I am angry."

"Whatever you say, but you sure seem angry to me."

"I do, don't I?"

146

"Yes. Unfortunately there's a car pulling into the lot at the moment, so we'll have to explore that area next time."

"OK, doc. Thanks for listening. See you in class tomorrow."

I hung up the phone and climbed up to bed, resolving to stay there and let Kevin face the music. Though I almost lost my nerve a few times—and even made an exceptional amount of racket on three separate trips to the restroom—I somehow managed to avoid surrender before finally falling asleep sometime after one thirty.

When I awoke the next morning, Kevin was seated at the desk outside our bedroom alternately typing and griping at the computer for running too slowly. He was dressed, but his hair was still damp from his shower, and a bowl of corn flakes sat wilting next to his briefcase on the desk.

I touched a button on his alarm clock and discovered that he'd gotten up at some point during the night and set it for 5:00 a.m. I couldn't decide whether to lie or apologize for not setting it, so I just said, "Good morning."

"Oh, hi, sweets," he called over his shoulder. "Too bad about last night, hunh? Guess we were both pretty wiped."

"Guess so."

"Well, at least I got this done," he added, nodding toward the printer.

I sighed as he pulled the printed sheets from the machine and begin to separate them from each other and their perforated edges. "About your alarm clock…"

"No problem. You forgot to set yours too."

Shit.

"That's what you get when you stay up too late," he teased as he shut his briefcase. "It would've been OK, though. I set it for you when I set mine— just in case I got out of here before you needed to be up."

"Well, I'm up now," I said, rising. "Can I fix you a real breakfast?"

"Thanks, but no time. I sure do love you though. Have a good day."

I watched his head disappear below the banister. *Yeah. Same to you.*

By the end of the day, I had gotten over my annoyance with myself and Kevin, and joined him and the kids on the living room floor.

"Anything new at work today?" I asked as he rolled toward me on the rug.

"No. But in my rush this morning, I forgot to mention that your dad called shortly after you went upstairs last night."

I feigned interest in Tyler's shoelace as Kevin squeezed my knee.

"He wasn't exactly thrilled when I told him you were indisposed, either. Said since you're not speaking to him, I'm supposed to tell you he's sorry if he 'offended your sensibilities' and that he'd like you to call him 'when you can find the time.'"

I rolled onto my back and held Lucy's hands as I lifted her in the air on my shins. "Did you happen to mention that you had instructions to hold *all* my calls?"

"Of course."

"Well, then you've done everything you can."

"So you're not avoiding him."

"Nope."

"Then why does he think you are?"

"Probably because that's what I normally do when I'm mad at him."

"Does that mean you're going to call him?"

"No—but only because I have nothing to say, not because I'm not speaking to him."

"I see. So, can you think of any reason he would think you're not speaking to him—even though you're not?"

"Of course," I admitted, as Kevin eyed me closely. "I really didn't want to bring it up since it was no big deal to me; but if you're that desperate to hear about it, I suppose I can tell you."

"That would be nice."

"OK. Well, after dinner on the tenth," I began, sitting up and placing Lucy on one side of my lap as Tyler crawled over to occupy the other, "while you were off enjoying your cigar, he and I had a brief exchange whereupon he informed me that Eleanor had invited us to join her family for Thanksgiving dinner. I told him that I was sorry, but you and I already have plans for Thanksgiving and would not be able to make it. He didn't like the sound of that and proceeded to point out that our being there would give us all a chance to get to know one another. I repeated that I was sorry, but you and I had agreed to spend every other Thanksgiving with your folks and the ones in between with mine. He then asked if we couldn't cancel for some other reason, such as illness or an emergency—and when I said yes, he pointed out that if we could cancel it for some other reason, we could, in fact, cancel it for him, as well. When I declined to do so—as politely as I could, mind you—he got upset and said he couldn't believe I could be so selfish."

"He actually said that?"

"Among other things."

Kevin grimaced gravely. "I'm guessing he was pretty disappointed to find he couldn't change your mind and just couldn't find the words to say so."

"With *his* vocabulary? Are you kidding me?"

"I'm not talking about his vocabulary, Jack, and you know it."

"Whatever. The point is I'm not upset with the man, but he does have reason to think I am."

"I understand."

"But?"

"But I think you should call him anyway. He's clearly feeling bad about how he behaved and would probably appreciate the chance to put things right."

"That's his problem. As far as I'm concerned, things are just find the way they are. If he thinks I'm selfish, that's his business. After all, we both know who the selfish one is and that he only said what he did because he hoped it would make me feel bad and induce me to change my mind. But alas, I don't and I didn't. The end."

"I understand how you feel, Jack, but I'd like you to reconsider."

"Why?"

"Because he's your dad—and he's trying to have a relationship with you. I mean, look at how much trouble he went to in order to join us for the ball."

"What trouble? Christ, Kevin, all he had to do was call."

"Twice."

I grimaced as I remembered having failed to ask Kevin about the tickets, and my dad calling back a few days later to ask him directly. "OK, twice," I admitted. "You still can hardly call that trouble. And I can't help it if I can't remember everything. I have a lot going on, you know."

"I know that. Nevertheless, he did call—twice. And he did go out and get a tux and drive all the way into the city. Doesn't that tell you anything?"

"Sure. It tells me he was out to impress Eleanor and thought taking her to the ball would do the trick."

"And you don't think it had anything do to with you?"

"No, I don't."

"If that's the case, why would he have contacted you in the first place?"

"For the same reason he invited us to Eleanor's for Thanksgiving—to show us off. To make him look like a great guy for having such a terrific family. It's just like when Ricky and I were kids. We barely existed when he was seeing someone, unless, of course, she took pity on us or had an unfulfilled maternal instinct—then we were suddenly prime assets. Well, I won't be his little Dresden doll anymore, and I won't let him take credit for me or you or the kids, because once he's got her hooked, we won't see or hear from him again unless and until she dumps him."

"Understood. And I'm not asking you to cozy up to him or his new girlfriend. I just think you should call the man. If you don't, he'll only continue to think you're avoiding him."

"I can live with that."

"Come on, Jack. Certainly you can manage a short conversation."

"Kevin, the man doesn't know *how* to have a conversation. All he knows how to do is instruct, inform, and critique. I'm not saying he does it on purpose. In fact, I'm convinced he can't help it. But I have all the professors I can handle at the moment, thank you. What I need is someone who is interested in me as a person; someone who won't evaluate and edit everything I say; someone who'll visit now and again, spoil my kids, and occasionally take you fishing."

"What about you?"

"What about me?"

"Why aren't you going fishing?"

"I don't want to go fishing."

"Well, neither do I."

"Then I guess it's a good thing this guy doesn't exist."

Kevin smiled. "I guess so."

Thirteen

I was in the laundry room running a load of whites the following Sunday when I heard the phone ring and, subsequently, Kevin's voice calling me from the kitchen.

"What *is* it?" I replied melodically.

"Guess."

Fearing it was my dad and having little time or patience for games, I continued to fill the washer. "Can't you take a message?" I pleaded when he appeared in the hallway with Lucy over his shoulder. "I'm supposed to be studying."

"Don't worry," he laughed. "It's only Katrine."

With a mixture of curiosity and relief, I dumped in the soap, closed the washer lid, lifted the freshly dried basket of darks off the floor, and killed the lights. "I'll take it upstairs," I announced on my way through the kitchen. "But this better not be a trick."

After trudging up the stairs, I dropped the basket on our bed and picked up the extension from the nightstand. "Hey, stranger," I said warmly once Kevin had hung up. "How've you been?"

"Better, thanks. I've been meaning to call and thank you for helping out when I was sick, but I've been so busy trying to catch up on my schoolwork that I haven't had time until now."

"I can imagine. How long were you out anyway?"

"A week and a half."

"Ouch."

"I know. My instructors have been pretty flexible in terms of my makeup work, but I'd really like to be fully caught up in time for finals."

"Good plan."

"I figured you'd approve," Katrine laughed. "So how was your Thanksgiving?"

"Nice and quiet—just the way I like it."

"That's good. Did you go anywhere?"

"No. We were planning to visit Kevin's folks," I explained as I dumped the laundry onto the bed and started to fold, "but by the time Thursday rolled around, we didn't feel like driving that far in the snow, so we stayed home and had a little dinner of our own."

"Sounds nice."

"It was. How about yours?"

"Don't ask."

"Is that 'don't ask' as in, 'I don't want to talk about it,' or is it 'don't ask' as in you do?"

"Maybe neither; maybe both. I'll let you know. So how are things otherwise?"

"Pretty good. The house is clean. Kevin's happy. The kids are well."

"I'm glad. I was worried they'd wind up with what I had."

"No sign of that so far. What about Rob?"

"Not a trace. Then again, given how little I see of him these days, there's not much chance he could have caught it from me."

"Really? What's he been up to?"

"Hanging out with Scott. He's out of work again, which means he has lots of free time to spend with his old pal, Rob."

"Well, I can see how that could be problematic, but I'm sure things will get back to normal once Scott gets back on his feet."

"I wouldn't bet on that."

"Why not?"

"Because he's moving in."

"You're kidding. How did that happen?"

"Easy. Scott told Rob he couldn't make his rent, so Rob offered him our spare room."

"And that's OK with you?"

"Hardly. I mean, Scott's all right and I'd like to help him out, but the timing is really lousy. I wouldn't mind so much if I knew he'd be gone by the time we get back from New York, but that wasn't part of the plan. And since Rob's letting him stay for free, there's no incentive for the guy to make other arrangements on his own."

"Did you mention any of that when you discussed it?"

"That's just it. We didn't discuss it. They discussed it, and Rob told me afterward."

"Maybe it never occurred to him that you'd object."

"You'd think *he'd* object. He should want to have the place to ourselves as much as I do."

"Guys don't always think of things like that—including Kevin, but once I've told him what I want or how I feel, he's generally more than willing to accommodate me."

"That's great, but what I want or how I feel doesn't carry much weight with Rob, and accommodation isn't exactly his strong suit."

"You should at least give him a chance," I said without conviction. "You never know; the man could surprise you."

"It's too late now. If I was going to say anything, I had my chance a week ago when he first told me."

"That may have been the optimal time," I allowed as I stacked the folded clothes back in the basket. "But there's nothing stopping you from reopening the dialogue. Just tell him you've given it some thought and that you're OK with having Scott stay there for a while, but you'd like him to make other arrangements for when you get back after the wedding."

"I don't know, Jackie. He doesn't like it when I question his judgment."

"Then the practice will be good for him."

"But it won't be good for me."

"What are you saying?"

"Nothing. Never mind."

"Katrine, does Rob hit you?"

"Of course not."

"Has he ever threatened to?"

"No."

"Then what did you mean when you said it wasn't good for you?"

"Oh, you know what he's like when he doesn't get his way; even if he gives in on this, I'll never hear the end of it."

I could find nothing in Katrine's words to suggest she wasn't telling the truth. She'd spoken quickly and firmly with genuine surprise and offered a plausible explanation with no extraneous detail or indignation to cast doubt on its veracity. In light of that, there was little to do but let it go and post a mental note for future reference. "Well, it's your call," I said to that end. "But the sooner he learns he can't have his way all the time, the better off you'll be."

From Katrine's silence, I figured I was about to be dismissed.

"Well, I should get back to work," I said, glancing through the doorway at my paper on the computer screen. "I'm glad you're feeling better, and I hope everything works out."

"Thanks. I appreciate it."

"No problem. Take care."

"Jackie, wait—there's something I wanted to ask you."

"Sure. What?"

"Would you mind if I came over?"

"Now?" I looked at the clock on the stand next to the bed. Kevin would be putting the kids down soon and heading off to bed.

"I know it's getting late," she continued, "but I don't think I can stand another minute alone in this house."

"All right. But you'd better bring that makeup work of yours, because I have a paper due tomorrow, and there'll be no one else awake to keep you company while I edit."

"That was fast," I called from the kitchen when Katrine arrived minutes later in a gray fleece sweatshirt and navy and white striped pajama bottoms. "Did you run all the way?"

"Nope." Katrine set her backpack on the recliner and smiled triumphantly. "But I did find *this* in Rob's change cup."

"What's that?" I asked in reference to the key ring dangling from her pointer finger, which she then spun around her finger like a pistol in the hand of a gunslinger.

"Spare to Rob's Nova. Scott's Chevette needed gas," she explained, "so they took that tonight instead."

"Well, I hope you left him a note. I wouldn't want him to worry."

"He wouldn't. He's actually hoping it'll be stolen."

"I meant about you."

Katrine tossed the key into her bag and sniffed. "You *must* be kidding."

I smiled grimly as I entered the living room with two mugs of hot cocoa and handed one down to Katrine, who now sat cross-legged on the floor in front of the recliner, having just swapped her sneakers for the fluffy gray slippers she'd pulled from her bag. "Oooh, thanks," she said, accepting the vessel with both hands and placing it under her nose. "Is it homemade?"

I nodded. "Only the best for you," I said, placing my own mug on the end table and taking a perch on the edge of the sofa. "I'm sorry if I upset you earlier," I continued. "I can be pretty pushy sometimes."

"That's OK. I know you're just looking out for me. Unlike Rob, who couldn't give a shit."

"I'm sure that's not true. His actions may not reflect it, but I'm sure deep down he wants you to be happy."

Katrine shrugged as she set her mug on the floor.

I watched and waited as she studied her slippers, and then the lamp, and then her slippers again. I didn't want to leave if she wanted to talk, but neither did I want to sit there all night waiting for her to open up when I had so much to do. With this in mind, I set a mental deadline by which she would have to start baring her soul before I ruled this crisis a false alarm and excused myself to work on my term paper.

"It wasn't supposed to be like this," she said finally, looking up from her mug. "Don't get me wrong—I knew it wouldn't be easy. I knew Rob would be busy, that he'd have duties and responsibilities on top of his schoolwork, and I'd have to find a way to fill the time when he was gone. I expected all that; I was prepared for it and actually looked forward to proving I had the maturity and discipline to make it work. But I did not expect to be completely cut out of major decisions, nor was I prepared to play second fiddle to his loser friends. I mean, it's like I don't even matter to him anymore, and I don't know what to do about it."

I shook my head. "I know I probably sound like a broken record, but you really need to talk to Rob."

"And say what exactly?"

"That you're not happy with the way things are and that you'd like to discuss some changes. Then tell him what's bothering you and how you'd like things to be different. And be specific. General terms may lead to a quick agreement, but they're open to interpretation and a bitch to enforce. What you need are clear expectations with measurable outcomes and a reasonable timeline. That not only gives Rob a better idea of what you want from him; it also gives you somewhere to negotiate from if he doesn't go for your first offer."

"I don't know, Jackie. This all sounds so businesslike. I really just want him to spend more time with me and to not make big decisions without consulting me."

"That's all well and good, Katrine, but what exactly constitutes a 'big' decision? And how much time is 'more' time?"

Katrine shrugged.

"That's why I say you have to be specific," I advised. "That's why you need approach it like a business deal. If you don't, you'll never get anywhere. And you start by assessing the current situation and deciding what kind of change you want to occur. For example, about how often is Rob out with Scott?"

"Nearly every night."

"Is that *nearly every night* as in five or six times a week, or is that an exaggeration?"

"It's *nearly* as in six, sometimes seven, nights a week."

"Christ! What are they out doing all that time? And how is he passing his classes?"

"I have no idea. The one time I asked about school, he just said he had it all under control."

"I see."

"Do you think he's lying?"

"What I think is irrelevant, Katrine. What matters is what *you* think and what *you're* going to do about it."

"What would you do?"

"What I would do can get you twenty to life in Stillwater, so I'm probably the wrong person to ask."

Katrine scowled. "I don't understand it," she said after a moment. "Things weren't like this in Europe. Rob always had time for me then."

"But other things were different back then, too, Katrine. Your relationship was new and exciting, and there were no old friends hanging around. You also didn't live together or see each other every day. I'm not saying you should accept this; I'm just trying to help you understand what's happening so you can better communicate with Rob."

I could tell she was no keener on that front than she'd been on the phone.

"Look, this doesn't have to be the big deal I think you're envisioning," I advised. "All you need to do is tell him there's something on your mind and ask him to make time to sit down with him and talk about it."

"What if he says he's too busy or wants to know what it is?

"He can't be that busy. If he says he is, tell him you understand and that you're willing to work around his schedule. Then ask him to pick a time that works for him, and hold him to it. If he wants to know what it's about, tell him you need to talk about schedules. Once you've got his attention—be it right at that moment or at some appointed time in the future—don't complain, criticize, or accuse. Simply explain that you'd like to spend more time together, and tell him what you had in mind."

"I can't do that."

"Sure you can. And once you've exhausted that subject, you can say something like 'I'd also like to talk about our finances' or 'I have some concerns related to our living arrangements,' then tell him you want to be more involved in decisions about the household or whatever."

"I can't say that."

"Then use your own words. Christ, it doesn't matter *how* you say it."

"Don't you get it, Jackie? It doesn't matter *if* I say it! It doesn't matter at all. He isn't the least bit interested in what I want, what I think, or how I feel."

"That's the real issue here, isn't it?" I asked gently. "It's not that he's letting Scott move in or that he's gone all the time. The problem is he doesn't listen to you or show you any respect."

"I guess."

"Has he ever?" I asked.

"I never thought about it before. Until we got here, everything seemed fine."

"Is that because you always wanted the same things? Or did you simply adjust your feelings, interests, and preferences to align with his?"

"I don't know. I never really thought about it."

I realized then it was time to get some things off my chest. I hated to think about how hearing them would make her feel—not to mention how it might change things between us, but she deserved to know the truth, and if I never saw her again, at least I'd know I'd been honest with her.

"Look," I said to that end, placing my mug back on the table. "I don't know whether you're looking for advice or just a sounding board, but there are some things I need to say. I should have said them a long time ago, but I was hoping I wouldn't have to. I was also afraid you'd get angry and never speak to me again. But I care enough about you to take that risk, and if you'll hear me out just this once, I promise—no matter what you do—I'll stick by you and never mention it again. Is it a deal?"

"Sure, Jackie. But, jeez, you're making me nervous."

"I'm sorry. But my words up to this point have been a big load of diplomatic excrement, and I have to set the record straight. The truth is, I think your relationship with Rob is a train wreck waiting to happen, and I don't think talking to him is going to change a damned thing. If I were you, I'd pack up what was mine, hand him back his ring, and get the hell out."

Katrine swallowed hard. "Listen, I know you and Rob have had your differences—"

"This isn't about me and Rob or our differences, Katrine. This is about you, your life, and what makes you happy."

"You don't think *he* makes me happy?"

"Considering you just spent the better part of an hour providing substantial evidence to the contrary, I'd have to say no."

Katrine shrugged. "Maybe I exaggerated things a little because I'm still angry about the Scott issue," she offered. "Or maybe I'm just tired."

"I know you're angry, Katrine. You have a right to be. I also know you're tired; I would expect that, too, given your recent illness. But I'm not telling you to leave based just on what you've said tonight; I'm telling you to leave because of what I've witnessed with my own eyes since the day we met."

"Such as?"

"The man treats you like dirt, Katrine. He tells you what to do, what to think, and how to act without any consideration for your feelings. He corrects your grammar, challenges your facts, insults your intelligence, and doesn't give a damn who's listening. He ignores you when it suits him, mocks you if your opinion differs from his own, and seizes every opportunity to undermine your confidence. He's a selfish, insensitive jerk, and you've got far too much going for you to waste any more time or energy on him or tolerate any more of his bullshit."

I watched tears flood her eyes, spill over once, and then recede.

"I'm sorry, Katrine," I said, handing her a box of tissues. "It kills me to have to say these things, but you deserve better than this."

"Well, that hardly matters now," she said coolly, after pausing to blow her nose. "It's too late to do anything about it."

"No, it's not."

"Yes, it is, Jackie—the wedding is less than a month away."

"So? People have called off weddings with less notice than that."

"But the invitations went out last week, and I'm supposed to pick up my dress tomorrow."

"So sell the dress and use the proceeds toward postage to issue retractions."

"But I'll never get what I paid for it."

That statement caught me off guard. I had always found it interesting how Katrine ascribed purchases and assigned possession in conversation. It was always *Rob's* house or *Rob's* money and *Rob bought* this or *Rob bought* that; occasionally it was *the* house or *the* car, but it was never *our* house or *we bought* this or that—much less *I bought* or *I paid*. So I found it funny that the Nova was still Rob's as of about an hour ago, but suddenly *she* had paid for the dress.

"Look, Katrine. If you're truly concerned about the finances, we can talk about that, too, but given what you stand to lose if you marry Rob, you'd be money ahead if you *paid* someone to take both him and the dress from you."

"But I gave up everything to be with him, Jackie. I have to go through with the wedding."

"No, Katrine. You don't."

"But how would it look if I don't? And what would I do?"

"Anything you like. That's the beauty of it, Katrine. For once in your life, you'd be free to make your own choices and decisions without any interference from anyone."

"You don't understand."

"Oh, yes, I do. Don't forget, I gave up a job, my friends, and a four-year scholarship for a guy who would degrade and threaten me on a regular basis, and when I finally walked away, I had nothing left but my clothes and a pathetic GPA. So there's not one thing about this that I don't get, except why you would put up with Rob's crap even one more day."

"What about my mother? She's been against this wedding from the beginning. If I call it off now, all I'm going to hear is 'I told you so.'"

"I guess you have to decide if you'd rather be happy or if you'd rather be right."

"But I don't even have a job, Jackie."

"So find one. You're an intelligent person, Katrine. You'll be fine on your own."

"But I don't want to be on my own. I just want things to get better."

"Do you really think that's possible? I mean, you've already established that talking won't change anything, and apart from that, all you've got is luck, magic, and prayer—none of which has proven very reliable. So how exactly do you think things are going to get better?"

"I don't know."

"More importantly, how long will you wait—how bad will things get— before you accept that they won't? Will you wait until you're married, when you'll need a court order to get back your freedom? Will you wait until you have kids and have to fight for them and child support as well? What if you can't afford a lawyer, day care, or a place of your own? What will be your excuse then? I don't mean to scare you, but you have to think about this stuff."

"I know."

"I just don't want to see you wait too long and live to regret it."

Katrine sighed. "I don't want that either," she admitted, "but I honestly wouldn't know how to leave him even if I knew that's what I wanted."

"It won't be easy. But I've done it, and so can you."

"That's right," Katrine said, apparently recalling our conversation on the balcony the night we met. "What made you finally decide to throw in the towel?"

"I got a glimpse of my future, and I didn't like what I saw. I had just had a fight with Steven about the outfit I had chosen to wear to a party, and I was walking to a pay phone after he drove off without me because I refused to go back to my apartment to change. There was this couple in the parking lot as I rounded the corner. The guy had the woman by the wrists, with them crisscrossed between her chest and his, and was pushing her backward against a car and talking to her through gritted teeth. I couldn't hear what he was saying, but she was clearly terrified. She must have noticed me and said something to him, because he looked over his shoulder, gave her one last big shove as he released her, called her a cunt, and told her to get in the car. She looked at me and did as she was told. That incident, plus nine million messages Steven had left on my answering machine that night, which included a mixture of apologies and professions of eternal love, insane rants on my questionable morals, and detailed descriptions of what he would do if I didn't call him back, convinced me I had to move on. It took a while to pull it all together, but by the time fall term ended, I had withdrawn from school, given notice to my landlord and my boss, and arranged to move in with my cousin in a town far enough away that it would be too inconvenient for him to visit. As far as he knew, we had made up by then, and when the time was right, I told him I had to quit school; I had run out of money and was moving in with my cousin."

"So he had no idea you were 'leaving' him."

"Nor any reason to come after me."

"Did it work?"

"It didn't stop him from berating me or insulting me for being an imbecile and running out of money, but it did keep him from hunting me down and killing me. Every now and then, he would call to ask when I was moving back, get mad when I'd say I didn't know, and then call me a few names and hang up."

Katrine nodded. "Why do you think you put up with him as long as you did?"

"I don't know. I guess I just didn't realize I had a choice. I mean, he drank too much, treated me like crap, and punished me if I complained; but he had good job, had never been arrested, and had never actually *beaten* me, so it never occurred to me to break up with him. What I didn't realize, and what I'm trying to impress upon you, is that you do have a choice, and you don't need grounds to leave someone. It all really boils down to just two questions: 'Is this what I want?' and 'Is this good for me?' With that in mind, you should not be asking 'What will I do without him?' but 'Is this what I want?' and 'Is this good for me?' If the answer to the first question is no, you owe it to him and yourself to say good-bye. Even if the answer to the first question is yes, if the answer to the second is no, you should still leave, because it would be silly and masochistic of you to stick around."

"I suppose you think the answers to both questions in my case are no as well."

"What I think is irrelevant. Although you've already admitted that things aren't what you expected them to be, so clearly the first question has been answered. What of the second?"

Katrine shrugged.

"Well, does he make you feel good about yourself?" I prodded. "Or does he make you feel bad? Does he make you feel smart and capable? Or does he make you feel stupid and small?"

"It varies."

"Well, it shouldn't. People who love us should never make us feel stupid and small. Even when we make mistakes or do dumb things, they should be there to comfort and reassure us and help us feel better about ourselves.

They should never rub our noses in our mistakes or use them to hurt us, and they most certainly shouldn't embarrass or humiliate us."

"But you and Kevin mock and harass each other all the time."

"Not really. Sure, we tease each other, but not with the intention of hurting or humiliating one another. With us it's a means of expressing affection—like flirting."

Shrugging, Katrine set her mug on the floor and absently wiped the cocoa mustache from her upper lip. "So what do you think would have happened if you'd stayed with Steven?"

"I'd probably be dead."

"You think he would have killed you?"

"More likely I would have killed myself."

"That's crazy."

"But it's true. That's what comes from constantly trying to please someone and failing at every turn. Steven was a lunatic, and anything could set him off, and it changed from day to day. One moment we might be talking, and the next he would be yelling at me and threatening to pound me senseless and leave my 'worthless ass' to die."

"How could you take that day after day?"

"That's just it. It wasn't day after day. It was irregular and unpredictable. That's what makes the situation so tricky. Abuse—physical or otherwise—isn't about whatever has upset the abuser at any point in time; it's about control and manipulation. Abusers are skilled and intuitive people who know what moves their victims and how to play to those motivations. So after they've beaten or terrorized the crap out of you, they'll switch gears and start apologizing, professing love and devotion, and promising to never do it again. They'll assure you they can change, and they may really want to; but the truth is, whether they mean them or not, they have to say those things. If they didn't—if they didn't show remorse, make promises, and deliver the goods now and then—they'd have no one to abuse, because their victims would have no incentive to stay and no qualms about leaving. I mean, let's face it, if all you had were bad times, you'd have no trouble calling off the wedding. It's only the memories of the good times and the hope they'll return that keeps you on that fence."

"But other women don't have to deal with this."

"*Assertive* women don't have to deal with this," I corrected her, "and that's because they won't take crap from anyone, and abusive men aren't attracted to them. They're drawn to patient, accommodating women who won't object to being yelled at, insulted, threatened, or slapped around here and there, who'll shoulder the responsibility for the abuser's mood and strive ceaselessly to avoid upsetting him. Their confidence destroyed, they'll eventually stop trusting their own perceptions, accept apologies and promises as signs of hope, and—all too often—get killed while waiting for things to improve."

"So how long after you moved away did he give up on you coming back?"

"Two or three months."

"That long?"

I nodded. "He called me one night," I recounted with a laugh, "to say he'd met someone. It sounded like a ploy, but I played along. With feigned disappointment, I congratulated him and told him he deserved to be happy. The idiot obviously never expected that; but what could he do? Later— when he found out I was getting married—he called again, this time to say I was a slut and that he knew I'd been cheating on him the whole time. I didn't bother to argue or defend my honor. I just let him get in his last lick and waited for him to hang up."

"Do you think he misses you?"

"Frankly, I don't care."

"But what if he's changed?"

"Highly unlikely. But if so, good for him and whomever he's with. Either way, it's got nothing to do with me."

"But—"

"Katrine," I said gently as I stood to refill my cocoa. "I know where you're headed with this, and I'm not going there with you. The bottom line here is that life is short, and *in for a penny, in for a pound* is not the way to live it. You have to decide when enough is enough and get out while the getting's good."

After reloading my mug and stopping by the laundry area to swap loads around, I returned to the living room to find Katrine lying down with her face to the back of the couch. With a shrug I continued through the living room toward the stairs and up to my computer.

Fourteen

"Hey, there," called a familiar voice as I approached the entrance of a local warehouse grocery store after my last final nearly three weeks later.

"Hey, yourself," I said upon turning around and finding Lynette walking toward me. "What are you doing here on a weekday?"

"Waiting for you. I called the house as I was getting off work, and Kevin said you'd be stopping here after your exam, so I thought I'd come by and see if you want to get lunch before you load your car with perishables and head home."

"OK, sure. Where would you like to go?"

"Over there." With grim determination she pointed toward a Chinese restaurant at the other end of the strip mall. "I've been craving egg rolls for half an hour, and it's driving me insane."

"You've been waiting here that long?"

"Actually, longer. But I spent the first ten minutes drooling over the Mexican place across the street and the next fantasizing about the pizza that was delivered to that travel agency."

I turned in the direction of her nod. "I see. Well, I'm OK with Chinese," I allowed, dropping my keys into my front pocket, "or any of the other ideas you've mentioned so far, but if you get a hankering for hamster on our way past the pet shop, you're on your own."

"Fair enough," Lyn agreed as we started down the sidewalk. "So how were finals?"

"Brutal. Fortunately, I'm fair-skinned, and I won't scar."

"You have such a knack for seeing the bright side."

"What can I say? My optimism is located on a recessive gene."

Lynette laughed. "Sorry I had to resort to stalking," she said with a hint of embarrassment. "You've been pretty hard to locate lately."

I thought about the phone I hadn't answered in a while and the machine whose tape by now was probably beyond full. "Sorry about that. Kevin's always after me to check our messages, but I just can't seem to remember."

"I know how it is. So what have you been up to?"

"Just homework and housework—the story of my life."

"I can relate."

Finding no one at the front counter as we entered the restaurant, Lyn decided to take a preemptive potty break. I had already gone before leaving campus, but figuring a trip to the restroom would be more interesting than standing in the empty lobby, I followed her anyway.

"So did you ever hear from your friend Katrine?" she asked from within the handicapped stall as I waited by the sink. "Last we talked, she'd been out of circulation for a while."

Standing before the mirror, I felt a twinge of regret. It had been weeks since we'd spoken and over a month since we'd seen each other. Not that this surprised me. Given how different things were from how they'd been a few years ago, it was more of a surprise that we still saw each other at all.

Even more amazing, however, was that we'd ever been close in the first place. We had so little in common—given her two-parent, middle-class background; her preference for country music and love stories over rock and nonfiction; and her irksome tendency to parrot the ultraconservative views of her husband and father—we were an unlikely pair. I had chalked it up to Tyler, with whom I'd been pregnant when we met, and Lyn's own as yet unfulfilled desire for a baby—and soon I found myself a member of her inner circle.

Initially, I had been thrilled to be accepted by her family and other friends. I thought it meant I'd transcended my underclass roots and took it as a reflection on my hard work, good manners, and positive attitude. I soon came to realize, however, that what I'd interpreted as acceptance was merely tolerance, and what I'd taken for approval was something closer to amusement. I also found that despite their Christian and "family" values, they regarded the poor with contempt and distrust and could not recount an event involving a person of color without mentioning that color in the narrative.

It was largely due to my exposure to their attitudes that my own political views began to crystallize. For example, I came to see the differences between conservatives and progressives as a matter of one's capacity for empathy. Social conservatives, I noticed, have a low capacity for empathy and thus cannot perceive as real or important anything they haven't felt or otherwise experienced themselves. As a result, they can't muster concern for the rights or needs of anyone but those whose values and experiences they share. Thus, they'll support laws and policies that suit their own lives and the lives of the people they identify with, but reject those that benefit people whose lives or perspectives are different from their own.

Progressives, on the other hand, have a high capacity for empathy and thus do not have to experience or witness something firsthand for it to be real or important. As a result, they can walk a mile in other people's moccasins—as it were—and support laws and policies that don't benefit them or people with whom they identify. Thus, they don't need to have experienced addiction in order to favor treatment over punishment. Nor do they need to have been hungry or sick to support programs and policies that help people in need.

This explained why the men in Lyn's family could routinely rail against environmental regulations, yet they threatened to picket the state capitol when the highway department wanted to build a staging facility near their hunting land. Protecting air, water, and wildlife was of no value if it prevented people like them from having fun or making a buck; but it was priority number one if it threatened their property or their way of life.

I tried not to hold any of this against Lyn—a feat made easier by the fact that she cared so little about social policy that such things never came up when we were alone. On those rare occasions when she would weigh in on some social or political issue—which was only in the presence of her kith and kin—her words sounded so rehearsed that you knew they weren't her own. As much as it pained me to do so, I resisted challenging these statements since doing so would have made me the rhetorical equivalent of a schoolyard bully. Instead, I accepted these and other tendencies as the result of her upbringing, just as she accepted my big mouth and curious nature as the consequences of mine.

Fortunately, we had other interests in common that gave us plenty to talk about. With junior enlisted military pay being what it was and credit not as easy to come by as it is today, we spent our time cooking and sewing rather than dining or shopping, and we taught ourselves how to make the things that our cohorts got from stores and restaurants. We had the kind of relationship that led strangers to mistake us for sisters and caused even people who knew better to assume we'd been friends our entire lives.

Things changed after she and Josh left South Carolina and never fully recovered even after Kevin and I got to Minnesota. Lyn was busting her ass trying to meet all the conditions Josh had placed on her fertility—finish school, find a job, save money to buy a house—and I wasn't about to get in her way. Plus, with college and my own offspring keeping me busy, I had little time to mourn the loss of her company as she cleared each of those hurdles and got pregnant. It saddened me somewhat, but I knew it was part of life—just like I knew her tracking me down today didn't mean things between us would be any different tomorrow.

"Yeah," I said finally, wondering how long I'd been deep in thought. "She called not too long after I spoke to you last."

"How was she?"

"Better. Although she wasn't too pleased with how things were going between her and Rob," I added, trying to sound like my usual dishy self. "She wanted to talk, so she came over and spent the night on the analyst's couch."

"So is she going through with it? The wedding, I mean."

"Probably. I can't say for sure, since she fell asleep as I was working on my paper that night and left sometime before I got up for the class the next morning."

"You mean she left without saying good-bye?"

I nodded. "And I haven't seen her since. I want to believe it's because she left town and assumed a new identity, but it's more likely because she decided to go ahead with the wedding and she can't bring herself to face me."

Lynette laughed as she joined me at the sink. "Sounds like I'm about due for an update," she said, snapping the sides of her adjustable slacks. "But can we get our food before you begin your review? I'm starving."

I held the door again as we headed back down the corridor and out to the lobby. Shortly thereafter, an employee appeared and escorted us to a table where we stopped briefly to order drinks before proceeding to the well-stocked buffet.

As we ate, I recalled for Lyn the fight and subsequent cease-fire I'd failed to mention last time we talked, as well as the events leading up to the night Katrine swiped the Nova.

"OK," she said when I'd finished. "So you still think the guy is wrong for her, and you finally got the chance to tell her. Mission accomplished."

"Not exactly. I mean, I rather hoped she'd do something *useful* with the information."

"Well, you know what they say: you can lead a horse to water."

"Yep. And I've done everything I can to convince her to leave the man. So about the only thing left to do is to convince Rob to leave her."

Lynette laughed. "You're not thinking of putting the moves on him, are you?"

"Are you crazy? I'd sooner swallow broken glass."

"Understood. But then, desperate times often call for desperate measures."

"Trust me—I will never be that desperate."

"Even if it had the potential to put an end to their engagement?"

"Even if it was *guaranteed* to put an end to their engagement."

"Some friend you are!" Lyn teased.

"Call me selfish," I offered, laughing along with her, "but there's a limit on how far I'll go for a friend, and seducing that man is well beyond it. Just the thought makes my skin crawl."

"So I gather. What I don't get is why you'd spend so much time with them given how badly you'd like to see him dead."

"It's not so much that I'd *like* to see him dead; I just prefer that to seeing him *alive*. And it's not as if we see them that much. Especially since Scott moved in with them."

"What do you think is up with him and this Scott, anyway?" Lyn wondered, laying her arms contentedly across her expanding abdomen and putting her feet up on the rungs of my chair. "Do you think there's something funny going on there?"

I giggled. "You mean, do I think they might be more than friends?"

"Actually, I was thinking Rob was fooling around and using Scott as an alibi, but your way works, too."

"I think we can exclude both theories. Knowing those two, they're more likely to be holed up somewhere watching *Babylon Five* than sleeping with one another or anyone else."

"That reminds me: does Katrine have any friends of her own yet? Besides you, I mean."

"Not really. Although, if I have anything to say about it, that's going to change."

"I knew you'd have something else up your sleeve," Lyn observed. "So what's your plan?"

"I don't have a plan, per se. I just think Katrine needs her own friends and outside interests. So, if and when I have the opportunity, I'm going to introduce her to Quinn, Sera, and a few other strong, self-assured women from Hamilton."

"Ah, so you're putting together a women's empowerment group."

I laughed. "Kevin called it a coven—but it won't be anything like that. I'm just thinking of getting them all together now and then with the primary objective of exposing Katrine to independent women and meaningful conversation. My hope," I added, wondering why I was telling Lyn all this when we hardly knew each other anymore, "is that by getting to know them and seeing how they interact, Katrine will come to realize that it's OK to speak her mind and learn to stand her ground. That way she'll be fine whether she stays with Rob or not."

"Well, good luck with that."

"Thanks. I'll let you know how it goes."

"Meanwhile," Lynette continued, "do you expect to see the newlyweds at your party on New Year's Eve?"

"Not really. Katrine expressed an interest when we first mentioned it to her, but that was before Halloween, and a lot has happened since then."

"And you're not worried that Rob will take the opportunity to confront you over what you said to Katrine?"

"If Rob was going to confront me, he would have done it already. The fact that he hasn't tells me either he doesn't care what I think of him, or she never told him."

"I hope you're right—on all counts."

Me, too. "So what's new with you?" I asked, anxious to change the subject. "Have you and Josh found a house yet?"

For the next twenty minutes or so, I listened as Lyn described to me the pros and cons of the various properties she and Josh had toured in their search for the perfect starter home. I, in turn, did my best to keep her chatting, in the hope she'd eventually get around to saying something that would explain the uptick in her interest in seeing me, as well as her decision to track me down in the middle of the week in the middle of December. Although I'd considered it, I discounted the idea of asking her outright, figuring that if the truth was unpleasant enough to keep her from telling me, it was probably something I didn't want to hear.

"So, aside from throwing a fabulous party," she asked when she'd run out of steam, "what are you and Kevin going to do over break?"

"I can't speak for him, but I'll probably spend it memorizing my children's faces so I won't forget what they look like during the last hellacious semester of my baccalaureate education. What about you and Josh? Do you have any plans for the next couple weeks?"

"Just the usual holiday madness—compounded by the impending arrival of my mother's entire reason for living."

"Think you'll have time for that *and* a few games of cards?" I asked with private trepidation. I wasn't sure I wanted to go down that road but decided to throw it at the wall and see if it stuck.

"That depends. When did you have in mind?"

"Friday and Saturday are both good—if you're available. Or even Sunday, as long as we don't make it too late. Either one should be good for us."

"I'm not sure," she stalled. "Let me talk to Josh and get back to you."

Fifteen

*A*s I had both feared and hoped, Kevin was not free to play cards that weekend. He had agreed to stand duty as a favor to one of the guys at the unit whose parents lived too far away for a day trip, and he thus was committed to being at the armory every evening from three to eleven. Not wanting her and Josh to reserve space on their calendar for a card party that was no longer an option, I rang immediately after I'd spoken to Kevin to allow them plenty of time to make other plans.

Although she claimed to be disappointed, she sounded more pleased than upset. This made me hate less the part of me that was relieved when Kevin said he couldn't make it, and it led me to wonder why she hadn't declined my invitation before we left the restaurant—or, for that matter, why she'd asked me to lunch in the first place. Nevertheless, before we hung up, we managed to flounder through a measured discussion about her upcoming baby shower and agreed to get in touch with one another if we found ourselves with free time between then and New Year's Eve.

Although I would attend her shower as planned, I resolved then to give up on the idea of cards completely. Kevin wasn't going to be around much anyway—owing to his willingness to swap duty to accommodate his colleagues whose families lived further away—and I didn't want to spend what little time we might have between terms gritting my teeth as Josh monitored Lyn's consumption of potato chips and griped about the tax code. Besides, if my diagnosis was correct, our friendship was terminal, and we weren't going to save it by squeezing in a game or two of spades.

So instead of playing cards, I spent the last two weeks of December obsessing about Katrine and Rob's big day and entreating the fates to effect its postponement or cancellation. Although I did my best to distract myself with housework and parenting, even with three stories to clean and two little ones to mess it up again, I would eventually run out of chores and, by midafternoon, find myself with nothing to do but brood. I didn't even have much in the way of Christmas shopping to divert me, since Kevin's family favored the Secret Santa approach to observing the birth of Christ—whereby each person gives one gift of a specified value to a member of the family and, in return, receives a gift of the same value from someone else. My family, on the other hand, preferred the Open Secret approach—whereby nobody gives a gift to anyone, and nobody ever expects to get anything in return.

And so the brooding continued through Christmas, threatening to ruin my New Year's Eve and prompting me to seek comfort from an old Russian friend and an Italian acquaintance.

"I should have never discovered martinis," I declared on one such occasion as I tried to pack three olives into my fourth glass of vodka and dry vermouth. "Howie" from the Marriott had warned me about the fine line between a great martini and a bad one, and the three I'd already poured down the drain had convinced me he was right.

Too cheap to waste any more booze and too stubborn to admit defeat, I declared my fourth attempt a victory and carried it and a book to the living room in hopes of obliterating any and all thoughts of the disaster brewing in Syracuse. The strategy was showing signs of success until Kevin arrived home with information that would guarantee I would think about nothing else for a very long time.

"Sorry I'm so late," he said, stomping snow from his boots. "I'd have been back earlier, but I got stuck in an unscheduled meeting with the unit staff."

"No problem. I'm just glad you survived."

The glass on the end table next to me appeared to catch his eye as he removed his coat and placed it in the closet. "Is everything OK?" he asked, correctly surmising that the liquid sitting with a trio of olives in a cone-shaped piece of stemware was not ice water.

"Yep."

"Are you sure?"

"Yep."

"And the kids?"

"They're great."

"That's good," he said, edging toward the kitchen. "I think I'll just go check on them, if you don't mind."

"Not at all. Have at it."

Returning to my book, I picked up my glass, drained it, and set it back on the end table.

A few minutes later, Kevin was back with his hands on his hips and concern on his face. "Jack?"

"Yeah?"

"Where *are* the kids? I've checked their room and the basement but can't seem to find them."

"Really?"

"Really."

Sensing from his tone that he wasn't enjoying my game as much as I was, I closed my book and set it next to my empty glass. "Take it easy," I said, wondering if he truly believed I was capable of harming or misplacing my own children. "Tyler is playing over at Timmy's, and Lucy is napping in our room. She fell asleep in the playpen while I was up putting away the laundry, and I didn't want to wake her up just to bring her down to her crib."

"OK. Then everything really is fine."

"Correct. I have the nursery monitor plugged in up there," I added, pointing to the receiver I'd moved from our bedroom to the kitchen, "so we'll be sure to hear her when she wakes up."

"Well, then I guess I won't worry," Kevin said, apparently satisfied that I was neither drunk nor filicidal. "So what have you been up to?"

"You're looking at it."

Kevin followed my gaze as I looked around the spotless house and eventually at the book next to my glass. "*Black Culture and Black Consciousness*?" he read off the spine. "Is that for school? Or are you finally gearing up for that big move to Harlem?"

Despite Kevin's attempt at humor, I could tell there was something still on his mind, and I wondered if it had anything to do with work and if he was planning to share.

"And how about you?" I asked as he joined me on the couch. "How was your day?"

"Fine. I mostly sat at the front desk checking no one's identification, since the only people entering or exiting the armory were duty staff like me."

"Sounds thrilling."

"You know it," he said with a sigh. "Meanwhile," he added, lifting my feet off the couch and laying them over his lap as he settled in beside me, "have you heard anything from Katrine?"

I shook my head. "Any particular reason to think I would have?"

"I just thought she might have called to check in or give you an update. That sort of thing."

"Well, that would have been nice, but I'm hardly her favorite person these days. Which would be fine with me, provided it meant she'd taken my advice and hopped a bus on the road to nowhere."

"Better she put Rob on one."

Say what?

"Hey, pal," I warned, having reviewed what I'd heard and decided he wasn't making fun of me. "I'll not have you speaking ill of that man in this house—that's my job."

"Maybe it's time to consider expanding the workforce."

"Seriously," I said, suppressing—for the moment—my exhilaration over the possibility that Kevin had seen the light with respect to Rob. "What happened today that has you talking like—well, me?"

"Well, much as I hate to admit it," he sighed again as he patted my knee, "it seems you may not have been far off the mark about Rob after all."

"No shit?"

"No shit."

Cool. Not far off the mark wasn't as good as right, but I was willing to give the man time to work up to it. *Baby steps,* I told myself. *Baby steps.*

"In fact," he continued, "from what I heard at the meeting today, you were probably dead right not to trust him."

Wow. Dead right was even better than right, and a term he rarely applied to my statements. Not that he often tells me I'm wrong; he just tends not to formally announce it when I'm right.

"I hate to say it," I offered, "but it sounds like things aren't going so well for him over at Warrior, Incorporated."

Kevin shook his head. "I just saw his fitness report. His evals suck."

"Really. Does he know?"

"Of course. He had to sign off on the paperwork. My question is, does Katrine know?"

"If I had to guess, I'd say no. Given how worried she's been about his activities of late, I doubt he would have told her anything about work that might give her concerns any traction."

"I suppose not. Still, I thought he would have mentioned at least one thing, since he was so proud of himself for it at the time."

"What was that?" I asked, still stifling my zeal. Much as I liked knowing he, too, now had doubts about Rob, I could see this wasn't easy for him and didn't want to compound his distress.

"Just before Thanksgiving," he was explaining now, "Rob and three navy options showed up late to formation. Staff Sergeant Kramer was annoyed with them all, but he was especially pissed at Rob, since, one, it was his third time that week, and two, he knows better. Anyway, after discussing it with the major, he decided to make an example of them and ordered all three to write an essay on the importance of punctuation."

"Punctuation? What the hell for?"

"Jackie, he meant punctuality."

"Oh my God!" I laughed as I heard the final syllables. "That is too funny!"

"Yeah, well, Jim didn't think it was so funny when all three of them turned in papers the next Monday outlining the proper use of commas, colons, and semicolons."

"I'm sorry," I said, trying not to choke, "but that's a scream!"

Poor Staff Sergeant Kramer. He was the nicest guy you'd ever meet, but he was by no stretch a scholar, which I suppose is why he was a member of the training staff and not a student.

"So were these morons at least smart enough to write a paper on punctuality and hand it in at the same time?" I asked when I had regained my composure.

"Oh, no. Rob convinced them that they were to follow orders strictly and precisely. And he had the nerve to walk in with a smug grin on his face, place his paper on top of the others on Jim's desk, and walk out without a word. Later, when Jim hit the ceiling and called him back to the office, Rob even had the nerve to stand before him and Major Henry and insist that he had done nothing wrong; he had only followed orders as they were given to him."

"Unreal. So what are they going to do to him?"

"At the moment—nothing. But a set of charges sheets were drawn up this afternoon for conduct unbecoming and insubordination."

"Are you telling me they're going to court-martial him? Over a prank?"

"No. The charge sheets are only being prepared to ensure that the incident is documented. They're going to be kept in a separate file along with a few others they've drawn up relating to his unauthorized absences and other things. The staff won't process or enter them into Rob's official file unless they have to."

"You mean, in case they have to cover their asses later."

"Basically."

"So how long have they been keeping this separate file?"

"Major Henry had it opened just a couple weeks ago, after Rob nearly destroyed one of the unit vehicles."

"Destroyed? How?"

"By failing to pay attention to detail. Apparently he took it on an errand to Fort Snelling at the first of the month and stopped for gas on the way back. Well, the fleet is getting pretty old, so we're required to check and adjust fluids levels every time we fill up."

"And he forgot?"

"Oh, no. He remembered all right. But when he went to top off the oil, he evidently poured it in with the transmission fluid by mistake."

"How the hell did he manage that?"

"Don't ask me. All I know is that the gears locked up a few blocks into its next trip. The staff sergeant, of course, followed the paper trail back to Rob, who denied having any clue as to what might be wrong with the truck. Later, after the staff sergeant had spoken to the mechanic and traced the purchase of the oil back to the receipt Rob had signed, he suddenly changed his tune to 'it was an honest mistake that could have happened to anyone.'"

"Anyone with an IQ below seventy, maybe."

Kevin grimaced in agreement. "Meanwhile," he continued, "the transmission had to be replaced, which cost more than the van was worth, but since the unit couldn't afford a new one, they were forced to repair it."

"They should make *him* pay for it."

"I agree, but they won't."

"How do they expect him to learn anything from his mistake?"

"I don't think they do. In fact, I don't think they expect Rob to learn from any of this, and frankly, neither do I."

"Why not?"

"Because right before finals, the dumbass missed formation again."

"You are kidding."

"I wish. And what's worse is that, instead of offering one of his usual excuses or blowing off the incident entirely, this time he sent Katrine in to explain how she'd set the alarm clock for p.m. instead of a.m., causing Rob to sleep right through morning muster."

"Did he really think that would make difference?"

"Apparently; but Staff Sergeant Kramer wasn't the least bit moved. I was at the desk when she came up to the office, and I remember wondering what the hell she was doing there. If I'd known what she was going to say, I would have tried to stop her, but I had no idea."

"So what did he do?"

"Well, at first all he did was stare at her. When he could finally bring himself to speak, he invited her to accompany him down the hall to have a chat with Major Weeks."

"Oh God."

"It wasn't as bad as you think. The major just pointed out at me and asked Katrine if she knew who I was. She said she did and that she's also good friends with my wife. 'Well, if that's the case,' Carl says, 'then you also know that Jackie would never walk in here making excuses for her husband. That's because she and Kevin both have the sense to know it wouldn't do any good. They also know that it's his responsibility, not hers, to see that he gets here on time.'"

If he only knew, I thought, casting my mind briefly back to our recent alarm clock debacle and feeling a bit like a fraud. "So how did she respond?"

"She said she was sorry and that she was just trying to help."

"Poor kid."

"I know. I felt bad for her, but what could I do?"

"Don't blame yourself, Kevin. It's Rob's fault for sending her up there—and hers, too, for going along with it."

"I know. I just wish I could have spared her the embarrassment. Then again, Rob could have done that himself if he hadn't been late so many times before. If this had been his first offense, they might have believed her, and they might have gone a little easier on her."

"True. So what does all this add up to?"

"Well, none of these things on its own is serious enough to land Rob in the brig, but together they've raised serious doubts as to his character and his fitness to continue in this program."

"And what are they going to do about it?"

"For now they're going to wait and see what develops. Meanwhile, I've been recruited to assist in our problem child's behavior modification and attitudinal adjustment."

"What are you going to do, Kevin? Spank him?"

"No, that's Carl's job. I just provide guidance and peer support."

"I thought you already did that anyway."

"I'm supposed to, but since I didn't know about all the shit he was pulling—I didn't have all that much to do. Now that I've been told, I'll be taking a more active approach to the role."

"Which means what?"

"Spending more time with him, being someone he can go to for advice or to blow off steam, which he's going to need since the staff is giving him not one, but two billets next quarter."

"Oh, sure—pile on more responsibilities. That should help."

"It's a test, Jack. Right now he has it pretty easy—with no billets or collateral duties—and yet he's still screwing up. The hope is, if we squeeze him a bit, he'll wake up and pull his shit together. Meanwhile, they're waiting to see how he performs at the field training exercises in February. It's a cakewalk for anyone with prior service, so he should ace it. If he does that, and *doesn't* commit career suicide by then, he'll be back on track for Officer Candidate School next summer."

"And if he doesn't ace it?"

"They'll probably still send him to OCS. In fact, about the only reason they wouldn't send him to OCS is if he fails out academically—which he might, since his grades this quarter were less than outstanding, and next term could be worse in light of his new billet responsibilities."

"I don't understand. Why would they bother to send him to OCS if he's so screwed up?"

"Because it will save them a lot of hassle. If they drop him at the unit level, he can appeal and keep them mired in paperwork for who knows how long. But if he doesn't pass OCS, he's out. No arguments. No appeals. He goes back to the fleet, and the unit is less one bad apple."

"So do you think he'll pass?"

"Not without some major effort. The leadership assessments alone will kill him. And if by some miracle he does better than they expect, the staff here will still have the charge sheets they prepared—which will give them leverage in the event that have to ask for his DOR."

"Rob—Drop on Request? Are you kidding me? He'll never admit he can't hack it."

"Especially since it would basically end his career," Kevin agreed. "Sure, he'd be allowed—well, forced actually—to finish out his current enlistment, but a DOR from this program, along with the accompanying adverse fitness reports, would ruin his chances for promotion as an NCO. Rob knows this, so I doubt he'll go down without a fight."

"Which means this could get pretty ugly."

"It could, but I don't think it will. They're giving him just enough rope to hang himself, and that's probably what he'll do with it."

"My, how the tides have turned," I observed. "Not three months ago you were carrying on about his stellar career, and now here you are predicting its fiery demise."

"Don't imagine that irony is lost on me. Of course, I stand by what I said back then. Rob performed very well during his first five years of service and has a right to be proud of that. But he did so under direct supervision in highly structured environments. Now that he's here—where he can basically do whatever he likes as long as he reports for muster every morning, stands all of his duties, and takes care of business in terms of his grades and his billet assignments—we're getting a pretty clear idea of who the guy really is, and that picture is not at all flattering."

"Well, if there is a silver lining to this, it's that the guy revealed his true colors now rather than after he was commissioned."

"Absolutely. Can you imagine if the Corps gave him his bars and put him in charge of a unit somewhere? The results would be disastrous."

"Poor Katrine," I sighed. "When she finds out, she's going to be devastated."

"I know. That's why I had to tell you what's going on. As the noose begins to tighten around his spindly neck, there's going to be a lot of stress in that household, and I suspect you'll be the one she'll turn to."

"I wouldn't bet on it. These days, you're more likely to see her than I am."

"Well, that's likely to change as well. The only place I really see her is at the armory lounge, and she's probably not going to be allowed in there much longer."

"Why not?"

"Because she's making some of the midshipmen uncomfortable."

"Uncomfortable how?"

"According to Staff Sergeant Kramer, some of them think she's coming on to them, and it's freaking them out."

"Coming on to them? That's ridiculous."

"Maybe. Maybe not. Keep in mind, we're not with her twenty-four hours a day, and these guys may have a very different picture of her than we do."

"Of course they do. They're horny, postadolescent males."

"I honestly don't think that's all there is to it, Jack. According to Jim, she's in there for hours—ostensibly studying or waiting for Rob—dropping innuendo all over the place. Maybe she is only joking, but it's entirely inappropriate in that setting."

"If it's true."

"Granted. But as you're so fond of saying, 'perception is half of communication.' So if she's making them uncomfortable, the situation warrants attention."

"I see your point, but they can't just *ban* her from the place. Do you have any idea how that would make her feel?"

"Look, we don't know they're going to do that yet. She may not even have time to hang out there this term, for one thing. And if she does, and if she continues to be a problem, they won't single her out. They'll just announce a policy change barring *all* civilians from the designated areas of the armory building."

"Well, that'll spare her feelings, but it hardly seems fair to anyone who might have to go up there for legitimate reasons."

"No one else ever goes up there, Jack."

"Ah. Well, I guess that will make it easier—unless she *knows* that."

"Which she probably does."

"Maybe I should talk to her. Maybe if she knew how people were reacting to what she's saying, she'd knock it off."

"I don't think that's a good idea," Kevin interjected. "Even if you only discuss her behavior, it could tip Rob off that people are talking about him."

"So what? I mean, much as I hate to stick up for the creep, maybe he should know what's being said. Maybe if he knew he was poised to lose everything he's worked for all these years, he'd straighten up, and none of this other shit would be necessary."

"Believe me—Rob has had plenty of indications that his behavior is unsatisfactory, and he knows damn well what's at stake. He knew it when he applied for this program, he knew it when he arrived at the unit, and he knew it every time he was late to formation.

"I guess."

"So can I count on you to keep this all under wraps? At least until further notice?"

"All of it? Even the part about punctuation?"

"*Especially* the part about punctuation."

"Fine," I groaned, lamenting the mileage I would *not* be getting out of that story for at least the foreseeable future. "But only because I love you, and I know you'll make it up to me."

"Really? And how will I be doing that?"

"By letting me watch and eat popcorn from a comfy chair when they toss his sorry ass out of there."

"You mean *if* they decide to toss his sorry ass out of here."

"Whatever. Meanwhile, can you do me the favor of conducting your black ops somewhere other than our house? I can't stand that man, and if I have to see him all the time, who knows what might escape my lips."

"Hmmm…that sounds an awful lot like extortion."

"It does, doesn't it? I guess that tells you how far I'll go to keep him away from me."

Kevin nodded. "And this," he added, pushing my feet to the floor and pulling the rest of me onto his lap, "tells you how far I'll go to get close to you."

Well, it's about time, I thought as he placed a series of kisses on the top of my shoulder and tugged my shirt out from the top of my jeans. *For a while there, I thought this guy was gone for good.*

Sixteen

To the surprise of many and the discomfort yours truly, Rob and Katrine not only made it to our New Year's Eve party but showed up ahead of schedule. So anxious were they to toast the new decade and introduce themselves as man and wife, Rob explained as Kevin greeted them at the door, that they'd taken an earlier flight from New York to ensure their timely arrival.

I should have been better prepared. After all, I'd been planning this party for two months and had thought of little else but it or Rob and Katrine for the last few weeks. Realizing upon hearing his emetic pronouncements, however, that I was in no shape to see or speak to them, I immersed myself in feeding Lucy and thus could manage but a friendly nod at the newlyweds as they followed Kevin past me through the kitchen and to the stairway.

It wasn't their presence, per se, that had me out of sorts; it was the uncertainty. For despite my protestations to Lyn, there was a chance Katrine had told Rob that I'd advised her to leave him and an ugly scene loomed on the horizon. Figuring even Rob had more class than to start something in front of our friends, I knew things would probably be fine tonight; but I also knew that our guests would have to leave sometime, and if he'd waited this long to confront me, no doubt he'd have the patience to wait a few more hours.

Whatever Rob knew—and whatever his plans to address it—things between me and Katrine were destined to be awkward. Although she hadn't said so, it was possible she'd been offended by what I'd said the last time we spoke. Even if she wasn't upset, she might find it hard to face me knowing I despised Rob and how he treated her. At the very least, it would be hard for her to look me in the eye after airing her own grievances about the man and then marrying him anyway.

Either scenario would explain why she'd been out of touch all month and why she had found it so easy to walk by me after not seeing me for so long. Not that my own behavior could have given the impression that I expected a tearful reunion; I just didn't see anything in hers to suggest that she would welcome one either.

On its face, their very appearance at the party suggested that things were fine and that it was only my guilty conscience keeping things from feeling normal. Unfortunately, acknowledging that did nothing to dispel my discomfort or quell the anxiety that had my neck and chest covered in hives.

I knew I would survive this experience, but I also knew it would take some serious effort to keep my head and not let my nerves drive me over the edge until morning—or at least until everyone went home.

It was with that in mind that I resolved to spend the evening on the main floor. Kevin would not have approved of this, I knew; but with the party in full swing, he wasn't likely to miss me. Aside from him, the only person who might notice my absence downstairs was Lyn, and she had Josh to keep her company. She also had my brother's wife, Bethany, who was also expecting, and to whom I'd made sure to introduce her since they were the only people besides Katrine that I expected to still be sober by night's end. Everyone else would assume I was busily playing hostess and would give little if any thought to my whereabouts until at least midnight.

That decided, I wiped down Lucy's high chair, placed a few toys on her tray, grabbed the phone, dialed Sera—who had vociferously declined my invitation to ring in the New Year in what she'd dubbed Lesbian Hell— and proceeded to chat about the party and what she planned to do when she finished her shift at eleven.

I was on the brink of telling her how she'd missed out on the opportunity to meet the Lovely Katrine when the girl herself appeared at the top of the basement stairs. Surprised, I changed the subject with a speed that was sure to leave Sera with a badly sprained—if not broken—neck.

Not wanting to further alienate Katrine but still unable to speak to her, I began to talk as if Sera was keeping me on the line instead of the other way around. At first this confused her as much as the sudden change of subject, but she soon caught on and assumed the role of chatty friend stuck at work while everyone else celebrated. Thus, I managed to remain on the line long enough for Katrine use the bathroom, pour herself a soda, and disappear down the stairs again.

I had just finished congratulating myself on the success of my strategy and thanking Sera for contributing thereto when I heard Kevin's voice and footsteps coming up the stairs.

"Gotta run," I said quickly before hanging up, grabbing the washcloth from the table, and placing it to Lucy's face as if I hadn't already washed it fifteen minutes earlier.

"Hey, sweets," he said merrily. "How's it going?"

"Great."

"Then what are you still doing up here?"

"Keeping an ear on the doorbell mostly, and satisfying the occasional request for a refill. That reminds me," I added, getting up from the table to remove a pitcher of margaritas from the freezer, "my tank is on E."

Kevin watched me pour the better part of a pitcher of what was basically tequila slush into the giant margarita glass on the table. "I think everyone who was planning to come is here," he advised, "so you may as well lock up and come downstairs. If anyone else does show up, they can either knock until someone hears them or learn to be on time."

"Seems fair," I admitted. "But I can't go downstairs just yet. I haven't put Lucy to bed."

"Why don't you let me do that? It's probably my turn to stand kid duty anyway."

"Don't be silly. I won't have any fun without you there, so I may as well put Lucy to bed myself and join you in the basement as soon as she's asleep."

Kevin crossed his arms. "You can't stay up here all night, you know."

"Actually, I could. So I'm guessing that what you mean is that you're not going to let me."

"You're right. I'm not. You're the hostess. You can't ignore our friends all night."

"Well, I *could*," I clarified again. "But I'm not ignoring anyone—I promise."

"Then why aren't you in the basement? And don't tell me you're playing bartender, babysitter, or doorman."

"What about bouncer?"

"Is this about Rob and Katrine?" Kevin prodded as I cleared the jars and other remnants of Lucy's dinner from the table.

"Why would you think that?"

"Gee, I don't know. Maybe because of the lukewarm reception you gave them when they arrived. Or maybe because Katrine is sitting in the basement staring off into space."

"That's not on me. My guess is she's taking tranquilizers to help her deal with reality of her situation. Now, can we do this later or at least take it somewhere else? I wouldn't want anyone to hear us as they're coming up to use the bathroom."

Kevin nodded. "Lead the way."

"Thank you."

"Look, Jack," Kevin began as we arrived in the playroom. "I know you're annoyed with Katrine, but you can't avoid her all night."

"Actually—"

"OK, I suppose you *could*," he corrected himself. "But you shouldn't."

"I'm sorry, Kevin. I don't want to avoid her. I just don't know what to say."

"How about 'congratulations?'"

"You must be kidding."

"It's the only polite thing to say under the circumstances."

"Maybe so. But after everything I said to her before Christmas, she'll know I'm full of shit."

"OK, so don't pretend to be happy for her. But would you at least make an effort to be friendly?"

"That depends," I allowed, having changed Lucy's diaper and handed her off to Kevin. "Does that request also apply to Rob?"

"No. In fact, it's probably better that you don't make any extra effort to get along with Rob. After all, we wouldn't want to give him the impression that something has changed and have him start to wonder why."

"So what you're saying is that I should be my normal hateful self when it comes to my least favorite person?"

Kevin laughed as we edged out to and down the hall, dimming the lights as we worked our way through the kitchen and toward the living room stairway. "Something like that," he said before stopping to train his bionic ears on the basement stairs and nodding toward the kitchen. "Sounds like we've got company."

"Hey, guys," Rob said as he approached. "I thought the party was in the basement?"

Kevin tipped his head toward Lucy, who was almost asleep in his arms. "We were just tying off some loose ends before things get too wild."

"Speaking of wild," Rob said quietly, "I just had an interesting conversation with Jackie's brother—or shall I call you Red?"

"Middle school hair disaster," I demurred when Kevin eyed me quizzically. "I'll explain when you get back from putting Lucy to bed."

Kevin nodded. "Meet you downstairs, Rob?" he suggested as if trying to induce my nemesis to leave the main floor and spare me another ass-kissing.

"Sure. Just as soon I score one of those fantastic margaritas I've been hearing about."

"Roger that," Kevin said as he backed away. "Jack, when you've finished there, can you find Tyler and send him upstairs?"

"Let's wait awhile. I want to make sure Lucy's down for the count. Otherwise he may just distract her, and the two of them will be up all night."

"You're the boss."

"All right, Copeland," I said when Kevin had gone. "What do you want? I mean, besides a margarita." *Kevin wants normal; I'll give him normal.*

"Nothing."

I considered him doubtfully as I removed the pitcher and a stein from the freezer. Setting the pitcher on the counter, I rolled the rim of the stein in the plate of salt nearby. "Sorry about the delivery system," I said, emptying the pitcher into the now frosted stein. "I'm out of stemware, so it was either that or a measuring cup."

Rob waved off my apology as he accepted the vessel and brought it to his lips. "That's good stuff," he declared after a sip. "Thanks."

"No sweat."

Reaching into the freezer again, I grabbed some more ice and dropped it into the blender. For reasons known only to him, Rob watched as I grabbed a bottle of tequila in one hand and the margarita mix in the other and poured while I counted to five, and then set the bottles down and ran the blender to the count of ten.

"It's good to see you again, Jackie," he announced as I topped off my own glass and returned the pitcher to its polar vault. "You look great."

"Thanks. I've been working out."

"Really?"

I laughed. "No."

"Well, it sure looks like you have."

"Then you either need to stop drinking or go have your eyes checked, because I am as fat today as I was when you were single."

"Don't be ridiculous. You're not fat. Now, I won't go so far as to say you're thin," he added carefully, "but Jackie wouldn't be Jackie without her trademark curves."

"Trademark curves?" I snorted. "That's a good one."

"Why is that funny?"

"I'm sorry, Rob. But you don't strike me as the kind of guy who appreciates curves."

"Why? Because Katrine is built like a model?"

"Among other things."

"Well, just because a guy likes prime rib doesn't mean he can't appreciate filet mignon."

Whatever.

"How's your friend Scott?" I asked, hoping to find a sore spot. "Has he found job yet?"

"No. But he's got some strong leads, so it shouldn't be too long now."

"That's good. He seems like a nice guy."

"I figured you two would hit it off. I mean, no offense, but he's a liberal, too, so it wasn't exactly a long shot."

"*No offense?*" I repeated. "Just what is *that* supposed to mean?"

"Just that I'm trying not to offend you."

"By referring to us as liberals, you mean?"

"Yeah. Is there something wrong with that?"

"Not in my book, but clearly there is in yours."

"What are you talking about?"

"Well, why else would you feel the need to say 'no offense'?"

"I'm sorry, Jackie. I just didn't want you to think I was attacking you."

"I have a newsflash for you, Rob. I don't mind being called a liberal. What I do mind is your suggestion that someone might be offended by the term, since it tells me you consider the word itself to be an insult."

"I guess I never thought of it that way before."

"That hardly surprises me," I fumed, preparing to unleash a plume of righteous liberal indignation along with a blast of personal wrath fueled by my disgust for Rob and accelerated by having waited over a month to find out what had become of Katrine. "You conservatives aren't known for your capacity to understand—much less care—how other people feel. You can't imagine anyone thinking differently from you or seeing things any way but the way you see them. That's why you're all about law and order when some stranger gets arrested but become the Lech Walesa of leniency when someone close to you is accused of wrongdoing. It also explains how you can grouse ad nauseam about all the deadbeats on welfare and disability, but you suddenly see the value of a safety net when you or someone you know can't work because of an accident or injury. Because if it affects strangers or people you don't respect, it's a waste of time, but when it happens to you or someone you admire, it's a totally different story."

"Get real, Jackie. Liberals are no different from conservatives when it comes to making policy that suits their own interests. Just look at the people calling for gun control who, because they don't need or want guns for hunting or self-protection, don't think anyone else should have them either."

"I hate to break it to you, man, but there are plenty of hunters and sportsman who support gun control. And the goal isn't to outlaw guns but to keep them out of the hands of people who would use them to commit crimes."

"Maybe that's what *you* want. But most liberals want to take them away from law-abiding citizens just because they personally have no use for them."

"Really? And just how many gun control advocates do you know?"

I waited as he paused to consider my question.

"That's what I thought," I said when he failed to answer. "Well, trust me—I know plenty, and not one of us wants to take guns away from law-abiding citizens. That's a myth perpetuated by right-wingers and the gun lobby to scare people into voting against reasonable gun control measures like background checks and waiting periods."

"You can't tell me there's no one out there trying to outlaw guns just because they don't think they're necessary."

"I'm sure they're out there—just not in the numbers that the gun lobby would like you to believe. But that's nothing new either. Conservatives have always exploited fear and ignorance by spreading lies and misinformation. Like the abstinence-only crackpots, who insist that sexual activity is never safe and refuse to teach kids about contraception and how to avoid sexually transmitted disease. They aren't interested in spreading the truth so that teens can make informed decisions about their health; they'd rather scare them with lies than give them the tools and information they need to protect themselves from pregnancy and disease."

"I don't think letting them get pregnant or sick is the goal, Jackie. Proponents of abstinence simply want to deter kids from having premarital sex because they believe it's unhealthy and immoral."

"I get that. And I respect their beliefs and their right to have them. But it's wrong for them to use lies and scare tactics to get others to do what they want—whether we're talking about gun control or contraception."

"So you would never stretch or twist the truth in order to convince someone to vote your way or to do something you wanted them to do?"

"Absolutely not. I may have opinions about this issue or that subject, but I don't need other people to agree with me bad enough to lie to or mislead them into doing so. I'm happy to let people do as they please provided they grant me the same courtesy. Unfortunately, social conservatives like to believe they have 'God' on their side, which gives them the right or duty to tell the rest of us how to live. Of course, it's easy for many of them to say, for example, that sex is immoral, because they have little or no sex drive themselves. They're like naturally thin people who credit diet and exercise with keeping them slim while condemning heavier people as lazy, gluttonous morons. They view their own size as the result of discipline and restraint without even considering that fat people exercise and watch what they eat as well. This allows them to see obesity as sign of a flawed character rather than of a faulty metabolism, which allows them to despise or disapprove of fat people. Similarly, those who call for abstinence credit self-control and moral superiority for keeping them from sleeping around when in fact it's simply a weak or nonexistent libido. So again, you have conservatives trying to stop other people from doing something because that something isn't something they're interested in themselves."

"So you think everyone who advocates for abstinence does so because they don't like sex?"

"Not all of them. Some do so because they're repressed. They're the ones who, despite their public condemnation of premarital sex, homosexuality, and other sexual behavior, have private urges and proclivities they consider deviant, which no one else knows of until their family members start going through their personal effects after their death. They're the senators who support antigay legislation despite their own affinity for engaging in anonymous sex with strange men in public restrooms, and the evangelists who rail against adultery despite having regularly harassed their secretaries or having had multiple affairs. These people know how dark their own hearts are and thus can't imagine others having normal, healthy urges that can be satisfied in normal, healthy ways. They only have their own secret kinks that they hide by vehemently opposing sexual activity of all kinds. Now, I could care less what these people do in the privacy of their own homes, dungeons, or bathroom stalls, but it offends me to no end when people like that try to dictate how the rest of us should live."

"That's the downside to living in a democracy, Jackie. Sometimes you're in the majority, and sometimes you're not."

"Understood. It's just too bad these people would rather fight to keep schools from teaching kids about contraception when they could be battling something more insidious, like poverty."

"And exactly how would you have them do that?"

"By supporting programs that help people acquire the skills and habits they need to achieve economic stability and promoting policies that don't benefit the rich at the expense of the poor."

"Poverty isn't about policy, Jackie. It's about good, old-fashioned hard work and ambition."

"It requires a lot more than that, Rob. It also takes confidence, social skills, and a fair amount of luck—all of which the poor often lack—not to mention good role models who can show them how to find and keep a job and to manage their money wisely. Unfortunately, conservatives would rather gripe about welfare queens than think about how to truly help the poor. They see poverty like some do obesity, as evidence of a flawed character and therefore unworthy of their energy or compassion. Like you, they think all it takes to make it is a willingness to work hard. They fail to consider all the other factors that helped them succeed. I'm not saying they don't work hard or that poor people are never stupid or lazy. I just think middle-class conservatives have a tendency to underestimate the role of other factors in their success and to overestimate the extent of their own struggle. So although they'd have to screw up pretty bad not to do at least as well as their parents, they're patting themselves on the back for a job well done. Of course, for people like that, screwing up means moving back to a basement in the suburbs; for people like me and Kevin, it's back to food stamps and free cheese."

"Seriously?"

"Seriously."

Rob raised his brows. "Katrine told me your mom died young," he said pensively, "and that your dad was out of work a lot, but I guess I'd never stopped to consider the implications those events would have had on your standard of living."

"And now that you have?"

"Let's just say it explains a few things."

"Like what?"

"Your tendency to support the underdog, for one. It's my experience that being disadvantaged makes *some* people more prone to advocating for others."

"*Some*?" I repeated, having detected a hint of condescension.

"Well, not me, anyway."

"You?"

Rob nodded. "My mom had to work two jobs to put food on the table after my dad had a stroke and could no longer work. And despite all that, I've never once felt that it was the duty of the middle class to advocate for the poor or help them solve their problems."

Although I didn't think this was something to brag about, I decided to let that remark pass. I was more interested in his history, for a change, than I was in his lack of compassion.

"Of course, I myself have never felt disadvantaged," he added with a shrug. "Maybe that's the difference."

I hadn't felt particularly disadvantaged myself as a kid, but I wasn't going to go there either. I had important data to mine, after all, and with midnight approaching, not a lot of time in which to prospect.

"I didn't know your father was disabled," I said, hoping to exploit his need for attention in order to satisfy my curiosity.

"Not very many people do. But we all came together the way a family should when there's a crisis. My older brother and eldest sister, for example, both dropped out of school to help pay the bills. My other older sister pitched in by keeping an eye on me and my two younger brothers while the others worked and making sure that we got to and from school every day and that we did our homework and our chores. Ray, Charlie, and I, meanwhile, did our part by foregoing sports, band, and anything else that required activity fees, uniforms, or transportation."

I could hardly believe my ears. It had never occurred to me that Rob and I had anything in common, or that he had ever gone without. I'd assumed from his manner and appearance that he'd come from the same world

Katrine did, and he'd had parents who played golf and held high teas. Relatively few people from that set enlist in the military, but I'd run across one now and then. Some join because they want a personal challenge or to serve their country, others because they want to kill. From his air and his clothing, I had assumed that Rob fit into one of those categories and, while I doubted he was lying, neither could I believe I'd been so far off.

Then again, he'd made a similar mistake about me. In fact, he'd known more about my background than I did about his and yet was still surprised to learn that one dead mother plus one unemployed father equals public assistance and USDA dairy giveaways.

"So you're not the only one who suffered," Rob said as I wandered back to the present.

So much for not feeling disadvantaged.

"I never said I suffered," I reminded him.

"But you did grow up in a disadvantaged home."

"I suppose I did. But I never said that either. You did."

"Fine. But you do root for the underdog."

The guy desperately needed to score a point off me for some reason, which made me wonder how many more times I could contradict him before he would give up.

"Yeah, well I think someone should," I said instead. I was growing bored with the game and ready for another drink and a serious change of scenery.

"Isn't it strange," he asked as he watched me withdraw the margarita pitcher from the freezer, pour the remainder of its contents into our glasses, and prepare to make another batch, "how people who grew up in similar conditions can come out of the experience with such widely varied attitudes?"

I didn't find it strange at all. In fact, as I loaded the pitcher with fresh ice, topped off the tequila and mixer, and switched on the blender, certain things finally started to make sense.

We both may have come from poor families, but our circumstances couldn't have been more different. For example, I was the elder of two children, while Rob was the fourth of six. With only one sibling who was several years younger than me and who, in many ways, was like my own child, I didn't have to compete for resources, attention, or space to the degree that Rob likely had. As the eldest, the only female, and a mother figure, I'd also had more control over the people and events in my life than

Rob probably did as one of several younger boys with a mother, two older sisters, and an older brother caring for him. This, I reasoned, accounted for the divergence in our attitudes toward and our treatment of others.

It also helped to explain Rob's political views. As someone who believed he'd pulled himself up by his bootstraps, he expected everyone else to capable of doing the same. The fact that his older brother and sister had actually yanked them up *for* him was, to him, irrelevant.

None of this excused his treatment of Katrine, of course. But it did make me curious as to the status of Rob's relationship with his family today. Were they close? Cordial? Estranged? And what, if anything, did the current state of things have to do with his and Katrine's decision to get married in New York instead of Minnesota? Was he trying to prevent his folks from coming in contact with Katrine's family? Or was the relationship between Rob and his parents and siblings such that they would not have attended the wedding even if it had been held in his hometown?

"Yes, it is strange," I replied upon realizing I hadn't yet. "And while you're correct in that I tend to root for the underdog, I've personally never felt disadvantaged in any way. In fact, I feel fortunate to be where I am, and grateful to the people who took an interest in me and for the experiences that shaped my values—even those that were ugly and unpleasant."

I could see from Rob's expression that gratitude and appreciation were the furthest things from his mind. He wasn't at all grateful for what life had dealt him. In fact, he regretted that he had not gone farther or done more, and he resented that others had not done better by him.

In a way, I felt sorry for him. Believing, deep down, that he wasn't as good as anyone else forced him to behave as if he was better than everyone else. Believing, deep down, that he deserved better that what he had, he would never be satisfied and never appreciate anything.

At least he was smart enough to know that echoing my sentiments would ring false and that speaking of his own true feelings would cast his character in an unfavorable light.

"And on that note," I said by way of ending our exchange, "I'm going to stop monopolizing your time and let you get back to the party."

Seventeen

_A_fter concluding my conversation with Rob, I followed him to the stairway and headed down to check the status of the food and refreshments. About halfway there, I ran into Lyn.

"Hey," she said as if she hadn't expected to see me. "I was just on my way up to use the bathroom and see if you needed any help before Josh and I take off."

"Take off?"

"Yeah. I'm really tired, and Josh and I have more house hunting to do before I have to be at work tomorrow afternoon."

House hunting? On New Year's Day?

Although her story sounded like a load of crap to my ears, I decided not to make an issue of it. I had enough on my mind without wondering why she and Josh were leaving early or why she couldn't just say they needed to go without making up some ridiculous story.

"OK, well, go ahead and take care of your bladder, mama," I said, forcing a hug. "And if I don't see you before you leave, happy new year."

Downstairs, I did a quick check of the bowls and plates on the refreshment table, munched on a few chips as I merged the contents of a few bowls to make room for two trays of champagne flutes, and made my way back upstairs and over to the hall closet. As I was scanning the shelves for what I needed and how many hands I would need to carry it, I felt someone standing behind me.

"Hello, Katrine," I said, without facing her. "What can I do for you?"

"You could stop avoiding me."

"Who's avoiding whom? You're the one who left my house without saying good-bye a month ago and couldn't even call to let me know how you were doing."

"Is that why you're mad at me? Because I didn't say good-bye?"

"Who's mad?" I asked, lifting a box off one of the lower shelves and turning around to carry it to the kitchen. "I'm merely pointing out that if you can walk out of here after the discussion we had and not speak to me for a month, then certainly I can walk around here without talking to you for a few hours."

We exchanged stares for a while before I shifted the box again and headed for the kitchen. Katrine followed and watched as I rinsed off the glasses and arranged them on trays on the table.

Kicking the now-empty carton under the table, I began pulling champagne bottles from the refrigerator and setting them on the table. "So, why aren't you downstairs with your new husband?"

"Because he's deeply entrenched in conversation over *the former Yugoslavia*," Katrine replied with an above-average impression of her self-important spouse that made us both laugh.

"Look, Jackie," she said after a moment as we moved the champagne to the table. "I want to explain something."

"There's nothing you need to explain to me, Katrine. You wanted advice, and I gave it to you. You chose not to take it, and I have no interest in the rudiments of your decision. Issue closed."

"But I want to tell you why I went through with it."

"Katrine, I don't *care* why you went through with it."

Without another word, I reached past her, grabbed my glass and the pitcher containing the remains of the margaritas from the freezer, and marched down the hall to the bathroom.

Sometime later—and several more pages into the Fay Weldon paperback I kept under the sink—there was a knock at the door. Realizing I'd been holed up longer than I'd intended, I got to my feet and surrendered the room to the anguished midshipman on the other side of the door.

As I walked past him toward the kitchen, my legs felt odd—a fact that I attributed in equal shares to the circulation being restored after having sat on the edge of the tub so long and to the tequila coursing through my veins.

A glance at the kitchen clock reminded me that it was closing in on midnight, while a quick scan of the table revealed that the champagne and glasses were gone. Assuming they'd been taken downstairs by Kevin or some other helpful person, I moved on to retrieving the hats and noisemakers from the spare room.

I was almost to the closet again when Katrine—or so I assumed from her fragrance—shut and latched the bedroom door. The room was dark save the glow of the streetlight leaking out from behind the shade, and I listened amusedly while my captor fumbled in vain for a switch plate along the wall nearest the doorway.

"You might as well give up," I said finally. "This place was built without overhead lighting, and all the lamps are standing duty in the basement this evening."

"That's ridiculous."

"You are correct. But so is this," I added, referring to her decision to ambush me "Now why are we here?"

"We're here so you can tell me what your problem is."

"I wasn't aware that I had a problem."

"Oh, come off it, Jackie. I know you're pissed."

"Do you?"

"Yes. And I would like to know why."

"OK. Well, when you've figured it out, feel free to let me know. Until then, I should get back to my guests."

"I don't think so."

I sighed as Katrine stepped forward and blocked my path to the door. I didn't think she would physically attempt to stop me if I tried to move past her, but I didn't want an already bad situation to escalate into something worse.

"What was I was supposed to do?" she demanded before I could decide whether to make a run for it or wait her out.

"If you're talking about the wedding again, I've already told you, it's none of my concern."

"I couldn't just walk away from him, Jackie. He would have been devastated."

"Bullshit."

"*What?*"

"You heard me. I said bullshit."

"*What's* bullshit?"

"This! You! Him! All of it! So why don't you just cut the crap and admit that you married Rob because you wanted to?"

"That's exactly what I did!"

"See? That wasn't so hard. At least, not as hard as, say, putting up with him for the next forty or fifty years. Good luck with that, by the way."

"He may not be perfect, but Rob really loves me—and I love him. Which is why I'm going to give this a chance. If it doesn't work out, fine; but at least I'll know I tried."

"So that's your plan? Marry a man who treats you like garbage and then cross your fingers and hope things get better? That's just about the dumbest thing I've ever heard. But, hey—if you think Rob is the best you can do, who am I to argue?"

Katrine folded her arms. "Why are you doing this to me?"

"I'm not doing anything to you. I'm simply letting you live your life."

Suddenly I saw the glimmer of tears streaking Katrine's cheeks. "Oh, Christ. Not this. Katrine—I am not doing this. Do you hear me? I'm *not*."

"Please, Jackie," Katrine sobbed. "Don't make me choose between the two of you."

"I'm not asking you to choose, Katrine. I'm not asking you for a goddamned thing."

"Then why won't you talk to me? Why are you shutting me out?"

"What exactly do you want me to say, Katrine? Congratulations? Mazel tov? Will either of those satisfy you? I'm perfectly happy to say whatever you like provided you don't expect me to mean it."

"You are not being fair."

"Fair?" I yanked the bottom of the shade and let it fly. It snapped up, flapping violently against the frame as it spun to a stop. "I'll tell you what's not fair! It's not fair of you to come over here, bare your soul to me, and then disappear for weeks without a word. It's not fair for you to leave me to worry and think about nothing but you for nearly a month because you're too big a coward to face me. It's not fair of you to ask for advice and then punish me when it's not what you want to hear. It's not fair that you would squander your mind, body, and soul on Rob, and expect me to be happy about it. Above all, it's not fair of you to stand there and accuse me of ignoring you and shutting you out when all I wanted was some time to deal with my own feelings so I didn't have to hurt yours."

Katrine lowered her head. "I'm sorry, Jackie. I didn't realize—"

"Obviously."

Crossing my arms, I faced the window and cursed my big mouth and all the tequila I'd consumed since Katrine and Rob arrived. Had I stuck with soda, I still may not have been able to feign happiness, but I could have at least kept my cool. Either way, I definitely wouldn't have found myself stuck in this dark room with no exit strategy.

Over my pounding heart and the dull roar coming from the basement, I suddenly heard footsteps in the hall outside the door. In a flash, Katrine pulled down the shade and dropped silently to the narrow path of floor between the bed and the wall.

Confused, yet unconcerned, I walked across the room to await a knock, and then unlatched and opened the door.

"Hey, Rob," I said without letting go of the knob. "What's up?"

"Not much. I'm just looking for Katrine. Have you seen her?"

I stared into the darkness behind me. "Not since I put out the champagne. Why?"

"I wanted to tell her that I'm driving a few of the guys over to another party."

"Oh?"

"Yeah. It's not safe for them to drive themselves, so I said I'd take them. I'll be coming back, of course. I just wanted her to know where I would be."

"OK. I'll make sure she gets the message."

"Thanks."

"No problem."

"What are you doing in here, anyway?" he asked with a nod toward the area behind me.

"Just getting some peace and quiet."

"Is everything all right?"

"Of course. Why?"

"Well, you're in here all alone, and, frankly, you seem upset."

"It's a New Year's thing," I lied. "Always makes me a little emotional."

"Do you want to talk about it? I could tell the guys to find another ride."

My skin started to crawl as he stepped forward, placed his hands on my upper arms, and looked at me the way a lion would a wounded gazelle.

Get your paws off me, I wanted to say, but couldn't for fear Katrine would realize his offer was more than a platonic gesture. As much as she deserved to know what he was capable of when he thought she wasn't around, I didn't want the party to turn into a circus. Fortunately, he saw my face, realized his mistake, and proceeded immediately to effect damage control.

"Don't be silly," I said as he released me—thereby sparing the good people of Minnesota the expense of prosecuting me for whatever crimes I otherwise may have committed. "I'll be fine."

"OK, then. Well, I guess I'll leave you to it."

"Thanks. And happy new year."

"Happy new year."

I watched him retreat down the hall, and then closed and locked the door.

"Well, that was interesting," I said as Katrine knelt by the window watching for the Nova's taillights to disappear from view.

"I know," she said, obviously not referring to her decision to hit the floor. "I'm sorry."

"Care to explain?"

"I'm not sure I can."

"OK," I said with a shrug as I faced the door. "Well, enjoy the rest of your evening."

"Where are you going?"

"I have to check on the kids and get some extra bedding. People are going to need something to sleep on when they finally crash, and I don't think Kevin would have thought to bring it down when—or shall I say, if—he put Tyler to bed. I guess I'll see you later."

Leaving her no opportunity to argue, I opened the door, walked through the kitchen, ascended the stairs, and slipped into the kid's bedroom. Pleased to discover Tyler asleep in bed, I adjusted his and Lucy's covers and pulled the door almost closed before heading over to retrieve the extra linen from the closet in the hall. As I did so, I thought about what had transpired downstairs and wondered what the hell Rob was thinking. Did he seriously believe I would welcome such an advance? If so, why? And had he really expected to get away with it if I hadn't?

Probably. After all, what had he done besides offer to console someone who claimed to be feeling down on New Year's Eve? His actions were clearly misinterpreted, he would say if confronted, and with no means to prove otherwise, I would look like a complete idiot.

Katrine's behavior, meanwhile, was as much of a mystery. What had possessed her to hide from Rob? Why wouldn't she want him to know we were talking? I could understand her not wanting him to know the subject matter, but surely we could have come up with a cover story that would have worked better than my pretending to be in the room all alone. At least then he would have kept his hands to himself.

I had just completed that thought when I heard someone on the stairs.

"What are you doing up here?" I asked as Katrine approached. "Is everything OK?"

She nodded. "I came up to apologize. It was wrong of me to say those things, and I'm very, very sorry."

"It's OK, Katrine."

"No, it's not. You've been nothing but a friend to me, and I should have known your intent was not to hurt me."

"I appreciate your saying that, but it's really not necessary."

"Yes, it is. Our friendship means a lot to me, and I just can't stand the thought of losing it."

"It means a lot to me too, Katrine. I hope you know that."

"I do now."

"Good. So now that I have enough sheets to rappel from the top of the Sears Tower," I said, hoisting the basket to my waist, "let's go downstairs and see what's going on."

"Do we have to?"

"Well, I suppose *you* don't, but I do."

"OK, but does it have to be right now? I mean, this very minute?"

Sighing, I strode back to the office, dropped the basket onto the chair, hopped up onto my desk, and crossed my arms. "All right, what gives?"

"What do you mean?"

I sighed again. "Look, Katrine, there is a houseful of people downstairs to whom I tacitly promised to provide food, amusement, comfort, and refreshment, so I don't have a lot of time for beating around the bush. Now, what do you want?"

Smiling, Katrine approached the desk. "I think the real question is," she breathed as she stepped between my knees. "What do *you* want?"

Her words sparked an electrical charge that erupted in my viscera and raced down my limbs and out my extremities, leaving a network of deliciously singed nerves in their wake. For a moment I sat paralyzed—unwilling to admit but unable to deny what she clearly seemed to know: I wanted *her*.

Whether she harbored reciprocal feelings for me or if this was an act of restitution, I could not divine. Nor could I tell if she working from a plan or acting on impulse—or that it even mattered. For whether hers was a discharge from a sighted weapon or an inspired shot in the dark, Katrine had me dead to rights, and there was little point in pretending otherwise.

Without a word or even a thought as to the other occupants of the house, I pulled her to me, pressed my mouth to hers, and guided her backward through the doorway to my bedroom.

"Not a bad way to welcome the new year," Katrine declared as she rolled onto her side and propped herself up on an elbow about forty minutes later.

"I'll say."

Recovering my bearings more slowly, I sat up, scooted sideways until my back was against the headboard, and began to pull myself together. "So how long have you wanted to do that?" I asked, only half joking, as I drew my knees to my chest.

"At least as long as you have."

"And who's to say mine wasn't an act of impulse?"

"Give me a break," Katrine said, shrugging her shirt back up over her shoulders. "I may have been born at night," she said as she fastened the buttons, "but it wasn't *last* night."

I suddenly and desperately wanted a cigarette, but even without a clock I knew I was more than a few minutes into my resolution. I'd planned to have one or two ceremonial good-bye smokes with my champagne before midnight, but the opportunity had obviously been lost along with my senses.

Not that I had expected quitting to be difficult. I already smoked so rarely that it hardly seemed worthy of deliberation, much less a resolution. Even Kevin, who often teased me about quitting—yet still would swipe one or two from me now and then to enjoy on his way to and from school—had chided me about choosing something more challenging after I'd told him of my plans to kick the habit.

Leave it to me to put myself smack in the middle of something like this only moments into the new year.

Suddenly I remembered the chewing gum I'd bought as a substitute, and I reached over to grab a pack from the top drawer of my bedside table.

"Want some?" I asked. "I'd offer you a smoke, but they're downstairs—along with the guests I'm so rudely neglecting this evening."

"I wouldn't worry about them if I were you," Katrine laughed as she rolled onto her back to tuck in her shirt. "They're someone else's problem now."

"What do you mean?"

"Well, when Rob called earlier—"

"Rob called here?"

"Yeah. Didn't you hear the ring?"

"No. I shut off the phones up here so if anyone called they wouldn't wake the baby."

Katrine nodded. "That explains why you didn't pick it up," she said. "Anyway, he called to see if I wanted to stay here or catch a ride with whoever was joining him and Kevin in crashing the army party in Maplewood."

"Wait a second—Kevin left?"

"Yeah. Along with everyone else from the unit. I told him I'd help hold down the fort while he was gone."

"What about my brother?"

"He and his wife left when Kevin did. Said to tell you good-bye."

"So *everyone's* gone?"

"Except us and the kids."

"So why'd you let me dig all that crap out if there was no one here to use it?"

"I guess I was stalling."

"That was sneaky."

Katrine raised her brows. "You're welcome," she said, rising from the bed and taking my hand. "Now let's go."

"Where?"

"Downstairs."

"Obviously."

"Oh, just get up, will ya? Christ, do you have to *plan* everything?"

Grudgingly, I let Katrine pull me to my feet and followed her to the kitchen, where we made mimosas from the leftover champagne and drank them with toast and scrambled eggs.

Eighteen

"What's this?" Sera asked as I unpacked two coffees, a sack of bagels, and a carton of cream cheese onto the front desk at the motel the following evening.

"A bribe."

"For what?"

"Listening without prejudice."

"Damn! You mean I missed something good last night?"

I nodded. "I told you it's a bad idea to skip my parties."

"I can't help that I had to work."

With a shrug, I slipped the lid off the cream cheese and peeled off the foil seal.

"Mmmm…honey—my favorite," Sera enthused as she sampled it with her pinky. "You must have something pretty juicy to tell me," she added, drawing a cracked wheat bagel from the sack and twisting it like a Rubik's Cube. "I haven't been treated like this since my mom tried to help me over my last big breakup."

I considered the modest spread before us as I pulled some napkins and plastic utensils from the bag. "Really?"

Sera nodded. "I live a fairly Spartan life."

"Yeah, right."

Sera followed my doubtful gaze to the red '77 Datsun 280Z parked out front. "Present vehicle excepted, of course."

"Of course. So your mom's cool with things, then?" I asked as Sera apprehended a knife and began to spread a generous layer of schmear on one half of her bagel. "With your digging girls, I mean."

"Oh, my mom's *way* cool with things. She's doesn't *get* it, of course, but she's the epitome of supportive. You know she even offered to prank call Sherri for me?"

"Did you accept?"

"No, but she did it anyway."

"That's hilarious."

"I know." Sera wiped the knife clean on the edge of the second ring and laid it across the rim of the cream cheese carton. "You would love her."

"I'll bet."

"So, are you ready?" I asked as Sera took her first bite.

"For what?"

"To fulfill your obligation."

"Oh, right," Sera laughed, recalling the bargain we had struck. "I almost forgot I'm under contract. So what were you up to last night? Robbery? Larceny? Assault and battery?"

"Try adultery."

"*Adultery*? You?"

Sera swallowed hard as I grimaced.

"Oh my God. With whom?"

"Katrine."

"You had *sex* with Katrine last night?"

I nodded. "At least I think so."

"You *think* so? You mean you don't *know*?"

"I know what we *did*. I'm just not sure you'd consider it sex."

"Hang on," Sera instructed tentatively. "You know about the birds and the bees, right?"

"Of course I know about the birds and the bees. It's the birds and the *birds* I'm having trouble with."

Sera grinned from behind her cup as she sampled her coffee. "So how did this happen?"

"Beats me. All I know is that one minute we were arguing, the next we were making up, and the next we were making out."

"Let me get this straight: you got naked with another girl—whom you previously weren't even speaking to—while hosting a party on New Year's Eve."

"Not exactly."

"Not exactly *which*?"

"We weren't exactly naked. Our shirts were unbuttoned, but they were still on."

"And your pants?"

"On."

"All the way?"

"All the way."

"OK," Sera stated with authority. "So essentially you got to second base."

"I wouldn't say that."

"Why not?"

"Well, for one thing, that makes it sound *intentional*."

"Would you have me believe your shirts came open by *accident*?"

"No. But it's not like I was *aiming* for that."

"Either way, if there was nothing going on below the waist—"

"Oh, now, I definitely wouldn't say *that*."

"You mean you—"

"Oh, yes."

"And did you—"

"Oh, yes."

"Wow."

"I know." I smiled and folded my arms atop the counter. "Katrine called it *outercourse*."

"Clever girl," Sera observed. "In less refined circles, we'd call that a dry hump."

"Ew! Sera, that's awful."

"Not to mention completely inappropriate. I mean, if you know anything about girl-on-girl action, you know it's *anything* but dry."

"Thanks for the visual."

"My pleasure. So back to how this happened," Sera continued. "You said you were arguing?"

I nodded. "She was upset because I'd been giving her a wide berth all night because I hadn't expected them to see them, and when they showed up at our party unexpectedly, I wasn't exactly thrilled to see them."

"Why not?"

"Well, to begin with, I've never liked the guy. I kept that to myself at first because we'd just met, and it really wasn't my place to say anything.

Unfortunately, by the time I'd gotten to know her well enough to express my concerns, Rob and I had fallen out, so I couldn't say anything without sounding vindictive and spiteful. Then, just before finals, she told me how he'd been behaving irresponsibly and making decisions without her consent. Figuring it for my one and only chance to speak my mind, I finally told her what I thought of the jerk and advised her to dump him."

"How did she respond?"

"She got defensive at first and tried to minimize what she'd said. Then I told her about my ex, and how men like him and Rob need to manipulate and control people, and how important it is to get away before things get too bad. She nodded, asked a few questions, and—"

"And married him anyway."

"Exactly."

Sera sighed. "Well, I can certainly understand the wide berth," she admitted. "Anyone in your shoes would have probably behaved the same way."

"I appreciate your saying that, but in light of last night's events, I'm not sure my motives have been entirely pure. I mean, I've always tried to be a fair and objective person, but I can't help but wonder if my opinion of him hasn't been colored by a subconscious attraction to her."

"Woman, you're the most objective person I know. If anything, you would have tried harder to *like* him because of how you felt about her."

"Well, I did try not to *dis*like him."

"Close enough. Though, in truth, I'd be more concerned if it was actually your distaste for him influencing your actions toward her. Disliking a rival is normal. Pursuing someone because you feel sorry for them, on the other hand, or to spite their current partner—however despicable he may be—is callous and opportunistic."

"Thanks, Sera. As if I didn't have enough to obsess about."

"You have *nothing* to obsess about as far as I'm concerned, Jackie. You advised Katrine to leave a man who treats her badly. Last I checked, that makes you the good guy."

"Even if I had a personal interest in the outcome?"

"Of course you have a personal interest in the outcome—she's your friend. So what if you *were* subconsciously attracted to her all along? Does that mean you shouldn't be honest with her? Does the fact that a doctor gets paid for operating mean she can't recommend necessary procedures? No. Maybe the consumer should get a second opinion and weigh all their options before taking action—as Katrine was welcome to do—but the bottom line is, you advised her in accordance with what you thought would be best for her. If you had another interest in the outcome, it was clearly secondary. And from where I sit, it was also likely irrelevant and mutual given the fact that she married the man *and* had sex with you shortly afterward."

"You do have a point."

"I *always* have a point. And in the words of Doc Mortenson," Sera added, "'Just because you have the hots for some guy's wife doesn't mean he's not a colossal asshole.'"

"I never heard him say that."

"Maybe you weren't listening."

"Or maybe you're making it up."

"Actually, I'm just applying the concept to a new situation."

"God bless the liberal arts."

"Amen."

"At any rate," I sighed, "Katrine finally got up the nerve to confront me and tried to tell me why she'd gone ahead with the wedding. I said I didn't care. Then she cried, and I told her to knock it off. Eventually I explained how I wasn't punishing her for marrying Rob, that I was avoiding her because I didn't want to say anything to hurt her feelings. By then it was close to midnight, so I went upstairs to get the extra sheets and blankets we would need for anyone who stayed over. The next thing I know, she's upstairs telling me how sorry she is and how much my friendship means to her. Well, I was glad we'd cleared the air, but I didn't think we needed all that. Anyway, not wanting to dismiss her feelings, I listened and waited for her to get to the point. When that didn't happen, I put the linens on a chair, sat down on the edge of my desk, and asked her what she wanted."

"What did she say?"

I leaned secretively over the counter toward Sera, who met me halfway. "'The question is,'" I quoted languidly in Sera's ear, "'what do *you* want?'"

"Are you serious?"

"Do I look like I'm joking?"

"Well, what did *you* say?"

"Nothing."

"'*Nothing*?'"

"Well, I didn't actually say '*nothing*'; I just said nothing."

"OK. And then?"

"And then I kissed her."

"You *what*?"

"I couldn't help myself, Sera. She was *this close* to me, and she smelled *so* good. What could I do?"

"Ask to borrow her perfume?"

I crossed my arms. "Need I remind you of your vow to listen without prejudice?"

Sera groaned. "OK, so you kissed her," she repeated with a sigh. "Then what happened?"

"Well, we stuck with that for a while. Then we worked our way over to my bedroom and, well, you know the rest."

"And you did all this with a houseful of people—including your two husbands and two small children—just two floors away?"

"Actually, the kids were sleeping down the hall, but the guys and our guests were gone."

"What happened to them?"

"Most went with Kevin to crash the army ROTC party. A few had gone with Rob to some place in Maplewood. The rest just went home. Of course, I didn't know any of that at the time, since Katrine didn't tell me until afterward."

"Interesting," Sera mused as she tore a fresh bagel apart over a napkin. "So how was it?"

"It was nice."

"*Nice*?"

"What do you want me to say? That it was a fabulous, soul-shattering experience that I'll remember for the rest of my days?"

"If that's what it was—yes."

"I suppose you want the gory details, too?"

"Details are good."

"I had no idea you were such a voyeur."

"Hey, I may be obliged to listen without prejudice, but you never ruled out lasciviousness."

"That'll teach me to skip the fine print."

"Damn straight," Sera laughed. "OK, you don't want to go into the details. So what's next?"

"Nothing."

"What do you mean *nothing*?"

"I mean, it happened. It's over. Check please."

Sera shook her head. "Not that I have a horse in this race, but is that really what you want?"

"Doesn't matter what I want. That's how it has to be."

"Why?"

"Because we're married, for one thing. And even if we weren't, it's… it's just a bad idea."

"Why?"

"Because she's nineteen, for Christ's sake."

"So? Last I checked, that's three years over the age of consent in Minnesota."

"Maybe so, but I'm certainly not going to take advantage of her."

"Take advantage of *her*? Jackie, you may be older, but that girl is no amateur."

"What does that have to do with it?"

"Nothing, I guess. I just don't understand why you're taking all the responsibility here."

"Because I should have known better, and I don't want to ruin things for her and Rob."

"But you don't think she belongs with Rob in the first place."

"True. But I can't have her leaving him for me or getting dumped because of me. And I'm not saying I'll never speak to her again. I'm just saying that nothing's changed between us."

"I see," Sera said, picking up her coffee cup and swirling the cold remains at the bottom. "So do you love her?"

"What kind of a question is that?"

"One that I hope will yield useful information."

Sera sighed as I shook my head. "Look, Jackie, there is no right or wrong answer here. I'm not going to call you a sap if you're in love with her, and I'm not going to declare you a jerk if this was just a roll in the hay. I'm just trying to get the lay of the land—so to speak."

"I guess on one level, I do love her," I admitted. "On another level, though, I could just kill her for putting me in this position. I mean, why couldn't she have just stayed downstairs? Why did she have to approach me that way? And why couldn't I have kept my hands to myself?"

"You really need to cut yourself a break here, Jackie. It's not as if you've been carrying on an affair behind Kevin's back, after all, or sleeping with his best friend—unless, of course, there's something you're not telling me. You were propositioned by a luscious young woman, and in your uninhibited state, you gave in to temptation. It's that simple."

"Simple?" I groaned as I put my head on the counter and covered it with my arms. "Sera, this is anything but simple. In fact, it's highly fucking complicated."

"OK, maybe it is complicated, but it also happens to be normal."

"Would you be so cavalier about this if I'd cheated on *you* instead of Kevin?"

"Depends on how I found out."

"Well, in that case, never mind."

"You mean you're not going to tell him?"

"Nope."

"How long do you think you can pull that off? I mean, look at you— you've got *spazz* and *guilt* running across your forehead like the stock ticker on Wall Street."

"That's only because we're talking about it. That'll go away once I leave here."

"And if not?"

I shrugged. "Kevin will be too busy to notice anyway. And even if he does notice, he'll just assume it has something to do with school or my dad."

"I don't understand why you wouldn't tell him, Jackie. Just a couple months ago you said this sort of thing wouldn't bother him."

"It won't—but it will *interest* him. A lot. And then he'll make jokes about it, which will keep me from forgetting it, and I can't have that."

"And what happens if he finds out later? Won't he be upset that you kept it from him?"

"You have to understand, Sera; Kevin does not get upset. He may feel love, thirst, hunger, frustration, and fatigue, but he doesn't have emotional responses to events like you and I do. I'm not saying he wouldn't be afraid if he were being chased by a wolf or doesn't get annoyed when someone cuts him off in traffic. He's just not the type to feel hurt or betrayed by something I did or didn't do. So were he to find out what happened and didn't like it, he'd simply tell me why and ask me not to do it again."

"I guess I'll have to take your word for it. Meanwhile, what about Rob?"

"What about him?" I stalled, because Rob was the part of the equation that made everything more complicated.

"Do you think Katrine will tell him?"

I winced. "I hope not," I admitted. "And not just because I don't want to be responsible for what happens between him and Katrine. The bigger problem at the moment is that he's having some issues at work that won't be made better if things go south for him at home."

"What kind of issues?"

Although I couldn't go into detail, I shared with Sera what Kevin had told me over winter break and how the situation could be complicated by what had happened on New Year's Eve.

"So although Kevin may not care that you had sex with Katrine," Sera summarized with the air of an attorney offering closing remarks, "or be hurt that you did so and didn't confess right away, there is a strong possibility he'll be annoyed with you for having sex with the wife of one of his colleagues, and even more so to know you had sex with the wife of a colleague who is currently on the military equivalent of 'double secret probation.'"

"That about sums it up," I said, laughing—despite my frazzled nerves—at her reference to one of my favorite lines from *Animal House*.

"Well, that explains why you're so freaked out."

I nodded. "I just don't want my actions to compromise the unit's position," I admitted. "Nor do I want to do anything to contribute to Rob's failure, because I couldn't bear to have something like that on my conscience."

"Does Katrine know that?"

"Which part?"

"Any of it."

"Let's see. No. No. And hell, no."

"Don't you think you should tell her? Before she spills the beans to Rob, I mean."

"That's just it. I can't tell Katrine anything, because she's not supposed to know about the double secret probation. Oh, sure, I could ask her to keep quiet about what happened last night and pretend I'm just trying to keep myself out of trouble, but I can't tell her the truth, which is that I'm afraid he'll lose his mind and blow what's left of his career to smithereens. And I certainly can't, in good conscience, demand that she keep her mouth shut on my behalf, because I honestly think that's a decision she needs to make for herself."

"Wow."

"I know."

"So what's your next move?"

"I have no idea. I'm going to give it some thought and see what I come up with. Once I have a plan, I'll give Katrine a call and set up a meeting."

"Seems sensible."

"If exceptionally broad."

"Well, you've got to start somewhere."

"I know. The next challenge will be finding a time and place."

"Couldn't you just invite her out to dinner one night after school?"

"No. I've always insisted that we eat dinner at home during the week, and Kevin would know something was up if I violated my own policy. Besides, any place that was quiet enough for us to have a meaningful discussion over dinner would also seem romantic, which may confuse things a bit. I think lunch—preferably outdoors and in broad daylight— would be the better approach."

"Christ, Jackie. Why don't you haul her into a cement cell and interrogate her under a high-powered lamp?"

"Good idea. I'll keep that in mind if we're forced to meet in the evening."

Sera laughed as she bagged up the remnants of our snack.

"Not to change the subject," I laughed, "but what are you doing over J-term?"

"Independent study. Doc Peterson is supervising my research project on the increase of female inmates in federal prisons," Sera explained as she tossed the leftover bagels into the fridge under the counter and then plopped down on the seat across from me. "What about you?"

"Creative writing."

"Really? I didn't even know that was offered this term."

"It's not on the Hamilton schedule. I'm taking it at William Marshall."

"*William Marshall?*"

"We can take classes there now," I reminded her. "And at St. Christopher's and St. Anne's. You can take them at any of the four schools and still get credit for it from your own."

Sera nodded. "I saw the newsletter. I'm just having trouble picturing you there."

"Why?"

"Jackie, have you ever *been* to William Marshall?"

"No."

"Well, the place is infested with rich kids with an abundance of social consciousness."

"So?"

"So let's just say it would be in your best interests to keep Kevin's vocation out of the conversation—especially this time of year when sunlight's scarce and the caffeine is plenty."

"Thanks for the warning."

"My pleasure."

"And now—much as I hate to," I said, rising reluctantly from the sofa, "I should mosey."

"I figured it was getting about that time."

Nodding, I retrieved my purse from the front desk and hung it over my shoulder. "Thanks for letting me bend your ear."

"No problem. Thanks for the bagels."

Nineteen

I waited a couple weeks to contact Katrine and invite her to lunch. In addition to giving myself time to plan a path through the mess I'd created, I wanted to let her process what had happened so we could have a reasonable chance at a rational discussion. I also wanted to give us both an opportunity to settle into our respective schedules and to put some distance between me and the event, in case Katrine had already told Rob and there was fallout to be managed.

We had appointed noon, but I broke with tradition and arrived early at the restaurant to establish my territory. I'd never been to Les Bougies—owing to my utter lack of knowledge of real French cuisine and my aversion to American corruptions of foreign culture—so I hoped it wouldn't be a mistake. Katrine had chosen it for its roughly equal distance from our respective institutions of higher learning, although I confess I was less concerned with *le proximité* than I was with *l'ambiance* or *le clientèle*.

The place was like a French version of the Olive Garden with a décor that, predictably, featured framed copies of vintage ads for products ranging from sewing machines and toys to champagne and soap. Little candles—hence the name—flickered here and there, while easel-mounted bistro boards boasted five varieties of croissants and announced *les specials du jour.*

After surveying the cozy, if cliché, scene and declaring it an acquaintance-free zone, I accepted the hostess's invitation to make myself comfortable and chose a table in the section nearest the patio. Through the glass of the, ahem, French doors, I could practically see the snowbanks receding as they melted in the unseasonably mild January air.

Katrine arrived a few minutes later, breathless and rosy-cheeked from her hike from the bus stop up the street. "I'm really glad you called," she said, arranging her backpack and gloves on the empty chair across from me. "I'm sorry if I was becoming a pest."

Pest?

Guiltily, I recalled the answering machine I was still avoiding and wondered if I should have resolved to kick that habit instead of smoking. From her comment, I realized that Katrine thought I was responding to one of her messages when I called to invite her to lunch. She hadn't mentioned that during our conversation on the phone, but it explained the eagerness in her voice then and the delight on her face now as she slipped off her coat.

"I guess I just really wanted to see you," she was saying as she laid it over her backpack and sat down to my right.

She'd just folded her hands after smoothing her hair when a waiter approached from behind.

"Hello, ladies," he said with the enthusiasm of Richard Simmons, "and welcome to *Les Bougies*. I'm Stan, and I'll be your server today. We are pleased to have you with us and trust you will find our menu and our service to your liking. If there is anything you'd like that you don't see on the menu, please ask, and we'll do our best to accommodate you. Meanwhile, may I offer you something from *le bar*?"

I considered offering *him* something from *le bar*—or perhaps *la pharmacie*—as he, without prompting, launched into a lively and lavishly detailed description of their best-selling wine and cheeses.

Katrine smiled at him as he spoke and asked far more questions than was necessary in my view, leaving me to suspect that she was deliberately engaging him to annoy me.

"What's your problem with Stan?" she asked as he practically floated back to the kitchen having promised to return with two goblets of water.

"I don't have a problem with Stan. I have a problem with his *enthousiasme*."

Katrine shook her head and sighed. "You're so cute," she said, squeezing my hand.

"Have you lost your mind?" I asked, withdrawing my hand as if it had been scalded. "What if someone from the unit was here?"

"Do you honestly think that's likely?"

"Likely? No. But I ran into two old boyfriends on the same day less than a week after Kevin and I moved here, so it's far from impossible."

"Fine. I don't know what the big deal is, though," Katrine continued as I scanned the faces of the staff and other patrons again to see if there were any I recognized. "It's not as if I kissed you."

Thank God.

"Seriously," she laughed when I didn't. "Can't friends show each other a little affection once in a while?"

"Sure, but around here, that means dropping off a casserole or sharing a case of beer."

Sighing, Katrine picked up the menus and handed one to me.

"So what are you in the mood for?" I asked, since I had no clue.

"I'm going to have the *salade Niçoise*, minus the anchovies."

"Me too." That decided, I closed my menu and set it off to one side. "So how's married life?"

"OK," Katrine replied as if unsure that the question was sincere. "Rob's still busy," she added. "In fact, he just started a part-time job as a desk clerk for a motel in Bloomington."

"Oh? Which one?"

"The one with the big blue sign across from the mall? Just off the expressway?"

"You mean the Lamplighter?"

"That's the one. He promised it won't interfere with school since he can study on the job, but I must admit, I have my doubts."

"I don't blame you. How often does he plan to work each week?"

"He'll pull the night shift on Mondays and Thursdays and a twelve-hour shift on Saturdays."

I couldn't imagine why Rob would take on a job with all the stress he was under. Nor could I understand why Katrine would go along with it given how little time he already spent with her.

I doubted they needed the money, since Rob earned exactly what Kevin did in wages and benefits. Not that we were rolling in the dough, but we did OK without a second income. Sure, they were both in school, but, like us, they received financial aid. On top of that, they had a smaller house, owned just one vehicle, and had no kids. If they couldn't make it without a second income under those circumstances, it was either because something from the past was putting a strain on their finances or because their ability to handle money left something to be desired. Still, it was their business, even if Katrine was now making it mine as well.

"So when is he planning to sleep?" I asked in accordance with that logic.

"In the afternoons, I guess—at least on the days he works. The motel has a lounge where employees can take their breaks and rest before and after their shifts, so he'll probably make use of that to save trips back and forth."

Katrine paused to request two *salades Niçoises*—both *sans* anchovies—and some sort of bread as Stan stopped to take our order.

"So what are you going to be doing all that time?" I asked after he had gone.

"Well, I'm hoping to get reacquainted with my violin, actually, since I prefer not to play when Rob's around. I'm also planning to gather and organize all my mom's favorite recipes in hopes of eventually putting them into a cookbook."

"Wow. You're going to be one busy woman."

Katrine nodded. "I'm also hoping you'll help me."

"I beg your pardon?"

"Now don't panic," she instructed in response to my surprise. "I'm not asking you for a huge commitment, just an hour or so a week."

"Doing what?"

"Helping me get organized and sketching out the illustrations."

"Illustrations?"

"Yes. I've seen you doodling on the score pad when we play cards, and I'd like to use some of your flowers and other doodads as accents in the book. We can work at your place if you prefer, and in return, I'm prepared to help out with the cooking, cleaning, and the kids."

I suddenly felt cut off at the proverbial pass. I'd marched into this meeting, tight as a drum, determined to reach an accord limiting the frequency of our contacts, and before I could make my move, Katrine sailed in with a plan guaranteed to do the opposite.

"So, what do you say?" she was saying now, having given me time to ponder her proposal.

"We can give it a try over J-term," I offered against my own better judgment. "If it's not working out by February, we can adjust."

Katrine blinked at me. "What the hell is J-term?"

"It's what the private schools in the area call the period in January when they all offer a handful of courses in a three-hour format. You earn the same number of credits as you would for the same class offered in a regular semester; you just have to go every day."

"And how many courses are you taking?"

"We're only allowed to take one. I chose creative writing."

"Sounds like an easy credit."

"That's what I thought. But since half of our grade derives from our oral and written reviews of other people's work, it's actually more painful than it sounds."

"Only if it's garbage—then you get to exercise your considerable wit telling people why."

"Excellent point. Way to spot the silver lining."

"Thanks," Katrine beamed. "So what do you plan to write about?"

"See for yourself," I replied, pulling a notebook form my bag and setting it on the table.

"*Obsolescence*, by Janet K. Thompson," Katrine read aloud from her angle. "Interesting title, but if that's the best you can do for a pseudonym, you might as well use your real name."

"That *is* my real name."

"Really? I always assumed it was Jacqueline."

"You were supposed to assume that."

"So where did Jackie come from?"

"My brother couldn't say Janet Kathleen when he was little, so he called me Ja-Kee."

"That's adorable."

I nodded. "Lucky for me it stuck, since I prefer it over Janet."

"Why?"

"Because my maiden name was Jackson."

"Oh, my."

"I know. Thankfully, I was already married by the time the other Janet Jackson gained any real popularity. As it was, I still got the occasional 'No, my first name ain't baby/It's Janet/Ms. Jackson if you're nasty' from Kevin."

"That's funny."

"I'm glad you think so."

"So no one put it together before that?"

"Well, my stepsisters and their friends would tease me about it back when she played Penny on *Good Times*, but our parents' divorce ended that nightmare. Go ahead and read it if you want," I offered, noticing

Katrine's eyes darting toward the paper as we spoke. "Just remember it's a rough draft."

"Your brother isn't dead," Katrine said after she had finished.

"Thank you for clearing that up for me. Although I confess, I had noticed."

"I'm sorry," she laughed. "I just assumed it was supposed to be autobiographical."

"Why?"

"I don't know. Maybe because the main character is a motherless guy named Richie—which, again, isn't much of a disguise if you're trying to conceal his identity."

"For your information, I chose Richie because it was the first name that came to mind."

"If you say so."

"Do you honestly think I'd share anything from my own life with a bunch of strangers?"

"We are still talking about you, right?"

I sighed. "Will you just stop being a smart-ass and tell me what you think? It's OK if you hate it," I added. "I won't hold it against you."

"Well, I don't hate it; it's just, well, kind of dark."

"I suppose I could brighten it up a little," I teased. "Maybe throw in a rainbow or two—or a few balloons. Unfortunately, all that cheery symbolism may keep the guy from trying to kill himself, and then we'd have no plot."

Katrine and I both laughed as Stan arrived with our food and two fresh waters.

"So how have you been?" Katrine asked when he'd left.

I didn't have to ask what she meant. "Not too bad, all things considered."

"Can we talk about it?"

"I think we *should* talk about it," I said as we sliced through the seared tuna and chilled vegetables on our respective plates. "I just don't know where to start."

"Me either," Katrine sighed. "Have you told Kevin?"

"No."

"Does that mean you don't want Rob to know?"

"That's up to you. I'm not keeping it from Kevin. I just haven't told him yet."

"Well, I haven't told Rob, in case you're wondering."

"I wasn't, but OK."

We each took a *croissette* from the basket and began to sample the so-called signature spreads that accompanied them. Basically a croissant in miniature, *croissettes* were a Les Bougies invention that—like the *Priazzo* introduced by Pizza Hut—were supposed to sound to the average American like authentic ethnic fare, even though there is no such thing as *Priazzo* in Italy, and the word *croissette* translates to "little cross" instead of "little crescent" in French.

They should have called them *bland* little crosses given their utter lack of flavor and texture, I told Katrine, who agreed. No wonder they served them with signature spreads.

"Are you sorry it happened?" she asked, with more curiosity than concern, a moment later.

"Not really."

Sighing, Katrine swept her curtain of sable waves over one shoulder and looked me in the eye. "Neither am I," she said, "But I'll be very sorry if this is the last time I see you."

"Why would it be?"

"Don't tell me you haven't considered it, Jackie."

"OK. I've considered it," I admitted, "and in some ways, it would be better that way. Then we could both pretend it never happened and get on with our lives."

"Is that what you want? To pretend it never happened, I mean?"

"Not necessarily."

It wasn't as if I could pretend it never happened if I'd wanted to. I could still feel the warmth of her skin everywhere it had touched mine and the outline of her lips everywhere she'd kissed me. I could still feel the weight of her body on top of me, the curve of her bottom in my palm as I pulled her toward me, and the shape of her nipple as it hardened against my tongue. Nothing short of global amnesia would erase those files, and, sadly, I'm not prone to head wounds.

Getting on with my life wouldn't be any easier. Even if we didn't live less than a mile from each other and Kevin and Rob were not in the same command, I would still think about Katrine and want to see her.

So, no. Avoiding Katrine would not help me forget what happened. At best, it would take away the temptation to let it happen again. And where's the fun in that?

That's right, I told myself, *willpower is meaningless if you're never tempted, and—at least in this case—the craving is as delicious as the drug.*

This is what we do—we masochists. We put our vices and other forbidden fruit just out of reach and force ourselves to resist their charms. Like a chocolate addict who buys a fresh box of truffles for a special occasion knowing it's only a matter of time before she's in the tub with the package celebrating national masking tape safety day.

"I can't even say I wouldn't want it to happen again," I heard myself confess. "I just think it would be best for everyone if it didn't."

"Which means we either agree to keep it cool, or we say good-bye."

I nodded.

"So which is it?" she asked.

"Well, as I recall, you have a cookbook to write."

"So I do," Katrine declared, grinning. "And as I recall, you have some drawings to sketch."

"Sounds to me like we're on the same page."

On the following Tuesday and every few days for the next few weeks, Katrine would arrive at the house with her backpack and a bag of groceries. Occasionally she would catch a ride with Kevin as he left the armory parking lot, but generally she walked from her house to ours via the grocery store, having taken a bus home from school.

If no one was home when she arrived, she would let herself in with the spare key that Kevin had stashed for her after coming home to find her reading on the steps one afternoon when I was running late, and she would busy herself with homework or chores before starting dinner. Sometimes she would play her violin for the kids while I cooked, but usually she would practice after dinner while Kevin or I did the dishes. I was pleased but not entirely surprised to find she was pretty good. Not that I would have known a good violinist from an excellent one, owing to my own lack of musical training; but I could tell Katrine had the skill to play professionally if the spirit ever moved her, and I envied her that option.

In addition to the obvious advantage of having a third person to share the cooking and kid detail, Katrine's presence conveyed other benefits for which I was grateful. For example, she would take messages when the phone rang without hassling me about returning the calls or prodding me to answer it myself. She would also help proofread my short stories and response essays and keep me company when Kevin was working late at the armory or studying.

If Rob was bothered by the amount of time she was spending away from home, I never heard about it. Katrine rarely mentioned him except when discussing schedules—a fact that I attributed as much to a desire to preserve her own dignity as to maintaining my sanity. Rob, for his part, never called or came looking for her, and on the rare occasions when he expended the time and effort to pick her up or drop her off himself, he accompanied her to the door only once, and then it was apparently for the purpose of conferring with Kevin on a unit matter.

This, of course, suited me just fine. We hadn't spent any time alone since the party and, thus, had yet to achieve a new "normal" since our exchange in the doorway to the spare room. Still, I wasn't sure if the man was deliberately avoiding me or if his new job and multiple unit billets were to thank for keeping him away. Either way, I was glad not to have him around pestering me and reminding me what a jerk he could be.

In accordance with the pact we'd made at Les Bougies, Katrine and I kept things cool in terms of our interactions. I couldn't tell if this was as difficult for her as it was for me; but I was glad she didn't intentionally test my will.

That is not to say my will wasn't tested. In truth, whenever she was near, I felt myself being pulled toward her as if by some invisible force, and every time she looked me in the eye for any length of time, I was reminded of how she had approached me on New Year's Eve. To my credit—and with a quantum of regret—I managed to keep these reactions to myself, and we carried on like sisters or roommates.

Although Kevin joked that coming home lately felt like entering a sorority with a day care, I wondered how he really felt about the frequency and duration of Katrine's visits. Especially when she started spending the night on the sofa rather than having one of us run her home at bedtime—or borrowing the car and bringing it back for Kevin in the morning—I worried he would find my hospitality excessive or decide that she had worn out her welcome.

"This is great," he announced without prompting one evening at the end of January as he and I did homework at the kitchen table. "Usually one of us has to tend the kids while the other hits the books. Having someone else around to put them to bed makes a nice change."

I eyed him warily. "Kevin, the kids are in bed. You put them there. Remember?"

"Yes. But only after Katrine read to them for forty-five minutes."

"True."

"And we rarely used to see each other even after the kids got to bed, because we're normally working in different rooms."

"That's because I'm usually at the computer producing my own papers rather than reading someone else's drivel."

Kevin nodded toward the pages in my hand. "That bad?"

"Worse." I sighed. "I can't believe this guy made it all the way to college without knowing the difference between object and subject pronouns."

"Must be an engineering student."

"In a creative writing class?"

"Could be spreading his wings."

"Sure—that would be my first guess."

"OK," Kevin laughed. "So maybe he figured it for an easy credit."

"Well, it won't be if I have anything to say about it."

"That's my Grammar Girl."

"So you don't mind Katrine being here so often?" I enquired as I resumed the bloodletting with my red pen.

"What's to mind? The house is clean, the food is great, and the kids are happy. Sure, I'd like to have you to myself more often, but it's not like that would be possible if she wasn't around. In fact, we've spent more time alone this month than we ever could have if she hadn't been here."

"That's true. She's been a big help."

Kevin nodded. "And best of all, she's not spreading hate and discontent at the armory."

"Shhh," I admonished, casting my glance toward the second floor where Katrine was studying. "She might hear you."

"Sorry. I just wanted you to know—it has not gone unnoticed."

"That's great, but this wasn't my doing. All I did was say yes when she asked if she could hang out here instead of sitting at her place watching Scott eat cereal."

"Well, however it happened—it's working. So thanks."

Twenty

T he transition from J-term to spring term was nearly seamless for me that year. Unlike the last—when I'd traded the daily three-hour class in January for a three-and-a-half-hour block of nothing flanked by two early morning and two late afternoon classes each day—this spring I got lucky with two late morning classes convening in consecutive slots on Tuesdays and Thursdays and a single midafternoon course every Monday, Wednesday, and Friday.

The switch to the new term was further eased by the fact that Kevin's schedule did not change. Being on quarters at the U, he would have the same courses and the same billets until the end of March when classes dismissed for spring break, which meant he was usually walking out of the house by seven in the morning and walking back in around half past four.

As a result of this odd yet welcome regularity, I found my schedule even roomier than I'd initially calculated. I had expected the elimination of a fourth class to net me about a hundred and fifty extra minutes a week and to save me untold hours of reading and writing over the course of the entire term. I had even factored in the hour or so I stood to gain by not having to cross campus to get from one building to another, as well as the fifteen or so extra minutes I'd shave off my commute by traveling after rush hour each morning and before rush hour every afternoon.

What I hadn't factored in was my improved efficiency. By working at home instead of on a chair in some busy hallway or at a table in the monastic library, I was less distracted and more relaxed. This enabled me to concentrate better and to absorb and process material more quickly. It also allowed me to outline my papers on the computer rather than by hand, thereby eliminating several hours of writing and revising, and saving countless trees.

I dedicated my extra time primarily to the kids. Although I dropped them off at day care at roughly the same time each morning as I had during previous terms, I was often able to retrieve them an hour or two earlier in the afternoon now, thereby easing my guilt over the time I spent away from them.

Farther from home, things weren't going so well. Saddam Hussein had refused to abandon his campaign to take over Kuwait, and coalition forces—comprised primarily of US, British, and Saudi troops—had begun the air assault that would ultimately lead to the ground war that would last only about one hundred hours.

Meanwhile, Katrine continued to turn up regularly in the afternoon or evening. She was even more anxious to be away from her place these days, since Scott had recently acquired a girlfriend to whom he'd extended Rob's offer of free shelter.

He'd met Liv—or the Sieve, as Katrine called her, owing to the numerous piercings adorning her face and body—outside the bus terminal downtown.

"She came west from Indiana en route to Las Vegas," Katrine had explained the day after Liv arrived, "where she'd hoped to become an exotic dancer, but she had to revise her plans when the trucker, who promised to take her to Denver, drove north instead of west out of Illinois."

"I gather this was not an issue of bad maps or faulty navigation."

"Nothing whatsoever. The guy just wanted a piece of ass and hadn't counted on her knowing geography. According to Scott, she played dumb as far as Madison, where she ditched the trucker while he was stopped for gas, and then hopped a Greyhound to the Cities, hoping to make some cash and a few friends before resuming her journey toward Sin City."

"So how on earth did she hook up with Scott?"

"She approached him in front of the hotel across the street from the bus terminal. He was walking to his car after a job interview when she approached him and asked for directions. She said she was new in town and was looking for a place to get a cup of coffee, and he offered to buy her one."

"What a guy."

"I know. The bastard won't even chip in for raisin bran at our place, but he'll buy coffee for a complete stranger. Anyway, so then over coffee, she tells him her hard-luck tale and proceeds to ask him if he knows of someplace she can stay."

"And, let me guess, he immediately thought of yours."

"You got it."

"Did he at least check with you?"

"Sure—as soon as they got there."

"You mean *in front* of her?"

Katrine nodded. "So we had no choice but to say yes."

"But you didn't even *know* her, Katrine. Don't you think Scott would have understood your not wanting some hitchhiking stranger under your roof?"

"Probably. I don't think Rob bothered to examine it from that angle. He was too busy playing gracious host."

"So you're stuck with them."

"At least until we can talk to Scott alone."

I shook my head. "I suppose the idiot thinks this is going to get him laid."

"Uh, actually, thought and *did*."

"You're kidding?"

Katrine shook her head. "They were at it practically all night."

"Good grief."

"Tell me about it. You don't know how close you came to waking up with me on your sofa this morning."

"I am going to have to get my own apartment," Katrine announced when she arrived at our place after school one week and two sleepovers later.

"Not again?" I asked, wiping my hands on the dishtowel that hung from my waistband as I met her in the living room.

"Hell yes."

"I don't understand. Are they doing this only when Rob's at work?"

"I wish."

"So how are the two of you coping when he's at home?"

Katrine set her bag at the end of the couch and followed me back to the kitchen. "Let's just say that the audio doesn't have quite the same effect on Rob that it has on me."

I cringed as Katrine mimed an erection with her hand. "Ew."

"I know! My first thought was 'Are you insane?'"

"Are you telling me you had a *second* thought?"

"Well, Rob said if we were busy ourselves, maybe I wouldn't notice what was happening in the other room. Of course, he was wrong, so after a while I told him to forget it. Then I dug out the earplugs he uses at the rifle range, which allowed me to sleep. Of course, when Rob's not home, I've got no reason to put up with that nonsense, which is why I'm here again tonight."

"Boy, those two really need to get a clue."

"I know. I'd like to give them one, but I don't know what to say."

"How about 'If you're going to keep sponging off of us, at least have the courtesy not to fuck so loud.'"

From the look on her face, I knew I was wasting my breath. Katrine wasn't any more likely to voice her dissent after hearing my two cents than she'd been before, and it really wasn't any of my business.

"So how's her job search going?" I asked instead.

"Not quite according to plan, apparently. She's been checking out her prospects with the various strip clubs in the area. Unfortunately, she's having trouble generating any interest among the local talent coordinators in her spiky black hair, pasty complexion, and electric blue nail polish—not to mention all the hoops, loops, and studs adorning her face and body."

"Well, you have to admire her pluck," I declared. "It takes a certain type of confidence to go up against Malibu Porn Star with that kind of ammunition."

"Confidence? I was thinking it was something closer to psychosis."

"Well, one often leads to the other. Does she have anything else going for her?"

"Well, she's kind of thin, but she's tall and leggy, and she has a pretty face."

"So she just needs a fake tan, a blond wig, a set of implants, and a little less metal, and she'll be on her way. Assuming, of course, she can dance."

"Oh, she can dance all right—I've seen her performing for Scott in the living room."

"I guess that explains the live audio you're hearing at bedtime."

Katrine nodded. "Although I still can't understand why she's still hanging around."

"You mean besides the free room and board?"

"Well, there is that. But she's been in town long enough to have met other people; you'd think she could have found a financially sounder, better-looking chump by now."

"Ah—but would any of them be as grateful?"

Katrine only shrugged then, and the subject did not arise again until a week later when we were preparing to work on her French econ paper.

Kevin had agreed to take the first shift with the kids that night, with the proviso that we would draft the paper quickly and then come down to put the kids to bed so he could use the office to study for the physics exam he was expecting in the morning.

"So what's new with Scott and the Sieve these days?" I asked as Katrine unpacked the notes she would use in her dictation.

"Not much," she laughed. "She's gone."

"What?"

"Gone. History. *Disparu.*"

"You are kidding."

"Nope. She left sometime Sunday morning before Scott was even out of bed."

"Ouch. How's he taking it?"

"Pretty hard, actually. He spent the next two days working his way through a bottle of gin and asking 'What's wrong with me?'"

"And did you tell him?"

"No."

"Why the hell not?"

"Because I didn't think he really expected an answer."

"Katrine. Katrine. Katrine," I said, shaking my head with each repetition. "When a guy like Scott gives you the opportunity to tell him he's a pain the ass and that his hygiene leaves a lot to be desired, you don't just let it pass."

"I had to, Jackie. I can't kick a guy when he's down."

"You don't have to kick him. You can tell him in a nice way that you find his odor and his behavior offensive."

"Yeah, right."

"You'd be doing the guy a favor, Katrine. After all, the sooner he gets a clue, the sooner he'll start taking regular showers, and the sooner he'll find someone else—and maybe a job."

"I agree. But people have to be in the right frame of mind to hear that kind of thing, and as of today, he was still in shock."

"I can't understand why; it's not as if he shouldn't have seen this coming. I mean, do women throw themselves at him so often that he can't tell when they're using him?"

"Sorry to interrupt your scholarly conversation," Kevin said as he approached the alcove, having escaped our notice as he ascended the stairs, "but I have a message for madam."

Katrine and I looked at one another.

"Are you madam, or am I?" she asked.

"Must be you," I replied. "He's never called *me* that before."

"I've never had to manage your calendar before," he informed me, handing over a small slip of paper. "You're meeting Lynette tomorrow after class."

"What? Where?"

"Rosedale. North Entrance. Two-thirty. Don't be late."

"Kevin—what the hell is going on?"

"She just called—apparently for the sixth time. She needs a new dress and would like you to help her find one."

"And?"

"And I made the date for you so you wouldn't have to take the time to call her back."

"Kevin, I am *not* going shopping tomorrow."

"Then I guess you will have to call her back after all, because she's expecting you, and it would be rude for you to stand her up."

"You're the one who made the date—you call her back."

"I don't think so."

"Then you're going shopping with her, because I have to pick the kids up at two-thirty."

"Actually, you don't *have* to pick them up until five, but since you're going to be busy, I'll pick them up at four-thirty."

"But Kevin—"

"It won't kill them to stay two extra hours," he insisted. "Some kids are in day care nine or ten hours a day, and they're none the worse for the wear."

"As far as you know."

"It's one day, Jackie. They'll be fine."

I scowled. "I love you, Kevin," I said as he headed for the stairs, "but that was a dirty trick."

"I know. Sometimes I surprise even myself. That reminds me," he added, "when's the baby shower again?"

"Why?"

"I'm thinking of taking the kids to my mom's that weekend so we won't be in your way."

"Don't worry about it. Josh's sister declared our house unsuitable for all the guests she wanted to invite and decided to have it at her place instead."

"No kidding."

"Nope. By the next day, she and her mother had taken over the entire affair and left me with nothing to do but buy a gift and show up."

"I'm sorry to hear that."

"Don't be. It freed me up for more exciting things—like painting the kitchen, watching it dry…"

"But you're still going, right?"

"Not unless you've invented a time machine."

"What?"

"It was last weekend," I explained. "In St. Anthony."

"Really? I knew your plans that day had something to do with Lyn. I just didn't realize it was for her *shower*."

"Of course you didn't," I said facetiously. "Since I so often bring a gift and dress like a nun when I'm popping out to meet a friend."

Kevin laughed. "OK. Well, make sure to wear something nice to school in the morning," he said as he headed back down the stairs, "since you're meeting one again tomorrow afternoon."

I turned to Katrine when he'd gone. "Well, I guess I'm going to the mall tomorrow."

"Looks that way."

"Were you planning to come over?"

"Why? Did you want me to come with you?"

"Are you kidding? I don't even want *me* to go with me. I was just looking for an excuse to cut things short."

"Sorry. Rob's off tomorrow, so I was planning to stay home."

"No problem," I said, prepping my fingers like a concert pianist. "We'd better get this show on the road. I have to get my ass into bed at a decent hour so I'm not a crusty bitch tomorrow."

"Well, now that we've discussed every house I've seen since January first," Lynette said the next day as I followed her across the plush mauve carpeting of yet another upscale store for mothers-to-be, "tell me what you've been up to lately."

"Writing mostly," I replied, postyawn, "and helping Katrine with hers."

"That explains why she's taken so many of my messages," Lyn observed as she read the wash and care instructions on the dress in front of us. "Does she ever go home?"

"When Rob's there. But he's gone a lot this term, and she'd rather hang out with us than sit at home alone or with his friend Scott."

"And you two don't mind having her around so much?"

"Not really. It's not as if all she does is take up space. She does all the cooking when she's over, and more than her share of the cleanup. She also runs errands, does laundry, and helps with the kids, so having her around is almost more to our benefit than hers. Besides, what kind of friend would make her sit at home alone or hang out with Scott the sponge all the time?"

"She doesn't necessarily *have* to do either. She could do something else—like get a job."

"I suppose she could, but there's no guarantee her hours would match Robs, and while I happen to see that as a prime advantage, for some reason she wants to be home when he is."

"Well, I'd like to be home when Josh is, too, but it doesn't always work out that way."

"What does this have to do with you and Josh?"

"Nothing. I'm sorry."

"Are you sure?"

Lynette sighed. "We had a fight this morning," she explained. "Josh wants me to cut short my maternity leave after the baby comes."

"How short?"

"Well, contractually I'm allowed to take up to six months and still have them hold my job, but Josh says I can only take a month, because that's all they'll pay me for."

"What about vacation time? And sick leave?"

"That *includes* vacation time and sick leave, plus ten days of actual medical leave."

"Wow. I guess I assumed you had more paid time off than that."

"Apparently so did Josh, which is why he says I'll have to work at least half time."

"That's not so bad."

"Not so bad?"

"Not as bad as full-time, I mean."

"Maybe not, but just look at my options, Jackie. To get the hours in that Josh wants me to work, I'll either have to work seven days out of fourteen and hire a sitter to stay with the baby between the time I leave for work in the afternoon and when Josh gets home in the evening, or work a twelve-hour shift every Saturday and Sunday, which lets me avoid the day care issue but keeps me from doing anything but work and sleep on weekends."

As was often the case in conversations with Lynette, I found myself torn between my personal beliefs and my desire to be supportive. Although I figured Josh was being typically miserly on the matter, I failed to see any tragedy in putting a baby in day care for what amounted to roughly three hours every other day.

"I wish I hadn't said anything," Lynette added, her eyes glazed with stifled tears. "But there I was, babbling about how nice it will be to stay home with the baby and how grateful I am to him for making it possible for us to go without my income for five months."

"So he didn't *know* you weren't getting paid for all six months?"

"Not until I opened my mouth this morning, at which point he informed me that we can't afford to go that long without my wages and still maintain a decent rate of savings."

"And what exactly constitutes decent?"

"Don't ask me. My contribution to our finances is limited to turning over my paystub every other week and buying groceries."

"Then maybe you should ask him to go over them with you," I suggested. "Maybe together you can find somewhere to cut spending so you won't have to work so much."

"He won't do that. He says having more than one bookkeeper screws things up."

"Well, as the resident accountant at our house, I won't disagree on that point. However, just because you don't manage the finances does not mean you shouldn't understand them."

"But if I'm not going to keep the books, there's no need for me to understand them."

I could tell from Lyn's tone that these words, like so many others she spoke in reference to her relationship with Josh, were not her own. When she first heard them, no doubt she was grateful; she had no interest in managing their money, and Josh's desire to run that show relieved her of any responsibility for their finances. She probably perceived Josh's willingness to tackle the job as heroic and likely never would've considered, much less minded, that he just wanted to be in charge. Likewise, she would never have expected her passivity in this area to come back and bite her in the ass.

With this in mind, I could see no point in continuing the discussion. Lyn would never push for what she wanted if doing so meant going up against Josh. Like Katrine, she preferred to avoid conflict whenever possible, no matter how much it might cost her in the long run.

"I'm sure we'll work it all out eventually," Lyn said, before I could find my own means of escaping the conversation. "Somehow we always do."

With a handful of hangers, she pointed to the fitting rooms. "I'm sorry for jumping on you about Katrine," she said as we headed that way. "I guess I'm a little jealous that she has so much time free time and that she gets to spend it with you."

"I wouldn't be too jealous if I were you. The woman shares a home and a bed with Rob."

"Good point," Lynette laughed. "So what's their place like, by the way?"

"It's your average fifties-era bungalow—at least until you factor in Rob's signature décor, which can best be described as Neo-Egotistical or Contemporary Self-Obsessed."

"Are you serious?"

"Oh, quite. You know how some guys have a place in their house where they display their military memorabilia and service honors?"

"Yeah. Josh calls it an 'I Love Me' wall."

"Right—well, Rob has taken the concept to a new level. For example, on one wall he's mounted not only the framed originals of his four promotion warrants, but also ten engraved plaques commemorating his dates of service at virtually every location since boot camp—including some bullshit school that lasted only a week. And that's just the beginning," I continued as we stopped before the row of fitting rooms. "His Meritorious Masts—you know those certificates of recognition they print up and frame in red plastic whenever some jarhead manages to piss for six months without missing the toilet bowl? Well, he's got one of them babies on practically every flat surface in the place."

Grimacing, Lynette handed over her purse, which I hung over my own shoulder. "That sounds obnoxious."

"Trust me, it's worse. In fact, the place is a virtual shrine. He's even got pictures. There's Rob in uniform doing this and Rob in uniform doing that. He's even got an eight-by-ten glossy of himself shaking hands with Casper

Weinberger. I'm telling you, it's got to be embarrassing for Katrine to ride along on an ego trip like that."

"How do you know it wasn't her idea?"

"Please, Lyn. Even the most devoted wife wouldn't go that far."

"I suppose." Lynette stepped out of the stall and over to the three-way mirror. "So, what do you think?"

"*Coming Attractions?*" I read from the tags hanging from her elbow. "Are they kidding? *Heavy Burden* would be more appropriate, as would *Interminable Financial Liability.*"

"Or in my case, *Wide Load.*"

Shrugging, I turned the tag over in my hand.

"Don't even bother, Jackie. At this point, price cannot be an issue. I shouldn't have put it off so long, but I didn't want to buy anything too early in case I put on more weight than I expected—which is good, because I have."

"I get that," I replied as Lynette smoothed the dress over her protruding belly and smiled. "And normally, I'd say go for it—if only to irritate Josh. But do you have any idea how many times you'll have to wear this in order to make the cost seem even remotely reasonable?"

"No. But I'm sure I'll get plenty of use out of it."

"With less than five weeks before you deliver?"

"I don't necessarily mean with this pregnancy, Jackie. For heaven's sake, we're going to have more kids. At least four if everything goes according to plan."

"*Four?*"

"Sure. You know what they say: the more the merrier."

"I hate to tell you this, but as the more experienced of us two, I must point out that kids are even less cost-effective than women's apparel."

"I don't care. The whole reason I agreed to wait so long to have kids was because Josh said that way I could have as many as I wanted. Besides, my mom is one of fifteen—and her family was poor."

"Maybe they wouldn't have been poor if they hadn't had so many kids."

"Maybe they didn't mind."

"Maybe not. But you have to wonder how your grandmother did it. I mean, my two keep me busy enough; I can't imagine what it would be like with one more, much less thirteen."

"It wouldn't be that bad. After all, by the time the fifth one came along, the first two would be old enough to help out with the others, and by the time the twelfth one came along, the eldest would be old enough to babysit."

"So the eldest gets stuck caring for a bunch of kids just because his or her parents wanted a big family. How nice for him—or her."

"Why do you always have to see the negative in everything? Why can't you focus on the positive?"

"Because there are few positives to having that many kids—especially for the mother. I mean, do you realize that to have fifteen children, your grandmother had to spend a hundred and thirty-five months of her life pregnant? That's twelve years. Even if you're only sick for the first three months, that's still four straight years of nausea and vomiting."

"Well, fortunately I haven't had to deal with that."

Leaving the dresses inside, Lynette stepped out of the stall again and retrieved her purse from my shoulder. "Well, I guess I'm ready to go."

"But you haven't bought anything."

"I know."

"Do you want to try different store? I think there's another one up on the third floor."

"No, thanks. I'm tired, and my feet hurt. Besides, you probably have studying to do."

"I can do it later."

"That's OK."

"Come on, Lyn. Let's try one more store—and I promise to keep my mouth shut this time."

"Really, Jackie. It's OK."

"But you said you needed to find a dress before next Saturday."

"Don't worry about it. I'll try again on the way to my doctor's appointment tomorrow morning." Sighing, Lynette eased herself down onto a bench outside the store. "You know, if this kid came a little early, I'd have a great excuse to skip the wedding altogether."

"That's true. Want me to run over to the pharmacy and grab you some castor oil? That's how my midwives finally got Lucy moving, remember?"

"Thanks, but waiting doesn't bother me all that much." Lynette added, "I just have to remind myself that babies are much easier to take care of when they're on the inside."

I forced a smile, wishing she would turn away so I could roll my eyes behind her back.

"OK, well, should we grab something to eat before we part company?" I asked, in hopes of making amends for running off at the mouth. "My treat?"

"I guess I wouldn't mind trying that new baked potato place we saw on the lower level. I could definitely go for some comfort food."

"Your wish is my command."

"So did you ever get around to starting your feminist intervention?" Lynette inquired, perking up a bit at the promise of carbohydrates as we headed for the escalator.

"Yeah. A group of us went to see *A...My Name is Alice* at the Ordway last month."

"Oh?"

"It's a musical revue," I explained when Lyn showed no sign of recognition, "comprised of various comedic skits and musical numbers. They all relate to the status of women in society and the everyday challenges we face."

"Sounds appropriate for the task. How was it?"

"The play itself was wonderful. It made you both think and laugh at the same time. I would have invited you," I added abruptly, "but we got the tickets on such short notice that I didn't have a chance to ask if you were available."

That wasn't strictly true. In fact, I had several days in which to call Lyn and invite her to join us. The problem was, as I told Quinn at the box office, I knew she wouldn't have enjoyed it even if she had been willing to risk Josh's disapproval by spending eighteen bucks for a ticket.

"It's OK," Lyn said as if she'd read my mind. "I probably wouldn't have accepted anyway. These days, I don't dare spend money on tickets to the dollar theater—never mind the Ordway."

That was about the response I expected, and it occurred to me as I walked to my car after escorting Lynette to hers that she needed the intervention as much if not more than Katrine did. At least Katrine didn't have to ask Rob for money anymore or take a ration of shit from him every time a bit of food passed through her lips. Maybe she didn't have much more say than Lyn about the management of their money, but at least she could buy a new pair of shoes when she wanted them without fear of violating some draconian financial plan.

Twenty-one

"What's wrong?" Tyler asked amid the engine sounds he was making as he drove a plastic building block like a truck along the top of my shin.

I was sitting on the living room floor with Lucy and her toys between my outstretched legs when he'd apparently decided to take the block off-road via my jeans. I'd been there since getting home from school a half an hour earlier, wondering how I would manage to finish my midterm research project with Kevin out of town.

It was now March—pistol team season—and he'd failed to mention the competition that required him to be in Iowa over the weekend, and his revelation just before he left that morning had left me too pissed off to speak, much less think clearly enough to make alternate plans before leaving for school. Now, with my anger having subsided and my senses having returned, I'd decided to sit down, take stock of the situation, and try to find a solution.

"Nothing," I replied, realizing only upon hearing his question how long I'd been silently pondering my predicament. "Mommy was just thinking about school."

"What about it?"

I smiled as he continued to drive the block over and around the various obstacles on the carpet. He didn't really want to know what I was thinking about, I knew—although I didn't doubt that he could understand if I told him. He just knew what usually came next when this type of conversation took place between me and Kevin and, like his mother, had learned to fill the void when a room had gone too quiet for his comfort.

"How come Maggie never comes over anymore?" he wondered before I could answer. "Is she mad at you?"

That's it, I thought as a solution suddenly sprang to mind. *I'll hire a sitter.*

It sounded extravagant and would only give me about six or seven hours after factoring in meals and other interruptions, but if I worked for a while after the kids went to bed that night, I just might be in a position to put on the finishing touches after Kevin got home on Sunday.

"No, she isn't mad at me," I laughed. "We just haven't needed her help for a while. Watch Lucy for me for a minute, OK?" I added, simultaneously patting Tyler's back and kissing Lucy's head as I rose from the floor. "I'll be right back."

It's not a perfect plan, I admitted as I walked over to the kitchen. Sitters aren't easy to find at the last minute—particularly if one hasn't called them lately—and Kevin might have his own work to do on Sunday if he decides to goof off with the team instead of studying when they're not shooting. *I guess I'll just burn that bridge when I get there,* I decided, as I picked up the phone and listened for the dial tone.

"Jackie?"

"Yeah?"

"It's Katrine."

"Yes. I recognize the voice."

"It didn't even ring."

"I noticed."

"Are you still mad?"

"I was never mad."

"Liar."

"Katrine, it was *Scrabble*."

"But you take it very seriously."

"Would you mind getting to the point?"

"Why? What are you doing?"

"Undergoing an inquisition. What are *you* doing?"

"You *are* still mad."

"No—I'm kidding. Now what did you want?"

"I'm just wondering what you're doing this weekend."

"Before or after my date with Peter Jennings?"

"Boy, you're really in a weird mood."

"I'm always in a weird mood," I snapped, turning to keep half an eye on the kids. "Now will you get on with it? My clothes are coming back in style."

"OK. I'm just wondering if you have any plans for the weekend."

"Of course I don't have plans. But Kevin sure does."

"Kevin? Isn't he on his way to Iowa with the pistol team?"

"That's right! No wonder he didn't show up for dinner."

"Jackie, are you OK? You're acting pretty strange—I mean, even for you."

"Sorry. It's just that Mr. Wonderful didn't tell me until this morning that he was leaving today, and I've got this major project due on Monday that, with him gone, I probably can't finish unless I can find a babysitter—which I probably won't since it's already Friday. Of course, with my luck, even if I *do* manage to find a sitter, the power will probably go out or my computer will crash, and I'll be stuck typing the paper manually by candlelight while Lucy pukes all over my presentation notes and Tyler paints the furniture with toothpaste."

"Whoa there," Katrine instructed. "I think someone needs to stop and take a breath."

"Katrine, I don't have time to take a breath. I need to find a sitter."

"Well, then, mission accomplished. Now, I can't promise there won't be a power failure or a computer malfunction, and I can't type—as you well know—but I can hold a candle, and I'm more than willing to help with the kids, the house, your project, and even Kevin's punishment, if you so desire—provided you supply the food, shelter, and companionship I was seeking when I picked up the phone to call you a few minutes ago."

"I don't know, Katrine. I know I make it all sound *incredibly* attractive, but are you sure you want to do this?"

"Why not? Rob's going to be gone all weekend anyway."

"That's right," I mused. In addition to being pistol team season, spring was also Field Training Exercise—or FTX—season, and this weekend featured the freshman component that Kevin had said would prove crucial to Rob's ability to redeem himself with the NROTC staff.

"So are we on?" Katrine prodded.

"If you're sure you don't mind."

"Then it's settled. I'll be over in five minutes."

"Five minutes?"

"Yeah—I'll have Rob drop me off on his way to the armory."

I looked at the clock. "You mean he hasn't left yet?"

"No. He's waiting for me to hang up the phone."

"Then do it!"

"Relax, Jackie. It's just the freshman Field Training Exercises. What's the big deal?"

"*It* is a big deal, Katrine. If he's not at the armory when they leave for the field, they're going to leave without him and hit him with another UA."

"Another what?"

"Never mind," I winced, realizing I'd already said too much. "Just hurry up; Rob cannot miss that bus."

Even without the Scrabble rematch—which I had consented to playing when Tyler went to bed and which Katrine had agreed to call a draw if no one had won by the time Lucy fell asleep—we would have accomplished little that evening. For less than an hour after I'd put her down, Lucy launched into screaming fit that, combined with an otherwise unexplained fever, made me suspect an ear infection.

Setting aside my project, which Katrine and I had been working on at the kitchen table, I changed Lucy's diaper and brought her into the living room where I could comfort her as we waited for the pain reliever to take effect.

As I settled into my chair, Katrine approached the stereo and tuned it to a classical station.

"What did you do that for?" I asked.

"I thought the soothing music might help put her to sleep."

"It's more likely to bore her death. Now do me a favor and put it back on ninety-seven. This kid likes rock."

"Oh, hush. Let's just try it for a little while."

I scowled. "You wouldn't be so bold if I didn't have an infant on my lap."

"You're probably right." Without remorse, Katrine sat down on the couch and tucked her heels up against her rump. "You really like being a mom, don't you?" she asked, grabbing a throw pillow and hugging it to her front.

"Yeah, I do."

"Did you always want kids?"

I nodded. "Never imagined adult life without them. My friends all thought I was nuts, but I always planned to have two or three."

"I guess that means you and Kevin have a bit more work to do."

"Not really. I've scaled things back somewhat since we got married."

"How come?"

"Well, Kevin never actively *wanted* kids himself. He figured his dad had done enough reproducing for the two of them and his eight siblings *combined*."

"*Eight siblings?*"

"Four brothers and four sisters, to be exact."

"Jeez—that poor woman."

"Women, actually—there were three."

"Not at the same time, I hope."

"No—although there was a bit of an overlap with the fifth kid, whom Dad had with his second wife, and the sixth, whom he had with his third; and as I recall, the conception of the fourth had something to do with his divorce from the first."

"Say what?"

"In other words, Marla got pregnant with Karla while Faye was still pregnant with Davy, and it was Faye's pregnancy with Julie that caused John to leave Ronna."

"Holy cow—how do you keep all that straight?"

"With my highly developed visual memory and detailed diagrams," I laughed. "Anyway, that whole mess apparently dampened Kevin's desire to procreate."

"I would imagine. Were you disappointed?"

"Of course. But I wasn't about to force the issue—if you'll pardon the pun. So we talked it over and decided on one."

"OK, so how did you wind up with two?"

I smiled at Lucy. "Let's just call her a bonus."

"For what?"

"For waiting so patiently for Kevin to schedule his vasectomy."

"I don't follow."

"Turns out, I was already pregnant with her when Kevin went in for his surgery. We didn't know it at the time, but once we found out, I had a pretty good time saying, 'Apparently you can get pregnant after sterilization surgery' to everyone we know who'd had one and watching their eyes widen in fear."

"I can imagine."

"So what about you?" I asked. "Are you planning to have kids?"

"No—although everyone seems to think I should. I don't mean to complain, but ever since we got married, it seems like all anyone, including my mother, wants to talk about is when Rob and I are going to start a family—which is ridiculous since she knows we're both in school, and she didn't think I should have gotten married in the first place. Then, when I tell them I'm not planning to have kids, they act like I'm selfish, crazy, or from another planet."

"I know exactly what you mean. My friend Stacey back in South Carolina used to get that kind of crap all the time. The worst of it came from the wife of one of the corporals in Kevin's command, who liked to say, 'I can't imagine never having kids. In fact, I don't think you can be a *real woman* until you've had a child.' When I would hear that, it was all I could do not to slap her ignorant face."

"I don't blame you. I mean, if she wants to define herself by her fertility, that's fine. But who is she to tell your friend—or anyone else—that she's nothing if she doesn't have children?"

I smiled as the words passed through Katrine's lips. This was the Katrine I'd met in October, fallen in love with in December, and come to know only in recent weeks. Thoughtful and articulate—this was the Katrine I found hardest to resist. More confident than the one I wanted to protect and more clever than the one I wanted to save, this Katrine had stolen my heart and made me wonder what might have happened if I'd run into her before I met Kevin.

"Well, if I knew I would enjoy it as much as you do," she was saying now, "I might not be so happy to rule it out."

"There's nothing wrong with not wanting children, Katrine. Some people simply aren't cut out for it. In fact, I've always felt that most of our social problems would cease to exist if more people recognized their own limitations and simply chose not to reproduce."

"I wish more people felt that way—and that those who didn't would keep it to themselves."

"Me, too. But failing that, you can only live your life as you see fit and tell anyone who tries to make you do otherwise to kiss your ass."

"That would be a whole lot easier if Rob wasn't one of them."

"I can see how that could make things a bit tricky. Didn't you two discuss this when you were dating?"

"No. I guess he assumed I wanted kids like everybody else. But at least he doesn't hassle me about it. In fact, the only reason I know he wants kids is that he talks about having them now and then, and how we'll raise them, and where."

"Those are some pretty strong indications the guy wants to be a father," I admitted. "Has he mentioned how many he'd like to have?" I asked for lack of anything better to say. Although I wasn't much interested in the procreative ambitions of Sergeant Robinson Copeland, neither did I want to jettison the subject until Katrine was ready to quit it herself.

"Not really. He's more interested in quality than quantity. I suspect that's because he's one of six kids from a family that never seemed to have enough of anything to go around. He doesn't want his own kids to live that way— where every day is a struggle, and your own parents and siblings can't be trusted to have your back because they're too busy trying to stab you in it."

As I listened to her, I realized Katrine was painting a different picture of Rob's childhood than he had painted for me last December. I'd gotten the impression from our conversation then that he came from a family that shared a "sink or swim together" culture where they all pitched in and did their share out of mutual love and respect. Katrine's version, however, made it sound as if Rob's family struggled on more than just the financial front and was characterized by envy and mistrust. This made me wonder to which of us Rob had lied—and why.

"One thing is for sure," Katrine was saying as I returned to our conversation, "if I do have kids, I'm *not* going to follow in my parents' footsteps. I am going to do *everything* completely different."

I laughed. "Everyone says that."

"Everybody?"

"Well, maybe not *everybody*," I admitted. "But close. And even those who don't say it often feel that way."

"How do you know?"

"Well, have you ever heard anyone say, 'My parents were awesome! When I have kids, I'm going to everything just like they did?'"

"No."

"I rest my case."

Katrine laughed. "So what about you?" she asked. "What are you going to do differently?"

"Hopefully, not die."

I regretted the words the moment they left my mouth and I saw Katrine's face drain of color.

"I'm so sorry," she said with horror. "That was an incredibly stupid thing for me to ask."

"Don't be silly. It was perfectly reasonable given the context."

"Really, Jackie. It was thoughtless of me and I apologize."

"I'm the one who should apologize. I should have just answered you, instead of being a wiseass. I'm sorry if I made you feel bad."

"You didn't—really. I just feel an idiot for not thinking before opening my trap."

"It's OK, Katrine. Honestly."

"I imagine you miss her," she suggested after a moment. "As frustrating as mine can be, I still can't imagine life without her."

"I don't miss her so much as I miss *the idea* of her."

"Do you think your life would have been better if she hadn't passed away?"

"I think it would have been different if she hadn't died, but I don't think it would have been better. Knowing my dad, they wouldn't have stayed together very long, and I still would have grown up in a single parent home. And since my mom had no skills or education, we still would have been poor—unless she remarried someone very different. And since my dad definitely would have remarried, if not Ricky's mom, then someone of equally sound mind and morals, there still would have been stepmothers, stepsiblings, and all the drama that comes with them. I may not have moved around as much, since once you're in public housing, you can essentially stay forever, but that may not have worked to my advantage either."

"Are you ever angry that things didn't turn out differently for you?"

"I used to be. Nowadays, I just feel adrift—like I don't know what I'm doing and there's no one there to guide or advise me and make sure I'm doing things right."

"I'd never guess you felt that way. You always seem to know exactly what you're doing."

"Trust me—it's an act."

I stood by Lucy's crib for a while after laying her down again in the playroom. Once satisfied she was OK, I went to the kitchen to pour myself a drink before heading to the living room to await Katrine, who had ducked into the bathroom with her overnight bag.

She finally appeared in a pair of flannel pajamas. Approaching the shelves by the stairs, she pulled one of my yearbooks from its spot and started flipping through the pages.

"Hey, that's you!" she said, pointing to a photo of me in my volleyball uniform.

"That's me."

"Most Valuable Server—Janet Jackson," she read—with a trace of laughter—from the list of honors in the side bar. "Not bad."

"Even if the hair was?"

Katrine studied the sun-bleached mullet gracing my head and frowned. "How come you're pictured with more than one team?" she asked upon spotting my unfortunately coiffed head with another group on the next page.

"I was officially on the junior varsity team that year, but since I was a sophomore at the time, I could also play with the tenth graders—which I did whenever they fell behind and needed a couple aces to catch them up."

"Is that legal?"

"It is as long as I didn't play in more than three games in one night."

"I see. And is the Quinn standing with you and the tenth-graders the same one who went to the play with us?"

"It is."

"Wow. She has really changed."

Haven't we all? I mused, as Katrine considered the page more closely.

"So how long have you known her?"

"Since middle school. I was the new girl, as usual, and she was the geek with four eyes and braces who got stuck with me as a lab partner. I'd seen her around school before but hadn't spoken to her until we wound up in the same science class. After that, we became inseparable."

"So you two used to be best friends."

I nodded. "And we had such a blast—biking, skating, babysitting, and shopping. She was so smart and up to then the funniest person I'd ever known. We used to take these marathon walks around the neighborhood—from one end of the development to the other and back—and talk our heads off. We could amuse ourselves for hours dissecting movies and books, parodying our classmates, impersonating celebrities, and inventing elaborate plans for what our lives would be like in the future. To see her now, I bet you'd never guess she once aspired to move to South America to raise llamas."

"Llamas? Where did that come from?"

"Beats me. She was always a little eccentric—especially about her hair. She hated to wash it in the shower—apparently shampoo and conditioner irritated her skin. So about every Saturday, she would lie down on the counter like a little kid and have me wash it for her in the sink. She also had a thing about breakfast. She wasn't picky about what she ate the rest of the day, but breakfast had to be hot and fresh. Unfortunately, since she'd never taken home ec and her parents didn't have time to cook in the morning, she'd have to settle for a bagel or toast—unless, of course, I happened to be around to make her something else."

"Why didn't you just teach her to cook?"

"I tried, but she was the epitome of hopeless."

"That is so sad."

"Not for me. Thanks to her, I got to eat something besides oatmeal or farina for breakfast."

"Like what?"

"It depended on her mood and what was in the fridge. If her parents had been shopping lately, I might whip up a couple omelets, some eggs Benedict, or waffles and hash browns, but generally she was happy with French toast, crepes, or scrambled eggs."

"Definitely not a cornflakes girl, then."

"Not by *any* stretch of the imagination. She would sooner have starved than eaten a bowl of cold cereal. In fact, she once walked to my house in the rain carrying an egg and a baggy of flour and sugar so I could make crepes, because they'd run out of bread and bagels at her place."

"I guess it's a good thing you lived so close."

"True. But I knew I'd eventually have to move away, so for her birthday one year, I gave her a makeover and told her to marry a chef."

"Good strategy. I hope she was as good to you as you were to her."

"She never cooked for me or washed my hair, but she always made me feel like the coolest thing going. She used to say I was the most creative person she knew and that I had more style and sense than any of the *bourgeois* brats at our school. Even though she lived in a big colonial on a cul-de-sac up the road from our subsidized apartment, she never let class be an issue and would immediately blast anyone who tried to make it one."

"So how come you don't get together more often?"

"We had a falling-out the summer before our senior year when I lost my virginity to her cousin. He didn't exactly have my consent, if you know what I mean, and she didn't believe me when I told her that."

"Oh my God, Jackie. That must have been terrible for you."

"It wasn't easy, that's for sure. But we worked it out."

"That's great, but I wasn't talking about you and Quinn. I was referring to the part about the rape."

It startled me to hear her call it that, although I knew that's what it was. I guess even that many years later, it still wasn't something I was comfortable talking about, or I wouldn't have characterized it as losing my virginity in the first place.

"I'm sorry," Katrine said, replacing the yearbook and joining me on the floor in front of the couch. "I'm sorry you had to go through that, and I'm sorry your friend didn't stand by you."

"Well, Sean was family, and sometimes people find it hard to be objective."

"I guess."

"In any event," I added brightly, "we've moved past it."

"But you're not as close."

"No, and I haven't really been that close to anyone since."

"What about Lynette?"

"Lynette and I have known each other a long time, and we've had a lot of fun over the years, but we've never shared the variety of interests or had the creative energy that I did with Quinn. Don't get me wrong, I love Lyn. But we don't seem to get each other lately, and I'm not sure I want to bother trying to force it anymore."

"I thought things seemed weird between you two at the Halloween party. I just didn't know either of you well enough to be sure—or to put my finger on what it was."

"I see. And how exactly did you know that?"

Katrine shrugged. "Maybe I'm psychic."

"Perhaps," I allowed, regarding her with amusement. "'O, Persephone,'" I quoted. "'Innocent of the underworld/How did it become your lot/To bear prophesies which can self-fulfill/And a soul which, sadly, cannot.'"

"What was that?"

"Just a bit of verse."

"I figured that. Whose is it?"

"Mine."

"I didn't know you wrote poetry."

"Well, now you do."

"Is there more?"

I nodded. "Unfortunately," I said, gesturing for Katrine to rise. "I have a paper to write."

"I thought we were on a break."

"How can we be on break when we haven't even started?"

"Good question," Katrine said as she grudgingly started to follow. "Maybe we should ponder that for a while."

"Actually, I don't think we're going to be pondering anything for a while," I groaned as I heard Lucy's cries coming from down the hall.

Katrine cringed. "Sorry."

"Don't be. That's what I get for running off at the mouth instead of working."

Twenty-two

The next time I heard Lucy crying was at six forty-five the next morning. Fearing her wails would wake the neighbors, their descendants, and all their dead ancestors, I instinctively flung back the covers, disentangled myself from Katrine, and raced to the crib.

I reached full consciousness only upon returning to the living room with a freshly diapered baby and a bottle of pediatric electrolytes, having nearly tripped on Katrine's ankles as she rolled over on the pallet we'd shared on the floor in front of the couch. Alarmed by the sight of her sleeping form and the memory of having awakened next to her, I carried Lucy to the recliner, where I gave her the fluids and frantically reviewed the events of the last few hours.

I remembered Lucy waking up just as we were making our way up the stairs, and running to the playroom to pick her up before her cries could disturb Tyler, who had insisted on crashing in a sleeping bag next to the crib for the night. "Thank goodness he's a heavy sleeper," I had said to Katrine after stepping over him to retrieve the baby. "Or we'd be entertaining him until oh-Christ-hundred this morning."

I recalled nearly losing at Scrabble again as we waited for the next dose of acetaminophen to take effect and calling it a draw when Lucy finally went back to sleep. "What do you say we get some rest, too," I had suggested upon returning to the kitchen where Katrine was reading. "We can hit the project full-bore in the morning."

"Sounds good to me," she had replied through a yawn as she started to follow me toward the stairs. "I'm bushed."

I hadn't expected that. I had assumed she'd pull some bedding from the closet and hit the sofa like she usually did when she stayed over. Of course, I had no reason to assume this since she'd yet to spend the night when Kevin was away, but neither did I have reason to expect things to be different just because he wasn't home.

"Why don't we stay down here," I suggested, believing the living room would prove less conducive to misconduct than my bedroom. "I'd like to be within earshot of the kids, so go ahead and make up your bed on the sofa, and I'll grab some bedding from the closet upstairs, and take the floor."

"I can't sleep on the couch and stick you with the floor."

"Then I guess we're both headed for the floor, since there isn't room for two on the couch."

"Fine," Katrine had said, heading for the closet. "You go get the pillows."

With a mock salute, I had done as Katrine instructed, shutting down the computer and the lights upstairs before returning to the living room to find her fashioning a pallet for two on the floor. Rather than waging a protest, I'd shut off the lights and crawled into the empty side of the pallet, vowing to keep my hands—and every other body part—to myself.

That's where the memory reel ended, I realized, as I raised Lucy to my shoulder for a burp. Other than the "good nights" we had mumbled to each other as I pulled up my covers and rolled over to face the edge of the pallet, we had not even spoken after the lights went out. At what point Katrine had curled up against me, I wasn't sure. Although I recalled a pleasing warmth radiating along my side during the night, I had not paused to consider its source. In fact, it was only after I'd woken up with Katrine's arm around my waist that I had a clue as to the source of the comfort in which I'd slept.

Watching her now as she shifted in her sleep, I could again feel that warmth against my skin. Like the events of New Year's Eve, the sensation had been burned into me like a brand—a sort of virtual memento I would keep and privately revisit again and again.

Accepting this, I turned my attention to Lucy, who was suddenly and vehemently opposed to being held. It occurred to me as I struggled to keep her on my lap that her fever had broken. She was now hungry for something besides water and ready to make up for lost time.

Relieved by my review of the preceding hours and Lucy's obvious improvement—and not wanting to wake Katrine as a result thereof—I took the baby, her toys, a bottle, and her infant seat upstairs. Four trips later—the first three with Lucy sucking her bottle while tucked inside my arm—I'd carried the swing, the jumper, the playpen, and various toys into my room and cordoned it off with the safety gate we kept at the top of the stairs. Exhausted but determined, I put Lucy in her seat and fed her some mashed banana, and then gave her a bottle and sat down to work on my project for however long the fates and the education fairies would allow.

Despite numerous adjustments to Lucy's location—seat, swing, jumper, playpen; seat, swing, jumper, playpen—I accomplished nearly two hours of work in the three hours before Tyler woke up. He'd apparently walked through the house and up the stairs—after using the bathroom, of course—to find me and sternly request a bowl of oatmeal. I tried bribing him with Kevin's strawberry frosted toaster tarts if he would help amuse Lucy upstairs and wait to have oatmeal tomorrow, but the boy was in no mood to negotiate.

I guess it's time for Katrine to wake up anyway, I figured, knowing we'd never pull off a hot breakfast without disturbing her. *We've got work to do.*

Having expected to wake her, I was surprised to find our bedding folded and stacked on the couch as I cleared the stairway.

"Katrine?" I called upon finding an empty kitchen.

"She's in the bathroom," Tyler informed me, pointing to the closed door in the hallway.

"Ah."

That mystery solved, I pulled out a pan, the measuring cups, and the wooden spoon as Tyler assembled the milk, the sugar, and the carton of oats I needed to fill his breakfast order. Then Tyler set out four bowls and spoons as I worked my magic at the stove.

Katrine wandered out to the kitchen exactly three minutes after I had sat down.

"Want some oatmeal?" I offered, raising a spoonful from Lucy's bowl as Katrine sat down across from me at the table.

"No thanks."

"Are you sure? It'll cure what ails ya."

"Oatmeal *is* what ails me," Katrine replied with a patient look at Tyler.

"What did you do?" I inquired of him, half-smiling.

"I just *ast* her to make me some," he explained, matter-of-factly gesturing with his free hand, "'cause I thought you were still sleeping."

"But wasn't *she* still sleeping?"

Tyler nodded. "That's why I *ast* her really *quiet*."

I shook my head and grinned apologetically at Katrine.

"Don't worry about it," she replied. "It was actually kind of funny."

"I'm glad you think so."

Tyler laughed with us as he continued to eat his breakfast.

"So this person you mentioned in the verse you quoted last night," Katrine said, leaning her elbow on the table and resting her jaw in her palm, "what did you call her?"

"Persephone. She was Greek goddess of the underworld."

"I don't think I've heard of her."

"That's understandable. She's not as widely known as the other goddesses, but like Artemis, goddess of the moon; Athena, goddess of wisdom; and Aphrodite, goddess of love and beauty, she was a daughter of Zeus. Her mother was Demeter, goddess of fertility, who—according to Jungian theorist Jean Shinoda Bolen—represents that part of a woman that wants to nurture and care for others and whose influence keeps us from killing our offspring—even when they drive us to the edge of madness."

Tyler laughed as I looked meaningfully from him to Lucy and back again.

"Anyway," I continued as I placed a spoonful of oatmeal in Lucy's mouth, "Persephone was taken from her mother by Hades—by clandestine arrangement with Zeus—to be his wife and queen of the underworld. Demeter was so angry and depressed after Persephone disappeared that she brought a terrible famine upon the earth that threatened the people until Persephone was found and returned. According to Dr. Bolen, the myth symbolizes the loss of purpose many mothers feel when their children grow up and no longer need them."

"What exactly did Demeter have against Hades?"

"Nothing. She just couldn't go on without her daughter. Anyway, as the story goes, for the good of humankind, Zeus arranged for the messenger god, Hermes, to locate Persephone and return her to Demeter with whom she could stay provided she hadn't eaten anything while in the underworld. Unfortunately—at least from Demeter's point of view—Persephone had eaten some pomegranate seeds and thus was required to spend part of each year with Hades."

"Did she want to?"

"One would assume so, since she ate the seeds. Then again, she initially denied eating them, so at least part of her wanted to go home, even if another part wanted to stay. She had reached a point, like all women do, where she had to start making her own decisions, and she didn't find it particularly comfortable. So, rather than openly choose her fate and risk displeasing someone, she allowed fate to choose for her. Thus, according to Bolen, Persephone represents the woman, or that part of her, that is receptive, compliant, passive, and adaptive. Persephone women, as she calls the archetype, tend to be sensitive individuals who are highly attuned to what others think and feel and who generally behave—at least outwardly—according to what others expect of them, which can give the impression that they're psychic or have a sixth sense."

"So *that's* what prompted you to think of her when I joked about being psychic last night."

"Correct."

Katrine seemed so comfortable with this aspect of the Persephone archetype that I didn't have the heart to say more. I saw no point to explaining, for example, that while their compliant nature may endear Persephone women to others in their orbit, it can be disastrous for them personally since power once relinquished is difficult to regain. Nor did I see the point in telling her that, even without someone breathing down their necks, Persephone women have trouble asserting themselves, making choices, and telling the truth, because they don't want to upset anyone or create controversy. No doubt she could see parallels between herself and Persephone already, and some things, I decided, were better left unsaid.

"Aren't you glad you asked?" I suggested instead.

"Of course," she said between yawns, "and I'll be even gladder after I've had caffeine."

Katrine took over with the kids as soon as she'd had her fix. She wasn't exactly a natural, owing, no doubt, to her lack of younger siblings and cousins and her dearth of babysitting experience. Still, she kept them amused by singing songs, reading stories, doing puzzles, building towers out of plastic dishes, and fashioning forts from blankets and furniture.

Thanks to her efforts—which also included taking them out to buy to ingredients for the lunch she and Tyler subsequently made—I managed to churn out a rough draft by dinnertime.

That evening, I performed the kids' usual bedtime rituals—hoping throughout that none would later need repeating—then sat down in the kitchen to review my work, unaware that Katrine had slipped outside for some fresh air.

A gentle "shhh" barely stemmed my panicked expletives when the wanderer unexpectedly opened the kitchen door a few minutes later.

"Sorry," Katrine offered. "I assumed you heard me on the porch."

Watching her drop solemnly into a chair, I capped my pen and poured two fresh cups of lukewarm coffee. "You don't look very happy."

"I'm just feeling a little overwhelmed."

"Considering you've been trapped here for nearly thirty hours, I'm not surprised."

"Oh, it's not that. I'm actually going to miss all this."

"You're either high or critically sleep deprived," I declared as I surveyed my disheveled domain, "because *no one* in their right mind would miss this."

"It may not be neat, but at least it feels like a home. My place feels more like a morgue or a museum."

"Have you considered redecorating?"

"You mean get rid of Rob's shit?"

"Well, I wouldn't necessarily toss it, but you could certainly store some of it."

Katrine shook her head. "Rob would kill me—which would be bliss compared to what I'd have to endure if he didn't. The one time I suggested we display his awards and other stuff in the spare room, I got a ten-minute lecture on pride and personal achievement. God only knows how long I'd suffer for shoving them in a closet."

"If I were you, just long enough to tape his mouth shut and pack my bags."

"Actually, he'd probably pack them for me."

"Either way, you win. Sorry," I added as Katrine grimaced. "I slipped."

Irked yet amused, she crossed her arms atop the table. "So how did you get so lucky?"

"In what respect?"

"In every respect. I mean, you have everything."

"True—but I got it all secondhand."

"You know what I mean. You've got brains, style, lots of friends, the kids you always wanted, and a man who not only loves you but actually listens to what you have to say."

"Well, I pay him for that, so it doesn't really count."

"Oh, is that how it works?" Katrine asked sharply. Reaching into her pocket, she withdrew a ten-dollar bill and tossed it on my lap.

Chastened, I picked it up and laid it on the table. "All right," I said with genuine contrition. "What's the matter?"

"Everything."

"Think you could narrow that down just a bit? I mean, I'd hate to waste an hour slamming the entire paper towel industry if it's only one brand's particular print that's bothering you."

Katrine's face eased into a smile. "You just can't help yourself, can you?"

"No. Meanwhile, I'm going to go out on a limb here and assume we're talking about you and Rob." It wasn't exactly a stretch, I knew, but I was just tired of beating around the bush, since—as was also the case during our last counseling session back in December—I had work to do, and the clock was ticking.

"OK, so what's the problem?" I asked when she nodded. *Aside from the fact that he's a colossal jerk, that is.*

"Well, you know I wasn't entirely happy with the way things were before we got married."

"Yes."

"Well, things haven't really gotten any better."

Really.

"In fact," Katrine continued as I held my tongue, "in some ways, things are worse. I see even less of him now, and he has little if anything to say to me. He used to talk about his classes and how things were going at work. Now he either doesn't want or have time to do that. I have nothing to do with the finances, so I can only assume the bills are paid, but I don't know where the money is going, much less what we can or cannot afford. We're not fighting or anything, since we're not together long or often enough for any conflict to erupt, and I try to avoid certain topics because I don't want to waste the time we do have together screaming at each other. Not that we've ever really screamed at each other, but you know."

I did. Like Persephone, Katrine was afraid to speak the truth for fear of how Rob would react, so she kept her head down and hoped for the best. "So you're walking around on eggshells trying to keep the peace," I paraphrased, "while he's stomping around crushing as many as he likes."

Katrine nodded. "I guess I thought when Rob saw how accommodating I was being, he would reciprocate by being more forthcoming."

I'd heard that one before—in different incarnations, of course. Like when my superstitious neighbor, Mona, asked me to remove the stray black cat that had taken up residence under her porch and subsequently confessed, "I thought if I gave it some food, it would eat and be on its way." And from the abused women I had counseled, who would say, "If I could just remember to do things the way he wants me to, he wouldn't get so upset."

These women were all thinking like people but dealing with animals.

"Men don't necessarily think or behave the way we do," I paraphrased again. "With some men—and women, to be fair—you give them an inch, and they'll take a mile."

"Kevin isn't like that."

"True. But then, I wouldn't put up with it if he was."

"So how did you get him to treat you the way he does?"

"I didn't do anything, Katrine. Kevin is who he is—as are most men. You can't go into a relationship planning or hoping to change the other person. If he puts away a twelve pack of beer every night before you're married, he's going to put away a twelve pack every night *after* you're married. And if he goes out with the boys twice a week before you have kids, he's going to go out with the boys twice a week after you have kids. Even if tells you otherwise—which he will if he wants to knock you up and lock you up—you can bet your ass you'll be home alone with a screaming baby at least two nights a week after you get out of the hospital."

"So you don't think people can change?"

"Oh, I know people can change. But they can only change if *they* want to, not because *you* want them to. Case in point: Kevin could have kept dropping his socks and underwear on the floor at night and leaving them for me to pick up the next day, for as much as I wanted him to stop doing it, he didn't quit until he wanted to."

"Which was when?"

"About a month after we moved in together—when he had to wear dirty briefs to work."

"Oh my God."

"Well, what did he expect? I mean, after asking him almost daily to put the damn things in the hamper and getting nowhere, I decided I wasn't going to enable him anymore and stopped picking them up. Instead, I left them on the floor and let them work their way under the bed as I made it in the morning. Then, when the time came to do the laundry, I washed only the clothing that was in the hamper and left the rest to fester under the bed. He apparently didn't notice how empty his drawers were getting—if you'll pardon the pun—or he might have figured it out sooner. Eventually, however, he found out the hard way, and I never had a problem again."

"Wasn't he pissed?"

"Of course—but it was his fault. I had told him after the first week or so: I'm not your mother, and I'm not your maid. I'm willing to do the laundry and the housework since I'm not currently working outside the home, but you can at least put your dirty clothes in the hamper and carry your dirty dishes to the sink."

"Didn't that make you feel like a nag?"

"Yep—which is precisely why I stopped repeating myself after the second week. He was a grown man, and he wouldn't have gotten away with that crap in the barracks. But he sure as hell wasn't going to stop leaving his clothes on the floor as long as I kept picking them up—just as Rob isn't going to start talking to you about finances because you stop asking him to. To bottom line it, you can't control Rob's behavior; you can only control your own. And if you continue to let him walk all over you, he will. Obviously it would be better if no one wanted to walk all over you in the first place, but as my story of Kevin's reform demonstrates, even a prince can acquire distasteful habits that have to be managed. You just have to decide what you want, how far you're willing to go to get it, and how long you'll wait before you give up and walk away. In short, you have to be willing to be the bad guy. You have to be willing to let people be mad at you. You have to be willing to be unpopular. We all get as much or as little as we are willing to settle for, Katrine, and for most people, that's usually about what we think we deserve."

Katrine nodded. "I know what I want. I just don't think I'm ever going to get it from Rob, no matter how long I'm willing to wait."

I couldn't have agreed more, although there seemed little point in saying so. She knew how I felt about Rob, and even though I hadn't brought it up, I had promised to forever hold my peace.

"What does that mean?" I asked instead.

"I don't know. I just know that things would be a lot easier for me if Rob was more like you."

"So you want your relationship with Rob to be more like ours?"

"Yeah. I guess."

"Then perhaps you should start by treating him the way you treat me."

"What does that mean?"

"It means not taking his shit, for one thing, the way you don't take mine. Think back to this past Friday, for example, when I was trying to put Lucy to sleep and you switched the radio over to that classical station and then refused to change back after I complained. You could have caved in at the first sign of resistance, but you didn't."

"I may have if you had protested much more."

"Maybe. The point is, you stood up to me—which I know you don't do with Rob. Think, too, about when you came back in the house tonight and I was making jokes when you were trying to talk seriously. You flung that ten-dollar bill at me with all the confidence of cowboy ordering a shot of whiskey in a saloon and risked pissing off the barkeep with your uppity words."

Katrine cringed. "I'm sorry."

"Don't be. You would have never gotten me to shut up if you hadn't put me in my place."

"But you couldn't have known I wanted to talk."

"True—my mind was elsewhere. Which is why it was perfectly reasonable for you to assert yourself—which you did in a clever and effective way. You need to do that with Rob. He may not like it at first, but he'll either get used to it, or he'll kick you out."

"And either way, I win—right?"

"Exactly."

Katrine smiled. "Thanks, Jackie."

"My pleasure. Now, I hate to be a taskmaster, but I need to get back to my project."

Katrine groaned again as she leaned over the table. "Do you have any idea how sick I am of this project?" she asked, punctuating each syllable by bumping her forehead on the table.

"Trust me—I'm sick of it, too; but if I don't finish it tonight, I may never get it done."

"I know."

"Tell you what," I offered, as she continued to sulk. "You help me finish editing this paper tonight, and I'll finish the presentation part myself Sunday night."

"And what exactly is in that for *me*?"

"Well, you get to decide what we do after we're done."

Katrine lifted her head. "I guess I can live with that."

"Great!" I said, standing. "Then let's get on with it."

We finished the paper around eleven, and, as promised, I left the rest of the plans for the evening up to Katrine. "My only request is that we not play *Scrabble*," I said as we put a pot of water on to boil. "If I see another letter—plastic, paper, or otherwise—it will be the death of me."

"You'll get no argument here," Katrine replied. "In fact, I'm happy just to sit here and chat."

"I don't mean to nitpick, but we've done plenty of that this weekend as well—which is why it took until now to finish my paper."

"I know. But I enjoy hearing about your other friends and about you and Kevin; and with school and everything else we have going on, we so rarely get the chance to just chill and talk."

"OK," I said, bracing myself for another counseling session. "Let's talk."

"Great. What should we talk about?"

"I don't know. It was your idea."

"Yeah, but you only just told me about this opportunity tonight. It's not as if I've had time to prepare."

"Fair enough," I said with relief. *At least now I know we won't be talking about Rob.*

"On second thought, there is something I've been wanting to ask you," Katrine admitted as we carried our tea to the living room. "It's kind of personal, which is why I haven't said anything in front of Kevin or the kids."

"What's that?" I asked, hoping that in escaping a discussion about Rob, I hadn't inadvertently set myself up for something worse.

"I'm just wondering if there's ever been, ah, anyone else."

"I'm afraid I don't follow. Are you asking if I've ever cheated on Kevin?"

"Yes and no. I mean, since Kevin, has there ever been anyone else, you know, besides me?"

"Just one," I admitted, excluding three crushes—including Quinn—that I'd survived over the years, since they'd all sprouted, flowered, and fizzled before I'd met and married Kevin.

"What was her name?"

"Melissa."

"What was she like?"

"Smart. Sweet. A lot like you, really. Only shorter and more direct."

"Where did you meet her?"

"At the base tennis courts in Yuma. I was working the board—you know, the wall with the white line running across it that allows you to practice without a partner. Anyway, she showed up and was hanging around waiting to use the space. Well, I'd been using that part of the court at the same time every sunny morning since Kevin had deployed, and I wasn't going to give it up until I was good and ready. So when she finally approached me to ask when I was planning to finish, I told her exactly that."

"What did she do?"

"Offered to play me for it."

"And?"

"And, figuring her for some officer's gym bunny trophy wife in her snazzy blue track suit and matching shoes, I decided to go for it. I probably should have examined her shoes more closely, however, since they would've told me she'd put in some serious court time. It also might have helped if I'd read the logo on her track suit rather than dismissing her because it looked too sharp. Instead, I accepted her challenge—which, after fighting the wall for half an hour was a very bad idea—and proceeded to get my ass kicked well and hard."

"Ouch."

"Exactly. Thankfully, there were no witnesses."

"So how did you go from competing to collaborating—if you'll pardon the expression."

"Pardon granted," I laughed. "After the set, I said good game and gave up the court, but she smiled and said she'd already had her workout for the day and invited me back to my place."

"*Your* place?"

"She was very direct."

"I guess so."

"Anyway, she followed me to a deli, where we picked up some lunch, and then back to *chez moi* where I learned she was in town helping to coordinate some weapons course on base. That's also where I learned she'd trained with the Olympic women's tennis team—hence the outfit I'd stupidly ignored—and where I discovered just how terrific Lil Miss looked *without* it."

"That same day?"

"And the next—and at every opportunity for the next three weeks."

"You slut!"

"Hey—sticks and stones, my friend. Sticks and stones."

"I cannot believe you."

I couldn't believe me either, at the time. Nor could I believe I was sharing it with Katrine now. But then, she had asked.

"You would have done the same thing," I told her. "That woman was amazing."

"For the record," Katrine added, "I would *not* have done the same thing, because I wouldn't have been at the tennis court in the first place."

"Not a tennis player, huh?" I observed. "And here I thought *all* you country club types played tennis."

"Not me. My mother was afraid it would interfere with my equestrian training or ruin my hands for the violin."

"Oh, heaven forefend."

"And how exactly did *you* get into tennis?" Katrine countered. "I didn't think non–country club types knew how to hold a racquet."

Grinning, Katrine swung her legs up onto the other end of the couch and arranged a pillow under her head in my lap. "So what ever happened to Melissa?"

"She went back to Quantico with the rest of her unit."

"She was a *marine*?"

"Yep. An officer, in fact."

"So she went back to Quantico and that was it?"

"Pretty much. Why?"

Katrine shrugged "I guess I assumed after all that you'd have stayed in touch."

"There wasn't much point, really. I mean, she was a marine, and I was married to one. Where was it going to go?"

"Have you ever thought of looking her up?"

"Nope."

"Never?"

"Never."

Not that I could have looked her up if I'd wanted to, given the tools available back then. For this was years before there was a computer in every home and more than a decade before the proliferation of Internet search engines and the rise of social networking. Back then, *looking someone up* meant dialing four-one-one; using your best guess as to the target's city, state, and area code; and hoping they didn't have a common name or an unpublished number. Compared to the technology available to stalkers of today, it was like using the constellations instead of GPS to take a road trip, or making popcorn over a campfire instead of in a microwave.

"So what else do you want to know?" I inquired as Katrine smiled up at me. "Or are we done playing twenty questions?"

"Actually, I think I'd like to play a different game."

My heart started to race as I caught her drift. I had vowed not to go there. As a condition of allowing myself to accept Katrine's offer to help me out, I had taken a solemn oath to keep my hands to myself. That's why I'd flown into panic mode when I woke up next to her this morning and why I had allowed myself not one drop of alcohol all weekend. And yet, as I stared down at her—and into those big, beautiful chocolate eyes—I knew there was no point in fighting it.

Things were about to get complicated. Again.

As she sat up and we started to kiss, I was already crafting the explanation I would offer my confessor.

The actions I am about to describe are indefensible…

Twenty-three

Katrine came down the stairway around eight the next morning as Tyler and I were at the stove assembling a record-setting stack of pancakes. After greeting him and Lucy with a kiss on the forehead and taking a swallow of orange juice from the glass I'd set for her on the table, she announced she was going home.

"Now?"

"Well, yeah. I have some cleaning to do, and I'd like to finish it before Rob gets home."

"All right," I said, not buying it but not wanting to push. "But if you can wait until after breakfast, I'll drive you. I need to run to the grocery store anyway, so it won't be any trouble."

"That's OK. You carry on—I could use some fresh air."

I watched Katrine purse her lips into a kiss and launch it into the air as she turned toward the door, but I waited until she'd unlocked the door before sending one back. She paused long enough to acknowledge the message with a grin, and then stepped outside and closed the door behind her.

It's just as well, I thought as I watched her through the window. I needed some time to get my shit together before Kevin got home anyway.

"Well, if we're not the awesomest pistol-packing college boys in the Midwest," he proposed as he burst through the kitchen door that afternoon, "then I'm the bastard son of Yosemite Sam!"

"You mean you won?" I played along in an exaggerated Southern accent à la Bugs Bunny in saloon girl drag.

"Shore 'nuff. That's one more first-place finish for the team, plus a none-too-shabby second for me in the two-gun aggregate."

"Congra-a-a-tulations, Kevin!" I replied in my best Don Pardo as I took a wooden spoon from the utensil crock and held it near my chin. "You are a shootist extraordinaire! And, because you have inspired us with your skill and sportsmanship, you shall be richly rewarded.

"That's right, Kevin!" I continued, nailing the legendary announcer's trademark tone and cadence, "because you're such a dedicated and capable marksman, *we* are sending *you* on a no-expense paid trip to your local Target where, in addition to fighting the weekend crowds, you will select—not one, but two—large packs of disposable diapers!

"Yes, Kevin! Since your wife was too stupid to pick them up while she was out earlier today, you are being given the distinct honor and privilege of choosing precisely which product will grace your daughter's bottom for the next two weeks! Well done, marine. You are amazing, and we salute you."

Kevin shook his head as I took a bow. "Sometimes walking through that door is like entering another dimension," he said to no one in particular as he set down his bags and continued on to the kitchen.

"Tell me you'd have it any other way," I said, turning back to the stove where I was heating soup and toasting cheese sandwiches.

Noting that a dinner was almost underway, Kevin set Lucy in her highchair. "So how did your weekend go?" he dared as he attached the tray and buckled her in.

"Fast."

"I'm sorry. I probably should have skipped the meet."

"And leave your *team* in the lurch?" I asked, expertly tossing and catching the toasted stacks of bread and processed American with a spatula. "Never!"

"OK, OK—you needn't rub it in."

"Of course I do," I said, reaching up to muss his hair. "In truth, I finished most of what I had to get done, despite the fact that Lucy had an earache and Katrine was feeling…uh…chatty."

"Oh, no—what did Rob do now?"

"Nothing that I know of—besides go to the FTX."

"Did you tell her you had work to do?"

"Yep. In fact, that's why I let her come over—so she could help."

"Smart."

"I know. Sometimes you get lucky." *Ooh,* I winced privately. *Bad choice of words.*

"Speaking of getting lucky," he said, hugging me from behind, "you smell great."

"You've been on the road too long, Kevin. I smell exactly the same as I do every day."

"OK. So I just missed you."

"I missed you too," I replied. "On another note, would you like some soup and a sandwich, or did the team stop to eat and take a victory lap on the way home?"

Kevin laughed. "Some soup and a sandwich would be great," he said, scanning the visible area for our older child—or so I assumed—who had yet to offer him his usual greeting.

"If you're looking for Tyler, he's in the basement," I explained as the phone rang. "I rented him a movie when I was out earlier and told him he could watch it while I made dinner."

I continued to set the table as it rang again.

"Would you mind getting that?" I asked, arranging the dishes and utensils before three of the chairs. "I'm a little busy."

Doubtfully, Kevin went to the phone and picked it up.

"Jack's Café," he announced as I pretended not to listen. "Hey, Josh. Yeah, I just got in. No problem. All afternoon? Really? Well, she's here," he continued with an irritated glance in my direction, "but apparently she doesn't always hear the phone."

Kevin shook his head as I acknowledged his remark with a sneer.

"So what's up?" he asked. "This morning? Really? That's great. Congratulations! OK, hang on," he instructed, reaching for the pen and notepad on the shelf. "Seven pounds, two ounces. Angelía Lisette. Sure, I'll tell her. And you tell Lyn I said 'Well done.'

"Hey, guess what," he challenged an empty room as he hung up the phone. "Jack?"

"In here," I called from down the hall. "Lucy needs changing, and I'm trying to find one of the old cloth diapers I saw floating around here recently."

"They're in the basement," Kevin replied as he walked to the stairs. "I didn't think you needed them anymore, so I put them with the car care supplies."

"Hey, big guy," he then called down to Tyler. "Can you go to the shelves where I keep the tools and bring me the towels we used to dry the car?"

"That's OK," I countered, handing Lucy to Kevin as I squeezed between him and the handrail. "I'll go."

"Why? It'll only take him a few seconds to find them."

"I know, but I can't do anything while I'm waiting, so I might as well go myself. Just do me a favor and mind the soup."

"OK."

"These are kind of dingy," I announced upon returning to the kitchen a couple minutes later with two light gray cloths, "but they'll do until we can get to the store."

"OK."

"Now, I'd planned for you to eat before your diaper run," I continued, retrieving Lucy from Kevin as I passed through the kitchen, "but since this was the last disposable, I'll just go now and eat when I get back."

Kevin sighed. "Jack, can we just slow down for a minute?"

"What for?"

"Don't you want to know who was on the phone?"

"I already know who was on the phone, Kevin. You said his name."

"What's going on?" Kevin asked as he followed me back to changing table in the playroom. "Why are you acting this way?"

"Acting what way?"

"Like you're pissed off."

"I don't know what you're talking about. I'm just trying to get Lucy changed and one of us to the store so we'll have a diaper to put her in when she's ready for bed."

"But the phone—"

"I know," I snapped as I folded the dirty diaper and taped it shut. "Baby girl. Angelía Lisette. Seven pounds, two ounces. I was standing right next to you when Josh called, remember?"

"But you were gone when I hung up, and I wasn't sure at what point you'd left."

"Well, I stayed long enough to gather the salient details."

Kevin nodded. "Josh said she was in labor for nineteen hours."

"Does he think that's some kind of record, or does he just want a medal for being there?"

"Excuse me?"

"Never mind."

"Jackie, what is with you?"

"Nothing is *with me*," I said as I pinned the sides of the cloth diaper together. "So Lynette was in labor for nineteen hours—big deal. I was in labor with Lucy for twenty-six hours and had to go under the knife to have Tyler. You didn't hear me screaming for accolades afterward."

Kevin sighed. "Where is this coming from?" he asked, running his hand over his hair.

Retrieving Lucy from the changing table, I grabbed a shower cap and my scissors from the linen closet and continued on to the kitchen. There, I laid Lucy on the counter while I cut the top of the shower cap open and then pulled the plastic material up and around the baby's diaper with the elastic edge on the bottom. Reaching into the junk drawer to my left, I located the packing tape, brought the front and rear of the elastic together, and taped them such that it fit snug, but not tight, around each of Lucy's legs. Finally, I gathered the plastic at each side of Lucy's waist, folded the excess forward, and taped it down. This Kevin observed in amused admiration, though it failed to dampen his interest in my response to the phone call.

"Come on, Jack," he urged as I completed Lucy's ensemble by snapping the crotch of her all-in-one t-shirt and pulling up her fleece pants. "What's going on?"

"I'm trying to minimize the potential for leaks."

"Not that. I'm talking about Lynette."

I shrugged as I hoisted Lucy back into her highchair. "What about her?"

"I just think it's strange that our friends just had their first kid and you don't find it worthy of commentary."

"Why should I find it worthy of commentary? Women have babies every day."

"Not this woman."

"Maybe that's the problem," I observed, turning off the burner under the soup. "Maybe if she hadn't waited so long, she wouldn't be so inclined to act as if she's giving birth to the messiah."

"I can't believe you said that."

"Why? Because she's my *friend*?"

"Yes."

"Then you need to catch up with the times, man, because as far as she's concerned, I am nonessential personnel."

"That's not true."

"Bullshit. If it wasn't true, she would have called me more than once a month after she found out she was pregnant, and I wouldn't have become just a convenient lunch date whenever Josh was busy. Oh, she may miss my smiling face when the stress of having a newborn starts to take its toll and that coldhearted ass of a husband refuses to help, but I won't hear from her until that happens, and as far as I'm concerned, that will be too soon."

"You don't really believe that."

"Yes, I do. I'm perfectly happy for her to get on with her life. It's about time, if you ask me."

"Look, Jackie, I don't know where you're getting all of this, but I do know that Lynette is your friend, and she is going to need you."

"Give me a break, Kevin. She's got forty million other people beating each other to death for the privilege of being there for her. She sure as hell doesn't need me."

Kevin shook his head. "I'm going to the store," he said, walking to the closet to retrieve his jacket. "Is there anything else we need besides diapers?"

I turned the burner off again and followed him. "I don't understand, Kevin. Why are you mad at me?"

"I'm not mad at you, Jackie. I'm just frustrated."

"Why? Because I'm willing to accept how things are, and you can't?"

"No—because you always expect people to disappoint you, and I don't think that's healthy. But since we don't have time to get into that right now, I'm going to run to the store and plan to get back to that subject later. So, again, do we need anything besides diapers?"

I shook my head.

"OK," Kevin said, pulling me close and kissing me lightly on the forehead. "I'll see you in a little while."

Once Kevin was gone, I took Lucy from her highchair and—violating at least six of my own rules surrounding child rearing—gated off a section of carpet in the basement, parked her and Tyler in front of a video with a bottle and a carton of tapioca pudding, respectively, and, leaving instructions for Tyler to call me if Lucy started to fuss, rushed back to the kitchen. I got to the sink just as my eyes began to burn and fill with tears. Not wanting the kids to hear me, I moved into the living room and started to bawl.

"Jack?" Kevin asked upon coming home to find me in the dark with wads of wet tissues strewn around the floor. "What's the matter?" he continued as he shut and locked the door with his arms still full.

I shook my head. "I can't do this anymore," I said, blowing my nose and flinging another glob of tissue to floor.

Kevin set the diaper packs on the floor at the end of the couch, and then sat down and took my hand. "Can't do what anymore?"

"There comes a point at which you have to admit you've had enough; when you have to accept that things will never change, and you have to give up hoping they ever will. Life just isn't the same for me as it is for other people, and I can't keep pretending it doesn't bother me."

"Jackie, what are you talking about?"

"That baby is going to have everything, Kevin—parents who'll love her, grandparents who'll spoil her, and a lovely and permanent home. She'll never have a stepmom who drinks or steals her allowance to buy booze. She'll never hear people fighting or the sound of glass breaking in the next room. She'll never be yanked out of bed and marched out of the house at two in the morning because someone's pissed off or threatening to call the police. She'll never have to sleep in a car or a camper, and she'll never feel like she's in the way. Her entire life will be about bubble baths, balloons, and birthday cakes—and I am going to hate her."

"No, you're not."

"Yes, I am, Kevin. I know it's not right, but she's not even a day old, and I'm so jealous I can barely function."

"Aw, Jack."

"That's why I forgot the diapers," I sniffed. "After Josh left the first message saying they were at the hospital, I completely lost the plot. I immediately put the kids in the car and went to the store. I was planning to go anyway—just not so soon. Of course, I wasn't thinking straight and forgot my list, so I was basically shoving stuff in my cart at random. I stayed out as long as I could to avoid Josh's updates, but eventually I had to go home. When I got back, I shut off the phones and unplugged the answering machine so I wouldn't have to hear anyone call or listen to any message that might come in. I can't stand the idea of hurting Lynette, but I can't bring myself to talk to her, because I'm so damned ashamed of myself."

"I understand how you feel, and I'm sure Lynette would, too, if she knew."

"Oh God—she can't know! I just couldn't bear for her to know what a monster I am."

"You are not a monster, Jackie."

"Believe me, Kevin. She would not understand. Lynette doesn't have an evil bone in her body, and she would never understand how someone could have such ugly thoughts."

"She may not have the kind of thoughts you do, but I'm sure she had some adjusting of her own to do when you had Tyler and Lucy. Besides, she knows your history, and anyone with that information would understand why this is so hard for you."

"I don't think so."

"Why don't you go visit them tomorrow?" Kevin suggested. "I'm sure once you've seen them, you'll feel a lot better about things."

"Kevin, I just can't. Lynette will expect me to hold the baby, but I won't be able to, and that will hurt her feelings."

"But don't you see? If you don't go see them, you'll do more than hurt her feelings."

"I doubt it. And even if I do hurt her, I don't care."

"You don't mean that."

"Yes, I do. Because it's not just the baby I can't stand—it's Lynette, too. I'm just so jealous of her I can't begin to be happy for her. I mean, she's had every possible advantage in the world and could always have anything she wanted. And now on top of all that, she has a baby, and everyone—including you—expects me to jump for joy. Well, forgive me, but I'm afraid I can't do that. I can't sit here and be happy that she now has the only thing I ever had that she didn't."

"I don't necessarily expect you to jump for joy, Jackie."

"Well, everyone else sure as hell does. Like at her shower, everyone kept saying how excited I must be that my best friend is having a baby, and wasn't it wonderful that my kids were going to have a new playmate. I wanted to tell them I didn't give a flying fuck if Lyn ever had her baby, that my kids already had playmates, and that if they needed any more, I'd call Hugh Hefner.

"Of course, I didn't say any of that," I added as Kevin suppressed a snicker, "because I have *manners*. You see, while her people are allowed to be as insipid, thoughtless, and self-centered as they like, people like me have no choice but to smile graciously. So that's what I did."

"I imagine it would have been quite some shower if you hadn't."

"It was a nightmare," I continued, sobbing. "There were over forty women there, Kevin. Aunts. Great-aunts. Grandmas and great-grandmas. Cousins, friends, and coworkers—not to mention her mom and *her* neighbors, friends, and coworkers. All of them fussing over Lyn as she cradled her belly and opened one lovely gift after another. I felt so alone I wanted to die. It was just like when I was in the hospital having Tyler, and all of those women kept coming to visit their daughters while I sat there listening to them ooh and ah over their new grandbabies. It was all I could do not to open my veins and climb into a hot bath."

Kevin clenched his jaw. "You know how I hate it when you talk like that."

"I'm sorry. It just…it just hurts so much sometimes. I'm sick of being happy for everyone else and tired of watching their picnics in the park. I want to *be* the ones for whom others are happy for a change; I want to be the idiots in the park. I want someone to take our kids for a week or two and bring them back completely spoiled. I want someone to make snowmen with them in December and watch fireworks with them in July. I want them to know Tyler's favorite Ninja Turtle and Lucy's favorite song, and for once I want to throw a birthday party where our family members outnumber our friends instead of the other way around."

"I know you do, Jack. And if I could make that happen, you know I would. But we're not going to change our families, so we're just going to have to make the most of what we've got to work with and not be preoccupied by what we don't."

"You sound just like my dad. I suppose next you'll be telling me to stop feeling sorry for myself and to be grateful that I have a brain that's smart enough to know I'm miserable."

"I wouldn't do that," Kevin cringed. "But he does have a point."

"So what are you suggesting? That I forget I lost my mom and just celebrate the fact that I lived to tell the tale? Congratulate your dad on giving you all those siblings and forget about the lives he shattered in the process? And what shall I tell Tyler the next time one of his friends goes to a movie with his grandpa, and he comes home begging me to ask one of our dads to take him to see it? That he's lucky just to have three granddads, and never mind that they refuse to give him the time of day?"

"Not necessarily."

"Well, good! Because I've had my fill of his 'count your blessings' bullshit. It's normal to feel bad when your mom is gone, and it's ridiculous to count your blessings when you know that any minute they'll be ripped from your grasp.

"You have no idea what it was like," I added. "Having to pretend I wasn't scared walking into yet another new school in the middle of the year; waiting for someone to trip me or make fun of my clothes; hoping they won't stick gum in my hair this time or throw my books down the stairwell; having to act so damned humble whenever Ricky and I got dumped on another doorstep; and always feeling like such a gigantic pain in the ass. And it was never enough to appreciate that people helped us out; we were expected to prove it every day. Even when it was just the three of us, I couldn't make him happy. If I tried to talk to him, I was told to be quiet. If I didn't talk, I was antisocial. If I hung around the house too much, I was in the way, but if I were gone too much, I didn't care about my family. Now tell me," I concluded, "how can he preach to me after all of that?"

"I don't know, Jack." Kevin admitted, holding me tighter as I stifled a new flood of tears. "I only know that I love you, and I can't stand to see you feeling so bad."

"Yeah, well, next time I'll try to finish crying before you get home."

"That's not what I mean."

"I know," I said as he wiped my face. "So did you still want that soup, or what?"

"Are you up to it?"

"Christ, Kevin, all I have to do is turn the burner on under the pan again."

"All right," he practically cheered. "That's the belligerent babe we all know and love."

"Keep up the sarcasm and she may never go away."

"Fine by me—as long as she's feeling better."

The next morning I joined Kevin in the bathroom as he was preparing to shave.

"Aren't you cold?" he asked as I sat down, naked, on the edge of the tub.

"No. Why? Are you?"

"No. But then I'm not sitting on icy porcelain."

I considered my perch for a moment and shrugged. "Say, Kev?"

"Yeah?"

"Have you ever wanted to fool around since we were married?"

"All the time," he laughed. "Haven't you noticed?"

That wasn't strictly true judging by the entirety of the last six months, but I wasn't about to quibble over details when things seemed to have gotten mostly back to normal.

"Not with me, you idiot," I said instead. "I mean with someone else."

"Not really. I mean, why go shopping when I've already got the best goods at home?"

I considered him skeptically as he shot a pile of shaving cream onto his palm and spread it over his face and neck. "Then what's with all the shit you talk about threesomes?"

Kevin laughed as he picked up his razor. "Just kidding around."

"So you're not really interested in being with someone else?"

"Depends. Who did you have in mind?"

Kevin laughed again as I rolled my eyes. "Where's all this coming from, anyway?" he asked. "I would've thought last night would have eliminated any concerns you had in this department."

I was as near as I'd ever been to telling him about me and Katrine, and I was wondering if I should take the plunge or walk back down the ladder. He'd been so supportive since coming home last night, and I felt closer to him than I had in weeks, so it seemed a shame to pass up the chance to make a full confession, take my licks, and clear my conscience.

In truth, I'd wanted to tell him all along. We had never kept secrets from one another, and I didn't want this to be the year we started. Unfortunately, as I told Sera in January, although Kevin wouldn't be upset about what had happened, there were a host of reasons why I held back.

Glancing at his watch on the vanity, I realized my confession would have to wait. I would need more than the twenty minutes or so we had before he had to leave for school to explain what I'd done and to address any questions—serious or otherwise—he might want to ask.

Not that I could explain it very well, since I didn't fully understand it myself. How could I be so head over heels for Kevin and still feel the way I did about Katrine?

"Just doing a status check," I said finally. "Just making sure you're still satisfied."

"Of course I'm satisfied. Aren't you?"

"Well, yeah. But what if that's all we have going for us?"

"What do you mean?"

"Think about it. We never play tennis or take walks like we used to. We never go out or talk much anymore. When we do talk, it's never about anything interesting, because we have nothing in common. So basically, we have no foundation for a relationship except sex and the kids."

"You could say that, I suppose, if things were that way by design. But the reason we don't spend much time alone together isn't because we don't want to—it's because we're too damned busy. As far as what we do not have in common—irrelevant. After all, it wasn't our similarities that brought us together in the first place. It was our mutual admiration for one another's body and mind—which, in my not-so-humble opinion, is a more than adequate foundation upon which to maintain a relationship."

"Well, I agree, but—"

"But nothing. Jackie, I don't know what goes on in that pretty little head of yours, but try to remember that our situation is temporary. As soon as we finish school, we'll go back to the fleet, where I'll have a normal assignment with normal hours and more time to relax and have fun."

"What if we don't get there, Kevin? It's over a year away."

"Yes, but we've already made it through the first three—which they say are the hardest, so it should be all downhill from here. And you'll finish school here in just a few weeks, which means no more homework for you and no more day care for the kids—unless you decide you want to keep them there part-time so you can work or whatever. Now, I know it's hard for you to be optimistic—especially when you're stressed out and sleep deprived—but things really aren't that bad, and they are only going to get better."

I studied him as I chewed the inside of my cheek. "You really missed your calling, you know. You should have been a therapist."

Kevin nodded. "Or a hostage negotiator."

Twenty-four

*A*s I returned to my car after my last class two days later, I decided I was ready to pay a visit to the hospital. I'd just gotten an essay back with a bright red A at the top, and one of my favorite songs was, oddly, playing on the radio. If there ever was a time to see Lyn and her progeny, it was while I was riding high, and few things made me sit so tall in the saddle as Elvis Costello and academic excellence.

A glance at the clock on the dashboard told me I had plenty of time to get home, grab the paper on which Kevin had written Lyn's room number, drive to the hospital, and spend an hour or so visiting before I had to pick up the kids. If the lights were with me, I might even have time to stop by a florist on the way. It was obviously too late to order a custom arrangement—even if I had thought to do so from a pay phone before I left campus—but I could do something nice with a generic bouquet when I got back to the house.

I hit the freeway at just the right time and was soon rounding the corner to our street with cluster of carnations, daisies, and sweetheart roses wrapped up on the seat beside me. Pulling up to the curb in front of the house, I shoved the gearshift into first, yanked up the emergency brake, grabbed my coat, my handbag, and the flowers, and made for the front door.

I was walking so fast that I failed to notice Rob sitting on the porch until I stepped on his shoe and nearly tripped.

"Hi, there," he said with smirk as I recognized him.

"Oh, hi, Rob," I breathed, retrieving my purse from the snow. "How's it going?"

"Great. You?"

"Fine."

It occurred to me that I hadn't seen his vehicle when I'd pulled up. *That's odd*, I mused, as I turned and fruitlessly scanned the street for the Nova. "Where's your car?"

"Around the block."

"Are you waiting for Kevin?"

"Actually, I was waiting for you."

"Really?" I wondered aloud, watching him rise to his full height in front of me. "Why?"

"Gosh, Jackie. You act as though you're not glad to see me."

"Not at all," I lied, backing toward the door. "I'm just surprised. It's not like you to show up here...alone."

"Nor is it like *you* to be so inhospitable. Aren't you going to invite me in?"

"What for?"

My mind raced to answer my own question. Was I in for an even more revolting replay of New Year's Eve? Had he found out about me and Katrine and decided to confront me about it? Or was he here about an entirely unrelated matter and just having fun making me uncomfortable?

"I just want to talk," he said finally.

"About what?"

"People. Places. Things."

"Look, Rob, this is a bad time. I'm really busy today."

"Funny, you never seem to be too busy for Katrine."

If I was uncomfortable before, I was stiff with dread now. Something about his demeanor made me feel vaguely like a character at the center of some gothic tragedy, and I wondered for a moment if I might go down in history as the first woman to die at the hand of another woman's jealous husband. I also considered what steps I could take to avoid becoming such a novelty but wasn't sure if my life was truly in danger or my fear was just the product of guilt and shame.

"What's the matter, Jackie? Cat got your tongue?"

Apparently, I conceded to myself as I looked up and down the block again. It was deserted except for an old man walking his dog two blocks down and across the street. I didn't know yet if I would need a witness or protection, but at his age, he would have less of a chance against Rob than I would and, at that distance, would be unable to come to my aid in time anyway. Therefore, resigning myself to whatever he had in mind, I unlocked and pushed open the door.

"After *you*," he insisted as he reached over my head and held it for me instead.

Warily I ducked under his arm and stepped past him through the door.

Various alarm bells continued their tentative ringing as I slipped off my boots. I knew better than to ignore them; doing so had cost me more than a few smacks from Steven in the past and the unwelcome attention of Sean before that. The difference, of course, was that I'd done nothing to deserve what had happened back then and, therefore, could have trusted my instincts. In the situation before me now, I was hardly an innocent bystander, and my conscience kept interfering with my emergency response system.

I thought again about the gothic tragedy angle and wondered if the newspaper would portray me as the victim of a crazed lunatic or the recipient of a cuckolded man's righteous vengeance. I wondered, too, as Rob plopped down on the sofa, if a killer's intentions could be altered in any way by the target's actions or demeanor and thus whether a little kindness might improve my chances of survival.

Forget it, I thought as I watched him arrange his gunboats at the opposite end of the sofa. *He may or may not want me dead, but I know it will kill me to be nice to this idiot.*

"So what can I do for you, Rob?" I asked through gritted teeth as I set the flowers on the end table and dropped my purse on the floor.

"Got anything to drink?" he asked, placing his hands behind his head.

"Of course." I tossed my coat onto the chair as I passed by it on my way to the other side of the room. "Time is all I'm short of at the moment."

"Gee, I guess I'll just have to sip it, then."

Whatever floats your boat, pal.

"I'm surprised you'd actually drink something I'd offer you," I added as I walked to the kitchen and opened the fridge.

"Oh, I think I'm pretty safe. You're far too sensitive a person to deliberately kill anyone, and far too many people know how you feel about me for you to expect to get away with it."

"Just the same, I'll let you open this yourself," I said, tossing him a soda. "That way if it makes you sick, you'll have no reason to blame me."

Slipping down the hall, I retrieved my craft kit from the linen closet, chose a vase from among those I kept above the fridge, and brought them to the living room floor. "So what's with the cloak and dagger act, Rob?" I asked, reaching for the package on the end table. "Do you really want something, or are you just trying to liven up an otherwise boring afternoon?"

"Well, I admit I'm enjoying myself, but in truth, there is a purpose behind my visit."

"And will I hear it soon?"

"You know, I never realized how comfortable your couch is," he marveled. "No wonder Katrine likes sleeping here so much."

"Rob, I really do have plans, so if we could speed this up a bit, I'd appreciate it."

"Is that for Lynette?" he asked, indicating to the vase that I was trimming in pink ribbon. "I only ask because I figure she's due about now."

"Well, congratulations on your excellent memory and math skills. Now, seriously—can we move this along?"

"You're a great friend, you know. Not just to Lynette, but to Kitty as well. You've made her transition here so much smoother than we'd expected, and I'm thankful."

Kitty? That was a new one. It alone was grounds for divorce in my book.

"You're welcome. Now will you stop screwing with me and get to the point?"

"I'm not screwing with you. I'm voicing my appreciation as any decent individual would."

"I see. Well, forgive me for pointing out the obvious, but you could've used the phone."

Rob nodded. "I could have sent a card, too," he admitted, resuming an upright position and facing me directly, "but I wanted to tell you in person that I know what you're up to."

"Up to?"

"With my wife?" Rob paused as if to let his words take effect.

I obliged with a prickly red flush that crept up my neck and settled in my cheeks.

"Don't worry," he added, delighted to have struck a nerve. "I don't blame you. Katrine is a beautiful girl. I'd just like to know one thing."

"What's that?"

"Why haven't you made a move on her yet?"

"Why haven't I *what*?"

"You heard me."

Wearing amusement as a front for my relief, I crossed my arms. "What makes you so sure that I haven't?"

"Please spare me the comedy," Rob sniffed. "Katrine would have told me if something had happened between you two."

"Would she now?"

"Yes. In fact, she would have been bursting to tell me and would have omitted no detail."

"If you say so," I laughed as I filled the vase with translucent aquarium rock. "But she has been over here an awful lot, so it's not as if I haven't had ample opportunity."

Rob shook his head. "You're not going to rattle me, Jackie. I've had training."

"And more than your share of time in the hot sun, too, from the sound of it."

"Still trying to humor me with that amazing Jackie wit," he observed with a laugh. "You must really like me."

"Actually, nothing could be further from the truth."

"Yes. Well, you've made that more than apparent—although where you got the idea that you're so much better than me, I'll never know. Still, I don't believe we have to be enemies."

"Even if I think you're an arrogant, controlling bastard?"

"Of course—since I think you're a judgmental bitch."

"Well, feel free to ask around. I'm sure you'll find you're not alone."

"No doubt," he agreed, collecting himself. "But you still haven't answered my question."

I was tempted to tell him the truth—if only to slap that smarmy smirk off his face—but I resisted. I would come clean to Kevin when I had the chance, but this jerk was Katrine's problem, and I wasn't about to speak for her even if it would take the bastard down a few notches.

"Look, Rob. I don't know how you arrived at this conclusion, but you're way off the mark on this one."

"Come on, Jackie—I may be busy, but I'm not blind."

"No—what you are is paranoid."

"Is that so?"

"Yes. I have no intention of sleeping with Katrine," I declared truthfully, having decided that this morning after talking to Kevin. From this day forward, I swore, I wouldn't be spending more than five minutes with her alone unless the kids were awake or Kevin was home. "I won't deny that I care about her," I added, "but as far as I'm concerned, we're just good friends."

"Funny, that's what she said about you and Melissa."

Melissa?

"Oh, now don't be angry with Katrine," Rob advised as I felt my face darken with a mixture of confusion and annoyance. "She just finds you so interesting that she can't help but go on ad nauseam about your fascinating life and your fascinating friends. Of course, I'm nowhere near as naive as she is, so I can tell what's been left out of the sanitized stories you feed her—and, if the mood strikes, relay them to Kevin or whomever else I'd like."

Although I was surprised Katrine had told Rob about Melissa, I was more daunted by the fact that he had managed to identify a key aspect of our relationship that Katrine had deliberately left out. And while the true nature of that relationship was hardly the weapon he thought he was wielding—since Kevin knew all there was to know about us already—I decided to leave Rob to his illusions in hopes of discovering what he was after.

"All right, Rob," I said with affected concern. "What exactly do you want?"

"That's an interesting question. I suppose I could ask you to stay away from my lovely and impressionable bride, but to be honest, I'm not the jealous type."

OK. So?

"So here's the deal," he added. "I'll agree to keep quiet about you and Melissa and anything that develops between you and Katrine. And in return, you agree to stop poisoning her mind against me."

"*Poisoning her mind?*" I repeated with more disbelief than derision. "Did you pull that from a copy of *Prepsychotics' Weekly*? Or have you just seen too many James Bond films?"

"So you deny trying to undermine our relationship?"

"I don't have to undermine your relationship, pal. You're doing an excellent job of that all by yourself."

"Am I? Well, you clearly underestimate how much of what you say comes back to me. Not that Katrine ever credits you as the source of all that bullshit, but it doesn't take a genius to know where it comes from."

No. It just takes a sexist asshole.

"Look, Rob, I'll admit to having advised Katrine to call off the wedding; but unlike you, I respect her wishes. So, despite my reservations, I've kept my mouth shut ever since."

"You've kept your mouth shut?" Rob laughed. "I guess I don't have to tell you why one might find that hard to believe."

"No, you don't. But it's true. And if you could—for even a moment—conceive of Katrine thinking for herself, you wouldn't be so inclined to blame me when she's unhappy with you."

"Katrine never had a problem with me until you started your shit—which stops. Today."

I don't believe this guy, I thought. *Who the hell does he think he is?*

"Aw, come on, Jackie," he urged, having mistaken my disgust for dejection. "You can still have your fun with Katrine. You just have to remember to respect her primary relationship."

It occurred to me, as I set the flower arrangement on the end table and cleaned up the scraps, that I'd been transported from the gothic tragedy to some surrealistic comedy.

As I understood it, and I wasn't sure I did, Rob was offering his silence on Melissa, which I didn't need, and giving me permission to sleep with Katrine, which I already had. And all he wanted was for me to stop running him down, which I no longer did.

It didn't make any sense. The guy was obviously in dire need of a reality check, but even if his facts had been right, the deal was not weighted in his favor. Had he miscalculated, or was he deliberately leaving something out of the equation?

"Look," I said, hoping to shore this up and still make it to the hospital before Lyn and Josh had another baby, "it doesn't take a genius to see your terms are a little lopsided. So why don't you cut the crap and tell me what you're really after?"

"Well, now that you mention it—and are in no position to negotiate—I don't mind telling you that, despite your distaste for me, I myself have felt something quite different for you since we met and would at some point like to see those feelings, shall we say, consummated."

I nearly gagged as I realized what he was suggesting "You must be joking."

"Why?" he asked. "Do you find it that hard to believe someone besides Kevin would find you attractive?"

"No. What I find hard to believe is that you're stupid enough to think you can blackmail me into sleeping with you."

Seriously, I thought as we stared at one another. *Even if Kevin didn't know about Melissa, I would have to be a total idiot to think sleeping with Rob would make his threat disappear, since all it would do is give him something else to use against me later. Either this guy thinks it's my first day at the poker table, or he's not playing with a full deck.*

In the moments that passed, Rob, too, must have realized he'd overbid, because his expression suddenly changed from one of cool self-assurance to one of forced amusement.

"You should have seen your face," he said, laughing. "As if I don't have better things to do than sleep with you. Who's the stupid one now?"

My cheeks burned again. Although I knew he was lying to conceal his ill-conceived attempt at extortion, it still stung a bit to see him having fun at my expense.

"OK, pal," I said with what was left of my patience, "You've wasted enough of my time. So, once and for all—will you please tell me what you want or get the hell out of my house?"

"Temper, temper."

Christ, I thought, sensing another round of arch-villain-isms coming on. *This guy takes longer to make a point than I do.*

"I don't really want anything, to be honest—other than your silence."

"Ah, yes. The 'No Poisoning Katrine's Mind' rule," I recapped. "Speaking of which, does it apply only to comments on your behavior and character? Or am I barred from questioning your sanity and intelligence as well? And while we're on the subject, if you think I'm such a bad influence on your wife, why don't you just tell her she can't see me anymore?"

"In a perfect world, I would. But there are certain advantages to having Katrine occupied that I'm not quite prepared to give up."

"Such as?"

"Such as the freedom to come and go when I please without having to explain and the ability to do what I like—where, when, and with whomever I want."

So that was it. While Katrine was trying to accommodate him by staying busy and keeping her nose out of the finances, Rob was seeing another woman—or women—behind her back.

"You son of a bitch."

"Ah-ah-ah, Jackie. You know what they say about people who live in glass houses."

I wanted to laugh at him. To tell the moron that Kevin already knew about Melissa. But what would have been the point? He hadn't believed a word I'd said so far.

So I decided to let the bastard think what he wanted. As long as he thought I had something to hide, he'd assume his secret was safe and maybe—just maybe—leave me alone. All I had to do was play along now and bide my time until I knew it was safe to tell the dumbass that the gun he was holding to my head wasn't loaded.

That was assuming, of course, he actually had a secret. His confession was really more of an insinuation, after all, and his demeanor was hardly convincing.

No. More likely this was bait. For while I didn't doubt that, given the chance, Rob would enjoy a bit of forbidden fruit, I doubted he had the time to screw around these days, much less someone screw around with. Moreover, it would be just like him to fabricate such a story hoping I would immediately tell Katrine. That way, when she confronted him, he could truthfully deny it and have both the evidence he needed to prove I was trying to turn her against him and an excuse to tell Kevin about Melissa.

It would have been a brilliant plan if it weren't for the myriad misapprehensions of its barking mad architect. So, for a change, words failed me.

"Well, it seems we understand one another," he declared as he left the couch, apparently satisfied by my silence that he'd achieved his objective. "I guess I'll be going now."

I scrambled to my feet and followed him to the door. Fighting the urge to slam it on him, I watched him step off the porch and onto the sidewalk.

"Good seeing you again," he added over his shoulder. "And thanks for the soda."

Storming back into the house, I grabbed the freshly prepped bouquet, my coat, and purse and ran out to the car. I would only have time for a quick stop at the hospital at this point and would still be later than I wanted to pick up the kids, but at least I would have made the effort to put in an appearance—as per my agreement with Kevin—before Lynette and the baby were discharged in the morning.

"Hard to believe," I said into the rearview mirror when I drove past Rob as he walked to his car. "Looks like you've finally met someone more fucked up than you are."

Although I was disgusted by my latest encounter with Rob, our conversation had at least two significant benefits. Chief among them was that it proved I wasn't wrong about just how vile and odious a creature he was. If I'd had any lingering concerns about my impressions of him being colored by my latent attraction to Katrine, they could now be put to rest. For I had not imagined or manufactured the words he said to me today, nor were they open to interpretation. Thus, while I was guilty of committing adultery with Katrine and deceiving Kevin, at least I could take some ironic comfort in knowing I had been honest and accurate in my assessment of my nemesis.

A second benefit I derived from my conversation with Rob was that it kept my mind too busy to obsess about my visit with Lynette as I drove to the hospital. This prevented me from winding myself up again, which in turn made it less likely I would make an ass of myself as I sat among the handful of other visitors who may have assembled there.

I entered the hospital planning to never see Lyn again. Kevin would not have approved, but he wouldn't have to know. I would just have to get better at checking and deleting messages, and soon it wouldn't matter. Her random calls would become less frequent—if they continued at all after today—and then eventually stop completely.

Perhaps I should have felt guilty—if not about cutting her loose, then at least about not being up-front about it. But how do you break up with a friend? Even if wanted to, you can't tell the truth, since that would lead to hurt feelings—which, if it's really over, is cruel, and if there's hope, seems manipulative and self-serving. And it's not like you can say there's someone else, as one would when spurning a lover. You might get away with the old "It's not you; it's me," but when the relationship is already dying on the vine, why would you even bother?

That I hadn't wasted much energy preparing for the event was fortunate, since things went even more smoothly than I'd hoped. With four grandparents, an aunt, and two young cousins in attendance, nobody cared that I didn't ask to hold the baby or that I hadn't weighed in on the issue of whether her eyes would stay blue like Lyn's or turn hazel in a month like those of Lyn's brother, Kent. And although my homemade offering made me feel rather like the Little Drummer Boy amid all the comparatively elaborate balloon bouquets, lollipop trees, and floral arrangements Lyn's relatives had brought, I consoled myself with the knowledge that they would eventually all be dead—the flowers and balloons, that is—and that mine would take less time to decompose. More importantly, thanks to all the commotion, I was also able to extract myself from the scene earlier than I had planned without appearing rude.

My duty done, I bid everyone good-bye and prepared to take my leave.

"What's she doing here?" I heard Josh ask as he suddenly appeared in the doorway.

Unsure of to whom he was referring, I turned around to see if I could identify the party whose presence was unexpected and unwelcome. Finding no one among the celebrants who would fit that that description, I looked at Lyn to see if her expression or the direction of her gaze might offer a clue as to the subject of Josh's remarks.

It was only then—as her face reddened and she turned away—that I realized it was me.

"I thought you talked to her?" Josh demanded of her, thereby confirming that I had reached the right conclusion.

Dumbfounded by this realization, I continued to watch as she sat frozen in his disapproving stare. "Talked to me about what?" I asked as the other visitors took turns looking at each other.

"Fine," Josh said when Lyn didn't answer. "If you won't tell her, I will."

"Tell me *what*?"

"Not here," he ordered with a nod toward the hall. "Outside."

Driven more by my curiosity than by deference to Josh, I followed him out to the hall. As I did so, I cast my mind back over the duration of our acquaintance in the hope of figuring out what I had said or done that would give him cause to eject me in front of such an audience.

"You're not welcome here," he said before I could make a sound.

"I gathered that. What I don't understand is why."

"I don't want Lyn to see you anymore. I could put up with you when it was just the two of us, but we have a child now, and we don't want to expose her to you, your foul mouth, your feminist venom, or your offensive liberal values."

Wow. Yet another bombshell I hadn't seen coming.

Or had I?

"Haven't you noticed that we've been avoiding you?" Josh asked. "Or that we never have time to play cards anymore? Or how, when we do get together, it's never just the four of us, and we always keep it short and sweet?"

Of course, I'd noticed that. I'd noticed that and more. Including the way Lyn had started turning up alone and out of nowhere lately and acting as if she had something to say but could never quite get around to it. And how she seemed more annoyed than usual when I offered my opinion or did something she considered outrageous—like refusing to dance with Rob at the Halloween dance or asserting myself with Kevin.

She'd been trying to work up to telling me I couldn't be part of her life anymore, and she blamed me—not Josh—that she had to end it. If I hadn't been such a bleeding-hearted, pinko feminist—or if I'd simply been willing to be quiet about it—Josh would have continued to look the other way and not forced her to kick me to the curb.

Of course, no one would have believed me if I'd said anything about it before today. Instead they would have accused me of being hypersensitive. Thin-skinned. Even paranoid.

Like Quinn, who—when I tried to decline her cousin's offer to drive me home that night because he gave me the creeps—said I was crazy to think I wouldn't be safe with him.

Or like Kevin, who dismissed my distrust for Rob as a consequence of his having tried too hard to make a good impression, only to realize two months later that the guy lacked judgment and respect for authority; and who—despite recent indications to the contrary—only yesterday had claimed Lynette needed me and chastised me for always expecting people to disappoint or desert me.

But what I'd seen was not the product of an overactive imagination or fear of abandonment. It was as real and as plain as the nose on my face. I just didn't know then what it meant.

"And in case you're wondering," Josh was saying now. "This decision is not subject to negotiation. I'm sure Kevin sees things differently since you have him wrapped around your little finger, but as a marine, a Christian, and a patriot, your very existence offends me. And while I may have taken an oath to uphold the constitution that protects your right to think and speak as you do, I am under no obligation to listen."

Wow.

"If you feel that way, why did you call us when Lyn went into labor?" I asked. "Or when the baby was born? And why did you come to our New Year's Eve party? Or the Halloween party?" *Why, why, why, why, why?*

"I called you as a favor to Lyn, who said you deserved to know, and because I thought she told you where we stood and that you'd have the decency to stay away. As far as the parties are concerned, I saw no harm in going to them since I have no issue with Kevin, the baby hadn't arrived yet, and I knew there'd be enough people around to keep you from bothering me."

Bothering him?

I would have laughed if the whole thing hadn't been so sad. How much time had I wasted putting up with that misogynistic bastard? How much energy had I expended biting my tongue when he said something unkind or unfair to Lyn? How hard had I worked to keep the peace with someone who, I realized now, not only despised me but didn't think I should exist?

And what about Lyn? How much guilt had I felt when I ignored or deleted one of her messages because I couldn't stand the tension between us but didn't want to make it worse? How many times had slapped on a brave face and put up with the patronizing smiles of her parents and other friends so I could be there for all her key milestones—including that nightmare of a baby shower and this train wreck of a hospital visit. And how stupid did I feel now, knowing I had done all of it for nothing?

It was a good thing I had already decided to end this relationship before arriving at the hospital. Having decided it was the last time I'd see these people made it that much easier to walk out of there with my head held high. Josh may have fancied himself the victor after our exchange, but like his fear of black people, gays, and poverty, it was all in his head. And while he definitely saw me as the loser in this, the only one to suffer would be Lyn—who would now have to live with having ejected me from her circle and endure whatever punishment she would receive for having refused to do it before today.

Not that I allowed these things to preoccupy me as I drove home that afternoon. Of greater import to me, now that I'd been formally excommunicated from the Church of Latimer, was what I was going to tell Katrine about my conversation with Rob, and when. Clearly she deserved to know about his visit, but just how to tell her, I had no idea. She already knew I disliked Rob and that I believed their marriage was destined to end in a fiery crash. Giving her more evidence would hardly change its course or convince her to step off the train.

Then again, I didn't have to treat the event like breaking news, I reasoned as I neared Miss Betty's Tot Spot. After all, it wasn't as if Rob was going to tell her anytime soon. Even if he thought it would upset Katrine to know I'd kept our meeting a secret, he wouldn't have spilled the beans, because, although he may not believe it, he would have had to manufacture something fairly evil and yet believable enough to make me look worse than he already did.

Thus, I resolved to bring it up if and when it became relevant.

Twenty-five

To my chagrin, my conversation with Rob became relevant in a big way when I found Katrine on the porch after school the next day.

"This is a surprise," I announced as I joined her at the door. "How are you?"

"How do I look?"

"Well, now that you mention it, like crap."

"I'd say that pretty much covers it."

"Ah. Well, come on inside," I instructed after popping the lower lock and extracting the deadbolt from the door jamb, "and you can tell me why."

Stepping through the door and out of my shoes, I shook off my jacket and hung it in the closet. "How come you didn't use your key?"

"Well, I knew you weren't expecting me, and I was afraid I'd startle you if I was inside when you arrived," she explained, taking off her own coat and laying it over the sofa. "I haven't been waiting that long anyway. In fact, I only just sat down after walking up from the bus stop."

"You came right from school, then?"

"Yeah. I was too wound up to wait around for Kevin. Plus, I thought it best if I told you this before he got home."

"Told me what?"

"I think Rob knows about us."

Us?

I confess, I had never thought of me and Katrine as an "us." Although I loved her almost as much and in nearly as many ways as I did Kevin,

I didn't expect her to love me in return, much less consider us an item. Rather, I assumed I was a diversion for her—a source of amusement or comfort to be tapped when things at home got boring or unpleasant. Perhaps I was selling myself short, but with little to offer in terms of commitment, I couldn't afford to be much more than a novelty anyway.

Maybe "us" was just shorthand, I allowed as Katrine and I sat down opposite one another on the couch. "I think Rob knows about us" was certainly a more efficient way of making a point than "I think Rob knows we've been fooling around now and then" would have been.

"What makes you think that?" I asked finally as I realized Katrine was awaiting a reply.

"Last night we were lying in bed, when out of nowhere he asks if there's anyone I've wanted to be intimate with since coming here. He then says he would understand if I wanted to see other people, since I hadn't really dated much before we met."

"OK," I breathed with a mixture of dismay and relief. "Well, I can see why that might have you a little freaked out, but I'm not sure that means Rob knows anything. After all, who besides one of us could have told him?"

"Nobody. But why else would he have brought that stuff up?"

"I don't know. Maybe he just thought he should say that in case something happened, so you wouldn't have to hide it from him or sneak around behind his back."

"But I wouldn't do that anyway."

"I hate to point this out, Katrine, but you already have."

Katrine's mouth fell open. "I can't believe you said that."

"Why? It's true."

"But it's not the same thing."

"Rob may not see it that way."

"How would you know?"

"I don't. I'm just saying he might not. But you obviously know him better than I do, so maybe he would. And maybe you were right before, and he does suspect there's something going on between us. It would be just like him to dance around the subject rather than confront it head on."

"You just can't resist, can you?" Katrine asked, shaking her head. "You just can't resist even the slightest opportunity to slam Rob."

"That was hardly a slam, Katrine."

"Really? Then what do you call it?"

"An unflattering, yet entirely accurate assessment of his character."

I crossed my arms as Katrine stared at me down. I found it ridiculous that she would stop to defend Rob's honor in the midst of a conversation over whether or not he knew she had cheated on him, and yet, I can't say I was surprised. Like the guy who stops to turn off all the lights as he's fleeing a house fire, Katrine had a tendency to miss the big picture in favor of fine details.

"All I'm trying to say," she said after a moment, "is that we have a potential disaster on our hands, and taking shots at Rob is not going to help."

"Trust me—if I wanted to take a shot at Rob, I could do a hell of a lot better than accuse him of being indirect. Meanwhile," I added, as long as we were off topic, "would you care to explain what—and more importantly, why—you told Rob about me and Melissa?"

Katrine's face burned a nervous red as her gaze shifted from me to the floor. "You never said it was a confidence."

"That's why you told him? Because I never asked you *not* to?"

"It wasn't like that."

"OK. Then exactly how was it?"

"Rob was just asking about the weekend when he got home on Sunday. So I told him what we did and what we talked about—or most of it."

"And while you were editing it, you couldn't have left out the part about Melissa?"

"I guess; but I thought it was funny how you met, and I knew he would, too. Besides, I didn't tell him you were physically involved."

"That was very kind of you, but apparently he figured that part out for himself—since he's now threatening to use it against me."

"What are you talking about?"

"Rob was here, Katrine. In fact, he was waiting on the porch when I got home from school yesterday and acting like an exile from Psychotics Anonymous."

"What did he say?"

"Well, first he thanked me for helping you adapt to your new locale. Then he informed me that my relationship with Melissa—not the edited version he admits you provided, but rather the fictitious yet somehow accurate one he crafted from it—is in danger of becoming public record if I don't comply with his demands."

"Which are?"

"To cease and desist with my campaign to turn you against him."

"Your *what*?"

"Oh, wait—it gets better. He also gave me permission to spend as much time with you as I like, and to sleep with you anytime I want."

"*What?*"

"That's right. Although he considers me a bad influence and would prefer that you not associate with me, he claims to have found certain *advantages* to having you occupied, which he is—quote, not prepared to give up, unquote—and which I'm required to keep to myself as a condition of his silence on the subject of Melissa and of you and me."

"So he's cheating on me?"

"That's how he made it sound."

"I don't understand. If you knew all of that, why didn't you call and tell me about this right after it happened?"

"Primarily because I was on my way out the door when he showed up, but also because when you're not over here, it usually means he's home, and I didn't think we would want him hanging around when we were discussing it. On top of that, I wasn't sure if he was telling the truth or just tossing me a rope to see if I would hang myself with it. I mean, the guy is convinced I'm out to break you up, and what better way to prove it than to feed me some bullshit he can honestly refute the moment you confront him with it?"

"Well, that makes sense, but then why didn't you tell me he knows about us as soon as I told you why I came here?"

"That's just it, Katrine. He doesn't *know* about us. He gave me *permission* to sleep with you but he's convinced I have yet to do so."

"Convinced? Are you sure?"

I nodded. "In fact, when I tested his confidence in that belief by suggesting that I had, he laughed and insisted it wasn't true, because if it was, you would have told him yourself. I suspect this may be what prompted your conversation last night," I continued. "Rob may have taken my taunting more seriously than he let on and decided to settle the matter by giving you a chance to tell him the truth."

"Maybe. But I still don't understand why you didn't tell me all this when I arrived. Couldn't you see how upset I was?"

"Of course I could. That's exactly why I *didn't* say anything right away. I didn't want to lend any weight to your concerns until I was sure they were justified. And while I'm inclined to think he doesn't have a clue about last weekend or New Year's Eve, we still don't know if he said you could see other people because that's something he thinks you should do, or because he was trying to see if you would admit to being involved with me."

"I see what you mean. So what are we going to do?"

"I don't know. I suppose you could just come out and tell him we've been intimate. That would eliminate his leverage and force things into the open."

"And what about Kevin?"

"You don't have to worry about Kevin. If you decide it's best for you to lay your cards on the table, he will be my problem, not yours."

"I don't know. I think the window has pretty much closed on that option after last night."

"I'm inclined to agree."

"So what's plan B?"

"We stop seeing each other, and you and Rob ride off into the sunset. That takes me out of the picture altogether, thereby eliminating Rob's excuse for obsessing about my intentions."

"I don't think I could go along with that."

"OK. So we don't stop seeing one another altogether," I offered. "We simply stop seeing one another *in* the altogether, and, meanwhile, you get Rob some professional help."

"I'm not sure I can do that either."

"I'm not suggesting you commit him, Katrine, or even send him to therapy. In fact, it would probably seem less suspicious and be as beneficial for you to make it about the two of you and ask him to go to couples counseling."

"I'm not sure that would work, either."

"It's worth a try. All he can say is no."

"And accuse you of putting me up to it."

"Why would he do that? If I were trying to split you up, I wouldn't recommend counseling."

"You would if you knew he wouldn't go and that his refusal would make him look bad."

This was beyond absurd, and I could see from the sudden interest in her shoes that Katrine knew it. *That's what you get for becoming involved with a teenager*, I chastised myself. *The next time you decide to fool around, make sure you do it with someone who was born before the advent of color TV.*

"Katrine, have you and Rob already talked about this?"

"No."

"I don't mean the counseling," I added in case she had misunderstood or was hoping to sidestep the issue by exploiting my lack of clarity. "I mean his issues with me or my so-called plan to break you up."

"He hasn't come right out and said you're trying to break us up, but there have been a few instances where I took issue with something he did and he suggested you'd put me up to it, and there have been times I objected to comments he made and he said you were a bad influence."

"So he's making me the scapegoat for any displeasure you express and virtually anything you say or do in your own defense?"

"I guess."

"Well, how convenient is that? You're never responsible for any of the things you say, so he never has to take you seriously."

"I guess."

"So where does this crap come from?"

"I'm not sure; but it may have something to do with what happened with him and Lori."

"Who the hell is Lori?"

"Rob's ex-wife."

"Rob was married before?"

Katrine nodded. She then went on to explain how Lori cheated on Rob whenever he was out of town and how she'd drained their bank accounts and decimated his credit before packing up and leaving him with nothing.

"That's terrible," I said, with feigned sympathy. "But you left out the part where she killed and dismembered twelve women between here and Florida," I said. "And the time she kidnapped and raped two nuns."

"What is that supposed to mean?"

"The woman *left* him, Katrine. Do you honestly think he'd portray her as a saint?"

"Are you saying he's lying?"

"I don't know if he's lying or not. What I do know is that there are two sides to every story, and if you think he's given you the unvarnished truth, you should contact the folks at Guinness, because it will be the first time such a thing has happened with a disgruntled ex-spouse."

"Come on, Jackie—what defense could she possibly have for everything she did to him?"

"I don't know. But that's not the point. The point is, you have to consider the source."

I could tell Katrine wasn't keen to examine Rob's motives, nor was she eager to discuss them with me. And although I couldn't have given a shit, since I had no dog in the fight, I thought it might help Katrine decide how to handle Rob if she understood his relationship with Lori.

"When did you first hear about all this, anyway?" I asked, in hopes of understanding it myself.

"Last night."

Last night? "Are you telling me that you've known this man for over a year and only found out last night that he was married before?"

"No. He told me when we started dating. He just didn't give me the details until last night."

"So after all this time, he suddenly opens up about his ex-wife and how she did him wrong. Didn't you find his timing a bit curious?"

Katrine shrugged. "I guess I didn't think it was relevant."

"I'm not trying to make you feel bad, Katrine, I just know people better than you do. And although taken in context with his offer to let you see other people, I can see how you might have assumed his remark about Lori were part of some new policy of openness he wants to establish with you, I think it was much more likely he was trying to arouse your sympathies so you'll stop calling him on his shit."

"Do you honestly think he would manipulate me like that?"

"To keep you in line? Yes, I think he would manipulate you like that. And to be frank, he probably did the same to this Lori. In fact, he probably treated her exactly the way he treats you in all respects, only she wouldn't stand for it and got out while the getting was good."

"Maybe she did," Katrine sniffed. "Or maybe it happened just like he said. Maybe he's still hurting from what she did, and that's why he can't treat me the way you think he should."

"Maybe. But even if he did nothing to deserve what she did, you shouldn't have to pay for it, Katrine. You shouldn't be held accountable for her sins, or have to sacrifice your liberty because she abused hers."

Katrine sighed. "Why do you have to make this so hard?"

"I'm not the one making anything hard. I'm just telling it like it is. Now, you have a decision to make, and I can't make it for you. So do tell him or don't tell him. I'll be fine whatever you decide, and I won't have anything more to say about you and Rob either way."

"What about Melissa?"

"What about her?"

"What if Rob tells Kevin about her?"

"Like I said, you don't have to worry about Kevin. He isn't going to be a problem."

"How do you know that?"

"I just do."

"He knows, doesn't he? About you and Melissa?"

"What Kevin does or doesn't know is not the point."

"Does he know about us, too?"

"What? No. Like I said in January—"

"Never mind what you said in January. I want to know, now: What does Kevin know about Melissa? And what does he know about us?"

As much as I would have liked to, I dared not tell Katrine what Kevin knew about Melissa. While it might ease her mind to know he had always known the true nature of our relationship and that it was useless as a weapon against me, that was the one card I had that would trump any Rob might play, and I couldn't risk putting it in her impulsive hands knowing she might, in a fit of pique, play it too soon.

"Oh, I get it," Katrine said when I hesitated too long. "You don't trust me."

That wasn't strictly true. I trusted Katrine not to deliberately hurt me, and I trusted her not to let Rob deliberately hurt me either. On the other hand, she wasn't experienced or guileful enough to know whether he was planning to cause me harm or what tools he might employ to do so.

"Well, if you don't trust me," she was saying now, "I guess I can't trust you either."

"Oh, come on, Katrine. Of course you can."

"Really? And just how would I know? After all, as you so eloquently pointed out, there are two sides of every story. So maybe Rob was right. Maybe you are trying to make him look bad so you can break us up. Maybe you've been lying to me this whole time, and you really are out to get him, just like he said."

"Or maybe it's you I'm out to get," I countered. "Maybe I'm trying to get you out of the way so I can have Rob the egomaniac all to myself."

Katrine shook her head. "If you're going to be sarcastic," she hissed, "I'm going to leave."

"And if you're just going to be absurd, you may as fucking well."

"Fine." Snatching her jacket off the couch, Katrine thrust her arms through the sleeves and yanked in over her shoulders. "But this is the *last* time I come to you for advice."

"Can I get that in writing?"

Grabbing my backpack and purse from the floor, I stormed out to the kitchen, expecting to hear the door slam behind me. Hearing nothing by the time I'd set them on the table, I turned around and found Katrine looking calmer, yet clearly not herself, standing where I'd left her.

"I'm sorry," she said quietly. "It wasn't supposed to be like this."

"I know." *Please take care of yourself,* I willed as she opened the door and pulled it shut behind her. *And if you need something, let me know.*

A moment later, Kevin walked through the same door holding Lucy in his arms and Tyler by the hand. "What's up with Katrine?" he asked, planting a kiss on my cheek as he entered the kitchen. "I said 'Hi,' but she didn't answer."

"Just some shit with Rob."

"Anything I should know?"

"I'm not sure."

"Well, let me know when you are," he said, handing off the baby. "I'll be happy to listen."

Twenty-six

Nearly four weeks passed with no word from Katrine. I knew this because, to my surprise, I managed to live up to my twin promises to keep the phones on and to check the machine for messages daily.

I'll admit my success in achieving this goal also had something to do with my hope that Lyn would call to apologize, thereby giving me the chance to tell her what I thought of her and that I wanted nothing more than to be there when she got everything she deserved in return for her lack of courage, loyalty, and basic human decency. Of course, the fact that she had not called during that time proved that I was correct in my assessment of her and, therefore, in my decision to cut her loose even before the scene at the hospital. *Good riddance,* I said, nearly every time I looked at the machine. *You don't fucking deserve me.*

An equal share of the credit, however, goes to my unwavering hope that Katrine would call. For all my frustration with her, I missed her more than I could possibly express and worried about her night and day. Having not seen or heard from her since our fight, I had no clue as to which course of action she had taken with Rob and no idea what fallout to expect as a result thereof.

In truth, I worried less about the price I would pay than how Katrine would suffer if Rob didn't care for what she did or said. Not that I expected Katrine to confront him about the so-called *advantages* he had spoken of, since, again, his peccadilloes—real or imagined—did not trump hers; but I also knew that arguments can take on a life of their own, especially when one of the contenders is a novice, and while Rob didn't seem like the violent type, given his actions of late, I wasn't sure what he was capable of or how far he would go to protect his interests.

As much as it pained me to imagine what lay ahead for Katrine, I vowed to stay out of it. No matter how much I missed her, she had to make her own way, and I had no right to interfere. Even if she came to me for help, as I had telepathically urged her to do, I planned to do only what was necessary to ensure her safety. By now I knew my limits when it came to resisting her charms, and while I couldn't blame her for my addiction, neither could I pretend, as junkies will do, that I could handle even a little hit of the good stuff now and then.

Thus, it was with a mixture of delight and trepidation that I responded to the sight of her waving at me from a picnic table near the armory parking lot one afternoon. With an affected calm, I returned the wave and walked over to where she sat with her backpack and a stack of textbooks. She looked beautiful and, more importantly, happy, and I genuinely hoped it wasn't just because she'd seen me.

"How's it going?" she asked as I approached.

"Good, thanks. You?"

"Same." Katrine smiled. "I heard your friend Lynette had her baby."

"Really? How?"

"The usual way, I imagine. Although I didn't press for details."

"I didn't mean *that*."

"I know," Katrine giggled. "But you left yourself wide open."

"So how did you find out?"

"I ran into Josh at the store the other day.

Of course. I had forgotten that they knew each other.

"So have you seen her yet?" Katrine asked.

"Who?"

"The baby?"

I nodded. "I went to the hospital before they took her home," I said, noting that the last time I'd seen Lyn was the day before I'd last seen Katrine. "She and Lyn both looked good."

"Are you all right?" Katrine asked. "You seem a little out of it today."

"Yeah, I guess I am."

"Any particular reason?"

Apart from the fact that I've missed you, and now that you're here, I can hardly breathe?

306

"Not really—although having to rearrange my day to bring Kevin his notebook didn't help."

"So that's why you're here."

I nodded again. "The guy flies out of the house so fast lately he practically forgets his head, which means at least once a week, he's either got to run back to the house before he gets all the way to school, or—as was the case today—I have to ride in on my white horse and save his forgetful ass. Meanwhile, I have a term paper due Monday that I had planned to write this weekend—that is, until I remembered Kevin's mom is expecting us *there* instead."

"Ouch."

"Tell me about it," I laughed. "So, yeah, I'm a little out of it today."

"Think he'd go without you?"

"Without the kids? In a heartbeat. With the kids? Could be a tough sell."

"Too bad."

I shrugged. "How about you?" I asked, noting the unseasonably warm weather. "Are you enjoying our early summer?"

"Sure. But only by military mandate."

"What do you mean?"

"Haven't you heard? I've been banned from the armory."

"Banned? You're kidding. Why?"

"Not sure. They claim it has to do with improving security, but I'm not buying it."

"Why not?"

"Well, you're the only other civilian I've seen go up there in two weeks, and I notice they didn't keep you out. I don't know what the real story is," Katrine continued with a shrug. "All I know is that I've been asked not to hang around in there anymore, so I'm out here—not hanging around."

"Ah. So, are you between classes or what?"

"No—just waiting for Rob. He's meeting me at the car when he finishes up today."

Upon hearing the name, I glanced back at the armory and breathed a secret sigh of relief. How I'd managed to avoid a collision with him during my trip through the building, I didn't know, but I was certainly grateful for my good luck.

"Well, I have a class at one," I added, "but if you'd like, I can swing by here afterward and pick you up on my way home if you don't want to wait."

"Thanks, but Rob has to work tonight, and if I don't want to have to take the bus to school in the morning, I have to drive him there myself."

"Makes sense," I mused, observing the books and notecards lying about. "Finals?"

"Yeah. Just one more to go."

"Kevin, too. And, boy, is he looking forward to spring break."

"That makes two of us. So are you guys going anywhere?"

I shook my head. "The private schools don't go on break for another week or so, and we don't get a full week because we're on semesters."

"Well, at least you only have finals twice a year."

Amen.

"Well, I guess I should get going," I said, suddenly aware I might be running late. "It was nice talking to you. Take care, and good luck with your exams."

"Thanks. I'll see ya."

Smiling from head to toe, I rushed to my car, pleased to know she didn't hate me.

I was *not* pleased, however, to see the dash clock—according to which I had precisely seventeen minutes to get to my own campus, park, and run to class before Doc Corrigan shut and locked the door.

With seconds to spare, I got to the classroom, only to find my efforts had been wasted.

Dr. Corrigan out of town due to family emergency, read the note that had been posted on the door. *Class to resume on Wednesday.*

"Well, that figures," I huffed, still winded from my sprint from the parking lot. "Good thing I didn't rush or anything."

Returning to my car, I imagined how I'd kill my unexpected hour of free time. I should have probably spent it on my blasted project, I knew, but I wasn't in the mood to think that hard. I contemplated picking the kids up early and taking them to the park, but I wasn't compos mentis enough to do that either, and, more significantly, they were presently in the middle of their nap. Finally, I considered going back to the armory to visit with Katrine, but doubting I'd be lucky enough to avoid running into Rob a second time around, I opted against that as well.

"Besides," I reasoned as I passed that exit, "she may be on her way home now anyway."

With that in mind, I decided to stop by Katrine's on my way home and invite her out for coffee. It had been great to see her looking so terrific and—apparently despite her issues with the armory leadership—sounding so confident. I hoped her attitude was genuine and not an act. For despite what our estrangement was doing to my appetite and sleeping habits, I hoped she was faring better in both departments. I wanted her to be happy, after all, and a chat over coffee might be just the thing to assure me she was doing well.

With this in mind, I took an early right off the main boulevard after leaving the freeway and drove up to the stop sign at the end of her street, from where I could see down the street to her house at the middle of the block. Sure enough, the Nova was out front.

Taking another right, I cruised down the street, pulled over behind the Nova, and parked. I didn't bother to lock the car but skipped up the stairs, rapped twice on the door, and then grabbed the knob and opened it.

"Knock, knock!" I called out as I peered through the arch into the empty living room. "Sorry to barge in on you like this, but I thought you might like to get some coffee!"

Hearing footsteps behind me, I turned around and froze at the sight of Rob wearing nothing but a pair of gym shorts and the proverbial smile.

"Well, hello, Jackie," he said with a strange absence of malice. "Long time no see."

A nod was all I could muster in return.

"And how have you been since our last chat?"

"Fine, thanks," I stammered. "You?"

He nodded to indicate the same. "And to what do I owe this honor?"

"I'm looking for Katrine," I pronounced, since it was the truth.

"So I gather. Well, unfortunately, she isn't here."

"OK. Well, I guess I'll just catch up with her some other time."

"Oh, now, don't go rushing off on my account," he said before I could follow through. "Come on in and visit for a while."

"Thanks, but I should get home."

"Don't be silly," he insisted, blocking my only means of exit. "Katrine would have my head if I didn't show you some hospitality. Now come on in and sit down."

Numbly, I let him herd me toward a presidential-looking wing chair, cursing myself for my ridiculous spontaneity.

"That's better," he said as I stiffly took my seat. "Now, what can I get you to drink?"

"Nothing, thanks. I honestly can't stay very long."

"I understand. But as long as you're here, I'd like you to meet a friend of mine," he urged. "Oh, Erin," he then called down the hall. "Come out here for a second. We have company."

We?

A moment later, *Erin* walked in wearing an off-white sweater and tan jeans. She looked about my height but weighed, I calculated, all of a hundred ten when soaking wet. She had rich golden-brown hair with amber highlights that she wore in a tousled bob with one side tucked up behind her ear. Her style, combined with a broad smile and animated but intelligent expression, reminded me of Meg Ryan.

"Hi," she said cheerfully as she extended her hand. "Erin Rollins. It's great to meet you."

"Jackie Thompson. Same here."

"Erin's one of the new midterm entries," Rob explained. "Kevin may have mentioned her."

"Yes. I think he did," I lied. "Navy option, right?"

Lucky guess, I mused when they both nodded.

"Well, I'll leave you two to get acquainted," Rob announced, clasping his palms together nervously, "while I finish getting dressed."

Erin nodded and sat down on the arm of the couch as he walked away. "So you're the better half of our illustrious Sergeant Thompson?" she asked. "I've heard a lot about you."

"From whom?" I wondered, although I wasn't sure I wanted to know.

"Some of the senior midshipmen."

I laughed. "Well, don't take what they say too seriously; they're probably too afraid of Kevin to say what they really think."

"I doubt that. Especially since they've seen him in tights."

"So you've heard about the Halloween party."

"Oh, yes." Erin laughed. "And seen the evidence. So what do you do while he's busy promoting truth, justice, and the American way?"

"Well, mostly I do my part to make life difficult for him, but I'm also a senior at Hamilton College in St. Paul."

"No kidding. I almost enrolled there myself. Unfortunately, they wouldn't take me as a new freshman until the next fall, which defeated the whole purpose of transferring in the middle of the year. But the U was willing to take me, and they had ROTC slots available, so I registered there instead."

"And how do you like it so far? ROTC, I mean."

"It's too soon for me to tell, really, but I'm sure I'll fall in love with it if my scholarship is approved."

Ah. "So you haven't officially entered the program."

"No. I've submitted my package, but I won't know anything until sometime next quarter."

"Well, I hope you get in. The armory could use some more estrogen."

"Tell me about it. Either way, I plan to be very careful in the ladies' room. A girl could lie unconscious for days in there before anyone would find her."

I laughed out loud. "So have you decided on a major yet, or are you still browsing?"

Erin nodded. "Computer science—same as Rob."

"Ah, so you two have classes together?"

"Just one this term. In fact, the final is tomorrow."

"Well, in that case, I should go and let you two study."

"Oh, we weren't studying. Rob was just having some trouble with his hard drive and asked me to come take a look."

"Nevertheless," I said, hoping to clear out before Rob reappeared, "I should get home. I've got kids in day care, errands to run—the whole boring suburban domestic thing…"

"OK. Well, it was great talking to you, Jackie."

"Same here. Maybe we'll run into each other again sometime."

"Sounds good."

"So how was your day?" I asked Kevin between bites at dinner later.

The events of my own had been on my mind all afternoon, and I could hardly wait for him to get home so I could grill him about my new acquaintance.

Naturally, there were some questions I would not be asking him but that nagged at me just the same. Like, was Erin one of the "advantages" Rob had referred to during his visit to our place last month? If so, was she aware of his intentions? More importantly, I wondered, did Katrine know of Erin and that Rob was spending time alone with her at their house?

Obviously I couldn't share what I'd witnessed today, since I wasn't sure what it meant. Rob's being home with Erin when he was presumably at school, though suspicious, proved him guilty of nothing. Katrine hadn't actually said from where he was coming to meet her, after all, so for all I knew, she knew. Even his behavior, which seemed to suggest—rather deliberately, in fact—that there was something going on between and Erin, did not prove they were more than friends. For all I knew, Rob had merely seized the opportunity to up the ante on his stupid spy game and made Erin an unwitting player in his psy-ops fantasy.

Erin, meanwhile, gave no indication that the two were more than classmates. Friendly and forthcoming, she'd been neither awkward with me nor unnerved by my arrival. And while her friendliness could have been as much an act as Rob's likely was, a lack of awkwardness would not have been so easy to fake.

If her actions suggested they were no more than friends, Erin's personality strengthened that perception. Lively and pretty, funny and bright, she likely attracted her share of admirers and would not have to scrape the bottom of the barrel. In short, whatever intentions he had in mind, Erin was too sharp to get involved with a married man—much less one as obnoxious as Rob.

Still, I was anxious to get Kevin's impressions of the girl and strengthen my hope that there was nothing going on between her and Rob.

"Guess whom I met today?" I asked after his typically brief and vague summation of his day.

"I give up. Who?"

"Erin Rollins."

"No kidding."

"You don't know who that is, do you?"

"Should I?"

"You're kidding, right?"

"Why? Is she someone famous?"

"No. But she does go to your school."

"So do about forty thousand other people, Jackie. Cut me some slack."

"OK, well, she's a freshman and a new ROTC candidate."

"Oh, you mean that new navy option we got in last quarter. With the punk haircut?"

"Well, I wouldn't exactly call it *punk*. But yeah, that's her."

"I see. Then I guess your little visit to the armory wasn't a complete waste." Smiling, Kevin picked up my hand, kissed it, and placed it under his own on the table. "Thanks for bringing me that notebook, by the way. You saved my life."

"I know. And you're welcome."

"So what was Erin doing at the armory today? Frosh don't muster during finals week."

"Well, we didn't meet at the armory," I admitted, kicking myself for failing to consider that detail. "We met at Katrine's."

"At Katrine's? I didn't know they were acquainted."

"Neither did I—since this was the first I've ever heard of her."

"So did Rob introduce them, or did they meet on their own?"

"I don't know."

"Katrine didn't say?"

"No. See, Katrine was at school."

"So it was *Rob* who introduced you?"

I nodded.

"At his house?"

"Yeah."

"And they were there alone?"

"Well, until I got there, anyway."

"And how did you wind up there, exactly?"

"My last class was cancelled, so I stopped in to see if Katrine wanted to go out for coffee."

"I thought you said she was at school."

"I had run into her near the armory earlier," I explained, fighting the verbal equivalent of an undertow, "and she had said she was waiting for Rob so she could drive him to work. Well, the car was out front when I drove by later, so I figured—since I'd already been to school and back—that she'd been to Rob's work and back. So I stopped in, and, well, she wasn't there."

"But *he* was?"

"Right. And so was Erin."

"Interesting."

"That's what I thought. Only I didn't want you jumping to any conclusions, which is why I tried to avoid explaining all of this until you had told me more about her."

"I see. Well, I don't know much about her except that she's someone who shouldn't be spending time alone with Rob if she doesn't want to give people the wrong idea."

Especially if it's the right *idea.*

Kevin sighed. "So are you going to tell Katrine?"

"Tell her what, Kevin? That Rob needed some help with their computer?"

"Computer? Since when do they have a computer?"

"Shit. I hadn't even thought of that."

"Well, they must've bought one," Kevin said decidedly. "Even Rob isn't dumb enough to concoct a story that could so easily fall apart."

"Actually, the story came from Erin, so it may be true."

"Unless she assumed they had one and didn't realize you knew otherwise."

"Either way, Katrine did not seem to know they were over there, and I am not about to be the one to tell her."

"What if she asks?"

"Kevin, if they're hiding something, they sure as hell aren't going to tell her they saw me, and therefore she won't have reason to ask."

"No. But if she does find out later or at some point becomes suspicious, she might come to you. What will you do then?"

"Plead insanity, I suppose."

"Well, that may be easy enough for you to prove, but why not go for ignorance first?"

"Great idea, Kev. If she asks, I'll just pretend it all looked perfectly innocent—I'm sure she'll have no problem believing I'm a complete idiot."

"OK, so maybe that *won't* work; but until we know otherwise, we have to assume it *was* innocent."

"But you don't think it was?"

"Well, something's keeping him busy this quarter. He's failing half his classes."

"Again?"

"Apparently. Of course, those grades were from midterm, so there's time for them to get better. But considering his less-than-stellar performance at the FTX, if his final marks aren't any better—or if rumors about him and Ms. Rollins start flying—Rob's going to be in deep shit."

"Well, they won't hear a thing from me. That much I can promise."

Kevin nodded as he washed the kids and I began to clear the table. "So, other than getting yourself wedged between a rock and a hard place," he asked, "how did things go for you today?"

"Fine, actually. If you discount the time I spent playing delivery boy. Which reminds me: it's payback time, buddy."

"Oh, shit. I get the feeling this one's gonna cost me."

"Sure is. You know the visit you promised your mom this weekend?"

"Yeah?"

"I'm afraid you're going to have to go without me."

Kevin shrugged. "That's OK with me, I guess," he said gravely, "but then who'll watch the kids while you work on your paper?"

I turned to argue with him but could only stare in shock and dismay.

"You are way too easy!" he laughed as a wicked grin spread across his lips. "Of course I'll take them with me. I'd planned to offer this morning, but I was in a hurry and forgot."

"You? In a hurry? Kevin, that doesn't sound like you at all."

"You'd better watch it," he warned. "There's still plenty of time for me to change my mind about this weekend."

"You wouldn't."

Kevin laughed. "No. In fact, I was thinking we might stay down there through next Friday instead of coming back this Sunday."

"You mean you'd let me have the house to myself for an entire week?"

"Of course. But I don't want to hear about any lingerie parties or pillow fights later—unless there are Polaroids."

I shook my head. "You're impossible!"

"I know. Ain't it great?"

Twenty-seven

B y Friday afternoon, I had all but forgotten about Erin and Rob and was running at full bore in panic mode over my dreaded term paper. Three false starts on the outline, combined with an ever-deepening disinterest in the subject matter, eventually drove me into the arms of the pint of Black Jack Cherry I'd originally planned to serve as a reward for a job well done.

Twenty minutes after cracking the carton, as I stared at the pile of books, seven pages of scribbled crap, and what seemed like thousands of three-by-five-inch notecards that lay on the floor—and which I desperately wanted to set on fire—the doorbell rang.

Praying it was a lost Schwann's driver offering frozen pizza in exchange for directions or sexual favors, I practically skipped across the room to answer it.

"Katrine," I said warily as I yanked the door open with my free hand and found her on the other side. "I didn't expect to see you here," I observed, closing the door behind her. "Shouldn't you be chugging beer on a beach somewhere in Florida?"

"Probably. But I'm not legal, remember?"

"Then how about some Black Jack Cherry?" I offered instead, scraping together the softened remains of my ice cream and holding it in front of her face. "Last bite."

"No, thanks. Cherries make me want to yack."

317

Shrugging, I sucked the spoon clean, dropped it into the empty carton, and set it on the already cluttered end table. "So what's up?" I asked, resting my rump on the edge of the couch.

"Not much. I had some time to kill, so I thought I'd drop by and see how things are going."

"How did you know I'd be here?"

"Kevin told me."

Oh?

"I ran into him at school yesterday," Katrine explained as she stepped between my bent knees. "When I asked him what he planned to do this weekend, he told me he and the kids were heading south today. I figured that meant you'd talked him into going without you."

I see.

"And just what are *you* up to tonight?" I inquired in a seductive tone as I looked from her to the stacks of paper behind her and back again. "Besides checking up on me, that is."

"I'm not sure at the moment. Why do you ask?"

"I was just wondering if you might like to stick around for a while."

Katrine smiled. "I could probably be persuaded," she offered, winding a lock of my hair around her finger. "What did you have in mind?"

"Homework."

"*Homework?*" Katrine repeated as she crossed her arms. "Are you serious?"

"I'm afraid so."

"I assumed you'd be done by now."

"Me, too," I admitted. "On the upside, I've done the research, so all we have to do is organize the material, type and edit the paper, and create a notes page and bibliography."

"Oh, is *that* all?"

"Come on—it'll be fun."

"No, it won't."

"OK, that was a lie. But you do kind of owe me for all the papers I typed for you this year."

Katrine sighed. "That's true," she allowed. "Speaking of which, it may interest you to know that I'll be typing them myself from now on, since Rob just bought a computer."

"No kidding?" I mused as if this was the first I'd heard of it. "What kind?"

"According to Rob, it's a state-of-the-art Packard Bell Legend I 286—whatever that means."

"I believe that's nerd for *expensive*."

"Could be. All I know is that it cost me my best excuse for coming over here."

I found that remark funny, since I hadn't seen her in weeks and hadn't typed a paper for her since a few weeks before that. "Don't be silly," I said anyway, ignoring the voice that was telling me to send her packing. "You don't need an excuse to be here. You're always welcome."

"Always?"

"Always."

"That's good." Katrine murmured, placing her arms atop my shoulders and crossing her wrists behind my head. "I was afraid I was going to have to be more creative."

"I have no problem with that. I like creative."

"Me, too."

"Perfect," I replied as I turned my face to the side and started to stroke her forearm with my cheek. "Then why don't we go upstairs and…get…creative…with…my…paper?"

Katrine yanked her hands back and crossed her arms again. "That was mean," she charged. "Really, really, really, really mean."

"I know—and I'm sorry." I admitted, hooking my thumbs through the belt loops on either side of her waist. "But I *have* to get down to business, Katrine. That sucker is due Monday, and it represents forty percent of my grade."

"But it's only Friday."

"I know it's only *Friday.* But I don't dare leave this to the last minute. Besides, Kevin took the kids with him so I could work—not play."

Katrine sighed. "You can be such a killjoy."

"True. But those are the breaks. So are you going to stick around and help me? Or are you headed home?"

Katrine sighed again. "I guess I can hang around and help for a while," she said, raising her arms as if to stretch. "And who knows?" she added as she pulled her sweatshirt over her head to reveal a spaghetti strap camisole. "Maybe with the right motivation, you could finish early."

Oh, my.

I'm going straight to hell, I decided two mornings later. Even before I'd opened my eyes—even before I'd felt the sun hitting my eyelids—I knew there was no way I was going to get away with what I had done with, to, and for Katrine over the last thirty-six hours. I may as well jump in a hole, douse myself with gasoline, and light the damn match.

Finding her still asleep, I got out of bed, pulled on a T-shirt and a pair of jeans, and ran out for doughnuts and a newspaper. I returned to find Katrine showered, dressed, and packed.

"You've been busy," I observed.

Katrine nodded. "I figured it was about time to get things back to normal," she said, nodding at the bag in my hand. "After breakfast, of course."

"Of course."

After making coffee and setting the table, we sat down across from each other and started sorting the paper.

"So how come you haven't asked me where Rob is?" Katrine asked as she tidied up the stack of circulars I'd set aside for Kevin to read later.

"Well, apart from the fact that I don't care, I assumed he was working."

"All weekend?"

"It wouldn't be the first time—and you do have a new computer to pay for."

"I suppose so."

"So is he?" I asked, less out of curiosity than obligation. "Working, I mean?"

"No. He's at home."

"So why aren't you?"

"Because he has company."

"Oh?"

"Her name is Erin Rollins," Katrine pronounced meaningfully as she pulled a frosted ring from the box on the table and prepared to devour it. "Now do you understand?"

"Well, I wish I didn't, but from your tone, I think so, yes."

"You sound as if you don't approve."

"I'm hardly in a position to approve or disapprove, Katrine. But it does beg the question: does he know what you're up to?"

"No."

"Then what does he think you're doing here?"

"Helping you with your project. I told him that you were under the gun, that Kevin was probably taking the kids to his mom's for the weekend so you could work on it, and that I was coming over here to see if I could help facilitate."

"To which he naturally replied," I proposed, "'No problem, honey. You run along and do that, and I'll just spend the weekend having sex with Erin Rollins?'"

"Not quite. He had his plans before I did."

"So where were you going to go if you hadn't run into me earlier this week?"

"Probably here, still. After talking to you and Kevin, I mean."

"I see. So how exactly did we get from 'I think Rob knows about us,' and 'what are we going to do about it,' to 'Rob is having sex with Erin while I'm here with you?'"

"Well, I sulked for a while after I left here last time. I was upset by what you'd told me, and I didn't know what to do. But eventually I worked up the nerve to ask him if he'd meant what he said about seeing other people."

"And what did he say?"

"He said yes, that he thinks it's perfectly healthy thing for me to do."

"And you bought that?"

"Why wouldn't I?"

"It just sounds a little condescending and placatory to me, but go on."

"OK. Well, from there we discussed what would happen if one of us ever wanted to have a relationship with someone else, and eventually we got around to talking about specific people—whereupon he admitted that he was interested in Erin."

"So he's decided since you've come around to the idea of getting more experience, he's going to get in on the action, too?" I asked. "Or was that the point all along—to get your consent so he could carry on his extracurricular activities without guilt?"

"Does it matter?"

"It would to me, but then, it's not about me."

"Well, at least this way he can't accuse you of spilling the beans," Katrine was saying as I contemplated the conversation, "since he effectively spilled them himself."

"Well, thanks for that, I guess."

Despite my disapproval with the outcome, I was impressed with how Katrine had handled Rob. She'd managed to induce him to share his intentions without inciting him to defensiveness or prompting him to draw conclusions of his own. I hadn't imagined she had it in her to pull off such a maneuver without letting her nerves or emotions dime her out.

I should have felt relief that I was no longer under any obligation to keep Rob's so-called advantages from Katrine, that she had managed to get information from him without making me a scapegoat, and that she was now aware of his intentions, even if they were, in my view, completely self-serving. Instead I felt an intense sense of foreboding and a sudden urge to warn Erin to watch her back.

"So how do you feel about this?" I asked after posting a mental note to find an excuse to run into Ms. Rollins and gauge how she was doing. "Is this all really OK with you?"

"Why not? After all, fair is fair, right? Why should I get to have all the fun?"

Although I didn't doubt that equity had played a role in Katrine's decision to accept Rob and Erin's relationship, neither did I believe it was the whole ball of wax. Clearly there were other things at work here, such as fear of losing Rob or a desire to seem sophisticated.

"Besides, she's just some girl from school," Katrine was saying with affected conviction as she selected another doughnut from the box. "Nothing special."

I couldn't say for sure, having only met her once, but my impression of Erin had been that she could be quite special. That Katrine would suggest otherwise either meant that she hadn't met her, did not know how much contact Rob was likely to have with her in the future, or had simply, albeit grossly, underestimated her appeal.

"I wonder how she feels right now," Katrine suddenly pondered aloud.

Nauseous is how I imagined how I would feel after a weekend with Rob, but I thought it best not to share that information at this particular moment.

"What do you mean exactly?" I asked instead, having realized I didn't know.

"Well, didn't you feel different after *your* first time?"

"*First time?* You mean this girl was a *virgin?*"

"Evidently."

"Aw, Christ!" I groaned. "This just gets worse and worse."

"Why does that make it worse?"

"Well, call me crazy, but I don't think having sex with someone else's husband is really the ideal way to lose one's virginity."

"Maybe not. But she knows he's married, so she must be OK with it."

"Yeah? And how OK will she be when he tosses her aside? And, more importantly, how will you be if he doesn't?"

"What?"

"Don't tell me you didn't think of that."

"I guess I didn't."

Well, someone should have. Especially Rob.

"Look," I said when I saw Katrine's face darken, "I don't want to fight about Rob, but he is *not* using very good judgment here. Not only could someone get hurt, but he could get in a lot of trouble over this."

"Trouble? With whom?"

"With the unit, Katrine."

"Jackie, what are you talking about?"

"I'm talking about laws, Katrine. Laws pertaining to people who fuck around. Specifically, laws pertaining to military people who fuck around with other military people."

"That's illegal?"

"Let's just say it's a little more than frowned upon."

"So what could they do to us?"

"Well, they can't do anything to you and me—we're civilians and therefore not subject to military rules and regulations—but they can do a hell of a lot to Rob and Erin."

"Like what?"

"Like kick her out of ROTC, for starters."

"Wait a minute—do you *know* Erin?"

"No."

"Then how do you know she's in ROTC?"

I knew that one might come back to bite me in the ass someday, but there was no way I could be more forthcoming as to my knowledge of Erin without making matters worse than they were at the moment.

"Well, I know *of* her, Katrine. I know *who she is*. I also know she'll have it easy compared to Rob if they get caught."

"What do you mean?"

"All they can do to her is deny or revoke a scholarship; Rob they can court-martial."

"Oh, my God," Katrine breathed. "Rob would kill himself."

"He might as well. Even if they just ask for his DOR and send him back to the fleet, his career would be over."

"DOR?"

"Drop On Request." *Like in* An Officer and a Gentleman, I was about to add until I realized Katrine had been about eleven when the film was released. "It essentially means he couldn't hack the program and had to quit," I offered instead, "which would probably keep him from ever seeing another promotion again."

Katrine's face turned ashen. "You're not going to turn him in, are you?"

"Don't worry," I assured her, shaking my head. "I think Rob is a royal shit, but I'm not looking to ruin his career, and I'm hardly in a position to throw stones. Now Erin, on the other hand," I added before polishing off my milk, "well, let's just hope Rob doesn't give her reason to feel differently."

Twenty-eight

Katrine lingered until almost noon that morning, pretending to proofread my paper about ten times before giving up and saying she was tired. Knowing how late we'd gone to bed the last two nights—and how tense things had been since we got up this morning—I couldn't disagree that she probably needed sleep and thus didn't bother to protest. I hated to let her leave in the state she was in, but there was little I could do to change things, and, with my project deadline nearing, there seemed little else to do but let her go. Thus, I shoved the situation aside and thrust myself full steam into finishing the paper for my research project.

Monday afternoon, after turning in the paper and finishing what little homework I had to do for the rest of the week, I decided to get a head start on the spring cleaning I'd originally planned for the following weekend. That night, I took down all the curtains and sorted them for washing. In between loads I mopped the floors and washed the walls, the windows, and the baseboards.

By Wednesday, after defrosting the freezer and returning the machine I'd rented to clean the carpets and furniture, I finally ran out of steam and flopped down in front of the basement TV. Finding nothing there of interest, I switched off the TV and walked upstairs in time to hear Katrine's voice leaving a message on the machine in the kitchen. Without hesitation, I picked up the receiver in hopes of catching her before she hung up.

"Jackie?"

"The one and only."

"We need to talk."

What a buzzkill, I thought. *She could have at least argued over the likelihood of my exceptional status before getting down to business.* "OK. What about?"

"Rob and Erin."

I should have guessed.

"OK, but can we meet somewhere? I've been alone in this place for almost four days straight with nothing to do but clean, and I've got a severe case of cabin fever."

"That's fine. I'll just need you to pick me up. Rob has the car, and I don't want to be out walking this late."

"Thanks for coming," Katrine said as she slid into the passenger seat a few minutes later. "I really appreciate it."

"Not as much as I do. For a moment there I actually thought I might become the first person to actually die of boredom. So where to?"

"I don't know. Let's just drive around for a while."

"OK. Shall we cruise through the rich neighborhoods and condemn the frivolous excess, or circle the parks and see if we can witness a drug deal?"

"I don't care. Just drive."

I could see this was going to be a lot of fun. "OK, so what about Rob and Erin?" I asked nevertheless.

"I need to break them up."

"Break them up?" I laughed. "Forgive me, Katrine, but what's to break up? I mean, after four days there can't be anything between them that time and a little penicillin won't cure."

"This isn't a joke, Jackie."

"I'm sorry, Katrine. But I think you're making more out of this than you have to."

"You don't know what you're talking about."

"Then maybe you should enlighten me."

"Look, I just don't want Rob to see her anymore, that's all."

"So tell him to get rid of her."

"I already did. But he refused. He says he doesn't want to hurt her feelings."

"Well, isn't that sweet! Who knew he could be so thoughtful?"

"Jackie, you're not helping."

"I'm sorry, Katrine, but he's feeding you a line of bullshit. He may say he's concerned about her feelings, but it looks to me like he's just keeping his options open."

"Maybe. But it won't matter what he's trying to do if I can make *her* not want to see him."

"Then maybe the best thing to do is to *let* him see her—that seems to work for me."

Katrine scowled. "If all you can do is make jokes, maybe you should take me home."

"OK. I'll stop. But I still think you're jumping the gun here, Katrine. I mean, if they've only been together for one weekend."

"Look, it wasn't just one weekend! OK? They've been together every weekend for the last three weeks!"

"*Three weeks?*"

"Yes! Are you happy now?" Katrine demanded as I pulled the car over near a playground and turned off the ignition. "Does it all finally make sense?"

"So you lied to me?"

"Isn't it obvious?"

"Why would you do that?"

"What difference does it make? He was still her first. So what if it wasn't last weekend?"

"Look, you deliberately led me to believe they hadn't been together before. Now I want to know why you lied."

"You want to talk about lies? OK, how's this? 'No, Katrine, I don't know Erin. I only know *of* her.' Does any of that sound at all familiar?"

I stared at the dash as Katrine exited the Toyota and slammed the door.

"Yes, it does sound familiar," I admitted, joining her at the front bumper. "But that was the truth. I *don't* know Erin. I hadn't even met her until early last week."

"Well, you certainly could have mentioned that little encounter last weekend. You also could have told me that you met her at *my* house and that you were introduced to her by *my* husband."

"That's true. But then apparently you already knew."

"Not until I got home on Sunday," Katrine seethed. "Erin was there, you see, and since Rob had told her where I was, she asked how you were. That's when she told me how you'd met."

"So you *knew* they'd been together that day?"

"Of course I did."

"And yet you let me believe you were waiting for him to finish up in the armory?"

"No, *you* let you believe that."

"So why didn't you correct me?"

"Why didn't *you* correct *me*?"

"What?"

"When you found Rob at home with Erin? When you thought he was at school—or more importantly, when you thought *I thought* he was at school—why didn't tell me right away?"

"Do you honestly think I could have told you, after the way we parted company last, that I'd been to your house and found Rob with Erin when you had just told me he was at school?"

"Yes!"

"And how would I have looked if there had been nothing going on between them?"

Katrine crossed her arms and leaned against the hood of the car. "I don't know."

"Well, I do. It would have looked like I was out to get Rob—again!"

"I wouldn't have thought that."

"Well, I couldn't take that chance."

"Even on Sunday? After I'd told you about them?"

"I didn't see any point in mentioning *then*. Since you'd left them alone together for the weekend, I hardly thought it mattered that they had been together before."

"Well, it did—and it still does. Because maybe if you'd told me what you knew, we could have talked about it then instead of arguing about it now."

"Sure. And maybe I would've told you what I knew if you had told me the truth about them in the first place. I mean, why tell me anything if you weren't going to tell me everything?"

"Because I was afraid of what you would think of me for letting it happen."

I didn't blame Katrine for thinking that. Especially knowing what I thought of her at the time.

"I feel like such an idiot," she was saying now. "I should have told you the truth from the start. Maybe you could've talked some sense into me, and Rob's career wouldn't be on the line."

I doubted that. But this was not a time to admit it. "Obviously we both could've been a little more forthcoming," I said instead, recovering my softer side. "But we can't change what's happened. You just have to decide what you're going to do next."

"What *am* I going to do next?"

"You're going to have to talk to Rob and tell him you want Erin out of the picture."

"I already did that."

"Well, tell him again—and again, and again—until he listens."

"Is that really the best you can do?"

"I'm sorry, Katrine, but I'm new at this. The only time I have trouble getting Kevin to do something is when there's dancing involved."

"Maybe I should mention that stuff you said the other night—about the trouble they could get into with the unit if they get caught."

"I'm not sure that's wise, Katrine. Would he expect to hear something like that from you?"

"Probably not."

I didn't think so.

"Let's get back in the car," I said, noting the advancing darkness. "I'm sure if we think about it long enough, we'll come up with a decent plan."

With a sigh, Katrine opened the door and climbed in. I followed suit.

"Now, tell me," I began as we pulled back onto the street, "does Rob have anything to hold over your head?"

"You mean, like us?"

"Well, yeah. Unless of course there's something *else* you haven't told me about."

"No. I told you on Sunday—"

"Katrine, you said *a lot* of things on Sunday."

"I know. But that part was true. He doesn't know."

"Good. Then all we have to do is make sure there *is* no *us* anymore. After all, you can hardly ask him to stop sleeping with Erin when you're still sleeping with me, even if he doesn't know you're sleeping with me."

"But it's not even close to the same thing."

"Exactly. It's worse—since he's not lying to you."

Katrine sighed and stared out the window as we pulled into the parking lot of the Laundromat down the street from her house. "Why are we stopping here?"

"Well, your car's out front, and I wasn't sure you'd want Rob to know where you were."

"Oh, it's OK. I'll just tell him you had cabin fever, so we decided to go for a drive."

"I guess parts of that are true. Can I assume from this he doesn't know I know?"

Katrine shook her head. "I told him I didn't want *anyone* to know, and now I'm glad I did. At least this way he doesn't blame you for my change of heart about Erin."

"Good point."

"What about Kevin?" Katrine asked as I swung back out of the parking lot and continued down slowly down the street. "Does he know about Rob and Erin?"

"He knows I ran into them at your house, so he suspects as much as I did at the time. But I haven't spoken to him since he called to let me know he'd gotten to his mom's, so he doesn't know what you told me on Sunday."

"What if he did know? Would he turn them in?"

"I don't think so. But I doubt he'd lie if he were asked directly. Why?"

"Well, if the unit found out, Rob would be sent back to the fleet, right?"

"Not if he were court-martialed, Katrine."

"But you said they might just ask him to DOR."

"They might."

"In which case, Rob would be sent back to the fleet, and we could start over again. Right?"

"Yes. But his career would be *over*, Katrine. He'd never see another promotion."

"I understand that. But I'm sure he could do something else if that happened."

"Maybe. But it's a hell of a gamble. And it's a moot point—Kevin won't turn him in. He wouldn't want to be directly responsible for ruining his career."

"OK. So what if I turn him in myself?"

"You can't do that, Katrine. He would never forgive you."

"He wouldn't have to know it was me."

"Are you willing to take that chance? And even if he never found out, could you really live comfortably with something like that on your conscience?"

"I guess not."

"I didn't think so," I said, shifting the car into park in front of her house. "I really hope this works out the way you want it to, kiddo. But let me say again, for the record: You would be much better off without this guy, and if you don't like what he's doing, you don't have to put up with it. You can just leave."

"I know. Well, thanks for keeping me company," Katrine joked as she unhooked her seatbelt. "Guess I'll see you later."

The phone was ringing when I stepped onto the porch. I threw the door open and ran to the kitchen without pulling my keys from the lock.

"Hello?"

"Hi, sweetheart. Where have you been? I've been calling all night."

"Sorry. I went for a drive with Katrine."

"Then you haven't been screening your calls or anything silly like that?"

"No—no. I've disabled my telephone avoidance system."

"Glad to hear it," Kevin laughed. "So is everything OK with Katrine?"

"Not exactly. Do you remember our conversation about him and Erin?"

"Don't tell me: we were right."

"Yes—but for the record, you don't know that. Katrine wants to handle it herself for now."

"OK. So what's she going to do?"

"I don't know. She's already asked him to tell Erin it's over, but he refused. I've told her to talk to him again, but I'm not sure she'll do it—or that he'll listen."

"He'd better listen. This is about all the unit needs to finally get rid of him."

"I know."

"Does she?"

"Well, I didn't tell her they've been watching him, if that's what you mean. But I did tell her what could happen if they find out about Erin. Unfortunately, that idea actually appealed to her."

"What do you mean?"

"She seems to think if she turned him in, they would drop him from the program, send him back to the fleet, and the two of them could live happily ever after. Lucky for him, I think I managed to talk her out that plan."

"I think that was wise—not to mention generous—of you, given how much you like him."

"You got that right," I said as I carried the phone to the door, took my keys from the knob, and locked it. "Meanwhile, I was wondering if you might be able to help resolve the situation."

"Ah…so you want *me* turn him in."

"Sure, Kevin. That way, when he shoots you, I can use your insurance money to publish a riveting account of what it's like to be a military widow in the nineties."

"OK, smart-ass. So what *do* you want me to do?"

"Talk to Rob. Get him to see reason on this thing between him and Erin."

"And how exactly do I do that without letting him know that I know?"

"Well, you could tell him you've heard rumors and just take it from there."

"I guess that might work."

"Then you'll talk to him?"

"I suppose—if only to keep him from screwing things up for Erin. She's a nice kid, and while she should have known better, I'd hate for Rob's stupidity to ruin her chance at a scholarship."

"I had a hunch you might feel that way."

"Well, you may have had me pegged, but now I'm in the dark."

"What do you mean?"

"I thought you hated Rob."

"I do."

"So why the hell are you trying to *save* his ass?"

"I'm not. The fucker can crash and burn for all I care—it's Katrine I'm trying to help. In fact, if I thought for a minute that Katrine would leave Rob if he got caught, I would not be asking for your help. Unfortunately, letting him hang himself is more likely to increase her devotion to him and make matters worse down the road. So, since I love her and want to see her happy, I have no choice but to help him straighten up and fly right—even if that means saving him from the court-martial he so richly deserves."

"Fair enough."

"So when are you coming back?" I inquired. "I know your mother is spoiling the kids rotten, and I need to know when I can begin reprogramming."

"That depends. Have you finished with spring cleaning?"

"Of course."

"Great—so how does tomorrow sound?"

"Bastard!"

"We'll probably come back on Friday," Kevin added, laughing. "There's a field mess at Major Henry's that day, and I should be there. I wasn't planning to go since, technically, I'm on leave, and they won't be expecting me. But under the circumstances, I think I need to be there. It'll give me a chance to talk to Rob about his grades and see what other shit may be coming down the pike."

"I see. So apparently you're not rushing home because you miss me."

"Of course I am. I was just so damned happy to talk to you that I forgot to mention that."

"You're a shit—you know that?"

"Uh-huh. But you love me anyway."

"Unfortunately."

"Great—'cause I love you, too. And I'll see you Friday."

I stared at the phone after I hung up and wished I could call Kevin back. I wanted to come clean about my relationship with Katrine—to tell him what had happened and why.

Not that I was any closer to explaining myself than I'd been the last time I wanted to tell him. Having thought on it since, I still couldn't comprehend what I was doing. In spite of our hectic schedules, I was mostly contented with my life. Sure, I felt washed up and ordinary much of the time, but at that point I would have taken the ordinary over insanity any day. And while I would have liked to have seen more of Kevin, as he had pointed out, there would be plenty of time for that in the future.

No. There was more to it than a need for attention, I knew, just as there had been more to it with Melissa. I just didn't know what the more to it was. I did know that being with Katrine made me feel alive in ways that I otherwise didn't, which made me want to be close to her in ways that I shouldn't.

As I considered this, I wondered if I'd ever find the words to explain myself to Kevin—to make him understand that my attraction to Katrine was more than physical, that when I held her, I was seeking to embody her. Although his life had not been perfect, he had no need to escape himself and thus may not comprehend my need to slip into someone else's skin now and then and leave my own behind. Thus, I vowed to do my best to make up to him what he did not know, to tell him what I could as soon as I could, and to stop tempting the Fates to take him away.

Twenty-nine

I could hardly wait for Kevin to get home from the field mess on Friday. I hadn't spoken to Katrine since Wednesday night and, while I assumed any disturbing or otherwise significant developments regarding Rob and Erin would have already come to my attention, I hoped Kevin could give me a sense of Rob's state of mind and of where things stood, if only temporarily.

"So how'd it go?" I asked when he was barely through the door that evening.

"About as well as I expected, I'm afraid."

"But you did give him the full deal, right? You didn't sugarcoat it?"

"Why would I do that?"

"Because if he continues to see Erin, he'll eventually get caught, and the unit will finally have everything they need to get rid of him."

"Well, although I'd prefer not to serve with him under the present circumstances, I'd still rather see him shape up than watch him go down in flames. After all, I've been tasked with the job of training the guy, and thus his failure is my failure. Which is why I told him, point blank, that if there was any truth to the rumors flying around the unit about him and Ms. Rollins, he'd better end it, double time, before people higher than me find out and bring him up on charges."

"And what did he have to say to that?"

"He said there was nothing going on between them. He went on to say that even if there was something going on between them, since MECEP

335

and ROTC students are integrated at this command, he and Ms. Rollins are effectively equals, and the rules pertaining to 'inappropriate relationships' wouldn't apply."

"And he's just arrogant enough to think that will fly."

"Which it might," Kevin admitted grudgingly, "if he wasn't married. The colonel has always said we're all equal by virtue of our status as officer candidates. Under that logic, Rob would have nothing to fear—at least from a purely 'inappropriate relationship' standpoint. Of course, he'd struggle to make that case today, since he's never accepted the colonel's policy and has taken every available opportunity to argue against it. And I see his point. He and I and all the other MECEP selectees are NCOs with at least four years of active service time who have committed to serving six more years, which we'll owe whether we graduate or not. So why should we stand on equal footing with a bunch of college kids who have never been to boot camp, held rank, or had any real responsibilities?

"Then again, if we're not integrated, what happens? Here you've got a group of people with active duty military experience but who, at the end of the day, are still enlisted personnel, and another group of people who have no military experience but who are only months away from making ensign or lieutenant. How do you structure the organization, and who outranks whom?"

"Does anyone necessarily have to outrank anyone in this case?"

"Spoken like a true pinko," Kevin laughed as he kissed my forehead. "Maybe you'd like us to carry flowers, too, instead of guns and ammunition?"

"I'm serious," I insisted, grinning along with him. "In this arena, does it really matter who's senior to whom?"

"Theoretically, no. Which is why I'm OK with our being integrated. My only problem with the policy is that the leadership wants to have it both ways. They say, on the one hand, that rank doesn't matter—that we're all officer candidates and therefore equal—yet they hold MECEP people to a higher standard because of our training and experience, and expect us to set an example for our ROTC 'peers.' So we're stuck with all the responsibilities of our official rank but afforded none of the respect or recognition that normally comes with it."

"I see what you mean. But it sounds to me like Rob wants it both ways, too," I observed, "by taking refuge in a policy to which he is so vehemently opposed. Isn't that rather like demanding a share of a lottery pool jackpot after forgetting to chip in for the ticket?"

"It is. But he won't get away with it. At the end of the day, Rob is an active duty marine, so even if their relationship doesn't constitute an 'inappropriate relationship' because of the unit's definition of rank, the fact that he's married makes it adultery, which is chargeable under the Uniform Code of Military Justice."

"Did you tell him that?"

Kevin nodded. "He responded by reminding me that other people at the unit—like Connie and Zane—are known to be intimately involved and, despite different class standing, haven't been charged or counseled, and thus he has nothing to fear regardless of what may or may not be going on with, or around about, him and Ms. Rollins."

"And did you point out that none of these 'other people' were married to someone else?"

"I did. I also told him perceptions count for a lot, especially at a small command like ours, but that just earned me a shrug. Maybe he was only feigning indifference for fear of confirming the rumors. Or maybe he's just banking on them never reaching the unit staff."

"Which they can't," I allowed, "since they don't really exist."

"True—but Rob doesn't know that."

"Are you sure?"

"Absolutely. Although he denied that the rumors were true, he never doubted their existence. In fact, it was almost as if he enjoyed the idea that people from the unit were talking about him that way."

"I'll bet. I'm sure it makes him feel like a big man on campus to imagine all those midshipmen thinking he's doing the new girl right under the unit's nose—and actually getting away with it."

"That's the part that concerns me," Kevin admitted. "Instead of thinking about the example he's setting for all those future officers or the black eye he's giving the command, this idiot's getting off on the thought of being seen as some kind of outlaw Casanova."

The following Saturday, said idiot arrived at our place with his wife in tow and an unexpected furrow on his brow. The guys were expected at a dinner that evening—an informal event for active duty personnel only—and in the interest of having another crack at Rob's seemingly impenetrable conscience, Kevin had suggested they ride together. Katrine had tagged along as far as our house, apparently in hopes of chatting with me until they returned.

The girl was glowing with what could only be described as delight, I noted, as she preceded her sullen husband through the door, which told me something big had happened and left me itching to find out what it was.

"Well?" I said after Rob and Kevin had left. "Don't just stand there looking like you've swallowed the proverbial canary. Tell me what's going on."

Katrine smiled triumphantly. "It's over."

"What's over?"

"Rob and Erin."

"You mean he broke it off?"

"Yep. Apparently he's more susceptible to my charms than I'd originally thought."

Either that or he's more worried about getting caught than Kevin *thought.*

"Was he at least decent about it?"

"He let her down easy, if that's what you mean. He blamed it on my lack of sophistication and what he called my 'pathological need for monogamy.'"

"And you're happy about that?"

Katrine shrugged. "At least now she's out of the picture."

I guess so.

"So when did this happen?" I asked, trying my best to be happy for her. "It couldn't have been too long ago, since you're still beaming."

"A few minutes ago, actually. Just before we left the house."

"*Your* house?"

Katrine nodded. "Rob didn't want to do it in the dorm, so he invited her over."

"Are you telling me he had this girl come all the way over to your place just to give her the old heave-ho?"

"Well, it's not as if we made her walk, for God's sake. Rob picked her up."

"So rather than going to her place or asking her to meet him somewhere, Rob drove all the way to campus, picked Erin up, and brought her back to your house to deliver the bad news?"

"Yes."

"And all that stuff about your lack of sophistication, he said that in front of you?"

"Well, not exactly. I was waiting in the kitchen."

"Then how do you know he said it?"

"I'm not just repeating stuff Rob claims to have said, if that's what you're getting at. I was only in the next room, so I heard it straight from the horse's mouth."

You mean the horse's ass.

"You don't look like you believe me," Katrine observed.

"Oh, I believe *you*; it's Rob I can't believe."

"Why not? I told you I could hear them."

"I know, Katrine. That's the problem."

"What do you mean?"

"I don't know. It just sounds a little staged to me. I mean, why would he bring her all the way to your house when he easily could've broken up with her somewhere else?"

Katrine shrugged. "I was so happy to know he was finally dumping her, I didn't really care *where* he did it."

"So long as you could be there?"

"Having me there was Rob's idea. He said he didn't want there to be any doubt in my mind that things were really over between them."

"And you didn't find that just a little *convenient*?"

I sighed as Katrine shook her head. I didn't know for whose benefit this little play had been staged, but I was sure it was a performance. Although it was possible Rob intended to stop seeing Erin, the way he'd gone about telling her seemed too convoluted to be the whole story. And while he had a knack for turning simple actions into grand gestures, even that manifestation of his ego could not explain why he'd gone to such lengths to show Katrine that he and Erin were over. Maybe the whole thing was a smoke screen so he could continue to see Erin on the sly. Or maybe he just wanted to highlight the sacrifice he was making in case he needed to use it against her later. Whatever the case, there was clearly more to Rob's little production than met the eye.

I would have pointed this out to Katrine, but I didn't see, well, the point. She was either naive enough to buy this crap or so thrilled by what she perceived as a victory that she didn't feel the need to examine things more closely.

"So how'd she take it?" I asked instead.

"Fine."

"Let me get this straight. This girl, whom you were so threatened by these last few weeks, sat there while Rob dumped her—essentially in front of you—and then just calmly walked out of your house and went home?"

"Well, no. We were running late to pick up Kevin, so we didn't have time to take her home. Rob's going to do that when we get back."

"Do you mean to tell me she's sitting at your house right now? By herself?"

Katrine shrugged. "Unless Scott came back."

Once again, I couldn't believe my ears.

"You two are unbelievable," I said, shaking my head. "Absolutely unbelievable."

"What's wrong?"

"You left that girl alone in your house after Rob dumped her for you and you're asking me *what's wrong?*"

"So?"

"So? You can't treat people like that, Katrine," I admonished. "It's not right."

"Treat them how, Jackie? We're just letting her wait there until we can drive her home."

"As if she has a choice!"

"Of course she has a choice—she could always take the bus."

I stared at Katrine. "What is wrong with you?" I asked, shaking my head again. "I love you more than you can possibly imagine, but these days, I hardly recognize you."

"But I only made him do what I wanted, which is exactly what you told me to do."

"I'm not faulting you for trying to hold on to what you want, Katrine—although God only knows why you want Rob—my problem is with how you're going about it."

"What are you going to do?" she was asking now as I stormed over to the phone.

"I'm not going to do anything; you, however, are going to call Erin and invite her to join us for dinner."

"But why? I told you, she was fine when we left. She wasn't upset or anything."

"Perfect," I said as I picked up the receiver and started to dial. "Then she'd probably love to join us for pizza."

"I don't think so."

"Why not?"

"Because I don't *want* her here."

"Have you no compassion at all?"

"Why should I have any compassion for her?"

"Because she's a human being, Katrine. And whatever she's done, she had your consent. And because, whether or not you're interested, I need to know she's OK."

"Fine. If you want to see her so bad—you call her."

"Forgive me for asking," Katrine said as I hung up a few minutes later, having secured an acceptance from Erin. "But what happens if the guys come back before she's gone? I mean, if they come in and find her sitting here, how are we going to explain it?"

I hadn't thought of that. I now pictured Rob's face as he walked in to find the three of us seated at my kitchen table. It amused me to imagine the fear that would grip him when he saw us all together, and even more to think what he might give away in the scene that ensued afterward.

I realized his reaction might not be as entertaining for others as it would be for me. Katrine, for one, would probably not enjoy the grilling Rob might give her when he arrived, and Erin would likely see little humor in having Kevin find out about her and Rob, should Katrine happen to mention it in the course of said grilling.

"You see?" Katrine added as she watched my face. "This is going to be a disaster."

"Not necessarily," I replied as I picked up my purse. "All we have to do is tell the guys what I told Erin: that you happened to mention that she was studying at your house, and I suggested we invite her over for pizza. That's what I would have done under normal circumstances, so Rob should have no cause for concern—besides his guilty conscience, that is—and thus no reason to create a scene. If it'll make you feel better, just tell Erin when we pick her up that Kevin and I don't know. That way she'll know not to say anything that would lead Rob to wonder—in the unlikely event, that is, that he and Kevin get back from their bonding session early."

I quickly dialed up Maggie, whom I had recklessly presumed to be available, and asked if she'd come stay with the kids while I ran some errands. Miraculously, I had enough karma still banked, as Maggie was both available and willing to walk over right away, leaving me and Katrine free to collect Erin, some pizzas, and something to drink unencumbered by children.

The three of us formed an awkward combo as we rode back from Katrine's. As hostess of our impromptu little fete, I tried to keep the conversation afloat, but due to limited input from my companions, I wound up babbling most of the way. Katrine, meanwhile, who had sulked like a kid being dragged by back to the store to return a piece of stolen candy until we reached her house, now seemed more edgy than cross and spent the return trip tracing the outline of her fingernails and staring out the window. Erin, for her part, spoke freely when asked a direct question but otherwise sat in sort of a stunned silence as we drove back to our duplex.

I understood her distress, of course. In addition to having just been so rudely shelved and left at the scene, she was now sitting in a car with a hostile acquaintance and one relative stranger. Add to that the fact that she had to mind her words lest she reveal the nature of her relationship to Rob and Katrine, and it was amazing she was functioning at all.

All of this made me wonder, as my companions and I carried the assorted bags and boxes to the kitchen, why Erin had accepted our invitation in the first place. Was she really OK with the situation, as Katrine reported, and just looking to pass the time, or was she after something else? With Katrine having briefed her on my knowledge of the situation—or, more accurately, my lack thereof—there couldn't be much else in it for her, no shoulder to cry on nor any ear to bend without dropping the dime on Rob.

Or maybe that was the point. Maybe Erin wanted to nail Rob's balls to the wall and figured mine was as good a place to start as any. Or maybe she was looking to unleash a few choice words on Katrine without Rob there to stop her.

She certainly hadn't come for the food, I later observed as I watched Erin pick at her plate. Not that I could blame the girl if she wasn't very hungry; my own appetite had been off these days thanks to my role in this bizarre drama, and I hadn't even slept with the leading man or been forcibly ejected from the production. Of course, this was a boon for me since it had helped me shed another six pounds of baby weight, but Erin didn't have as much to spare.

Still, she looked pretty good for someone who'd been so thoughtlessly discarded only an hour or so ago. Although she was definitely less chatty tonight than she had been the day she and I first met, she didn't appear wounded or devastated in any way. In fact, aside from her subdued demeanor, Erin did not behave at all like a jilted lover, which made me wonder if Rob had actually meant less to her than he had led Katrine to believe, or if she was just putting up one hell of a front.

Whichever was the case, with eating and the conversation both having ground to a halt, I concluded it was time to drive Erin back to Katrine's. Thus, I decided to forego the vodka I'd picked up until after I returned from that errand, and I excused myself to apprise Maggie of our plans.

"Mommy, why's Daddy mad at Mr. Rob?" Tyler asked as I interrupted the board game that was in progress in the playroom.

Needless to say, I was more than a little surprised by the question. Kevin and I had never been particularly careful about what we discussed in front of him; neither had we felt the need to avoid certain topics in his presence. Not that I didn't think he was swift enough to understand what was said; I just didn't expect him to be paying attention. Now with the former having been confirmed and the latter having been dispelled, I decided we'd have to be more discreet in the future.

"He's not really mad at him, buddy," I explained after posting that mental note. "He just wants to help Mr. Rob; that's all."

"Well, OK, but he sure looks mad to me."

"What?"

Tyler nodded authoritatively as he went to the window and pointed at something just out of my field of view. "And Mr. Rob looks pretty mad, too."

I didn't have to look to know they were back. Still, I took the two steps required to reach the window to see how much time I had before they reached the door, and I found the Nova parked out front with Kevin and Rob sitting inside. The engine was still running, I could see, and it was clear—apparently even to Tyler—that they were having a heated discussion.

Although I had briefly reveled in a vision of this exact situation just a few hours ago, I hadn't really considered it an actual possibility. With the spouses and midshipmen having been excluded from the event—thereby leaving the active duty marines to make merry without regard for silly things like standards of decorum—I assumed the guys wouldn't be back until well into the evening. Now, with my powers of prediction having failed me, I went back over what I'd told Katrine and hoped to hell that I was right.

Even on second thought, I could see no reason why the plan couldn't work. Rob knew how I treated people and therefore should have little trouble believing I had asked Erin to join us upon learning she was in the neighborhood. And while he may not buy Katrine's explanation as to *how* I came to know Erin was at their house, he could hardly accuse her of telling me about the affair without admitting to it himself. Thus, he would have to wait until they were alone to interrogate his wife, by which time, I hoped, our actions would have convinced him that he didn't need to anymore.

These assurances did little to quell my panic, however, when I saw Kevin opening the passenger door. In fact, it was with unusual speed that I felt the familiar lump rising in my throat, the hives spreading across my chest, and the accompanying urge to pee.

At least now I won't have to drive, I realized with perverse delight as I backed out of the playroom—after getting the thumbs-up from Maggie that all was well in hand—and bolted to the kitchen for something to steel my frazzled nerves.

I arrived there in time to see Kevin walking through the front door. "Hey, Jarhead," I chirped in case Erin and Katrine hadn't heard him. "What brings you back so early?"

"Gray Nova."

I took stock of my companions as Kevin laughed to himself and shut the door. Erin, I noted happily, seemed fine. Although she was as surprised as I was by his arrival, she also seemed enlivened by it. Whether this was because she was comforted by the fact that she was about to see a familiar face or because she was actually hoping for a confrontation, I could not say. All I knew for sure was that the girl didn't seem upset when he walked in and, given how she laughed at his joke, suddenly seemed more at ease than she had all night.

The same, of course, could not be said for Katrine, who was now watching me with a combination of terror and anger as I, in turn, watched Kevin hang up his coat. "Where's Rob?" she called from the other side of the wall that separated the dining room and living room.

"He's waiting in the car," Kevin replied as he strode over to the aquarium to feed the fish. "He's in a bit of a hurry to get home for some reason," he added. "Said to send you right out."

"Terrific," Katrine muttered without taking her eyes off me. "Now what?"

I shrugged. "You go out to the car, I suppose."

"And what about Erin?"

With Kevin in the living room at my twelve o'clock and Erin at the table to my eight, I could see them pondering Katrine's query and trying to decipher its meaning with the equally small yet distinctly different sets of information in their possession.

"We'll see she gets home," I replied casually, hoping to pass off Katrine's question as a purely logistical inquiry for Erin's sake while announcing her presence for Kevin's.

"But Rob's expecting her to be at our place."

"So tell him you spoke to her and that she decided to head back to campus on her own."

"But won't he think that's strange?"

"I don't know why he would. She knew you'd be here, after all, and he knows she's intelligent enough to find and use the phone book if not your bulletin board."

"I guess."

By now, Kevin had finished with the fish and was standing by the aquarium with his hands at his waist and eying me like Desi Arnaz would have regarded Lucille Ball.

"But you'd better move it," I advised guiltily, "or he'll be in here looking for you."

"She's right," Erin interjected. "It'll be a lot easier for you to explain why I'm not at your house than it will be to explain why I'm at Jackie's. You'd better take off."

Although Katrine had nodded in response to my instructions, she suddenly appeared apprehensive after Erin seconded them. I wondered if this was because feared she might not be able to convincingly explain why Erin wasn't at their house or because she doubted the wisdom of leaving her alone with me and Kevin.

Either way, she had hesitated too long, for Rob suddenly burst through the door. "Where the hell is Katrine?" he asked of no one in particular as he did so.

"She's on her way out," Kevin replied, walking over to the entryway as if to keep Rob at the door. "She and Jack were just finishing up their conversation."

"That figures," he exclaimed as Katrine appeared under the arch and started walking his way. "You want to get a move on?" he demanded. "We've got things to do."

"I know. I'm sorry."

"Where's your coat?"

Katrine looked around the living room. "I must've left it in the kitchen," she replied. "I'll be right back."

"No—I'll go get it. You wait here."

Kevin started for the kitchen ahead of Rob, as if the two-step advantage he had over the other marine would be enough to prevent disaster. "Well, hello, Ms. Rollins," he said as he and Rob cleared the archway with Katrine in their wake. "I didn't realize you were here. How are you?"

"Fine, thanks, Sergeant T. And you?"

"Likewise."

"I'm glad to hear it. And you, Sergeant Copeland?" Erin inquired as the startled Rob nodded at her.

"Fine," Rob replied, glancing repeatedly from me to Erin as he put his arm around Katrine, who had pressed herself up to his side.

"Yes, just fine," Kevin echoed. "And what are you ladies up to this evening?" he asked, just as thrown by the situation as Rob but without the fear or guilty conscience to deprive him of the power of speech.

"You're looking at it," I said, pointing to the empty pizza box with what moments ago had been a fresh vodka martini but was now an empty vessel. "Just deep-dish and dialogue."

"I see."

"And do you object?"

"Are you kidding?" Kevin asked with an affected swagger. "I just came home to a blonde, a brunette, and a redhead: how could I possibly object?"

Although Erin and I laughed along with Kevin, neither of the Copelands seemed amused. Katrine's problem was obvious: after finally achieving solo status following her stint as one of two, she was likely none too eager to be included in the full-spectrum harem Kevin had described. Rob, meanwhile, was clearly too thrown by the whole situation to comprehend Kevin's remark right away, much less find the humor in it.

"Yeah," he said finally, struggling to appear at ease. "How could we possibly object?"

Finding this even less amusing coming from him than she had when it came from Kevin, Katrine stormed out of the kitchen and down the hall to the bathroom. Rob followed—more to find out what was going on, I imagined, than to comfort her—and urgently sought admittance.

"Boy, you guys can really throw a party," Erin observed after Rob had breached Katrine's sanctuary. "I can't remember when I've had such a lovely time."

I raised my glass. "Well, if you like our cheap little slapdash affairs," I observed, "just imagine what we can do when we've had time to plan ahead."

"Speaking of slapdash," Kevin interjected. "How *did* you throw this all together?"

"Well, Katrine mentioned that Erin was at their place tonight, and, thinking that sounded kind of boring, I invited her to join us for some pizza. I figured you and Rob would be out for a while anyway," I added, "and that I'd have her back at Katrine's before you two got here, but I apparently miscalculated."

"I'm sorry," Kevin murmured, having since realized why Rob had wanted to come back so early. "If I'd known what was up, I'd have tried to talk him into staying out awhile longer."

Erin looked from Kevin to Jackie and back again.

"You guys know, don't you?" she asked quietly. "About us, I mean?"

We both nodded.

"Rob doesn't know that, though," Kevin added. "He thinks he's got everybody fooled."

"So he didn't tell you?"

"Uh, no. I told him I was concerned about some rumors I'd heard at the armory and what might happen if they were true, but so far he's admitted to nothing."

"Rumors?" Erin repeated as the color began to drain from her face. "About us?"

"Well, rumors of rumors, actually," I offered.

"I don't understand."

"Rob *thinks* I've heard rumors about the two of you," Kevin clarified. "But the rumors don't really exist. I only pretended they did so I'd have an excuse to counsel Rob on the subject."

"Why?"

"Long story." Kevin sighed. "Suffice it to say, I'm trying to save his ass."

Erin nodded. "But if Rob didn't tell you about this, and you haven't really heard any rumors, how on earth did you know?"

"I told him," I admitted. "And Katrine told *me*."

Erin shook her head. "So she actually let me sit here and sweat over what I could and could not say in front of you, knowing full well that you knew everything?"

"Well, she only knows *I* knew everything."

"And she hasn't figured out yet that if you know something, Kevin probably does, too?"

"I'm gonna go with 'no.'" I joked. "Since communication isn't exactly a hallmark of their relationship, she probably doesn't expect it to be a feature of any other."

"So what *does* she think Kevin knows?"

"Nothing, to my knowledge."

"Last we talked," I explained, figuring this was more my department than Kevin's, "I told her Kevin suspected—which was the truth at the time—and I just haven't rushed to correct that perception. So you see, she kind of had to tell you we didn't know. Otherwise you might have said something that would have told Rob that we do."

"And?"

"And Rob doesn't want me to know."

"Why? What does he think you'll do?"

"It's not that he's afraid of what *I'll* do. It's that she told him that she hadn't told me, and she's afraid he'll find out she lied."

"And what does she think *he'll* do?"

"Who knows?"

"And more importantly," Kevin added. "Who cares? What matters is that you're OK."

"Oh, I'm fine," Erin laughed. "I'm just tired of her bullshit."

"How did you get involved with these two, anyway?" I asked. "If you don't mind reliving it, that is."

"Three weeks ago," she explained, sotto voce as she glanced toward the hallway, "Katrine approaches me in the hall at school, claiming that Rob was attracted to me and wanted to get to know me better."

"Katrine?" Kevin wondered aloud.

Erin nodded. "She set everything up—when we'd meet; where we'd meet; she even lit candles, for fuck's sake."

I could just imagine Katrine flitting around fluffing pillows and setting out votives with a fresh, romantic bouquet.

"I'm still not entirely sure what happened," Erin admitted, taking a gulp of her flattened soda. "All I know is that one minute she's casting me for the romance of the century, and then next I'm *persona non grata*."

"The irony here," she added, "is that I was only in this out of curiosity in the first place. In fact, when he 'broke up' with me, I was dumbfounded. I couldn't believe he actually thought it was necessary or that he'd go to so much trouble to do it. From my reaction, I'm sure they thought I was absolutely crushed, but in truth, I was just trying my damnedest not to laugh."

"So *that's* why you didn't mind when he left you at their place afterward."

Erin nodded. "It was actually a relief," she explained, "not to have to ride back with them again right away. I don't think I could've kept a straight face or held my tongue any longer."

"But why did you wait at their place? Why didn't you just take a bus back to your dorm?"

"I considered that after Rob and Katrine left, but then you called, and I thought, 'why not just hang out at Jackie's for a while and save myself the bus fare home?'"

I was impressed. Erin was obviously smarter—and saner—than she'd been given credit for; and though I had doubted it when I heard it earlier, I was convinced she would be OK.

"Speaking of home," she said to Kevin. "I should probably be getting back to my dorm. Would you mind walking me to the nearest bus stop?"

"Not at all," he replied. "I can even drive you back to campus, if you like."

"Thanks, but I wouldn't want you to go to any trouble."

"Oh, it's no trouble," he insisted. "I'll just need a couple minutes to use the bathroom, and we can go."

"All right then—why not? Do you mind if I wait in the car, though? I want to be out of here before the Axis Powers emerge from their conference."

"No problem. In fact," Kevin said, tossing Erin the keys on his way to the stairs. "You can warm her up for me."

"The Ford or the Toyota?" she asked as she considered the cluster of notched metal tabs with the faded Wonder Woman figurine adorning its central ring.

"Either one. I'm not picky."

Erin shrugged and picked up the backpack she'd wisely brought with her. "So why did you really invite me over for pizza?" she asked as I walked her to the door.

"I was worried about you. Katrine had told me what had happened earlier, and I just couldn't stand the thought of you sitting over there dealing with it by yourself."

"But you don't even know me."

"I know. But you seem like a decent person—irrespective of your inexplicable affiliation with Rob—and I thought you deserved to be treated like one."

Erin smiled. "Thanks, Jackie."

"My pleasure."

Thirty

"Where's she going?" Katrine asked as she and Rob emerged from the bathroom in time to see the back door closing on Erin.

"She needed to get home, so Kevin's driving her back."

"He doesn't have to do that," Rob interjected to Katrine's obvious consternation. "We would have been happy to take her."

"It's not a problem, Rob. I'm sure he doesn't mind."

"But Katrine and I are leaving now anyway, so we may as well do it ourselves."

"That's OK," Kevin informed him, having returned from the basement. "My car's already warm, so you two can just run on home."

I could tell Rob didn't much care for the way he was being dismissed, but I knew he wouldn't do anything about it. His defining feature—the one that likely had made him such an exceptional marine out in the fleet but that rendered him a jerk in other settings—was his absolute belief in the concept of rank. Thus, while he knew Kevin socially, his training prevented him from challenging a more senior marine.

"Fine," he said with only a trace of disdain. "Whatever you say."

"Great," Kevin replied as he opened the back door. "Then I guess I'll see you tomorrow. And, Jack, I'll see you when I get back."

Provided I'm still alive, I thought as I poured another martini. I didn't even bother with the shaker. I just swirled a drop of vermouth around in the glass and added ice and vodka.

"What the hell was she doing here?" Rob demanded of me the moment Kevin shut the door.

I had seen both sides of Rob's personality in action before but had yet to witness the transformation from one to the other. Thus, I was taken somewhat aback by his seemingly instantaneous shift from *Dr. Kissass* to *Mr. Snide.*

"I don't understand, Rob. Is there some reason she shouldn't have been? Some reason you don't want us to be acquainted?"

Rob's nostrils flared as he faced Katrine. "I thought you said she was *out* of this?"

"She *is* out of it."

"Then what was Erin doing here?"

"I told you," Katrine insisted. "We invited her to join us for pizza."

"That's right," I agreed, crossing my arms. "So whatever it is that I'm not supposed to be *in*, you'd better shut up before I figure it *out*."

"Do you really expect me to believe that you decided out of the blue to invite Erin over here for pizza when she just happened to be studying at our place?"

"No. It was when I heard that she was studying at your place," I explained, hoping I wasn't about to contradict anything Katrine had said, "that I suggested that we invite her over for pizza."

"You see?" Katrine asked bitterly as I breathed a mental sigh of relief. "I told you."

At the sound of her voice, Rob turned on her like an armed gunman in a hostage situation. "What's your issue?"

"My *issue* is that you never listen to me. With anybody else you take their every word as gospel, but let the same words fall from my lips, and it's all just wasted breath."

"That's not true!"

"Isn't it?" Katrine challenged. "When was the last time you took something I said seriously? And when have you ever done something I wanted you to do, just because I asked you to do it?"

For Christ's sake, Katrine, I thought as she sounded off. *Why can't you quit when you're ahead? I mean, isn't it enough that we got the bastard to dump Erin and to believe our story about how she got here? Must we go for the whole pot tonight?*

"Oh, come on," the bastard was saying now as he took a seat to Katrine's left, "I do that all the time."

"No, Rob, you don't."

"If I may," I interjected, hoping to avert a protracted game of "did not/did so." I wasn't sure if Katrine had stumbled onto this topic by accident or if she'd engineered it to occur in front of me. What I did know is that it had the potential to be even less pleasant than its forerunner, and I wasn't interested in being either a participant or observer. "I think what *matters* here, Rob, is Katrine's perception that you don't listen to her."

"Oh, really?" he sniped. "Well, since you're such an expert on communication—and the premier authority on our marriage, apparently—maybe you should sit down and join our little chat. That way you can tell us *both* what's wrong with our relationship for a change."

"No, thanks. In fact, I'd prefer you take this all back to your place, if it's all the same to you."

"Come on, Jackie. You know how much Katrine values your input, and how will I ever know whether you're as wise and insightful as she claims if I never get to witness it for myself?"

"Stop it!" Katrine shouted, pounding her fists on the table. "Stop talking about me as if I'm not here."

"Katrine, you need to calm down."

"Because you say so, right? And what Rob says, goes? Well, I'm sick of being told what to do. And I'm sick of being patronized and sick and goddamn tired of being taken for granted."

"I don't take you for granted."

"Yes, you do! You never ask me what I want, and you don't care what I think. You just say and do whatever you want and expect me to go along with it."

"That's not true. If you'd just talk to *me* once in a while instead of Jackie, you wouldn't feel that way."

"You don't want to hear what I have to say, Rob. You just want to pat me on the head and expect me to follow you and be happy."

"You *were* happy until Jackie came along."

"No, I wasn't! It only seemed that way because I always went along with what you wanted."

"Why would you do that?"

"Because I trusted you. I trusted you to know and want what's best for us. I trusted you to care what I think; to consider my feelings and our future, and to do what's right."

"I do want what's best for us, and I do care what you think.

"Well, you have a funny way of showing it, Rob. Because you never ask. Just like you never asked if it was OK for Scott to move in, or if I minded you getting a second job, or if I thought we should buy that new PC. Meanwhile, you're failing out of school and risking your career with your carelessness and total lack of respect for authority."

I could see that Rob was about as thrilled to have these things said in front of me as I was to be hearing them.

Too bad, my sense of justice interjected. *Let's not forget that this is the same man who—in addition to treating Katrine like crap—tried to blackmail you and offered to trade the use of her body for your silence.*

"I don't think it's fair to lay this all on Rob," I said, nevertheless, as I took a seat on Katrine's other side. "You could've spoken up about all this long ago, but you didn't. Even after I told you to talk to Rob, you chose to keep things to yourself rather than confront him with your concerns. It's time to take responsibility for that and for the role you played—albeit passive—in letting things get this bad. I mean, you can't expect the man to read your mind, after all—at least not until you've been married as long as me and Kevin."

"Speak of the devil," I declared as Kevin opened the back door and stepped inside.

I thought you were going to get rid of them, he conveyed with his eyes as he leaned down for a kiss after forcing a smile at our guests.

I'm trying, I replied in the same manner.

"Well, I guess I'll go relieve Maggie," he said, this time aloud, "as long as you're still occupied."

"Sounds good."

I retrieved twelve dollars from my purse after Kevin disappeared and waited for Maggie to emerge from the playroom, whereupon I handed her the cash and walked her to the door.

"So what needs to happen now," I instructed, returning to the table and facing Katrine, "is for you to start telling Rob what you want and need from him."

"Why? So he can turn around and ignore me anyway? Or maybe so he can actually do what I want and make me feel guilty for it afterward?"

"No one ever said asserting yourself would be easy, Katrine. Even when you're experienced at it, it can be pretty fucking difficult. But as the saying goes, anything worth having is worth fighting for, and you probably wouldn't want anything that isn't. So you have to ask yourself which matters to you more: getting what you want and having your needs met, or avoiding criticism and controversy."

Rob nodded righteously.

"Don't think for a minute that this gets you off the hook," I warned him. "You haven't lifted a finger to make things better here. If anything, you've been exploiting her reticence to advance your own interests and maintain the status quo. It's time you stop that and start showing her some respect."

"What are you talking about?"

"Don't give me that. I've seen the way you treat her—remember? Now, maybe you don't mean to hurt her feelings, but that's the net effect. So you need to stop and consider her feelings before opening your mouth and to take the time to say what you mean and explain things—as many times as necessary—until she understands and is satisfied with your reasoning. Stop taking advantage of her passivity and quit using shame and humiliation to get her to back down."

Katrine shook her head as Rob stared at the table. "You may as well save your breath," she said. "He's not interested in any of this."

"Yes, I am. And I think Jackie's right."

"Oh, come off it!"

I chewed my lip, unnerved by the shift in Rob's stance. I was no more convinced of his sincerity than Katrine was, but I saw no harm in humoring him. We had achieved our primary objectives, after all, and the remaining work to be done wouldn't be accomplished in one night, so why not leave Rob to his illusions if it brought the discussion to a peaceful close?

"It's just a matter of patterns," I continued toward that end, "which in your case are neither healthy nor effective. So the two of you need to develop some new ways of communicating that will allow you both to be heard and understood, and that will lead to outcomes that are mutually satisfying."

Rob nodded. "I see what you mean," he announced. "I never realized it before, but now that you've pointed it out, it makes perfect sense."

"Oh, give it a rest," Katrine scoffed. "Nobody's buying your bullshit."

"Now, hang on a second," I urged, hoping to prevent another spiral and steer the discussion toward some semblance of a conclusion. "I know this is out of character for me and you probably don't want to hear it, but for the moment at least, I think you should take Rob at his word."

"Are you kidding me? After everything that's happened, are you seriously falling for this sycophantic garbage?"

"I'm not falling for anything," I said meaningfully. "I just think that under the *circumstances* you should give him the benefit of the doubt."

"I see," she seethed. "And is that because he's been kissing your ass all night? Or is it just that you're feeling guilty for playing doctor with me?"

Rob stared at Katrine as if she'd confessed to murder. "What did you say?"

Katrine suddenly covered her mouth as if she'd only just heard the words herself. *Oh, my God,* her eyes said to me. *Jackie, I'm so sorry.*

I crossed my arms and eyed her with disbelief. I knew I had annoyed her by defending Rob, but I never imagined she would lash out at me for it, much less cut her own throat in the process.

I couldn't fathom what she hoped to accomplish by her remark. She certainly wouldn't score any points with me that way, and although telling Rob about our affair might dampen his newfound affinity for me, it wouldn't win Katrine his allegiance. In fact, even if her words succeeded in quashing the goodwill Rob was showing me this evening, neither that nor the satisfaction it might bring could possibly be worth the harm it would do to their relationship.

Then again, maybe that was the point. Maybe she'd decided the relationship wasn't worth saving and was going to let it bleed out like wounded game.

Assuming, that is, that the remarks were premeditated. In truth, judging by the timing of her outburst and her unspoken apology afterward, Katrine had spoken with little forethought and no regard for the repercussions. Those repercussions were on her mind now, however, as she watched me over the hands she still held to her mouth as if she didn't trust it to stay silent on its own.

I could've shaken her for her thoughtless words, but while that may have made me feel better—at least temporarily—it also would have been counterproductive. We would eventually discuss what had happened, but for now I needed to control the damage wrought by Katrine's verbal lacerations and prevent further complications.

The situation, I decided, called for a combination of verbal misdirection and sleight of hand. If we played our cards right, we stood a chance of passing off Katrine's words as a desperate attempt to rekindle the animosity between me and Rob and not the extemporaneous confession they happened to be. That meant convincing Rob that Katrine was apologizing for losing her temper and casting aspersions on my character, and treating the part about playing doctor as something she'd contrived to upset him.

"Let's get something straight right now," I said to that end as Rob looked on. "I have not now nor would I ever put my own interests before yours; nor would I ever sell you down the river. So don't imagine for a second that I would suggest that you give Rob the benefit of the doubt for any reason other than because I think he deserves it. You may not like it, but that's how I feel, and I won't be made to feel guilty for it or blackmailed into saying otherwise. So before you go stirring up shit between me and Rob, you'd better make sure you've got the wherewithal to ride out the storm on your own, because I will not be there to give you shelter."

Katrine nodded. "I understand," she said, grasping my subtext. "And I'm really sorry. I was angry with you for defending Rob, and I spoke without thinking. Please forgive me."

I smiled. "Already done," I said, patting her forearm protectively before lacing my fingers on the table in front of me. "Now, where were we?"

I watched Rob as he continued to stare at Katrine. "What the hell was that all about?" he demanded.

Katrine shrugged. "Just clearing the air."

"Just clearing the air? Huh? And what was that crap about playing doctor?"

Katrine's eyes drifted left until they came to rest on me.

You're going to blow it, I warned telepathically. *Answer him now or you're going to blow it. Tell him you wanted to hurt him; tell him you wanted to piss him off. Tell him anything; just tell him something before he wonders why you're looking at me and figures it out for himself.*

I fought to stay calm, as Katrine faced Rob, and tried to imagine why she wasn't talking. Obviously she had reconsidered her initial confession or she wouldn't have accepted the line I'd thrown her, but now it seemed like she wasn't sure—as if she suddenly couldn't decide whether to continue the ruse or smack Rob in the face with the truth.

Whatever she was thinking, she was running out of time. As I had pointed out to her psychically, the longer she was quiet, the guiltier she looked, and the more likely Rob was to draw the obvious conclusion. She needed to come up with an answer to this question soon if she didn't want to wind up facing several others.

"I don't know," she said finally, tossing her hair over her shoulder.

It was a stroke of genius, I observed, and quite impressive in its simplicity. It not only allowed Katrine to avoid lying—which was handy since she wasn't any good at it—but it also forced Rob to choose between pushing for a better answer, thereby proving himself the asshole he'd been pretending not to be, or letting it go and feeling like a eunuch. Even if she didn't get away with it, she would at least have bought herself more time to weigh her options and devise an alternate course of action. It was also a daring move, I concluded—one that Rob, judging from the way he was looking at her, did not appreciate.

"*I don't know?*'" he repeated. "What do you mean, *I don't know?*"

"I mean, I don't *know.*"

I could see Katrine was just yanking his chain now. She knew from watching him fight with me how much Rob hated to be dismissed and was dodging his questions as much for sport at this point as for self-preservation.

Unfortunately, I feared, her fun would be short-lived. For Rob would eventually tire of dancing around the ring and, as she should have also recalled from watching us fight, put an end to the match with one good blow below the proverbial belt.

"Why do you have to be such a child?" he jabbed as if on cue. "I mean, you're a grown woman, for Christ's sake, so why don't you knock it off and tell me why you said it?"

"Fine! I'll tell you why I said it: because it's true!"

I held my breath as Rob looked from Katrine to me and back again. "Are you kidding me?" he practically choked. "After all the shit you put me through over Erin, are you seriously telling me you've been sleeping with Jackie?"

"That's right! Just like you told her I could. Are you happy now?"

"Hell no, I'm not happy! Christ, Katrine—how could you do that? How could you lie to me?"

"Lie to you?" she sniffed. "Why, I never lied to you, Rob. I never once told you I wasn't sleeping with Jackie."

"Maybe not; but by not telling me that you *were*, you lied to me just the same."

"Fine," Katrine sniped suddenly, yanking me out of my analysis. "So I lied. Big deal."

"*Big deal?*"

"Now Rob," I interjected. "I know you're upset—"

"Can it, Jackie. No one was talking to you."

"You may as well talk to her," Katrine snapped, crossing her arms defiantly atop the table, "because I have nothing to say."

"Oh, yes, you do!"

"No, I don't."

"I'm pretty sure she means it, Rob," I observed as Katrine crossed her arms and fixed her gaze on a point on the wall above the stove. "I don't think she's going to talk."

"I told you to stay out of this."

"I know. But she's obviously upset, and so are you, so why don't we just take a break and come back to this after you've both had a chance to cool off?"

"Did you not hear me?"

"I did. I'm just saying it might be better to talk about this later."

"And I'm telling you to shut the fuck up."

"That's enough!" shouted a voice from behind me.

Kevin.

I froze as he appeared, wondering how long he'd been within earshot.

"Why, Sergeant Thompson," Rob said with relish. "You're just in time."

"So it seems," Kevin agreed, approaching Rob with narrow eyes and a clenched jaw. "In time to see you out, that is."

"What?"

"I'm sorry. Was that too cryptic? It means you're leaving."

"But—"

"But nothing." Striding over to the door, Kevin grabbed the doorknob with one hand and beckoned to Rob with the other. "Now, don't make this harder than it has to be," he said. "Just grab whatever you had with you and get the hell out."

"But I can explain."

"Let me make something crystal clear for you, Sergeant Copeland," Kevin said, retracing his steps back to the table. "I don't care what you think of her or what she's done; you do not get to talk to her like that in this house. Not for any reason. Now, I'm prepared to let you walk out of your own volition—just as you did the last time you insulted her—but I am equally prepared to remove you by force. Do we understand one another?"

Rob looked at me and then Katrine, who was sitting in stunned silence and staring at the table. "Fine," he said, yanking the cuffs of his shirt down with both hands as he stood to put on his coat. "Come on, Katrine."

"What do you mean, 'Come on, Katrine'?" she demanded. "I'm not going anywhere—not with you, anyway."

Kevin shrugged. "You heard her," he said. "Hit the road."

Rob took a long look at all of us again and shook his head. "Whatever."

"I'm glad you see it that way," Kevin observed. "Now if you would be so kind as to follow me, I'll see you out."

"Don't bother."

I stared in stunned silence as Rob headed toward the front room under Kevin's careful watch.

"This is your last chance, Katrine," he announced as he opened the door. "Are you coming or not?"

"No."

"All right. Well, I guess I'll see you around."

Katrine looked at me as she heard the door close. "So what happens now?" she asked as Kevin set about locking up.

"It's probably not a good idea to make that decision right now," he replied. "Things may look a little different once everyone has calmed down and thought things over. In the meantime, you can stay here if you like."

"Thanks, Kevin. I appreciate that."

"No problem. Meanwhile, I think it's important that we keep these arrangements quiet for the time being. It won't do you or Rob any good for this to get around the armory. It will only set people's gums flapping and increase the odds that the staff will find out about Rob and Erin."

"Rob and Erin?" Katrine repeated. "You mean you *knew*?"

"I'm afraid so."

"But how?"

I raised my hand. "I told him—after our drive last weekend."

"*What*?"

"I had no choice, Katrine. The situation was making you miserable."

"And you thought telling Kevin would change that?"

"Indirectly. I thought if Kevin spoke to Rob and reminded him of what could happen if he's caught, he would wise up and stop seeing Erin. Which is exactly what happened."

Katrine sighed. "So he really didn't do it for me."

"It doesn't look that way, sweetie. I'm sorry."

"It's OK. I should have known there was something else going on when he changed his mind so suddenly. I guess I wanted so badly to believe he was doing it for me that it never occurred to me there might be another reason."

Thirty-one

Although we weren't yet sure how long Katrine would be staying, I persuaded Kevin to assist in prepping the basement for her habitation. Katrine had said she'd be happy to crash in the living room, but I convinced her to stay downstairs where she wouldn't hear the kids, whose body clocks did not distinguish between weekend and weekday mornings.

I was careful not to linger too long in the basement after Kevin had gone upstairs to put the kids to bed. As much as I wanted to confront Katrine, I was more anxious to talk to Kevin and explain what had happened tonight before Rob got to him at school on Monday.

It wasn't that I wanted him to hear my side first. Although I felt there was more honor in confessing something he didn't know than there was in admitting to something he'd *already* heard, in truth, I just wanted him to hear from my own lips why Rob was so upset with me and that I had in fact deserved it.

Assuming, of course, that he didn't know already. I wasn't sure how much he had heard before speaking up, after all, and while he had leapt to my defense and behaved normally afterward, that didn't mean he hadn't heard every incriminating word. And so it was with a mixture of fear and contrition that I ascended the stairs and, after checking on the kids, approached the entrance to our bedroom.

"Do you want to tell me what that was about?" Kevin asked as the creaking of the floor announced my arrival.

He was standing in front of the window with his body at an angle to the pane, and I could see his face reflected in the glass that separated him from the darkness outside.

"Which part? The part where Rob was swearing at me? Or the part where he walked in and found Erin in the kitchen?"

"All of it. I mean, I get that he was annoyed when he walked in and found Erin consorting with the enemy, but I don't understand how things escalated to shouting—especially when the last time I passed through the kitchen, it seemed like you were trying to help the two of them work things out."

So he hadn't heard.

Although that knowledge should have filled me with relief, instead it filled me with dread. For if Kevin was still willing to talk to me after hearing Katrine's confession, there was a chance my sins would be forgiven. But now that it was clear he knew nothing of our transgressions, I feared the news would push him right out the door.

Still, it had to be done, so I sat down and motioned for him to join me on the bed.

"I don't know how to tell you this," I began as my heart threatened to beat through my chest. "But everything that happened tonight was my fault..."

And so began my tale of how the happily married wife of the most decent man on earth got involved and fell in love with the wife of one of his colleagues. I made no excuses for my actions other than my weak will that rendered me a slave to her charms and my infuriating tendency to immerse myself in temptation.

"And you couldn't tell me this before tonight?" he asked when I had finished. "Or at any point in the past four months?"

"I wanted to—and there were many times I almost did—especially when I was feeling close to you. But then something about the situation wouldn't feel right, and I'd decide to put it off again. Like when we were getting ready for school that morning after my meltdown over Lyn. I almost told you then, but we were on a schedule, and I didn't want to hold you up."

"Well, I admit this has been a busy term, and we haven't had much time to ourselves."

"I'm not trying to make excuses, Kevin. Honestly. I just didn't want to say anything until I knew there'd be ample time for me to explain."

"Explain?" Kevin repeated. "Did you think you were going to upset me?"

"No. I was pretty sure this wouldn't upset you. But neither did I think you'd understand."

"Why?"

"Because I've always had a sense that you think this sort of thing for me is about the kinky sex."

Kevin stared at a cobweb that was strung across three rows of the pine paneling covering the walls and ceiling around them. "I guess I can see how I might have given you that impression," he admitted. "I do have a tendency to tease you about it."

"Not to mention a penchant for lechery."

"But that doesn't mean I think your relationships are meaningless. That's just my way of letting you know I'm comfortable with how things are."

"Really?"

"Of course. I don't claim to be an expert on how it works, but whenever someone captures your fancy, it's obviously more than a sexual attraction."

"And you don't have a problem with that?"

Kevin shook his head. "The only thing I have a problem with is the secrecy. After all, you've never kept anything from me before, and it concerns me that you did this time."

"Me, too. And I'm very sorry."

"I am, too—for whatever part my lecherous teasing may have played in your reluctance to tell me."

"You don't have to apologize, Kevin. I'm the screwup here, not you."

"You are *not* a screwup."

"Where have you been, man? I've been explaining myself to you for six years—eight if you count back to before we got married."

"That doesn't make you a screwup," Kevin argued, reaching over the bed and squeezing my hand. "It makes you talkative."

I smiled. "You've always been so good—so tolerant and patient—it kills me to think you might take this as a reflection on how I feel about you. Because I've loved you since I met you, and I love you more and more each day."

"I know that, Jack. I wouldn't be here if I didn't."

"Honestly?"

"Honestly."

"And the second you doubt it, you'll leave my ass, right?"

"Right."

"Promise?"

"Promise."

I smiled as Kevin patted my hand and kissed me on the forehead. "Does this mean you won't be teasing me anymore about lingerie parties and threesomes?"

"What do you think?"

I shook my head. "You are so wonderfully uncomplicated, Kevin."

"Well, you know what they say: opposites attract."

I awoke to the sound of ringing a few hours later. Kevin and I had moved under the covers after our conversation, and after an hour that left me feeling both healed and exhausted, we had fallen asleep in each other's arms. Thus, it was with some difficulty that I reached beyond the sleeping form that still encircled me and over the edge of the bed to pick up the phone.

"Hello?" I groaned.

"Jackie, it's Erin. I'm sorry to wake you up, but I wanted to warn you that Rob's on his way over, and he is not happy."

"Over *here*?"

"Yes."

Rubbing my eyes, I slid out from under Kevin's embrace and over to my own side of the bed. "How do you know?"

"Because he told me."

"When?"

"A few minutes ago. He showed up at my building around midnight, after he couldn't reach me by phone. He had left a couple messages on my answering machine while I was at the library, asking me to meet him for coffee. Not wanting to get dragged into this drama again, I ignored his messages and started screening my calls. The next thing I know, he's downstairs buzzing me on the intercom. I told him to go home, but he refused, claiming I owed it to him to see him, because his involvement with me had cost him his marriage."

"What?"

"It didn't make sense to me either since, last I knew, he'd 'broken up with me' to save his marriage, but whatever. Anyway, so I told him I was busy, but he threatened to keep buzzing me until I agreed to go down and talk to him. I probably shouldn't have gone given the state he was in, but I was afraid if I didn't let him in, someone would eventually call security, and I knew it wouldn't be good to have the campus police involved in this."

"Good thinking. So what did he want?"

"To say he was sorry for what had happened and that things are truly over between us."

"You are kidding me."

"I wish."

"So what did you say?"

"Same thing I said yesterday. That it was fine with me and that I understood."

"Did he accept that?"

"Actually, he seemed rather surprised by that," Erin recalled with mock amazement, "and a little disappointed—as if he was expecting me to throw myself at his feet and beg him to change his mind."

"No doubt he was. In fact, if you had protested at all, he probably would have changed his tune and asked you to run away with him."

"That was my feeling, too—especially given his falling-out with Katrine earlier."

"And what did he tell you about that?"

"Only that he'd been asked to leave after losing his temper and that Katrine had refused to go home with him. I got the impression there was more to it, but I didn't press for details."

"I see. So having failed lure you into his arms with his wounded animal routine, the jerk has decided to launch the mother of all efforts to reclaim his bride, eh?"

"That's about the size of it."

"Terrific. Well, I guess I'd better rally the troops. Thanks for the heads-up."

Sighing again, I hung up the phone and crawled back over and nudged Kevin's side. "Hey, Jarhead," I coaxed as he stirred. "Time to get up."

"Nooooo," he moaned in reply. "Sleep now. Get up later."

"I'm afraid not, sweetheart. Copeland's on his way over here, and I'm not sure I'll be able to handle him myself."

"Sure you will," he offered through a yawn. "Just take my .38 with you, so you can shoot him if he gets out of line."

"Great idea. I hear the prisons are lovely this time of year."

"You won't go to prison for defending your home. Just make sure the body lands on the *in*side of the doorway."

In spite of Kevin's protestations, I managed to get him downstairs before Rob arrived. In fact, I had just finished waking Katrine and putting the kettle on to boil when I heard the Nova up front, followed by footsteps on the porch.

"Who is it?" Kevin called through the door to after a series of heavy knocks.

"It's Rob. I want to talk to Katrine."

"You can talk to her in the morning when we've all had some sleep."

"No. I want to talk to her now."

"Rob, go home," Katrine urged, having joined Kevin at the door. "I'll see you tomorrow."

"No—you'll see me tonight."

"I don't want to talk to you now."

"Of course you do. You've been calling the house all evening."

Katrine looked guiltily toward the kitchen where I now stood with my arms crossed, having just set out three cups of tea to steep on the counter. "I was just checking to see if he was OK," she said. "He was so upset when he left here earlier, I was afraid he'd do something drastic."

"Is that right?"

"Yes. But I stopped calling when I got our machine for the fifth time in a row, and I never left a message."

"Then how did he know you called?"

"Because the playback system has message assistant software that announces each call and the number it came from before playing the message, even if you don't leave one."

I see. "Well, you may as well let him in," I said, suddenly not caring what she did, "before he starts banging again and wakes the kids."

With a shrug from Katrine, Kevin opened the door and let Rob inside. "That's far enough," he instructed, pointing to the tiles on the floor. "You can talk to her from the foyer."

"Not in front of her," Rob replied, nodding toward me. "Tell her to get lost."

Kevin shook his head. "You want to try that again?"

"I'll say it however you like," Rob offered, "but either she leaves or we go outside, because I am not going to talk to Katrine in front of her."

Kevin faced Katrine. "Well?"

"Fine," she said to Rob, grabbing her jacket from the closet. "I'll talk to you outside—as long as Kevin comes with me."

"Fine."

I returned to the kitchen as the three of them walked out the door, and I wondered what the hell Rob had to say. His refusal to talk in front me, I knew, had less to do with not wanting me to hear their conversation than with isolating Katrine. Obviously he intended to make some big emotional appeal for her to come home and didn't want me to remind her, by my mere presence, of her other options. He probably imagined a scene akin to what one would find in an old family film—where some poor hound has to choose between the kid who just found her and the one she'd somehow gotten separated from. It would be just like him, I concluded as I squeezed the sodden tea bags and tossed them into the trash, to assume Katrine couldn't think for herself and to try to win her back not by making an attractive offer but by limiting her choices.

Not that I minded being left out of the conversation. In fact, the only reason I hadn't left the room when Rob instructed Kevin to tell me to get lost was that Kevin had already objected, and I wanted to present a united front. A second later and I would have been on my way to my room, leaving Katrine to fight her own battle with Kevin standing by making sure *someone* got killed.

It wasn't that I didn't care what Katrine did any more. I was just tired of all the drama in the air and ready for something lighter to waft on through.

That wasn't likely to happen anytime soon, I lamented as I remembered I hadn't given Katrine any details about Erin's call. There simply hadn't been enough time between it and Rob's arrival to do much more than get everybody out of bed.

That was lucky, I decided as I carried the tea to the table. If we had been more organized when he appeared, Rob might have realized Erin had tipped us off that he was coming. I could only hope this would occur to Katrine and that she wouldn't mention the call or otherwise convey to Rob that they were expecting him.

"So what was that about?" I inquired when she and Kevin reappeared several minutes later.

"He wanted me to come home with him," she replied "I told him I need more time, that there are issues we need to address, and that I wanted to see evidence that things could change before I would agree to come home."

"Good for you."

"I'm not so sure it was good for me, actually."

"Why not?"

"Because he said forget it; that if I didn't leave with him, he was going back to Erin."

"Oh, really?" I laughed. "Well, I wouldn't worry about that. He's only trying to scare you."

"What if he wasn't, Jackie? What if he's on his way over there again right now?"

"Then you'll know you made the right decision not to take him back."

"Thanks, Jackie. That's a real comfort."

"I'm sorry, Katrine, but it's the truth. Meanwhile, if it will make you feel better, we can check in with Erin a little later and see if Rob ever showed up."

"How will that make me feel better? I mean, you don't expect her to tell you if she takes him back, do you?"

"She's not going to do that, Katrine. I told you, she's not interested."

"That's not what Rob said."

"Rob's full of shit. He just wants you to feel threatened by her so you'll fall in line."

"So you say."

"What is that supposed to mean?"

Katrine shrugged. "Maybe you're wrong. Maybe Erin's lying."

"Maybe. But Rob has a lot more reason to lie than she does, Katrine. But if it makes you feel better to look at it that way, go ahead. I just think your energies would be better spent planning your future and deciding whether or not Rob is the one you want to spend it with."

The remainder of the morning passed without a word either from or about Erin or Rob. Katrine and I distracted ourselves with laundry and the kids on the main floor, while Kevin studied for an exam in the office. Finally, as I was setting out lunch just after one o'clock, the phone rang.

"It's me again," Erin said as soon as I finished my greeting. "How's it going?"

"A little tense, but otherwise OK. How about over there?"

"About the same."

"Why? What's happening?"

"Well, Rob was here again. He buzzed my dorm about an hour and a half after we hung up. I wouldn't let him up of course, but I did go downstairs just to avoid the scene he made last night."

"So what did he want?"

"To get back together."

"Did he say what changed his mind?"

"No, but I figured striking out with Katrine probably had something to do with it. Anyway, I told him I wasn't interested and to leave me alone."

"And that was it?"

"Not quite," Erin added gravely. "As I was walking back to my room, he caught up with me. Apparently he'd slipped into the building behind another student after I left him in the commons. There was no way I was going to open my door with him there, so I walked past my room and down the hall to another stairway, with him walking beside me the whole time telling me how much he loves me and wants me to give him another chance. He was so wrapped up in making his case, he didn't even notice we'd gone down two flights of stairs until we were standing in the commons again. I told him I was sorry, but I wasn't interested. Then he starts to beg, tells me how he's ruined everything and that if I don't change my mind, he'll have nothing to live for. I didn't know what else to do but stand there and listen. Eventually I decided I'd heard enough and told him to go home."

"And did he?"

"Sure—after calling me a cold-hearted bitch and unleashing a string of obscenities that brought the entire commons to a standstill."

"Oh, my God—this guy has really lost the plot."

"Tell me about it. It wasn't until one of the other residents threatened to call security that he finally shut his mouth and left."

"Did he happen to say where he was going?"

"No. But he did mention something about driving off a bridge. I don't recall which one it was because at that point, I was no longer listening."

"All right, well, thanks for the update. You hang in there, and I'll talk to you later."

As I expected, it wasn't long after I'd hung up with Erin and shared the details of the call with Kevin and Katrine that Rob showed up asking to see her. As she had during his last visit, Katrine put on her coat and went outside to meet him, only this time with Kevin watching from the living room window.

"He asked me to come home again," she said when she returned. "He said he realized when he got back to Erin's dorm that he was making a mistake and that he'll do whatever it takes to convince me to come home. I told him that nothing had changed since this morning, that we have issues to resolve before I'll even think about moving home."

"And?"

"He said fine—and then threatened to drive off a bridge."

"Well, at least he's consistent."

"What do you mean?"

"He said the same thing to Erin when she left her place."

"You didn't tell me that."

"I didn't see any reason to. He's only trying to push your buttons again."

"How do you know that?"

"Because people who really want to die don't talk about it, Katrine; they just buy a gun—or drive to a bridge—and get it over with."

Later that evening, I was surprised by a visit from Erin, who arrived on her bike while Kevin and Katrine were away retrieving some clothes and other items from her place.

"I'm sorry I didn't call," she said between gasps. "I left my dorm in kind of a hurry and then forgot to take your number with me."

"Why? What's going on?"

"Rob's been calling and leaving message after message since early this afternoon. He finally quit about forty minutes ago, but I was afraid that meant he was on his way over, so I hopped on my bike and got the hell out of dodge."

I was heating water for another round of tea when Kevin and Katrine returned from their supply mission to her and Rob's place. Both were obviously surprised to see Erin, who, having calmed down enough by then to utter complete thoughts without pausing for air, immediately began to fill them in.

After assembling another pair of mugs on the counter, I watched Katrine as Erin described how Rob had harassed her all day with messages that ran the gamut from casual invitations to bizarre reflections and from demands and remonstrations to rambling pleas for forgiveness. I hoped the conversation would convince Katrine that Rob was coming unglued and motivate her to start thinking in terms of an exit strategy, but from her face, I could not tell if any of it was sinking in.

"I don't want to get anyone in trouble," Erin concluded with a shrug, "but if this doesn't stop, I'll have no choice but to involve the police, and we all know where that will lead."

Katrine shrugged. "Why don't we call them now?" she asked. "I mean, if he's going to get himself busted anyway, why don't we just turn him in and get it over with?"

"I don't think that's a good idea," Kevin observed. "There's a lot at stake here, Katrine, and I don't think we should do anything until we've explored all other options."

"In the meantime," he continued, facing Erin, "did you save any of the messages Rob left, or have you already erased them all?"

"Oh, no. Each of these has several messages from him," Erin explained as she pulled five cassettes from her coat pocket and set them on the table, "some over twenty minutes long. I was forced to screen my calls, so there are also a few messages from other people mixed in there, but I kept everything, which is why there are so many."

Kevin nodded approvingly. "Keep those in a safe place," he instructed as he pocketed two of the tapes. "I'll take these with me."

"Where?"

"To see Rob."

"Great idea," I declared emphatically. "I'll get your coat."

"I don't mean now, silly. In the morning."

"But you have class in the morning."

"As does he. So I'll just leave a little early and catch him outside the armory before muster."

"But what if you miss him?"

"Jackie, listen to me," Kevin said patiently. "With the possible exception of Erin herself, no one wants this shit resolved more than I do; but I haven't had a good night's sleep in days. So if you'll please give me a kiss and let me go to bed, I promise I'll be ten times more intimidating in the morning."

"I'm going to take off, too," Erin said after Kevin had collected his toll and exited. "If you need to reach me for anything, I'll be at my sister's place."

"Where's that?" I inquired as she scribbled a number onto the pad by the phone.

"In Bloomington. She and her husband are a little on the dull side, but that'll be a welcome change after all of this."

Katrine turned in a few minutes later, and I thought it was strange she hadn't had much to say either before or after Erin's departure. Chalking it up to a combination of factors, not the least of which would have been annoyance at having Erin's woes eclipse her own, I bid her good night and broke out the homework I'd neglected all weekend.

Thirty-two

With Kevin having left early to catch Rob in the morning and Katrine having been asleep when I left, I didn't see either of them again until after school the next day, when I arrived at home to find them standing in the living room with Katrine's belongings piled up on the floor next to the front door.

"Hey, guys," I said guardedly, setting my own stuff on the chair by the stairs. "What's going on?"

Kevin looked at Katrine, who moved over the window and stared up the street. "There's been a development," he replied when she failed to. "A couple, actually."

"I see. Well, no one's wearing black," I observed as I kicked off my shoes, "so I gather Rob is still alive."

"Yes."

"So are you going to tell me what's happened, or are you going to make me keep guessing until I figure it out?"

Kevin looked at Katrine again, who continued to stare out the window. "Rob's on his way over," he said carefully. "And Katrine is going home."

"*What*?"

Kevin nodded. "She's decided to give him another chance."

"Another chance to *what*?" I demanded, facing Katrine. "Screw you over again? Because you *know* that's what he'll do. It's all he knows *how* to do."

"Now, Jack," Kevin said, taking me gently by the shoulders and looking me in the eye. "I know you're upset, but this is what Katrine wants, and as her friends, we have to support her."

"It's OK," Katrine assured him as a yellow convertible pulled up to the curb. "I didn't expect her to be happy for me. I only hope," she added, stepping around me as I watched Rob disembark the vehicle and begin his trek to the front door, "that one day she'll understand."

Rob did not come in but stood on the porch and accepted Katrine's things as she handed them out to him.

"Well, I think that's everything," she said as she apprehended the last item in her pile. "If I've forgotten anything, please let me know."

"Will do," Kevin said. "You guys take care now—and good luck."

Letting Kevin get the door, I watched Katrine follow Rob to the car, where he was now arranging her things in the trunk. "Son of a bitch," I breathed as the two of them climbed into the front seats and drove away. "I can't believe she's going back to him."

Kevin shrugged. "I guess he offered the right incentive."

"You mean the car?"

"No—a DOR."

"A DOR? When the hell did that happen?"

"This morning."

"Because of the tapes?"

Kevin shook his head. "Didn't need them."

"Because of his scores?"

"Nope."

"Look, pal, could you be a little more forthcoming? If you haven't noticed, I'm in the wrong frame of mind for twenty questions."

"I'm sorry, Jack. It's just that a lot has happened today, and I'm not sure how to tell you."

"How about chronologically? I've always found that to be an effective way of relating a sequence of events."

"No kidding?" Kevin replied with mock wonder. "I'll have to give that a try."

"Thank you."

"Well, as I'd planned," he began as we each claimed opposite ends of the couch, "I tracked Rob down at school before morning muster. Contrary to what I expected, he wasn't the least bit hostile and actually seemed quite upbeat. I asked him how things were going, and he said 'great' and invited me over to see the new car he'd apparently bought last night when we thought he was at work. I'd seen it pull in to the lot while I was waiting for him, but I never imagined he was in it, so I hadn't paid much attention."

"So you *did* almost miss him?" I interjected playfully.

Kevin laughed. "Almost," he acknowledged. "Anyway, Rob said he was going to surprise Katrine with the car when she got out of class this afternoon. I said she may not be interested in talking to him in light of his actions yesterday, and I proceeded to share what I knew about them and the messages he'd left on Erin's machine. He acted as if he knew nothing about them and accused you of conspiring with her to spread lies about him, so I told him I had them on tape and offered to play a few. I guess he realized then that the jig was up, because he asked me why I had them. I told him Erin had given them to me; that she'd come over to our place last night after he drove her out of her dorm with his insane ranting."

"What did he say to that?"

"Nothing. He just stared at me. That's when I advised him that if he intended to make the payments on his sweet new ride, he needed to leave Erin alone, effective immediately. I added that he was not to speak to her—in person or by phone—from this day forward, nor should he try to contact her through any third parties. I said provided he agreed to these terms, I would keep what I knew to myself, but failing that, all five tapes would be turned over to Major Henry, who would happily treat him to a court-martial and dishonorable discharge. I then asked him if he had any questions. When he said no, I said 'Good' and told him to have a nice day."

"OK, so you told him not to see Erin anymore, and he didn't refuse," I paraphrased, turning sideways on my cushion and arranging my feet on Kevin's lap. "That doesn't explain his DOR or why Katrine took him back."

"True."

"So what happened?"

"I can't tell you that part yet. We need to wait for Erin. I have to discuss it with her, too, and I would rather not have to go over it twice."

"Are you serious?"

"I'm afraid so."

"So when will she be here?"

"In a couple hours or so."

"Are you kidding me? You know I can't wait that long. I'll die of suspense."

"I doubt it. Besides, you're the one who told me to tell you chronologically."

"Oh, come on! You should know better than to listen to me."

"And you should be careful of what you wish for."

I crossed my arms. "Fine," I sighed. "So how about we skip around instead."

"Well, that would be a great way to pass the time, I suppose, but isn't this place kind of small for that much activity?"

I groaned as I got his joke.

"It won't kill you to wait," he urged, patting my knee as I tried not to laugh. "Between dinner, the kids, and homework, we should have plenty to keep us busy until Erin arrives."

"If you say so. But any nails or other parts I manage to chew off in the meantime are going to be on your conscience."

Erin arrived as Kevin was just finishing his dinner and I was arranging mine into something resembling a cubist nude. We'd picked up the kids from day care together for a change and fed them before sitting down to the stuffed pork chops I had made while trying to pass the time. I had continued to badger him about the events of the day, and, to my intense consternation, he had deftly deflected each of my attempts to learn more than he was prepared to tell.

By the time we had cleared the table, put away the leftovers, done the dishes, and wiped the counters, I was exhausted from trying to get him talking and from pondering the various scenarios I could invent on my own. The kids were now playing down the hall with Maggie, whom Kevin had hired so we could devote our full attention to the discussion we had planned to have with our guest.

"Hello, there, my fellow civilian," she said to me as I opened the door. "What's cooking?"

Fellow civilian? I wondered to myself. *What the hell is that supposed to mean?*

"Well, you're looking awfully chipper," Kevin observed, "for someone who just lost an all-expenses-paid trip through the U of M."

"I know."

"So you're not devastated?"

"Hardly. Naturally I'm disappointed about the scholarship, but it wasn't mine yet anyway, so I can't be too upset. Plus, I have plenty of other options."

"That's terrific," I interjected as I paused from clearing away their dishes. "I'm incredibly happy for you—now, would someone mind telling me just what the hell happened today?"

Erin stared at Kevin. "You mean you haven't told her?"

"I was waiting for you," he explained. "I figured she'd have some of the same questions you would, so I decided to talk to you at the same time and conserve my energy."

I nodded. "At the expense of my nerves, of course."

"So I see. Well, as you've probably figured out," Erin offered as we assembled at the table, "I won't be receiving an ROTC scholarship. The unit staff found out about my relationship with Rob and decided that I'm not officer material, so they called headquarters and withdrew my package from consideration."

Wow. They don't waste time, do they?

"So how did they find out?"

"I have no idea. That's why I'm here. As far as I knew when I left for school this morning, everything was fine. Kevin had called me at my sister's house after speaking to Rob and said that he'd agreed to leave me alone. So I finished getting ready and hopped on my bike to go to school. Next thing I know, I'm in Major Henry's office and minus one scholarship."

"My God, Kevin," I exclaimed. "What on earth happened over there today?"

"Well, after I'd spoken to Rob and called to give Erin the all clear," he explained, "I headed over to the armory for morning muster. I had considered calling our place and giving Katrine a heads-up about Rob's new purchase before she left to catch her bus to school, but figuring I'd see her before he did anyway, I decided against it and went upstairs.

"When I got there, Sergeant Weeks pulled me into the major's office and said they'd received a call from a young woman asking about Erin. She had said she'd seen an altercation between her and someone who looked like a marine at her dorm yesterday and that Erin hadn't been seen since she left the building a few hours later. She added that she didn't know Erin very well, but she thought she was in ROTC and wanted to make sure she hadn't gone missing."

"Did they say who she was?" Erin asked.

Kevin shook his head. "I just assumed it was someone who lived your building."

"But no one in my building knows me well enough to be that concerned, and I haven't lived there long enough for anyone to be familiar with my routine. Besides, I don't know how anyone in that place would know I'm in ROTC. I don't have a uniform yet, and I never wear my PT gear in or out of the building."

I closed my eyes. "I don't believe it."

"What?" Kevin and Erin asked simultaneously.

"It was Katrine. The woman who called the armory was Katrine."

"How do you know?" Erin wondered.

"Think about it: she knows you're in ROTC, she knows Rob made a scene at your place yesterday, and she knew you weren't going back to your dorm last night. So she had all the information the caller had this morning—plus motive *and* opportunity."

"That's true," Kevin conceded. "And come to think of it, she didn't seem entirely on board with the plan last night. So I wouldn't be surprised if she decided to take matters into her own hands and set this disaster in motion."

"But how could she be sure what would happen?" Erin asked.

"She's not a stupid girl," he replied. "She knew the unit's first priority would be your safety; she also knew they'd want to know more about any 'altercation' involving one of their marines."

"Which is why they hauled you into the office first thing this morning," Erin realized with a sigh. "So what did you tell them?"

"That you were fine, that I'd just spoken to you a few minutes ago, and that you were on your way in to school. They couldn't take my word for it, of course, since for all they knew, I was the guy you'd had the altercation with and might very well be responsible for your disappearance. Unfortunately, I didn't think of that before I opened my mouth; I was so eager to allay their concerns and distract them from the fact that one of their marines had been seen at your building that it never occurred to me that I was making myself look guilty in the process."

"Well, as they say," Erin said, "no good deed goes unpunished."

"You can say that again."

"All right—enough with the clichés!" I commanded. "What happened next?"

"Well, as I feared the moment the words fell from my mouth, they started asking how it was that I had spoken to Erin this morning and whether I had been at her building yesterday afternoon. I told them no, but I knew who was, and I'd been in touch with Erin this morning to tell her I'd spoken to the jerk and had instructed him to leave her alone.

"It didn't take them long to figure out who I was talking about," Kevin added, "since only one of the marines here would have fit that description or would have required such counsel."

"So *you're* the one who dimed us out?" Erin laughed. "That's hilarious."

"I'm glad you think so, because it's killing me."

"Don't be silly, Kev. I wasn't really sure I wanted to be in the military in the first place. Naturally, I would have preferred to make the decision myself," Erin admitted, "but I wasn't necessarily going to accept the scholarship if I was offered one, so don't sweat it."

Kevin sighed. "Well, that makes me feel better—although not much."

"Anyway…" I prodded.

"Right. Well, once they realized who was involved, they wouldn't let it drop. They asked me about the incident at the dorm, what had preceded it, and why I was involved. I tried to minimize the situation, hoping to convince them the problem had been resolved, but they smelled blood and wanted details."

"I'm not surprised," I observed. "They've been looking for an excuse to get rid of him for a while now, and this gave them just the ammunition they needed."

"Exactly. So, sensing what was coming and that there was little I could do to stop it, I gave them everything—including the tapes, which were still in my pocket."

"I was wondering how they got ahold of them," Erin mused. "I figured you'd turned them over, but I wasn't sure under what circumstances."

"What do you mean?"

"Well, Rob had speculated here and there that he was being monitored— as if the staff was out to get him. I assumed he was just being paranoid— that is, until this Saturday, when you said you were trying to 'train' him. Remembering that, and not knowing you very well, when I saw the cassettes on the major's desk this morning, I took you for some covert operative and decided I'd been sacrificed to the God of Good Order and Discipline."

Kevin and I laughed.

"I don't mean to embarrass you," I explained when Erin turned red. "It's just that that was fucking funny."

"Trust me," she replied. "You can't make me feel any more ridiculous than I do already. So what exactly happened after you spoke to the major? I assumed they talked to Rob, but no one said a word to me about it."

Kevin nodded. "They brought him in a few minutes after they finished with me. He denied everything, of course; said he knew nothing about any incident at the dorm and that he barely knew 'Ms. Rollins.' Eventually they told him that they knew about your relationship and that he had a choice between dropping from the program or facing a court-martial."

"Did he have anything to say to you during this time?" I wondered. "I mean, he must have thought you'd double-crossed him."

"Oh, no. They had made it clear at the beginning that they were investigating a report from someone who had witnessed an incident between Erin and an unknown marine yesterday."

"So essentially, they told him what they told you."

"Right—and when they told him they knew about him and Erin, they explained how they came by their information—so he had absolutely no reason to think I had sold him down the river."

"That's good," I observed. "So did he finally cop to it then or continue to deny it?"

"Actually, neither. Instead, the fucker turns into F. Lee Bailey—saying they were wasting their time; that fraternization doesn't apply in this case because he's not an officer yet; that even if he was, the charge would never stick because Ms. Rollins is not officially a member of the unit; and that even if she was, he wouldn't outrank her because they are considered equals at this unit. He then went on to say that even if this went to court, he'd never be convicted, because what I'd said was hearsay, and even if they got Erin to testify, he would argue that she's just an 'unstable erotomaniac' out to destroy his life."

"Oh, my God!" I exclaimed. "That is hilarious. Talk about the pot calling the kettle black!"

Erin appeared confused. "Are you saying there really *is* such a thing?" she asked. "That wasn't something Rob just made up?"

"Well, it was obviously something he made up about *you*," I replied, "but that's what makes it so damned funny."

"I still don't get it."

"Erotomania is a form of psychosis," I explained, "whereby a person imagines someone is in love with them. The object of this disorder may be known to them either directly or tangentially or may even be a stranger or a celebrity. Either way, the erotomaniac will become delusional to the point that he or she will interpret ordinary behavior and basic civility as expressions of secret love and adoration and reject evidence to the contrary as something the object must do to conceal their secret passion."

"Well, however ironic and funny that may be to us," Kevin interjected, bringing us back to the point, "it failed to amuse the major. In fact, having had it up to here," he added, illustrating the frustration level in question with a gesture that only approximated a salute, "he pulled out the secret file and the tapes and laid all their cards on the table—at which point Rob folded his hand and tendered his DOR."

Erin raised her brows. "No wonder they had so little to say to me when I got there."

"What do you mean?" I asked.

"Well, they didn't tell me any of this. They just said that recent events had forced them to withdraw my package from consideration and sent me on my way."

"So they didn't even tell you why?"

Erin shook her head. "And I didn't dare ask. I mean, it was obvious that something had gone terribly wrong since I'd spoken to Kevin earlier, but he wasn't there to explain. Plus, by then I'd seen the cassettes on the major's desk and figured I'd been shafted in the interest of national security, so I just left the armory and went on with my day. Eventually I caught up with Kevin on his way to his car this afternoon, but he was with Katrine and couldn't talk. He said to come over tonight since she wouldn't be around."

"Too bad you didn't know about this mystery caller then," I observed. "You could have had some fun with her and that lousy excuse for a conscience."

"Speaking of which," Erin said furtively, "when is she due back? It may sound petty, but I'd rather not be here when she returns."

"You've got nothing to worry about there," Kevin assured her. "Evidently Rob made his pitch like he'd planned this afternoon, and she accepted his offer. The two of them drove off in a pretty yellow convertible a couple hours before you arrived."

Erin shook her head. "I don't get it," she admitted. "Why on earth would she go to all that trouble to get him to DOR if she was just going to take him back anyway?"

"Beats me," I replied. "But this puts her in the driver's seat in more ways than one, which means Rob may be in for one hell of a ride."

It was just over a week after Katrine left that Kevin ran into her on campus. Although Rob was no longer welcome at the armory, he still attended classes thanks to the benevolence of the commanding officer at the local reserve unit to which he'd been assigned while awaiting orders back to the fleet. Thus it was that Katrine was able to finish out the term as well and was around when Kevin left his last class that afternoon.

"What can I do for you?" he asked as she accompanied him to his car.

"Nothing. I just knew you'd be coming this way, so I came by to say hello."

"Oh, is that right?"

Katrine nodded. "So how's Jackie?" she asked. "I've been wanting to call and ask her myself, but I wasn't sure she'd be happy to hear from me."

"Well, how awful for you. It must have come as a terrible shock to discover that you're actually capable of thinking of someone besides yourself."

"Jeez, Kevin. I expected Jackie to be annoyed with me, but what's your problem?"

"I don't have a problem. I just don't like seeing her the way she's been since you left."

"What do you mean?"

Kevin stopped walking as they reached the Ford. "I mean she's not herself, thanks to you. In fact, some days it's all she can do to put one foot in front of the other."

"*Jackie?*"

"Yeah. For some reason she still cares about you and worries if you'll be OK. I keep assuring her that you'll get *everything* you deserve, but you know how obsessive she can be.

"By the way," Kevin continued, having tossed his book bag onto the passenger seat after unlocking the driver's side door, "if Rob's wondering about his CDs, he'll be happy to know Jackie's decided against melting them down. So unless she changes her mind or uses them for target practice this afternoon, I'll bring them to school with me tomorrow."

"That's OK, Kevin. There's really no rush."

"Maybe not for you, but I'd like them out of the house as soon as possible. That way they won't be lying around reminding her of you, and they'll be right where you want them when you're packing up to start your new life with the now and forever Sergeant Copeland. So, they'll be in the backseat of my car tomorrow morning—assuming no one else gets to them first."

"Thanks, Kevin. But that's really not necessary. I'll just come by and pick them up myself tonight when Rob's at work."

"No, you won't. In fact, I don't want you anywhere near our house again," Kevin added. "Understand?"

"I guess."

"Good—I'm counting on it."

"Why would you do that?" I asked after Kevin related the conversation to me as we made dinner that evening.

"Because she's bad news."

"Do you think I don't know that?"

"No."

"Do you think I can't handle her?"

"No."

"Then what is this about?"

"It's about me knowing what she's like and not wanting you to have to deal with her."

"Thanks, Kevin, but I can take care of myself."

"Well, excuse me for trying to make things easier on you."

"Is that what you were doing—by making me sound like a nervous wreck?"

"Of course not. That was just me trying to wind her up. I thought you'd be amused."

"Oh, yeah. I'm really fucking amused. It just tickles me to death to have her thinking I'm on the verge of a nervous breakdown. I only wish I could have seen the satisfaction on her face when she realized what an emotional cripple I've become."

"Trust me—the look on her face was not satisfaction."

"I'm sure it will be by the time she finishes processing it."

"I doubt it. But even if I'm wrong, what does it matter? I mean, why should you care what she thinks of you?"

"I don't care what she thinks of me. I would just like to preserve as much of my dignity as I can, and I can't do that with you making me sound like a basket case. Think about it, Kevin: would you want any of your old flames thinking you'd fallen into the gutter over them?"

"No—but if one of them had used me like she did you, I would want her to feel *ashamed*. Not that she has the capacity to feel shame," he admitted, 'but I thought it was worth a shot."

I see. "Well, I guess I understand now what you were trying to do," I admitted, regretting my initial response to his tale. "Of course, I would have preferred you'd painted me more pissed off than stressed out, but I appreciate your looking out for me."

"It was my pleasure, Jack."

Thirty-three

For the next month, Kevin and I juggled, as we had for the past two years, the kids, the house, and our homework—often on separate shifts. Deadlines and weekends came and went as the days grew longer until, finally, I finished spring semester and graduated—not on the dean's list as I had hoped but, as I told Sera a week after commencement, with a respectable grade point average.

"Are you going to look for a job now?" Sera asked as we enjoyed the bruschetta and chianti that kicked off our celebratory dinner at Bar Domitiana that evening.

Unlike Les Bougies and others of its ilk, Bar Domitiana had not sacrificed authenticity in the interest of making a buck off gullible Americans. Rather, both the atmosphere and the food were suited to folks who had grown up eating spaghetti at home and wanted to enjoy a meal in a place that reminded them of their Neapolitan grandmother's kitchen.

"Not yet," I replied, having made this assessment. "I'm just not comfortable with the idea of spending forty-plus hours away from the kids after having been in school for the past two years. I'll still keep them in day care part-time so they can see their friends and I can maintain my sanity, but I just can't stand the thought of spending even less time with them now than I was while I was in school. Besides," I added, loading a slice of the toasted bread with a spoonful of the diced tomato and garlic concoction in the bowl before me, "I wouldn't feel right taking a job that

I know I'm going to quit when Kevin graduates and we move to Quantico next year."

"So what are you going to do with yourself in the meantime?"

"Write, hopefully—maybe draft a sketch or two, or float a couple of short stories—and try to get back in shape."

"Well, that should keep your mind off Katrine. Then again, after what she pulled last month, she should be the last person on your mind anyway."

I wished I could be so rational. As I'd confessed to Sera when we discussed the events of the past spring by phone last week, however, I missed Katrine terribly and thought about her every day. Although I hadn't been in the mood to share every detail then, I had managed to bring Sera up to speed on the status of things with Katrine—how she'd left Rob after telling him about our already defunct affair; and how she'd gone back to him after having destroyed his career by surreptitiously alerting the unit staff to his liaison with one of the female midshipmen in the command, with whom she'd previously given him consent to consort.

"I know," I conceded. "I really must find a way to get her out of my system."

Sera shook her head. "I don't understand. What on earth is it about this girl that you are having so much trouble letting go? I mean no offense, but knowing how she operates, I can't imagine a single reason why you would want her around."

"I didn't say I wanted her around, Sera. I said I have to find a way to get her out of my system—that means I *don't* want her around."

"No—it means you *do* want her around, but you know you *shouldn't.*"

I shrugged as a server came into view carrying what I presumed to be our meals. Sera was right, I acknowledged to myself while he set a plate of pasta in front of each of us and arranged a dish of roasted peppers next to the bread. Knowing that the arrival of the food would not derail the brewing inquest, I skewered a bundle of penne as soon as he had gone and braced myself for Sera's next run at my psyche.

"So what is it?" the future lawyer asked, swaddling her fork in fettuccini.

"I wish I knew. I mean, it's not as if she was my first," I laughed. "Or even the best."

"Oh, is that right?"

"I'm sorry," I said as she absorbed my meaning. "I should have told you a long time ago."

"I agree. In fact, I've been dying to ask ever since you told me what happened with Katrine, but I didn't want to push."

"I appreciate that."

"So why didn't you tell me?" she asked as she dragged a pepper across her plate. "I mean, we've known each other for two years, for God's sake; you'd think it would have come up."

"Not necessarily. In fact, it probably would have *never* come up it hadn't been for this thing between me and Katrine."

"I don't understand why. You've known I was gay from day one."

"And?"

Sera shrugged. "I guess I assumed that would have made it easier for you to tell me."

"Well, it didn't. In fact, in some ways it actually made it harder. After all, the few lesbians I know don't appreciate my kind. Many of them think that identifying oneself as bisexual is a cop-out; that people like me are just gay women who aren't willing to come out of the closet and subject ourselves to the discrimination they face; that we want to have our cake and eat it too."

"And you thought I might fall into this category?"

"No. I just didn't want to take the chance."

"I see. Well, let me say, for the record, that I *don't*. I happen to view sexuality as occurring along a continuum; that we are all born with an innate tendency to be attracted to all kinds of different people for all sorts of different reasons, at different times in our lives; and that we drift in one direction or the other in response to our changing needs and interests and in response to the messages we receive—be they positive or negative—from our family and peers and society in general. So although I accept that people you've described are entitled to their opinion, I also happen to think they're full of shit."

I smiled and tipped my glass. "Here, here."

"That said," Sera continued, "I still can't believe it took you so long to tell me. I mean, I've known about you and Katrine for months now. I would have thought you'd have figured out I was cool with before now."

"Oh, I've known you were cool with it since January. I wasn't ready to talk about it then."

"And now you are?"

"I think so. I just don't know what to say—especially about Katrine. I mean, with everyone else, when it was over, it was over. I mean, I loved them, but I knew at the outset they wouldn't be around forever, so when the time came, I said good-bye and moved on. But this thing with Katrine is different. I can't say I love her more than I did the others or even that I expected more from her than I did them. In fact, having been down this road before, I probably expected less. So I don't know why letting go is so much harder with her, but it is, and I don't know what to do about it."

"Are you sure this isn't just a memory issue? I mean, maybe letting go then hurt just as much as it does now, but it seems worse this time because you've had a chance to get over the others."

"Maybe. Or maybe I'm just a sore loser," I laughed. "I mean, I've been kicked to the curb before by guys who didn't want to be tied down— like Joe Cochran, from whom I got my one and only Dear Jane letter, which I subsequently copied and hung all over the school after marking his grammar and spelling errors with red pen because I felt the entire student body should have the chance to learn from his mistakes. But the only time I've been dumped for someone else was when Wayne Davies dumped me for that butt-faced Libby Moline in eleventh grade—which stung a little bit, but I figured if he was going to ditch me for a slut who looked like the ass end of a shaved pug, I didn't want him anyway."

"Well, I won't go so far as to say you're a bad loser," Sera observed with a combination of amusement and disbelief, "but you certainly have issues with rejection."

"That's what I'm talking about."

"Understood—but I really don't think that's what's going on here."

"Why not?"

"Because Katrine didn't really reject you, for one thing. You broke it off with her before she even left Rob—remember? And, thus, before she ever took him back."

"Hey—you're right."

"Of course I'm right. As I've said to you many times, I'm rarely anything else."

I laughed. "Including modest."

"But of course."

"OK," I said, laying my utensils across my plate and wiping my mouth. "So maybe I just need to give myself some more time."

Sera nodded. "And a smidge of distance wouldn't hurt. I mean, I don't think her living only blocks away from you is helping very much."

"Me either. But they'll be gone soon enough. Rob managed to get a temporary assignment assisting a local recruiter so he could delay his transfer, but they still should be gone by the end of the summer."

Sera eyed me sideways. "Can I assume that means you know what she's up to as well?"

"No, but she seems to want to tell me pretty bad."

"What do you mean?"

"Ever since Kevin pulled his Sir Galahad act, she's been calling the house every few days or so, usually in the morning after he's left for work. I wasn't sure it was her at first because she wouldn't say anything at all, but I had a feeling it was her. So when the phone rang yesterday and I was sure it wouldn't be Kevin—I said 'Hi, Katrine' instead of 'Hello.'"

"And what did she have to say?"

"She said she was sorry for everything and that she missed me. I told her I missed her, too, but it would be best for all concerned if she would stop calling and move on with her life."

"Have you told Kevin?"

"Hell no."

"Why not?"

"Because he'll make some big-ass deal out of it—that's why not."

"Is that the only reason?"

"I have no intention of seeing her, if that's what you're getting at."

"You'd better mean that, woman, because there's a limit to what a man will take—even one like Kevin."

"I swear," I vowed upon finishing my last swallow of wine, "if she calls again, I'll tell him what's going on and have him sort her out."

By the end of June, Kevin had finished the last quarter of his junior year and was temporarily free from both homework and unit responsibilities. Although he would still have to attend pistol team practice and competitions so as to avoid getting rusty over the summer, he planned to otherwise avoid anyone and anything even remotely connected to the armory.

Thus, he was visibly annoyed to spot a familiar gray Nova stopping in front of the house one sticky Sunday afternoon just a couple hours before he was due to leave for a tournament in Madison.

"What does he want?" Kevin asked as Rob exited the car and started walking toward the shady swath of lawn where we were reading and watching the kids playing in the inflatable pool we'd bought the weekend before.

"Hello, Kevin," the subject said before I could answer. "How have you been?"

"Fine, thanks," Kevin said as he rose from his lawn chair and set his book on the seat. "What can I do for you?"

"Nothing. But I'd like a word with Jackie, if you don't mind."

"I don't mind if she doesn't mind. What's this about?"

"Ask her—I'll bet she knows."

Kevin looked at me. "Well?"

"Well, what?" I replied from my chair. "I have no idea what he's talking about."

Rob shook his head. "Yes, you do."

"No—I don't."

Crossing his arms, Rob faced Kevin sternly. "Ask her what my wife is doing with *her* sweatshirt."

"That's it?" I sniffed as I stuffed my hands in the back pockets of my jean shorts. "You want to ask me about a sweatshirt I lent Katrine last winter? Christ, Rob! Nice to see you're managing your paranoia."

Rob shook his head again. "Nice try—but you're not getting out of this that easy."

"Oh, really?"

"Yes, really."

Kevin put his hands on his hips. "Now, hold on just a second," he directed. "Jackie, what the hell is he talking about? What sweatshirt?"

"One that Katrine borrowed from me at some point, apparently."

"At some point, my ass," Rob interjected. "I'm sure you know *exactly* when you gave it to her, and it was *not* last winter."

"So what are you accusing me of, Rob? Falsifying vestments?"

Kevin nodded. "It's a fair question, Rob. Just what *are* you suggesting?"

"You mean you still don't get it?"

"I'm afraid not."

"Well, then allow me to show you!"

I shrugged at Kevin as Rob marched back to the Nova.

Kneeling down to retrieve a few toys Lucy had launched from the pool, I watched him pull a cadet blue bundle from the front seat and storm back toward me. I had barely resumed standing again when Rob hurled said bundle at me from several steps away.

"I found *that* in the convertible last night," he announced as I caught the projectile.

"OK," I said, shaking it out to reveal a hooded sweatshirt bearing the Hamilton seal. "So?"

"It is yours, right?"

I shrugged. "Either that or Katrine's been sweating up the sheets with some new Hamiltonian while you're off conning kids into camouflage all day."

"You bitch!" Rob hissed, his face so red I thought it might burst.

"All right—that's enough," Kevin said as he stepped between me and Rob before either of us got a well-deserved smack from the other. "So it's her shirt. What's your point, Rob?"

"My point is that Katrine didn't have that when she left here two months ago."

"How do you know?"

"Because we put all the winter clothes away when we heard we were going to Arizona."

Kevin considered Rob's logic. "Well, maybe Katrine kept the sweatshirt back," he offered. "Maybe she planned to return it before you leave."

Rob glared at me. He apparently hadn't thought of that—and clearly didn't buy it—but having failed to sway Kevin, he turned around and stalked back toward his car.

"Good thing he's such a prick," I observed as I arranged the shirt over the back of Kevin's chair after the Nova sped away. "Otherwise I'd have been stuck buying another one of these."

Kevin nodded. "And just when did you buy that one?" he asked, indicating the item in question while stooping down to pick up the next batch of toys to be flung from the pool.

"I beg your pardon."

"This is the first time I've seen it, so I'm wondering when you bought it."

I stuffed my hands in my pockets again as Kevin stood up and faced me. "What are you asking me exactly?"

"I'm asking you when you bought the sweatshirt."

"Aren't you really asking me when I gave it to Katrine?"

Kevin shrugged. "I suppose I am."

"I see. Well, like I told Rob," I pronounced deliberately, "it had to have been last winter."

"Then why haven't I seen it before?"

"As if you'd remember if you had. And since when do you keep track of what's in my wardrobe?"

"I don't—that's why I'm asking."

"No, Kevin, you're not asking. You're accusing."

"And you're avoiding the question."

I couldn't believe what was happening. It wasn't like Kevin not to trust me, and even though I deserved it, the shock of it left me suddenly speechless."

"You're seeing her again, aren't you?" he asked when I didn't reply.

"Is that really what you think?"

"What else should I think?"

I shook my head. "I don't give a damn what you think," I said, retrieving Lucy from the pool and wrapping her in a towel. "I'm going inside."

"Why?"

"Because I'm *not* going to stand out here and argue with you. It was bad enough having Rob accost me in front of the entire neighborhood," I added, taking Tyler by the hand after he'd dried himself off. "I'll be damned if I'm going let you do the same thing."

"So that's it?" Kevin asked, following me through the front door. "You're not even going to try and explain yourself?"

"Explain myself?"

"OK, bad choice of words."

"You're telling me."

"Nevertheless," Kevin continued, sotto voce, so as not to upset the children as we reached the kitchen, "I would like you to tell me what's going on."

"Would you really? Or are you just looking for your out?"

"My out?"

"Oh, don't give me that," I breathed, buckling Lucy into her high chair as Tyler climbed aboard his booster. "Do you honestly think I didn't see this coming?"

"See what coming?"

I shook my head as I placed a sipper cup and a handful of graham snacks in front of each of the kids and set the box on the counter. "This," I stage whispered, edging toward the living room. "Your grand exit."

"Jackie, what the hell are you talking about?"

"You know exactly what I'm talking about! So why don't you spare me the drama and your manufactured motives and get the hell out?"

"What?"

"You heard me. You're off the hook, man. You don't have to be here anymore."

"I'm not here because I *have* to be, Jack. I'm here because I *want* to be."

"No, you don't. Oh, maybe you did at first, but I knew that wouldn't last. I knew you'd want out eventually. So go ahead—now that you've found an excuse and won't have to feel like a shit—get lost. I won't blame you, and neither will anyone else."

"You'd like that, wouldn't you? You'd like nothing better than for me to leave you right here and now so you can sit back all smug and say you knew it was coming. Because that's how you operate."

"Well, gee, I guess you've got it all figured out."

Kevin shook his head. "And I tried to be the one—the *one* left standing when the smoke cleared. I tried to show you things could be different, that you could believe in people, and that you could trust them not to hurt you or desert you. But you don't want me to be different. You'd rather drive me away than believe that I love you—just so you can be right."

I crossed my arms. "So you *are* leaving, then? I mean, that is your point, right?"

"For now I am, yes," Kevin replied, glancing obviously at the clock on the stove, "but only because I have to be on a bus to Madison in twenty minutes."

"So what does that mean?"

"It means we'll finish this when I get back at the end of the week."

Sure, I thought as Kevin picked up the bags he had packed before we took the kids outside and delivered a peck to my cheek. *Have a nice life.*

Thirty-four

I knew I couldn't afford to keep the duplex after Kevin moved out. However generous he might be in terms of finances, I wasn't about to accept anything from the man except child support. This left me no choice but to adjust the plans I'd made to include either taking Tyler and Lucy out of day care, finding a job, leaving the city, or all of the above. Thus, I spent the evening of his departure scouring the paper for every viable housing and employment opportunity within a one-hundred-mile radius of South Minneapolis.

As I conducted my research, I avoided the phone. I didn't know if Kevin would have access to one himself while he was away, but since I wasn't keen on discussing our issues by phone anyway—and since I didn't want to talk to anyone else—I set the answering machine to pick up every call without even having to hear it ring.

Upon reviewing my prospects, I decided to head for Wabasha. As I told Sera on the phone later that night, "Job or no job, I have to get out of the Twin Cities. The place was already too crowded for me and two ex-boyfriends, so there is definitely not enough room for them, me, Katrine, and an ex-husband."

"He is *not* your ex-husband," she replied. "You haven't even finished your argument yet, for Christ's sake."

"OK—so there's not enough room for me, the ex-boyfriends, Katrine, and my *estranged* husband. Is that better?"

"I suppose. Although since it's only been a few hours since he left, and, more importantly, he said he's planning to come back—I'm not even sure that's appropriate."

"You and your technicalities. No wonder everyone hates lawyers."

"Only until they need one, baby. Only until they need one."

I couldn't help but laugh.

"Seriously though," Sera continued, "I don't understand why you let things get to this point in the first place. I mean, why didn't you just tell Kevin you weren't seeing her?"

"Because it wouldn't have mattered, Sera. He had obviously decided I was guilty."

"If that's true, it was only because you were being so evasive."

"Evasive? I told him I'd lent her the sweatshirt last winter. What more could I have said?"

"I don't know exactly, but you could have been a little more forthcoming, I think—and a lot less defensive. I mean, I hate to admit it, but you even had me thinking you were up to something when you told me what happened with the sweatshirt today—and I was standing right there with you when you bought the damned thing at the bookstore."

"Are you serious?"

"Hell yes, I'm serious. After all, having bought it last fall doesn't prove you gave it to her then, and having lent it to her then doesn't prove you haven't seen her recently. That's not to say I think you're hiding anything. I just mean that by addressing only the issue of when you bought or lent Katrine the sweatshirt, you left open the issue of whether you were seeing her again, which—combined with your combative attitude—is what makes you look so damned guilty."

"I take your point. But the way I see it, there was little I could say that *wouldn't* make me look guilty. Rob never actually accused me of seeing Katrine, after all; and even after Kevin asked him directly what he was suggesting about the sweatshirt, he refused to spell it out. So with that in mind, and knowing I hadn't seen Katrine since she went back to him, I figured he was either having another paranoid delusion or trying to discredit me. Either way, I was not about to dignify his insinuations with a response—much less one that might lead him or Kevin to conclude that 'the lady doth protest too much.'"

"What about after Rob left?"

"I probably could've handled that part better, I suppose. I was just so shocked by Kevin's sudden change in demeanor, I didn't know what to say. And then when he outright accused me of seeing Katrine behind his back, I realized it was too late."

"Too late?"

"Yes. The man will never trust me again, Sera, and there's nothing I can do about it. It's my own fault, I know. If I hadn't lied to him about Katrine in the first place, this wouldn't have happened; but I did, and now everything is different."

"It doesn't have to be."

"Sure it does. Kevin deserves someone he can trust, and I no longer fit the bill, so it's time for us both to move on."

"So that's it? You're going to split up over something that never even happened?"

"Looks that way."

"Can't you at least wait until Kevin gets back and see what he has to say once he's had a chance to think things over?"

"Why bother? I already know how this is going to go, so I may as well be prepared."

"OK, so plan for Kevin to move out if you decide to split up and for you and the kids to stay where you are."

"I would, but that would mean waiting for him to find his own place, and I really don't want to drag this out any longer than is necessary. Besides, the kids and I will have to move eventually anyway, since I won't be able to afford this place without my own income, and any job I get will likely mean moving to the suburbs. So, in order to avoid that and the accompanying cultural death, I'm gonna make like a shepherd and get the flock out of here."

"Well, I'm certainly not going to argue with you, but I think you're being a bit hasty. I mean, Kevin's a good guy, Jackie, and he deserves a chance to realize he jumped the gun on the sweatshirt issue and the opportunity to apologize. He shouldn't be punished eternally for one minor lapse in judgment."

"He's not the one who should apologize, Sera. I am. And I'm not punishing him for anything; I'm setting him free."

"Have it your way. Just tell me you'll think about what I've said."

"OK, I'll think about what you said. In the meantime, should I go for a Colonial or Victorian?"

"Woman, you are impossible!"

"No—I'm just determined."

"Po*tay*to, po*tah*to. And why Wabasha, for Pete's sake? It's so…*rural*."

"Because I can rent a house for about half the cost of this duplex, and because it's a quaint little river town with artisans and wildlife, which seems like a great place to raise kids."

"Well, gosh—then what on earth are you waiting for?"

"Nothing. In fact, I may call around tomorrow and set up appointments to view a few of these places in the paper. No need to waste time, you know?"

"Why not? That's all you're going to be doing when you get there—unless, of course, you know how to crochet."

"Very funny."

"I'm not trying to be funny, Jackie. I honestly want to know what you think you're going to do in Wabasha."

"Write."

"Write *what*? Order tickets at the local diner?"

"If that's what it takes to survive, sure. But I don't think it will come to that, because the cost of living is much lower—which means I'll have more breathing room when it comes to finances and, thus, more time to decide what to do if the writing thing doesn't pan out. That'll be the hard part, really," I admitted. "There are many things I could do if I don't become a writer. Unfortunately, I won't know which of them I'd like best until I've tried them, and by then I might lose my chance to try the rest. As Sylvia Plath put it as Esther Greenwood in *The Bell Jar*, I feel like I'm sitting in a tree full of ripening fruit wondering which to pluck knowing that the longer I wait to choose one, the fewer I'll have to choose from."

"Oh, my God. I cannot believe you're sitting there quoting Sylvia Plath."

"Actually, I'm *paraphrasing* her. And what's wrong with that?"

"Jackie, the woman gassed herself."

"I know that."

"Then you also know hers are not the sort of ideas you should be immersing yourself in at this point in time."

"Sera, hers are not the kind of ideas I would immerse myself in *ever*—I learned that much when I read the damned book back in 1983. Her fans would probably have me shot for saying so, but in my opinion, the woman probably would have lived if she hadn't taken herself so seriously."

"That's a relief. For a moment I thought I was going to have to start conducting hourly oven inspections."

"Not necessary—mine's electric."

I began packing the next day. I started with my textbooks, which I had stacked according to size and subject before placing them in the boxes I'd scavenged from the grocery store after dropping the kids off at day care that morning. I was just moving on to the paperbacks when I noticed a yellow convertible parked out front and Katrine starting up the walk.

For a second I sat stunned on the floor. I couldn't imagine what had possessed her to show up today. Even if she'd somehow gotten wind of Kevin's trip to Wisconsin, it took a certain kind of nerve—if not a total lack of sense—for her to pull this after he had told her, in no uncertain terms, to stay away.

"It's open," I shouted irritably, having been startled by the knock at the door. Although I had fully expected to hear it, the sound proved that my eyes had not deceived me, and it set my heart to beating with such force that I thought it just might explode.

Bracing myself for her entrance, I resumed packing and tried to appear aloof. It would not do for Katrine to know I was still carrying a torch for her, or for her to get the idea that she was at all welcome.

"What's wrong?" I asked without looking up when I heard her step through the doorway. "Or shall I say, what's wrong *now*?"

"Nothing."

"Then why are you here?"

Katrine shrugged. "I just stopped in to say hello," she replied, observing the stacks of books and boxes that occupied the room. "What are you doing?"

"What the hell does it look like I'm doing?"

"Packing."

"Funny—that's exactly what I *am* doing."

"But why?"

"Because I'm moving, Katrine. Now what do you want?"

"I don't want anything. I told you, I just stopped in to say hello."

"Don't you mean 'good-bye?'"

"I'm sure that's what you expected since we're supposed to leave for Arizona soon, but things just aren't working out like I'd hoped, so I'm filing for divorce and staying here instead."

I slapped a strip of tape across another box of books and set it beside the others. "Does Rob know that? Or is it going to be a surprise?"

"No, he doesn't know yet. But he will once I've spoken to a lawyer."

"And will that be before or after he leaves the state? It's a fair question," I observed when Katrine scowled. "After all, you wouldn't be the first woman to leave a guy without informing him of her plans, and you certainly wouldn't be the first to ditch Rob without telling him either."

Katrine crossed her arms. "Maybe not," she allowed. "But I wouldn't do that to Rob even if I thought I could get away with it."

"What does *that* mean?"

"Well, he'll have to know I'm staying behind before he leaves, right? I mean, it's not as if he won't notice I'm not in the car with him when he drives away."

I shook my head. I knew damn well that circumstances would not prevent Katrine from keeping her plan to leave Rob under wraps if that was what she really wanted to do. Of course, I saw no reason to point this out right now. If Katrine was actually going to leave Rob—and I was not at all convinced she would—she would have to do it on her own terms and in her own way, without my advice, consent, or support.

"So what plans have you made?" I inquired instead. "For when he's gone, I mean."

"Well, our lease doesn't expire until the end of August, so I'll stay in the house for now, and if I can't find something better by the first, I'll just renew the contract for another year. With my background in chemistry, I can probably get a job as a pharmacy tech, which should pay enough to cover my expenses, including a class or two at the university each semester."

I see.

"So what, if anything," I asked as I used a black marker to label the six cartons I'd packed so far, "does this have to do with me?"

"Nothing."

"Then why are you here?"

"I told you: I just wanted to say hello. I tried to call first to make sure it was OK, but your machine kept picking up, so I decided just to take my chances that you were here."

"Well, I am, as you can see. Unfortunately, I'm also busy. So if you don't mind, I'd like to get back to work."

"No problem. In fact, maybe I can help."

"I don't think so, Katrine."

"Why not?"

"Because you shouldn't even *be* here, that's why not. So if there really isn't anything you need, you should go."

"Actually, there is *one* thing."

Of course there is.

"What's that?"

"A gun."

"A gun? What the hell for?"

"Protection."

"From whom?"

"Rob. I'm afraid of what he'll do when he finds out I'm not going to Yuma," she explained. "You know irrational he can be."

I nodded. "Unfortunately," I said, recalling his behavior yesterday, "yes. I do."

"So could I borrow one of yours?"

"No way."

"I won't keep it loaded. I just want to have it in case he doesn't take this very well."

"I don't care if you planned to keep it loaded or not, Katrine. I am not giving you a gun."

"Why not?"

"Because despite Kevin's belief in achieving peace through superior firepower, I think it's dangerous to have one in the house—especially yours—and I won't be responsible for putting one there."

"Can I ask Kevin?"

"No."

"Why not?"

"Because he's not here."

"Well, where is he?"

I stared at Katrine. It never occurred to me that she wouldn't know Kevin was out of town. Rather, I had assumed his absence was the reason for her presence.

"Wisconsin," I replied finally, trying not to choke up as I recalled the circumstances of his departure, "at a pistol team tournament against UW–Madison."

"So when will he be back?"

"I'm not sure. And if it's all the same to you," I added, bowing my head to surreptitiously dab the corners of my eyes with my shirt, "I would prefer you didn't tell your nut job of a spouse he's away. I'd hate to have to explain to the authorities how I mistook him for an intruder in broad daylight—especially at such close range—if he suddenly decided to pay me a visit."

"Don't worry. I don't even plan to mention I was here."

"Great! Then I won't bother to send my disregards."

I arrived home from collecting the kids from day care that afternoon to find the front door unlocked. After weighing the odds that I had left it that way myself as a result of my mental fog against the possibility that someone else had been in the house while I was out—and after kicking myself for tempting fate and blowing good karma with my joke about intruders—I decided to take my chances and go inside.

"Daddy!" Tyler shouted as he pushed past me and ran to Kevin, who had risen from the recliner as Lucy and I stepped through the door.

"Hey, Jack," he said carefully after giving the boy a good squeeze. "How's it going?"

"What are you doing back?" I asked as I set Lucy on the floor and watched her follow Tyler into the playroom. "Did the other teams find out you were competing and decide not to show?"

"No," Kevin laughed. "I just realized in the van last night that you are more important to me than some shooting match. So when we got to the hotel, I told Staff Sergeant Kramer I had to go, and then hitched a ride to the bus terminal and caught a Greyhound back to Minneapolis."

I stared at Kevin.

I knew better than to think he'd ditched a tournament and gone to all that trouble to make up. That kind of thing only happened in perfume commercials and movies—and then only to women who looked like Michelle Pfeiffer or Cindy Crawford. No, either the man had come back to give me the boot, or he'd gone completely out of his mind.

"Well, welcome home," I said for lack of a better response. "I wish I'd known you were on your way back. I would have made sure we were here when you arrived."

"It's no problem. I did try to let you know I was coming back early, but I guess you were screening calls again, because I kept getting the machine on the first ring."

"Yeah," I said with a shrug. "I wasn't in much of a mood to talk."

Kevin nodded. "So what's all this?" he asked, indicating the boxes in the corner.

"I was just getting a few things out of the way. You know—stuff we don't really need on a daily basis anymore."

"Then you weren't planning on taking off before I got back?"

"Of course not. I was, however, preparing to take off *when* you got back."

"Why?"

"Because I figured that's what you would want."

"Jackie, I was upset. That doesn't mean I wanted to leave you—or for you to leave me."

"OK."

"You don't believe me."

"Actually, I do."

"You don't sound like you do."

"That's probably because my nonverbals are contradicting my verbals."

"Your *what* are contradicting your *who*?"

"My *nonverbals* are contradicting my *verbals*," I repeated with a laugh. "That's how you know when someone's uncomfortable," I explained, "when their nonverbal behavior fails to correspond with their verbal communication. It's usually because they're lying, but in my case it's because I'm trying to look calm when, in fact, I'm a wreck.

"So, would you like some iced tea?" I offered suddenly, marching past Kevin in a beeline for the kitchen after realizing I was still standing by the front door. "I don't know about you, but I am just dying for something cool and refreshing."

Kevin nodded again as I buzzed by him. "Sure," he said, turning on his heel to follow me. "A dose of your home-brewed iced tea would be great."

I looked at the clock on the stove as I filled two tall glasses. It was apparent I would not make my appointment to see the Colonial in Wabasha tonight without explaining it to Kevin within the next few minutes. Thus, I decided to sneak off and reschedule for later in the week, by which time I would know whether I really needed to exercise that option.

"So what happens now?" I asked after placing the sugar canister and a glass of tea at one end of the table and taking a seat at the other.

"That depends. What do you *want* to happen now?"

"I don't know, Kev. What do *you* want to happen now?"

"I want to be with you."

"Even after everything I said yesterday?"

"Even after everything you said yesterday."

I shook my head. "I think you need counseling."

"You think *I* need counseling?"

"Well, we *know* I do. So if you want to stay with me, you *must*."

"Perhaps. But I can't help it, Jack. I love you."

"I know you love me, Kevin. The question is, do you trust me?"

"Of course I do."

"Then why did you accuse me of seeing Katrine?"

"Because I was afraid, and I lost my head."

"Afraid of what?"

"That you'd get hurt again. You were such a mess after you ended it with her last time, and given what she's capable of, I figured the next time might be even worse."

That was fair. But things couldn't possibly be any worse as far as I was concerned. Even as angry as I still was at Katrine for what she had done to Erin last spring and as disappointed as I had been to realize she had learned nothing from the events of the past six months, I missed her as much now as I ever had. It made no sense, of course, but even knowing she was still incapable of thinking of anyone besides herself hadn't made it any easier for me to keep my distance this morning. In fact, it had taken every drop of energy I had to resist the urge to tell Katrine why I was packing and invite her to spend the night.

Had I given in to that urge, of course, things would be a lot more complicated than they were at present. For instead of making up with Kevin, I would likely be watching him pack his things.

"I understand how you feel," I heard myself say with surprising conviction, "but you don't have to worry about that. I'm not seeing Katrine, nor do I have any plans to in the future."

"I know that. I realized last night that it only looked that way because I'd put you on the defensive. I shouldn't have done that to you, Jack, and I'm very, very sorry."

"It's OK. I didn't really handle things much better myself."

Kevin smiled. "So do you really think I'm looking to escape?" he asked. "Or have I managed to convince you that I'm in this for the long haul? You don't have to answer that," he added, reaching across the table to take my hand as my face, neck, and shoulders turned a deep red, "unless, of course, you expect your verbals to contradict your nonverbals."

Thirty-five

"So who was on the phone?" I asked as Kevin joined me on the back porch one steamy Monday evening in mid-July.

"Rob."

"Rob?"

Kevin nodded. "He received his fitness report from Colonel Keane this afternoon," he explained amid the chorus of car horns and kids' laughter coming from the ice cream stand a few blocks away, "and he doesn't want to sign it."

"Why?"

"Because it stinks."

"Well, what did he expect after what happened this spring?"

"I don't know what he expected exactly, but Rob feels he's entitled to marks in keeping with his service record, which was officially spotless when the major accepted his DOR."

"So he thinks he should walk away from here unscathed?"

"Well, I wouldn't say he's entirely unscathed, Jack. He did have to give up MECEP."

"OK—so he won't get to be an officer. Boo-hoo. That doesn't mean he should be allowed to slither off to another unit and pretend nothing ever happened. The leadership at his new command should know what kind of a marine he is, and without a fitness report that accurately describes his skill and character, they won't have a clue."

"I understand what you're saying, Jack, but when the major agreed not to press charges against him last spring, he lost any grounds he had to give him adverse marks. Rob knows that, which is why he doesn't want to sign it."

"So now he has them by the balls, instead of the other way around?"

"Not quite. They can always submit the report without a signature."

"Really?"

"Sure. Although with no evidence on record that he's ever received any formal counseling or nonjudicial punishment and with no charge sheets on file, it may not hold up on review."

I shook my head. "It should have never come to this," I said. "They should have never let him off with a DOR in the first place. In fact, they should have prosecuted him—even before the matter of Erin came to light—for the insubordination and unauthorized absences. That way he would have been out of both MECEP and the Corps before he had a chance to ruin her life, and this damn fitness report would not be an issue."

"Perhaps. Unfortunately, the unit couldn't afford the publicity that may have brought. We were already under so much scrutiny due to the Gay and Lesbian Alliance's weekly protests of DOD policy prohibiting homosexuals from serving in the military. And with the university's board of regents threatening to strip our funding and boot us off campus for violating their charter's nondiscrimination policy, the last thing we needed was for a scandal like this to hit the press and provide more grist for the mill."

"So instead they let the problem fester until they had enough to bury him with, and then they offered to make it go away if he would?"

"Pretty much."

"So what did you tell him?"

"I told him it doesn't matter; signed or unsigned, it'll go on his record. I also told him it made sense to sign it; if he truly felt that report was inaccurate or unjustified, he could always file a rebuttal or move to have it blackened out when he gets to his new command."

"Is that true?"

"Yes."

"I don't understand, Kevin. Why would you help him like that? After everything you've said about not wanting him in the same sacred corps as yourself, why on earth would you go and tell him how to save his ass instead of just letting him twist in the wind?"

"Because he was talking about hiring a lawyer, Jack, and I didn't want it to come to that. Don't get me wrong," Kevin cautioned. "I want him out of the corps as much as ever, but letting this thing become a federal case isn't going to do anyone any good. Besides, I happen to know that anyone he might approach about blacking out that report will be smart enough to contact the marines and other personnel who served in his unit during the period covered to investigate his claims."

"Meaning you."

"Exactly. Of course, by then all the higher-ups will have retired and settled into civilian life, while the junior personnel—those who make it through the gauntlet and actually wind up staying in the service, that is—will be few and, probably, too far flung to find. I, on the other hand, will be right out in the open where they can find me, and that's when everything I know about Rob will be best put to use."

"Wow, Kevin. I had no idea you could be such a scheming son of a bitch."

"Me either."

"So why did he call you of all people?"

Kevin shrugged. "Apparently he still considers me his faithful brother-in-arms, despite my affiliation with the Great White Bitch of the North."

The following week, Kevin received word that Rob had signed and returned his fitness report as advised. With that matter resolved, he and Katrine would soon be heading off to Arizona, where Rob would either confirm or dispel the impressions that members of his new command had formed of him after reviewing his record and by virtue of the verbal and written information they no doubt had exchanged with Major Weeks and the colonel.

I realized, as Kevin relayed this to me, that in the wake of his early return from the pistol team meet last month, I had not told him of Katrine's visit or her plan to leave Rob, and with the girl apparently having taken my advice not to ask him to lend her a weapon, neither had I thought to mention it since. Given how much time had elapsed since Katrine's visit, however, and knowing that he would be no less shocked to hear that Katrine had left Rob despite her advance notice, I thought it best to simply let the matter drop.

As the summer waned, however, I became increasingly curious as to whether Katrine would have the ovaries to follow through with her plan.

Although I told myself repeatedly that it was none of my business, with the new school year approaching and Rob finally detached from the reserve unit, it was all I could do not to pick up the phone and satisfy my curiosity once and for all.

The only solution, I decided upon catching myself dialing for the fifth time, was to pick up the kids early and let them provide the distraction I needed to stop obsessing. It sounded like a perfect plan, and as I loaded the kids' sand pails, swimsuits, and towels into the trunk of the Ford—which Kevin had left instead of the Camry today, owing to the fact that he'd agreed to drive a couple incoming midshipmen to Fort Snelling for haircuts later—I had high hopes it would work. Those hopes were dashed, however, when I found myself taking the scenic route to Miss Betty's and realized I'd been duped.

"This is ridiculous," I thought as I parked in front of the Laundromat on the south end of Katrine's block. "Even if she isn't here, it won't necessarily prove she's gone with Rob."

Yeah, but if she is *here* I argued back as I got out of the car and stepped onto the walk, *it will mean she's left him, and I won't have to worry about her anymore.*

I was just taking the argument around the corner and up Katrine's street when the sight of a yellow convertible stopped me short. Having assumed that Rob would've taken the new car with him since Katrine would not be able to afford the payments alone, I didn't know what to make of this development. I did not have long to ruminate over it, however, as a moment later I spotted Rob tromping down the front steps toward the driver's side door.

Relieved I hadn't ventured any closer, I snapped about-face and strolled back around the corner and into the Laundromat, where I plopped down onto a molded fiberglass chair that faced inside, flipped open a ragged copy of *True Story*, and hoped the windows behind me were too high off the ground for Rob to recognize my head should he be driving that way.

After a few minutes, I decided I was behaving even more ridiculously than when I'd talked myself into this excursion. Rob's car wasn't even facing my direction, I reasoned, which meant he might not even come this way. In fact, for all I knew, he wasn't even planning to drive the car but had simply come out to retrieve something from it. With this in mind, I dropped the magazine back on the stack and walked out of the Laundromat toward the Ford, where I found the object of my disaffection leaning against the hood.

"Well, hello, there, Mrs. Thompson," he said as I approached. "Long time, no see."

"Not long enough, as far as I'm concerned."

"As I figured."

I sighed as Rob pretended to admire his perch. I should have known better than to think the old beast would go unrecognized, and I kicked myself now for not thinking of that when the warring factions in my head had hatched this plan almost an hour ago.

"Doing some laundry, are you?" he asked finally. "Or was this a head call?"

"Actually, a little of both. You see, I was on my way to the grocery store, having run out of detergent in the middle of doing a few loads this afternoon, when I realized the only money I had with me was a handful of change. Not wanting to write a check for just the detergent, I decided I'd just pop in here and grab a couple boxes from the vending machine instead."

"Whereupon you were suddenly overcome by an urge to use the restroom."

"Exactly."

"Well, that explains what took you so long."

So long? I thought, wondering exactly how long he'd been waiting, and if maybe it wasn't the car that had attracted his attention, but the sight of me retreating down the block.

"Yeah, I guess so," I said finally. "Although I wouldn't have dawdled if I had known I had company."

Rob nodded irritably. "So where is it?"

"In the back, off to the right. Make sure you turn the door hanger to 'occupied' though," I advised facetiously, "because that lock has seen better days."

"Not the bathroom," Rob snapped. "I meant the detergent."

Oh, that. "The machine is busted," I replied, conveniently recalling the *out of order* sign I'd seen taped to the front of it. "Guess I'll have to write that check after all."

"Guess so."

I stared at Rob. I wasn't about to get any closer to the car with him still leaning on it, but neither did I want to stand in the street all day in a contest of wills.

"Well, go ahead," he instructed suddenly, nodding to the driver's side door to his left. "Go get your detergent."

"I'm afraid I can't do that with you on the hood," I pointed out. "Well, maybe I could—but it would be fun for you only up to the point where I slammed on my brakes."

"Oh, I don't know. I think I might enjoy visiting you in Stillwater after they put you away for attempted manslaughter."

"Trust me—if they ever lock me up, the charge will not include the word *attempted*. Now if you don't mind, I need to go get the kids."

Rob nodded. "Now see, *that* I believe," he said. "That crap about needing detergent, not so much; but when you say you have to pick up your kids, that I can believe."

"Great. Then get your ass off my car."

"Sure," he replied, hopping up onto the hood. "Just as soon as you tell me what you're really doing here."

"Excuse me?"

"Oh, come on, Jackie. We both know you didn't come here to buy detergent or use the head. So why don't you just give it up and admit that you were on your way to see Katrine?"

"Fine. I'll admit I was on my way to your house," I confessed, figuring it would be more expeditious to humor Rob than to fight him, "but it was to see you, not Katrine."

"Is that so?"

I nodded. "I've wanted to come by for a while now but couldn't work up the courage. I only convinced myself to come today because I knew it might be my last chance."

"If that's true, then why did you park down here?"

"So I could escape without being seen if I lost my nerve—which is exactly what I did when I saw you come out of the house a few minutes ago, and which is how I wound up hiding in the Laundromat."

Rob crossed his arms. "And what did you want to talk to me about? Or was your plan just to stand by and gloat?"

"Of course not. Believe it or not, I do not take pleasure in other peoples' pain, and I am not at all happy with how things have turned out."

"No, I suppose you wouldn't be, since you still lost the girl."

I shook my head. It was just like Rob to think I'd regret only that aspect of the situation that affected me. Having no capacity for empathy himself, he could not imagine me feeling bad for any of the other people he'd hurt or taken down with him or wishing he had simply behaved differently in the first place.

"That's really all I really wanted to say," I said, knowing that anything else would just fall on deaf ears. "So can I go now?"

"Not yet. There are a few things I'd like to discuss as long as you're standing here."

"Like what?"

"Well, for starters, I'd like to know how you plan to live with yourself knowing you've ruined my career."

"After *I've* ruined your career? How the hell did I do that?"

"Oh, come on, Jackie. Do you really think I don't know who convinced Erin to confess?"

"Erin didn't confess, you moron. In fact, she didn't say anything even after they yanked her scholarship application—after somebody else reported seeing you acting like a homicidal maniac at her dorm."

"Bullshit. That's just the story they cooked up to cover her ass. I know she turned me in, I know it was you that convinced her to do it, and I know you did it to punish me for convincing Katrine to come home."

"I hate to break this to you, pal, but I broke up with Katrine long before she ever left you."

"Is that so?"

"Yes! And even if I hadn't, she didn't come back to you until *after* you were busted, which means I had no reason to encourage Erin to turn you in."

"According to you!"

"What do you mean, *according to me*? I was there when you picked her up."

"Maybe—but you were not there when she told me she was coming home."

"Which was when?"

"The day before. She told me outside your house that night that she was giving me another chance. She only stayed over to say good-bye and because I had to work anyway."

"Is that what she told you? Or is that what you wanted to hear? Because as I recall it, Katrine was ready to turn you in herself that night after you pulled that stunt at Erin's dorm. So there is no way she would have agreed to come back to you then—not for love or money."

"Say whatever you want, Jackie. The bottom line here is that you're the reason I had to choose between a DOR and a court-martial, and I will never forgive you for that."

I shook my head. "Are you seriously going to stand here with a straight face and suggest that this is my fault? Even if Erin had confessed and I had been the one to talk her into it, it was still you who violated not one, but four different codes of military conduct."

"Maybe—but that was none of your concern. I told Kevin I would leave Erin alone, and I meant it. So you didn't have to go behind his back and have her turn me in. You could have just left well enough alone."

"So you actually think I could talk that girl into ruining her own career?"

"Yes—I do."

"Man, you are some piece of work," I said, shaking my head again. "You think because you need to control everyone in your life that I do, too. Well, I have news for you pal—I don't. Nor would I have deliberately tried to ruin your life."

"Of course not. You're far too honorable and decent for that."

"That's right. So blame me if you want, Rob, but let me assure you: if I'd had anything to do with your DOR, I'd be only too happy to take credit for it."

I could see that made sense to him and that he didn't like it.

"Whatever," he said then, instead of arguing. "Just let me make one thing clear: you are not to contact Katrine again—not here, not in Arizona, not ever."

So she hadn't told him. Interesting. "And just what makes you so sure she's even going with you to Arizona?" I asked. "Last I heard, she was planning to stay right here."

"Only until I find us a place to live. She'll be joining me just as soon as I've made the arrangements."

"Is that what she told you? Boy, that girl can come up with some whoppers, can't she?"

"What are you talking about?"

"I think I'll defer that to your wife. She should be the one to tell you the rest. But just in case she's a tad elusive when you ask why there's no 'Arizona or Bust' sign on her car window yet, you might want to ask about the attorney she hired to help her navigate the interstate divorce laws— that should jog her memory."

"What?"

414

"Yeah—and while you're at it, you might want to ask her about that telephone call you and I discussed a moment ago. Oh, I know you think that's something the unit dreamed up after I convinced Erin to rat you out, but I promise you, it wasn't. So be sure to ask Katrine about that, too, since she had all the information that the caller did and was alone at my place when the call was made. My guess is she wanted to make sure you two had to leave the area, because she didn't think the tapes would be enough to keep you from seeing Erin—but I'm sure she'll deny it."

I watched Rob slide off the hood as my words sunk in. I couldn't believe I'd said all those things to him, and for a moment I almost regretted it since I wasn't even sure they were true. But then I thought about everything Rob had said and everything Katrine had said and decided it no longer mattered.

I backed the Ford away from the curb before taking off so as to steer well clear of Rob, who was now bent over the convertible vomiting on the tire. *Serves you right,* I said into the rearview mirror as I drove away. *You've been making me sick for almost a year now; it's about time I returned the favor.*

I wondered all the way to Miss Betty's, to the park, and basically the whole afternoon, if, when, and how I would tell Kevin about my encounter with Rob at the Laundromat. On the one hand, I was anxious to tell him Rob was still in the area and even more so to share his theory about how I had conspired to ruin his career. He would get a charge out of the fact that Rob believed me to be the force behind his DOR when in truth Katrine had orchestrated the whole thing.

On the other hand, I reasoned, it might be better to keep my clandestine excursion to myself. For although Kevin would find the story enlightening and humorous, he would eventually inquire as to how I had arrived at the Laundromat in the first place, which would compel me to tell him about Katrine's last visit—and, more importantly, why I hadn't bothered to mention it earlier—or find another way to account for my presence there today.

Still, I wasn't wild about the idea of keeping yet another secret from Kevin. Even if I hadn't deliberately concealed Katrine's decision to divorce Rob or the manner in which I'd learned of it—and even though I wasn't covering up any wrongdoing on my part—I was extremely uncomfortable at the thought of withholding yet another piece of information from him, especially in light of our recent difficulties concerning Katrine.

I continued to contend with these issues as I fed the children an early dinner of chicken nuggets and peas while prepping the steaks and veggie kebabs I planned to grill for me and Kevin in observance of his birthday. Thus, I felt more than a modicum of relief when he called to say he would be late getting home from his weekly visit to the armory this evening.

"What did you forget about *this* time?" I asked cheerfully as I impaled a mushroom and shoved it behind the onion, pineapple, and green pepper already on the skewer.

"Nothing. It's just that the colonel suddenly decided we were all due for some forced fun," Kevin explained, "and arranged for us to take on the army folks in a game of basketball tonight. I hope you weren't planning anything special for dinner," he added, "because the game doesn't start for another hour, and the major's buying us pizza afterward."

I looked at the tray of beef and skewers I'd just finished putting together. "Well, I was," I admitted with genuine understanding, "but it's nothing that can't wait; so I'll just make myself a salad for now and put this back in the fridge for tomorrow night."

"Sounds good. Thanks, Jack."

I took the kids out for a long walk after dinner in hopes that they would be worn out and sleeping soundly by the time Kevin got home, and I could tell him about the day. Although I still didn't know how I would approach the matter of my conversation with Rob, I felt he had to know. For while odds were slim that he would hear about it from Rob or someone else later on, I preferred to face the music now rather than have it unexpectedly kick me in the ass at some point in the future.

All was going according to plan, as far as I could tell, when the phone rang at eight forty-five. Having put the kids down barely fifteen minutes before and being up to my elbows in fresh dishwater, I was more than a little annoyed at the interruption. Knowing Kevin wouldn't risk waking the kids to tell me he was on his way home, I shook the suds off my hands, wiped them on the nearest towel, stormed over to the receiver, and picked it up.

"Hello?" I asked without masking my irritation.

"Jackie?"

"Yes, Katrine?"

"Oh thank God."

"Thank God what?"

"You've got to come over here right away."

"What for?"

"It's Rob—I think he's dead."

"What do you mean you think he's dead?"

"I mean I think he's *dead*!" Katrine repeated as she began to cry. "There's blood all over the place, and I don't think he's breathing!"

"Have you checked his pulse?"

"No!"

"Well, do it."

"I can't!"

"You have to!"

"Why?"

"Because you might be able to save him! Now do it—if only so you can say you did!"

My heart began to race as I heard Katrine drop the phone and, a moment later, start screaming. "Oh God! Oh God! Oh God!"

"Katrine," I shouted when the girl returned to the line. "You need to get ahold of yourself right now!"

"But what if they think I did it?"

"Did what?"

"Shot him."

"Well, did you?"

"No!"

"Do you know who did?"

"I think *he* did. He was the only one here before I heard the gun go off, and he was alone when I found him afterward."

"Found him where?"

"In the living room," Katrine sobbed. "I'd gone down to the basement to watch TV, because he kept playing the same damned CD over and over, and I just couldn't take it anymore. I mean, he *knows* I hate the Velvet Underground!"

I sighed hard. "Katrine, will you *please* try to focus?

"OK. I'm sorry."

"It's all right. Now, how long has it been since you called the police?"

"The police?"

"You mean you haven't called them?"

"Oh God."

"Katrine, I have to go."

"What? No!"

"Katrine, listen to me! Someone has to call the police. Now I want you to stay right where you are and wait for them. I'll be there as soon as I can."

"Please come now."

"I can't do that, Katrine. Kevin's not here, and I can't leave the kids alone, so I'll have to make arrangements for them first, but I will be there as soon as possible."

I clicked over to the other line in case Katrine didn't hang up right away and started to dial just as Kevin walked in the door. Sighing with relief, I hurriedly waved him inside as the emergency operator picked up.

"I need to report a shooting," I continued as Kevin looked on, "on twenty-second avenue and—shit! Kevin—what's their address?"

"Whose address?"

"Rob and Katrine's!"

"Jackie, what is going on?"

"Rob just shot himself," I explained quickly, "and Katrine panicked and called me instead of nine-one-one, so I've got to get an ambulance over there in case she's wrong and he's not dead!"

Without a word, Kevin took the phone from my hand and gave them the address.

"This is Kevin Thompson," he reported. "No, we're not calling from the scene. The victim's wife called here in a panic, so we're calling for her. Yes. The victim is a white male, about twenty-six years old. I do not know his condition. Please, just send someone right away. If they need more information, I'll provide it when I get there. Yes. Please. Thank you."

Kevin turned to me as he replaced the phone on the cradle. "What the hell happened?" he asked as I grabbed my purse and keys.

"I have no idea. I had just put the kids to bed and started dishes, when all of a sudden Katrine's on the phone screaming that Rob is dead."

"But Rob was supposed to be on his way to Arizona by now."

"That's what I thought, but apparently there was a schedule change. Now I've got to get over to Katrine's before she loses it completely. Can you get someone to come stay with the kids? Maybe call Maggie or something?"

"Yes. Go. I'll meet you there in a little while. Don't expect me right away, though," Kevin warned. "I still need to notify the MPs at Fort Snelling, and I should probably try to track down someone from the unit."

Thirty-six

I found Katrine sitting on the front porch steps leaning over her lap with vomit splashed over her shoes. Neighbors were peeking through curtains, I noted, and stepping out onto their own porches as the sounds of emergency sirens drew closer.

"Where are you going?" Katrine asked as I stepped over her and opened the door.

"I'm just going to see if there's *anything* I can do. I'll be right back."

"Oh my God!" I gasped as I returned to the porch just seconds later. "What the hell did he use? It looks like a bomb went off in there."

Katrine shook her head. "It was a forty-four, although I don't know how he knew where to find it."

"Whose is it?"

"Mine."

"*Yours?*"

"Well, sort of. Scott actually bought it, so I guess technically it's his."

"Rob's best friend bought you a gun?" I asked, having all but forgotten about the sponge over the course of the summer. "How the hell did you get him to do that?"

"Does it really matter now?"

"Not to me. But the police are probably going to ask, so why don't you tell me so I won't look so surprised when they do? Too late," I added as two city squad cars come flying down the street followed by an ambulance. "Come on—let's get out of their way."

Kevin made it over to Katrine's about twenty minutes after the police arrived, and he found me and Katrine resting against the right rear quarter panel of the Ford. With all the emergency vehicles and rubberneckers crowding the street, he'd had to park down by the Laundromat, and I could not help but shake my head at the irony as I spotted him coming up the sidewalk.

An official in street clothes approached us just as he did.

"Sergeant Thompson?" he asked, having apparently scanned him for signs of military life.

"Yes?"

"I'm Detective Carnes. The MPs said to expect you. How are you?"

"I've been better."

"I can imagine."

"So is he…?"

"Oh, yeah. A guy can't use his brains to redecorate the walls like that and live to tell the tale."

I put my arm around Katrine's shoulder as what was left of the color drained from her face. "Do you mind?" I demanded. "This is his wife!"

"Sorry, ma'am. I didn't know."

"It's OK," Kevin said to my chagrin. "We understand. I'm told it was suicide. Is that true?"

Carnes nodded. "He left a note," he said, "although seems more like a poem to me. Said something about being 'set free' and 'yesterday's clouds.'"

"That's not poetry," I announced, recognizing the line. "They're lyrics—from Lou Reed's second album with the Velvet Underground."

"Interesting," the detective observed indifferently. "I'll be sure to mention that in my report. In the meantime," he advised, tapping his notebook with his pen, "we'll need to collect your statements, so stick around."

Having given my statement to a kinder, gentler detective, Katrine and I gathered—under the supervision of another officer—some clothing and a few other items from the bathroom and bedroom, and we headed back to my place, leaving Kevin to deal with the local and military police.

As Kevin had failed to mention, it was not Maggie whom we encountered when we got there. She had been out on another job already when Kevin called at nine and would not be available for at least another two hours. Apparently, however, after Kevin explained why he needed her so late, her mother had leapt to his aid and offered to come watch the kids herself.

Fortunately, as I observed when she had gone, Mrs. Fisher had not made this gesture out of morbid curiosity, and rather than ask a slew of questions when Katrine and I arrived, she offered her condolences and showed herself out.

"I couldn't help but overhear," I observed when Katrine and I were alone again, "when you gave your statement, that you told the detective you and Rob were separating."

Katrine nodded. "Like I told you a few weeks ago," she said as we gravitated toward the kitchen, "I hired a lawyer and was planning to divorce Rob rather than go with him to Arizona."

"Did he know that?"

"What do you mean?"

"Did Rob know you were divorcing him?"

"Well, he shot himself, so he must have. Right?"

"I had assumed so, but had you told him?"

"Not yet. I decided to wait until he got to Arizona to tell him," Katrine admitted, "so I wouldn't have to deal with his reaction."

"So how do you think he found out?"

"I'm not sure. All I know is that the gun was in my drawer, and he never would've found it if he hadn't gone through my things—which he would not have done without provocation."

"So you think he found out you were leaving, and then went through your things, found the gun, and decided to shoot himself?"

"Yes."

"Without even confirming it? Or confronting you?"

Katrine shrugged. "I guess."

"That doesn't make any sense."

"Well, it's the only explanation I can come up with."

Some explanation. I wouldn't go so far as to say she was lying then, but things definitely did not add up. I couldn't imagine Rob not confronting her with the things I'd said before deciding to kill himself. Yet Katrine denied—as she had to the detective—having even spoken to Rob about her plans prior to his suicide. Although she had led the officer to believe their impending separation was consensual, it did not follow that she would lie about what had transpired that evening. In fact, Katrine was far more likely to invent an argument than to conceal one, since that would have lent weight to the theory that Rob had killed himself and thrown suspicion off of her. No, the girl was obviously missing—or hiding—something; I just couldn't figure out what.

"You say he went through your drawers?" I asked finally as Katrine shifted her weight from one foot to the other.

"He must have, because he used Scott's gun."

"Which you say he wouldn't have known about until he found it there."

"Right."

"And were there, perhaps, other things in your room that might have given you away?"

"Just some forms that my lawyer needed me to complete in order to calculate my settlement demand."

"Well, that probably would have done it, don't you think?" *That combined with my damned mouth that sent him to snooping in the first place.*

"But the papers were underneath my jeans," Katrine argued. "The gun was on top."

"In the same *drawer*?"

"Well, yeah."

So you stored both his motive and his method together for him, huh? Nice going, Katrine. You may as well have provided instructions and drafted his damn note.

"Scott's not going to get in trouble, is he?" she asked. "Since it was his gun, I mean?"

"I don't think so. It's fairly obvious that Rob committed suicide, so they won't have that much interest in the gun as long as it was registered."

Katrine sighed. "I hope you're right," she said. "I tried to call him tonight—while I was waiting for you, I mean—to tell him what had happened, but he wasn't home at the time."

"Wasn't *home*?"

"He got his own apartment shortly after Rob dropped out of MECEP. He thought it was best under the circumstances to give us back our space. He knew by then, too, of course, that Rob wasn't all that stable, which is why he agreed to buy the gun when I asked him about it."

"Hang on: the two of you knew Rob wasn't 'all that stable,' yet you brought a forty-four into the house anyway? Don't you think that's just a little bit—I don't know—cavalier?"

"Well, it never occurred to me that Rob would find it. After all, he wouldn't have even known I *had* it if he hadn't gone rummaging through my things."

Which he wouldn't have done if I had kept my trap shut.

"I realize that," I admitted. "I guess I just would have expected you to be more cautious about how and where you stored the thing—in light of his condition, that is."

"But Rob shouldn't have even been here today. He was supposed to leave two days ago, but he kept changing his plans because he didn't want to leave without me."

"I don't get it, Katrine. Why would you need a gun if you weren't going to tell Rob you were divorcing him before he left?"

"That's just it. I had every intention of telling him when I asked Scott to buy the gun. It's just that by the time I realized I *couldn't*, it was already in my drawer."

"I see."

"So you really don't think Scott will get in trouble over it? The gun, I mean?"

I shook my head. "But if it will make you feel better," I offered as I started toward the stairs to check on the kids, "give him a call. It'll be all over the television by morning—and if I know the news media, even if they leave out his name until his parents can be notified, they'll make sure to mention that he was a marine, and that will give it away."

"Thanks for the warning."

After checking on the kids, I came back downstairs and crept quietly through the kitchen toward the bathroom so as not to disturb Katrine, who was still on the phone with Scott. Upon returning to the kitchen, however, it seemed from her tone that the conversation was nearing its end, so I lingered at the entrance, hoping Scott wasn't taking it too hard that Rob had ended his life with the weapon he had bought.

Although I did my best to ignore the conversation in the kitchen, I was suddenly all ears when I heard Katrine say, "I love you, too."

For a moment I stood there, stunned by the thought that there was something going on between Scott and Katrine. After all, the guy was a greasy-haired slacker with terrible body odor and breath to match—last I knew, anyway—and he was Rob's best friend. Then again, he may have learned a thing or two about hygiene since March, I reasoned, and loyalty can be a fleeting thing when it comes to your best friend's girl.

Don't be ridiculous. Why can't a woman show her husband's friend some affection without it being interpreted as evidence of impropriety?

Because that's generally what it is.

"Excuse me?" Katrine asked, having spotted me in the hall. "What did you say?"

"Nothing. Just talking to myself."

"About what?"

"I'm not sure now, owing to the fact that you startled me."

"Well, perhaps you wouldn't startle so easily if you weren't eavesdropping so intently."

"Eavesdropping? Why on earth would I be doing that?"

"You tell me."

I stared at Katrine. *This really takes the cake*, I thought. *I'm standing here trying to respect her privacy, and this chick accuses me of invading it. It's almost too much.*

"Look, Katrine. I wasn't eavesdropping. I just didn't want to hover in the kitchen while you were talking to Scott, so I was staying out of your way."

Katrine nodded. "Were you, now?"

"Are you saying you don't believe me?"

"I guess I am."

It occurred to me as I watched Katrine cross her arms that the girl was overreacting in a big way. She obviously had something to hide, I decided, and the best way to get her to give it up would be to let her think I'd got her dead to rights.

"Fine," I said as if admitting to the charge. "So maybe I did hear a few things."

"As if there was any doubt."

I shrugged. "So how long has this been going on?"

"Since June."

"So, about the time you decided you needed a gun?"

"I guess."

"And would that be before or after you decided to leave Rob?"

"What difference does that make?"

"None to you, I suppose."

Katrine crossed her arms. "I don't know what that's supposed to mean, but whether I started seeing Scott before or after I decided to leave Rob is none of your business."

"You're absolutely right. You're a grown woman, and you're entitled to make your own mistakes."

"What makes you so sure it's a mistake?"

"Please, Katrine—that's the only kind of decision you know how to make."

"How dare you!"

"How dare I what? Talk to you that way? I'll talk to you any way I please in my own house, thank you. Especially now that I know what a lying sack you are."

"*What?*"

"Well, it's true, isn't it? Did you not stand here barely a month ago and tell me that things between you weren't working out the way you'd hoped and that you were going get a job, your own place, and be independent? And did you not just admit that you aren't doing *any* of it on your own? That you are in fact *doing it* with the best friend of your suddenly and conveniently deceased husband? Because in my book, that makes you a lying sack of whore trash."

Katrine glared at me. "Rob was right. You *are* a judgmental bitch."

"*Judgmental?* Katrine, you *hurt* people. You have *damaged* them with your lies. If pointing that out makes me judgmental—that's fine. But I'd rather be a judgmental bitch than a walking disease—which is exactly what you are for anyone who comes near you."

"Is that so? Well, what about you, Jackie? Shall we take a look at your crimes? Because as I recall, you've lied to Rob, too—and to Kevin as well—both before and since we broke up. And don't think I don't know what made Rob go digging through my dresser. I know damn well you had something to do with that, because you were the only one who knew of my plans besides Scott, and Rob would not have thought to go through my things on his own. So don't go shoving your self-righteous bullshit down my throat, because if Rob hadn't found those papers and the gun, the crazy fuck would still be alive today, which makes you just as liable for this as I am."

I shook my head. I could not dispute most of Katrine's diatribe, for it was true right down to the ground; but I could not believe the utter lack of remorse in the girl's tone.

"Jesus, Katrine! Have you no conscience? Have you no shame?"

"What for? I didn't pull the trigger—Rob did. And given how most people felt about him, he did us all a huge favor."

"You are unbelievable."

"No, I'm exactly what you wanted me to be," Katrine insisted, approaching her bag on the kitchen table as if she were preparing to leave.

"You always said I should do what makes *me* happy, that I should do what *I* want. Well, that's exactly what I've been doing, and, to be frank, I suspect the only reason you're so upset is that I don't want *you*."

I pointed to the door. "Go fuck yourself, Katrine," I fumed. "And make sure you use a condom—you wouldn't want to catch anything."

Kevin returned home just before midnight. Finding the house completely dark, he switched on the living room light, causing me to shield my eyes with the pillow I'd been holding in my lap.

"Hey, honey," he said, taking a seat beside me. "Are you all right?"

"I guess."

"Where's Katrine?"

"I don't know. And to be honest, I don't care.'

"Why? What's happened?"

"It shouldn't have come to this," I said, squeezing the pillow to keep from crying. "I know I joked about it all the time, but I never meant for Rob to die."

"I know that."

"I just wanted him to go away."

"Look, we all know how unstable he was, Jackie. This was not your fault."

"Yes, it is, Kevin; at least in part."

"Why do you say that?"

"Because I'm the one who told him about the gun, and I'm the reason he found it," I admitted, wiping my face with the back of my hand as I felt a tear escape down my cheek. "Scott bought it for Katrine this summer. She told him she needed it in case Rob went off the deep end, only he had no reason to go off the deep end because Katrine hadn't told him yet."

"Told him *what* yet?"

"That she was going to leave him."

"How do you know that?"

"Because she came over here and told me so while you were in Wisconsin for that pistol team tournament last month. She said she wouldn't be going to Arizona with Rob, that she planned to stay in the Cities, get a job, and go to school. She told me then, too, that she wanted a gun in case Rob didn't take it very well. I told her I wouldn't give her one and that it would be a bad idea to ask you as well, but apparently Scott was a little more accommodating."

"So you think Rob shot himself because Katrine was leaving him?"

"I know he did."

"How?"

"Because he just found out today."

"How do you know that?"

"Because I'm the one who told him."

"What? When?"

"This afternoon—when Rob confronted me outside the Laundromat near their house. I wanted to see if Katrine had followed through on her plan to stay behind," I admitted, "or if she had gone with Rob to Yuma after all. I don't know why it even mattered. I guess I hoped she had learned to stand on her own two feet, and I wouldn't have to worry about her anymore. Anyway, I was under the impression that Rob was on his way to Yuma already, or I would have never gone near that area in the first place. I swear I was going to tell you about all this when you got home tonight, but then you had the game, and then Katrine called, and, well, you know the rest."

"So what did he have to say to you?"

"He wanted to know what I was doing there. Since he was supposed to be gone, when he spotted the Ford outside the Laundromat, I guess he figured I was planning to sneak over to his house—which I was, but not for the reason he had in mind. Anyway, in the course of the ensuing argument, he said that I was to blame for ruining his career, that I'd gone behind your back and convinced Erin to turn him in as punishment for taking Katrine away, and that he would never, ever forgive me."

"But you weren't seeing Katrine anymore by then—and he'd been busted before she went back to him."

"That's how *I* remembered it, too. But according to Rob, Katrine had already agreed to take him back that Sunday night."

"Do you believe that?"

"I didn't at first, but in retrospect, it would explain why he suddenly stopped harassing her and Erin, and why he so readily agreed to leave Erin alone when you confronted him the next morning. It would also explain why he was so convinced I had talked Erin into turning him in, since he would have assumed Katrine had told us the same thing she told him."

"I suppose. But why *wouldn't* she just tell us the same thing she told him? I mean, why lie?"

"I'm guessing she figured I wouldn't let her spend the night if I knew she was going back to him, and then she wouldn't have been around to discuss how we were going to get him to stop harassing Erin. I think she hoped we'd opt to turn him in, and when we didn't, she decided to take matters into her own hands."

"So what kind of an outcome do you think she was looking for, exactly?"

"I'm not sure. Either she agreed to go back to Rob just to calm his vibe until she could figure another way out of the marriage, or she really wanted to make things work. Either way, getting Rob transferred out of the area would make her life easier."

"OK, so let me see if I have this straight," Kevin said, shifting to the other end of the sofa and facing me. "Katrine promises to go back to him, listens to us make plans to pressure Rob to leave Erin alone after we opted against turning him in like *she* suggested, waits until we're all at school, and then calls the armory and says just enough to pique the command's interest—and then stands by and lets him blame you for ruining his career?"

"That about sums it up, yeah. Anyway," I continued, "we argued that point for a while until he finally ordered me to stay away from Katrine from that day forward. Well, I had no intention of doing otherwise, but I was so incensed by his attitude that I just couldn't contain myself. I laughed at him and told him that Katrine wouldn't be going to Arizona; that she had hired an attorney and would be divorcing his ass just as soon as he crossed the state line; and that she was actually responsible for ruining his career, because she was the one who called the unit that morning to report Erin 'missing.' As a capper, I added that if I *had* been responsible for destroying his career, he would have known it, because I would be only too happy to take credit for it."

"Wow."

"I know. I'm not proud of myself for losing control like that, especially since I didn't even know how much of what I was saying was actually true, but he made me so angry that I couldn't help myself."

"I understand, Jack. And now I understand why you feel responsible. But even if Rob did this because he found out Katrine was leaving him, it's still not your fault—or even hers."

"OK, so maybe he didn't do it *because* of me, but he couldn't have done it without the gun, and he would have never found the gun if it weren't for my big mouth."

"How do you figure?"

"He went snooping. I imagine he wanted to see if I was telling the truth before he discounted what I said or confronted her with it. Either way, he obviously found the gun, which Katrine had stashed in her drawer along with the divorce papers."

"So you think Rob shot himself after finding the papers and the gun in Katrine's drawer?"

"Right."

"And what was Katrine's take on the situation?"

"Pretty much the same."

"And Rob never confronted her with what he found? They didn't argue?"

"Not according to her. Although I wouldn't be the least bit surprised if she'd left that out given what else I've learned about her tonight."

"Such as?"

"That she's been sleeping with Scott."

"*What?*"

I nodded. "For over a month."

"How do you know that?"

"She was *worried* about him," I reported with mock sympathy, "and whether he would get in trouble, since it was his gun that Rob had used. I told her I didn't think so, as long as it was registered. She was fairly preoccupied over it though, and since she hadn't been able to reach him earlier, I suggested she call him and let him know what had happened. So while she did that, I took a moment to check on the kids and use the bathroom. Next thing I know, I'm three steps from the kitchen hearing her saying 'I love you.'"

"You've got to be kidding me."

"That was my reaction, too, at first; but then I thought, well, he was Rob's friend, and the three of them lived together for a while, so maybe it wasn't what it looked like. I probably wouldn't have thought any more about it if she'd just hung up and moved on, but she got pissed off and accused me of eavesdropping, which told me something was up."

"So what did you do?"

"I did the only thing I could do at that point—I bluffed. I pretended that I had figured out that she and Scott were involved and asked her point blank how long it's been going on."

"And?"

"'Since June,' she says—as if it was absolutely no big deal."

"Jesus!"

"I know."

"Did Rob?"

"I don't know. Although finding the gun and the divorce papers may have been enough to put him over the edge, I suspect there was something more, say a letter, a photo, that told him not only what she was up to, but with whom."

"But she didn't confirm that?"

I shook my head. "I didn't know about her and Scott when she was talking about the gun and the papers, so I didn't think to ask if Rob had found them out, and once I had busted her on her relationship with Scott, well, let's just say the conversation took a decidedly different turn."

"I see. So Rob either shot himself because he found out Katrine was leaving him, or he shot himself because he found out she was leaving him for his best friend."

"Pretty much—although I don't think she was leaving Rob *for* Scott as much as she was using Scott to get away from Rob."

"That would be more her style, wouldn't it?"

I nodded. "I just can't believe I thought she may have finally grown up and decided to stand on her own two feet. How could I have been so stupid?"

"You weren't stupid, Jack. It's what you wanted for her."

"You should've seen her," I marveled. "There was no remorse in her voice whatsoever. I'm not saying she's wrong to want to be free of Rob, but as much as I hated him, I'm at least sorry he's dead. In fact, I would have never opened my mouth today if I'd thought for a minute that what I had to say would lead to something like this."

"I know that, Jack. And this really is *not* your fault. No matter what you said or what he may have learned afterward, it was still Rob who pulled that trigger. You have to remember that."

"I'll try," I agreed, wiping my face on my shirttail again. "So, what do we do now?"

"Well, first I think we need to call Erin."

Erin.

"She's going to hear it eventually anyway," Kevin added. "It may as well be from us."

Thirty-seven

"I can't believe they actually had the nerve to pull that crap in front of us," Kevin said to me and Erin as he recalled watching Scott guide Katrine over to accept the flag from the honor guard after draining his first beer in silence at the Jack of Diamonds bar following Rob's funeral. "I can still see them, sharing that single umbrella, talking to Rob's parents in the rain."

"I know," I agreed, shaking my head. "It was all I could do not to walk over and smack her in the face. In fact, if I weren't so damned well-mannered, I would have told Rob's folks *exactly* what a comfort Scott has been to their daughter-in-law over the past several weeks."

"I'm glad you didn't," Erin replied. "They deserve to live in peace."

"But they deserve to know he stabbed their son in the back! He should be made to suffer."

"Jackie, the man is with Katrine. Believe me—he's going to suffer."

"He sure is," Kevin laughed. "Almost makes you want to warn the guy."

Erin nodded. "Too bad none of us gives enough of a shit to bother. Speaking of not giving a shit," she added. "I was surprised at how few ROTC people showed up today. I expected more of them to come."

Kevin rolled his empty glass back and forth within his palms until he spied our waitress and signaled to her for another hit. "Me, too," he said grimly. "But then, maybe they didn't feel it would be appropriate under the circumstances. I'm still not sure we should have gone ourselves."

With our table having fallen silent again after the delivery of the next round, I heard *Wheel of Fortune* coming back from commercial on the TV over the bar. Grabbing the seat with both hands, I swung my chair around in time to catch Pat Sajak chatting up the player who would be starting the next round.

"Jesus—where do they find these people?" I griped after the contestant had rattled off her vital statistics to include her occupation and children's names. "It's as if the producers had made *boring* a qualification for participation."

"They're introducing themselves, Jack," Kevin observed, "not auditioning for *Comic Relief*. Besides, how exciting can they make themselves sound in ten seconds or less?"

"I don't know. But just once I'd like to hear someone recite a bio that doesn't sound like someone's gag-worthy holiday brag letter. I mean, honestly. Instead of these insipid morons—all of whom apparently work for a *major corporation* and whose crowning achievement involves a capacity to give birth to live young—it would be refreshing to see a bunch of parolees, starving musicians, and homeless people up there. Not only would that make the show more interesting for me, but it would also put that prize money into the hands of some people for whom it might really make a difference."

Kevin grinned as I returned my chair to its original position. "Feel better?" he asked, patting my knee.

"You know what else gets me?" I added. "It's the way she portrays herself as such a victim."

Kevin looked up at the TV. "*Victim?*"

"Not her," I sighed, nodding with the back of my head at the screen behind me. "Katrine. The poor thing!" I whimpered. "Controlled by her mother—that witch! Neglected and mistreated by Rob—that bastard! And eclipsed and betrayed by Erin—that home-wrecker!"

"Tell me about it!" Erin laughed. "She wasn't singing *that* tune when we were playing footsie last spring."

We?

"Oh my God," I breathed as I stared at Erin. "Are you saying Katrine was *there*?"

Erin looked from me to Kevin and back again. "I assumed you knew that already," she said carefully, "or I wouldn't have mentioned it—at least, not in quite that way."

"No. No. It's OK. I, uh…I'm glad you told me."

"Are you sure?"

I nodded. "Of course, I would have thought someone would have told me before now," I added, eyeing Kevin curiously as he drained his second beer, "but as the saying goes, better late than never."

"In truth, she was only there the first time," Erin explained, "and there never was a third."

I see.

"I had assumed we'd remain friends afterward," she continued, "but obviously that wasn't going to happen. Which is a shame, because I was really into her."

"Excuse me?" I said, nearly choking on my own breath.

Erin looked at Kevin. "You mean she didn't know that *either*?"

"Know what?" I demanded when Kevin shook his head. "What are you talking about?"

"Jackie, I'm gay," Erin confessed. "I suppose I shouldn't have expected you to know that either, but there it is."

Wow.

"That's why it didn't really bother me when Katrine made Rob dump me," she added as Kevin raised his glass at the waitress. "He just didn't trip my trigger."

"If that's the case, why did you sleep with him in the first place?"

"Well, this is going to sound silly, but that was actually part of a much larger mission. You see, I've suspected I was gay for a long time, and for the most part, I was OK with it. Of course, I knew life would be easier if I was straight; but I wasn't planning to work or live anywhere that my sexuality would be an issue, so I didn't worry about it at all. Then I got to college and started thinking about a career in the military, and since gays aren't allowed to serve, I knew I would have to decide whether to subjugate my sexual identity or pursue another career. I really couldn't talk to anyone about it, of course, since this isn't exactly the kind of thing you can discuss with either military personnel or lesbians if you're looking for objective commentary, so I elected to do some research and joined ROTC, with the hope of finding out if military life suited me well enough to sacrifice or conceal my sexuality."

"So that's what you meant back in June when you said you weren't even sure you wanted to join the military?"

"Exactly. I had given myself until my scholarship results came back to make a decision," Erin recounted, "but then my package was withdrawn, and the decision was made for me. In the meantime, having never so much as kissed a guy before, I decided to take a test drive, if you will. After all, I didn't want to forego a military career on the grounds I was gay if there was even a remote chance I really wasn't."

"Makes sense."

"I thought so, too—and the plan probably would have worked if I'd just steered clear of Sergeant Psycho and his nutzoid bride. Not that it would have been easy to avoid them. With Rob at the unit and in one of my classes—not to mention Katrine's omnipresence at the armory lounge—I was bound to meet them one way or another. As it turned out, though, it was Katrine I spoke to first. I found her incredibly attractive, if a bit awkward, but I told myself I hadn't joined ROTC to pick up women— especially married ones—and decided to keep my hands to myself. Well, I no sooner got that sorted when she's suddenly coming on to me, and I'm vigorously reminding myself that her husband is a marine and that I don't want to die."

"You are kidding me."

"If only," Erin laughed. "I tried skirting the issue at first, but I finally had to tell her that, while I was flattered by her attention, I wasn't looking to break up any marriages."

"So how'd she take it?"

"Pretty well, I assumed, since she immediately offered to make it a threesome. I, on the other hand, was dumbfounded, since it was quite literally the farthest thing from my mind. But then I thought, why the hell not? After all, if I'm going to sleep with a guy anyway, there may as well be a girl there, too."

Kevin shrugged as the waitress approached with his next round. "Seems logical to me."

"Of course it does," I replied. "They don't call you King *Leer* for nothing."

"True."

I waited as our empties were removed and replaced before nodding for Erin to look at Kevin, who was now watching the curvy blonde walk back to the bar. "See what I mean?"

Erin laughed. "So we arranged to get together at their place one night and try things out," she continued. "But as I feared, things didn't click between Rob and me. In fact, if Katrine hadn't been there, things would have gone absolutely nowhere. Thinking the problem was at least partly down to my feeling somewhat like an interloper, I decided if the opportunity ever presented itself again, I would give it another whirl—and this time try not to let my thoughts hang me up. Well, the opportunity did present itself again—in the form of an invitation to spend the next weekend at their place. Bizarrely enough, however, only minutes after I arrive, Katrine's heading out the front door holding an overnight bag and telling us to have a good time."

"That must've been the weekend Kevin had the kids at his mom's place—when Katrine told me you were spending the weekend with Rob."

"Probably. At any rate, I was alone with Rob for almost the entire weekend, and I couldn't have enjoyed myself less if he'd driven pins and needles through my eyes, which is why, after careful consideration, I've decided I'm never sleeping with another man as long as I live."

"I understand what you're saying," I laughed, "and I wouldn't dream of trying to change your mind, but maybe you just picked the wrong guy. I mean, we are talking about Rob, after all—and not to speak ill of the dead, especially immediately after his funeral—but I can't imagine why a straight woman would sleep with him, much less a gay one."

Erin grinned. "Well, had I not been so enchanted by Katrine," she admitted, "I definitely would have never considered it myself."

I stared into my glass. I had fought to appear undaunted by Erin's confessions, but with the complete tale having been told, I began to feel myself sinking into a familiar abyss.

"I'm sorry," I said finally. "This is all just a lot for me to absorb."

"I understand. And if this is going to bother you—if knowing I'm gay is going to change things between us," Erin added, clearly mistaking the cause of my introspection, "just say so."

"You're kidding, right?"

"No. Why?"

"Because Katrine and I were a little more than friends."

"No kidding."

I nodded. "Up until I heard about you and Rob, that is, when I decided things were becoming too complicated for me."

"You're serious."

"'Fraid so."

"This is unbelievable," Erin exclaimed. "You, me, Scott—I mean, is there anyone she hasn't slept with yet?"

"Yeah," Kevin sighed. "Me."

Erin laughed. "That's a relief!" she said I rubbed his shoulder. "With all the other shit that's come out today, I half expected you to say the opposite."

Kevin shook his head. "Not this guy," he said, standing to make a head call. "It may have sounded good to me last fall, but these days I'm only too happy to have missed that boat."

Erin smiled as he walked away. "He's really something, Jackie. An absolute gem."

"Tell me about it. I don't know if he's my reward or I'm his punishment, but he is most definitely a keeper."

"And how do you know you're not *his* reward?"

"Because I know what I'm like, and that man deserves a medal for putting up with me."

"Does that mean there have been others besides Katrine?"

"Only one—at least since he and I've been together. I dated outside my gender in high school," I joked, "but Kevin really is the only man for me. In fact, if he hadn't come along when he did, I may have surrendered my sword and joined the other side permanently."

"I don't know why—the options there aren't necessarily any better."

"No?"

Erin shook her head. "You know how some women are always whining that all the guys they meet are either married or gay?" she asked. "Well, I can relate to that—only in my case, all the girls I meet are either married or straight—and those who aren't are tomboys who want me to be their femme. I'm looking for a woman who's in touch with her femininity and who also happens to want to get in touch with mine."

"Well, forgive me for saying so," I said, as I nodded back at Kevin, who was leaving the bar holding a fresh beer and shaking a handful of coins at the Galaga and Missile Command games flanking the back door. "But your appearance and demeanor don't exactly scream *lesbian,* so there may be plenty of women out there who are interested in you but who aren't sure whether their attentions would be welcomed."

"I suppose. But then why was Katrine willing to risk it?"

"Katrine's different. She has this ability to sense what people want, sometimes before they do. She doesn't actually *care* about them, mind you; she only knows that making people happy and earning their approval is necessary if she's going to get what *she* wants. So she'll say, do, and become whatever she must in order to keep people around—at least as long as it suits her. Once she no longer needs or wants someone, she loses all interest in what they want or like. Add to that the fact that she has no conscience and views the truth as an elastic concept that can be shaped to fit a particular moment, and you have someone who can act on her every whim without regard for the consequences. She's like a sociopath—a drop-dead gorgeous sociopath—but a sociopath just the same."

Erin watched as I emptied my soda as if it was a shot of whiskey. "She really hurt you, didn't she?"

I nodded. "And the funny thing is that I never saw it coming. One minute I was fine, and the next I was flattened."

"And yet, you seem more awed than angered by the whole thing."

"I guess I am. Although I am pretty angry—and sad and disgusted—I'm also surprised and unnerved. I mean, I'm generally a lot swifter than this. I can usually spot trouble from a mile away. But then Katrine comes along and waltzes right through my security systems as if they didn't even exist."

"Like a computer virus or worm exploiting a flaw in a firewall."

"Exactly. And I should probably thank her for that, really. At least now I know where my weaknesses are, and can take steps to bolster my defenses."

"Or," Erin offered, "and I'm just spit-balling here, but maybe the lesson to take from this isn't that your security needs improving, but that it needs to be scrapped altogether. After all, the strongest defenses are essentially useless against perniciously toxic people like Katrine. And like pesticides and antibiotics, they tend to be devastating to non-harmful organisms, and can make it challenging for decent people to get to know you."

I grimaced as I considered what Erin was saying.

"Don't get me wrong," she added as I did so. "You've been nothing but kind to me, but the day we met at Rob's place you were very guarded. I realize, of course, that there was a lot going on that day that had nothing to do with me; but I also remember thinking, both then and since, that you're about the most well-defended person I've ever met, and wondering what someone like you has to be afraid of."

I felt myself blush. I wasn't used to spontaneous character assessments—apart from the kind my father made—and I honestly had no idea how to respond.

"Well, that's my two cents," Erin interjected, sparing me an awkward reply. "For whatever it's worth. The important part is that you survived—unlike Rob, may he rest in peace."

"Yes," I agreed, happy to have something to say for a change. "And meanwhile, thanks to his life insurance, Katrine won't have to work and instead can devote her time feeding her ego and quenching her ceaseless thirst for attention."

"And how do you envision her doing that?"

"Well, it won't be by becoming an actor, or singer, or dancer. You have to have actual talent for that. So I imagine she'll have to settle for doing porn, since sex seems to be the one thing she excels at. Of course, she could never settle for being just a member of the cast. She'll expect a starring role and will stop at nothing to get it. So she'll have an affair with, say, the producer or director of her films. When that gets old, she'll become the mistress of some mafia boss, against whom she'll later testify in a celebrated, televised trial before ditching him for the judge or his lawyer.

"Or maybe she'll become a high-priced dominatrix," I continued, "and hook up with some foreign dignitary who likes having his genitals covered in hot wax while being strangled with panty hose and whose gardener she bangs while he's in meetings. Either way, she'll have a pretty good time of it—provided her looks hold up and her wits stay sharp."

Erin laughed. "You've obviously put a lot of thought into this."

"Not really. In fact, I could do a lot better than that if I had more time to prepare."

"Of that I have no doubt. So what happens when her looks start to fade? Will she settle down with some nice sap and have a bunch of kids?"

"And share the limelight? I doubt it. Unless, of course, she can find a way to use them as a source of attention, like by becoming the stage mother from hell and turning them into child stars or developing Munchausen syndrome by proxy and spiking their apple juice with antifreeze."

"Ouch."

I nodded. "Yeah—that may have been a bit harsh."

"No—not that," Erin laughed. "Kevin. He just smacked his arm on that stool," she explained as he made his way back to the table. "It looked like it really smarted."

"It sure did," he admitted, rubbing his left wrist. "It's a good thing I've had four beers, or I might have actually felt it."

I shook my head. "So what's next for you?" I asked after Kevin took our empty mugs to the bar, having failed to spot our waitress on his way back to the table.

"I'm considering a career in law enforcement at the moment, actually. I have a feeling computers are going to be a big part of the investigative process down the road, and I'd like to be there when the whole thing takes off."

"Sounds like a great plan to me."

"Me too," Kevin agreed heartily as he returned to the table. "What are we talking about, anyway?"

I shook my head again. "Well, that's my cue for a potty break," I announced, slinging my purse over my shoulder. "Keep your eye on the jarhead for me, will you? I'll be right back."

Having held it while Kevin was away from the table, I rushed into a stall and out again, washed up, and set my purse on the counter to dig for change. I had just exited the ladies' room having located the necessary coins when Kevin came back down the hall.

"Ah, Monsieur Thompson," I said, à la Inspector Clouseau. "Returning to the scene of *le grime*?"

"You know how it is once you pop that cork," he laughed, as I inserted four coins into the machine. "So who are you calling?"

"Shhh," I said, placing my fingers to his lips. "Sera?" I confirmed. "It's Jackie. What are you up to right now? Because I want you to come have a beer with me, that's why. Oh, come on! You have a full year to study for the bar—surely you can spare an hour today. What if I told you there's someone here I want you to meet? No, this is not a trick. Yes, I promise. Her name is Erin Rollins. Yes, she's cute. Yes, she's batting for your team. Yes—really. Excellent. We're at the Jack of Diamonds on University. OK, great. We'll see you in a few."

Kevin put his hands atop my shoulders as I hung up the phone. "There you go again," he scolded, "poking your cute little nose in where it doesn't belong."

"*Au contraire*. You know as well as I do that my nose has never been little, and it is most definitely not cute."

Kevin pulled me to his chest. "Still as feisty and argumentative as ever," he observed, planting a kiss on the top of my head. "It's nice to know some things never change."

Epilogue

Over the years, I've thought a lot about what Erin said to me the day they put Rob in the ground. At first, of course, I wondered mostly about how she knew I had trust issues. But eventually I got around to thinking about my tendency to keep people at arm's length—especially Kevin, who, of all people, did not deserve to be held hostage to the sins and transgressions of Sean, Steven, or my father—and whether the costs associated that strategy were outpacing the benefits.

I've thought a lot, too, about the last time I saw Rob, and how things might have turned out if I hadn't lost my temper, Katrine hadn't lied, and Scott hadn't bought her a gun. Maybe he would have set off for his new command and settled into his new job, and would still be walking the earth today—perhaps a little wiser from having lost his shot at an officer's commission, or at least a bit less smug for having done so.

And I've thought a lot about the night I met him and Katrine, and how despite having chastised Kevin for judging the girl by her cover as we drove home from the party, I had done exactly that in spades. Had I not assumed—from her youth, beauty, demeanor, whatever—that she was not only naïve and helpless but also innocent and guileless, I likely would not have taken up for her so forcefully, and Rob would still be around to annoy and offend feminists all over the world. Divorced from the toxic teenager, I can even imagine him married again—this time to someone he considers his equal, who understands and soothes his need for attention and reassurance, and who loves and trusts him enough to tell him when he's being an ass or an idiot.

And I've thought about who I am, and the person I still want to become. I'd like to say I'm a new woman with nothing but joy in my heart and love for all of humanity. But although no one reading this would know any better if I lied, I'm inclined to tell the truth: I still find it hard to trust, and to not look for disaster around every corner. But I give more of myself, accept more from others, and I hope others won't disappoint me rather than assume they will. It's a process, and I'm making progress.

Kevin and I are still married, and approaching the end of our third decade together. He has retired from the Marine Corps and is harassing me full-time now—that is, when he's not hunting, playing golf, or enjoying a cigar on the back deck. Tyler and Lucy, I'm pleased to report, are healthy, well-adjusted adults who respect their parents and almost always remember our birthdays. Both went on to college and both are working. Neither of them is in a committed relationship, but I'm doing my best not to blame myself.

Sera and Erin, who met on the day of the funeral, are also still together, and—thanks to a recent change in Minnesota law—are soon to be married. Erin proposed the day Governor Mark Dayton signed the bill making it legal for them to get hitched, and is currently fielding calls from their wedding planner, while Sera is drafting the prenup. You wouldn't think people would need either a wedding planner or a prenup after more than twenty years together, but there you have it. Apparently getting married has only gotten more complicated since 1990.

I wasn't completely off target with my predictions about Katrine. From what I've seen in the press, she is still an attention whore who uses people with abandon. She's neither in porn nor in bed with the mob—as far as I know, anyway—but she has appeared in one now defunct reality TV series, which is practically the same thing. I sometimes wonder if she thinks about what she's done or regrets any of it. My money would be on a big fat 'no,' but I've been wrong before—and more than once—so for all I know, she is consumed with remorse and just hides it exceptionally well. But I doubt it.

Meanwhile, here I am—alive and well, and living with myself. My skin is a little thinner, and yet I'm none the worse for the wear.